W9-CMT-025

Even the ice-cold water could not drown the spark between them . . .

Carefully, he lowered her upper body down into the cool swirls of water. Her tresses caught in the whipping motion of the stream and the soap bubbles drifted away. Jocelyn dropped her head back a little more, allowing Dash a moment to rinse the soap from her. He took his time, unmindful of his own uncomfortable position. Over and over he ran his fingers through the heavy strands until there wasn't a bit of the harsh soap left, then he lifted her upright.

Finally Jocelyn opened her eyes and gazed up at him. Her eyes were a startling shade of green; guileless and fringed by dark lashes that held droplets of water sparkling like diamonds.

"Finished?" she asked in a throaty voice that nearly took Dash's breath from his lungs.

He nodded, mute, transfixed by the sight of her.

"Good," Jocelyn whispered, and then, before Dash realized her intent, she lifted her hands and pressed them hard against his chest. "Because now it's *your* turn . . ."

Stolen Dreams

SUSAN ANDERSON

CHARTER/DIAMOND BOOKS, NEW YORK

STOLEN DREAMS

A Charter/Diamond Book / published by arrangement with
the author

PRINTING HISTORY
Charter/Diamond edition / September 1990

ISBN: 1-55773-386-4

Charter/Diamond Books are published by The Berkley Publishing
Group, 200 Madison Avenue, New York, New York 10016.
The name ''CHARTER/DIAMOND'' and its logo are trademarks
belonging to Charter Communications, Inc.

PRINTED IN THE UNITED STATES OF AMERICA

10 9 8 7 6 5 4 3 2 1

Prologue

An inky blackness cloaked the rolling lands of the Cotswolds as low-lying thunderclouds caged the heavy night
air against the damp earth. Soon the elements would rage
like angry gods.

But there was more than one storm brewing this night,
Dashiell Warfield knew. Mounted atop a powerful ebony
stallion who snorted in impatience, Dash waited silently,
wishing he were anywhere but this snaking country road.
There could well be blood shed on this spooky night. Even
the beast beneath him sensed the danger. The horse
scraped a hoof atop the ground, shook his bulky head,
then blew out a long breath. Dash ran one gloved hand
across the horse's neck, soothing him. Then the clatter of
hoofbeats in the distance shattered the silence.

It was time.

Dashiell Warfield heard the pounding of hooves coming
ever closer, and the sound filled his heightened senses with
a roiling mix of anticipation and dread.

As though in a trance, Dash reached up and pulled a
black half-mask down over his eyes and nose. A simple
gesture, but it transformed him nonetheless. To be recognized would be his death. Dash did not fear a load of
shot slamming into his body. In fact, he knew he would
probably meet his end in such a manner, but he was not
yet prepared to die. He had a quest to see to completion,

and if nothing else, Dashiell Warfield was a man of his word.

He turned his face northward, his gray eyes narrowing as he centered his thoughts on those pounding hoofbeats. But instead of the hollow black of the night, he saw other images, other times. He remembered only too well the pain of poverty, and was prepared to do what he must to help the less fortunate in life. But though he'd been determined to aid others, his recklessness had led to murder. It mattered not that Dash hadn't pulled the gun that killed his close friends. What mattered was that he should have known better than to help incite the riot that had led to such devastation. Such flashes of the past were his living hell. Life would relentlessly continue, but Dash's spirit would remain as bleak as the land surrounding him. He wondered again if there would ever come a time when he could lay to rest the ghosts of his past and leave behind the secret life he now led.

"Ho, Dash," a man whispered from behind, cutting into Dash's thoughts. "I don't think it's the midnight coach coming toward us. I hear only two horses instead of four."

Dash nodded; he'd already had the same thought. After a beat he whispered lowly, " 'Tis probably Robert Mowrey's coach, and we both know what a cheat Mowrey is. He leaves his young bride at home while he cavorts about London Town with his wenches. Mowrey deserves to be brought down a peg or two. We'll take his vehicle and be quick about it. We've no choice."

"But if the midnight coach comes along behind—"

"Then we'll stop it as well," Dash cut in. His order left a bitter taste in his mouth, and the brace of pistols strapped to his waist felt heavy indeed. Dash yearned for a warm fire and a tankard of potent ale. But such amenities would have to wait. He knew the midnight coach would be carrying a cache of gold—and soon, if Dash's plans went forward, he would have that cache in his hands.

Beneath a flickering flash of staticlike lightning, an ornate coach rambled into view along the narrow lane. Dash held up one black-clad arm, signaling to his band of highwaymen. Silent, they allowed the coach to pass them by. And then, like pale shadows in the night, they fell in behind the swiftly moving vehicle.

One

Jocelyn Greville jumped nervously as a loud clap of thunder reverberated across the darkened land outside the coach.

"Blast!" her thin companion muttered, pulling his coat tighter about his bony frame. "I demand an explanation for why you've dragged me out on such a night, Jocelyn."

Jocelyn gave her cousin what she hoped was a reassuring smile. "I told you, Charles, we're running an errand for my father."

Charles did not appear mollified. "I can hardly believe such a thing. Your father would certainly not want his daughter out and about on such a night!" Charles's fair hair caught the light of the lantern as he leaned forward on his seat, his brown eyes narrowing. "He wouldn't want you anywhere but in bed at such an hour. Why, the clock struck midnight a good forty minutes ago!"

Jocelyn let out a long sigh, not listening as her cousin, a few months shy of his nineteenth birthday, continued his tirade. She didn't want to listen to her cousin's chatter. Not tonight.

Unconsciously, she moved her right hand to the missive she'd surreptitiously tucked beneath her leg before Charles had climbed into the coach after her. It was a hastily scrawled message, one penned on her father's crisp parchment, the very paper he reserved for special occasions. Jocelyn had no doubt but the paper held a very important message for the man she was to meet . . . whoever *he* was.

Jocelyn only knew she must brave the oncoming downpour and meet this mysterious figure.

Alexander Greville, a physician of incomparable skill, was very well known for his desire to help the less fortunate people of England. Only this afternoon she'd overheard her father arguing with her grandmother, Amelia, about his clandestine meetings with a group of Radicals. An argument within the Greville household was not such an uncommon thing, Jocelyn knew. Her father often clashed wills with Amelia, a fiery Georgian woman with a sharp mind and silver tongue. But this particular disagreement had left Alexander in a foul mood, and soon after, he'd sat down and penned the missive Jocelyn now carried.

Jocelyn remembered the scene well; her father, pacing back and forth within the great study, and Amelia, resplendent in a frosty gown of satin, her pale blond hair swept up in an elegant style, as she unhurriedly buffed her nails and eyed her son.

"My dear boy, if you don't sit down and take a moment to catch your breath, you'll find yourself prostrate on the floor, and I'll be left with the odious task of reviving you," Amelia said in that deep-throated voice of hers that came from stolen moments of sneaking a smoke or two from one of her many hand-carved pipes.

Alexander turned on his heel, his features twisted with impotent rage. "There must be something we can do! Though the Treaty of Vienna has been signed, the expenses of the war have plunged our country into debt! Soldiers and sailors are without employment, and yet the Prince Regent continues to squander our resources on luxuries. Pah! 'Tis a crime, I tell you!''

Amelia, though concerned for her son's state, leaned back in her chair, saying, "You needn't give me a history lesson, Alexander. I know exactly what is transpiring. A revolution may be imminent. But I must warn you now: do not involve yourself with Thistlewood and his firebrands. You've no place in the midst of revolutionists. The Spencean society is naught but a group of miscreants, every one of them far too thirsty for blue blood.''

Alexander nearly choked on air. "How do you know of the society?" he demanded.

Amelia didn't bat an eye. "My dear boy, I know more than you think, and perhaps more than I should. The machinations of that Radical body aren't as hush-hush as all of you would like to believe.''

Clearly distressed, Alexander gave his mother a penetrating stare. "For pity's sake, Amelia, to what channels have you pressed that ear of yours now?''

"Worried?" Amelia questioned. "Well, you should be. Can't say as I wouldn't be nervous if I were in your shoes. I've connections in London, dear boy, and they've clued me in to what you've been doing. Fortunately, this person isn't involved in the government, and he has assured me he'll keep his lips sealed as to what he's heard about you and the Spencean society. Do us both a favor, Alexander, and cut your ties with that lawless lot. No good ever comes of covert meetings.''

"But you're wrong!" Alexander thundered. "I can hardly let things continue as they are, and by God, I *can* help force a change!''

Amelia dropped her hands to her lap. "Certainly you can try, but you'll find yourself dangling at the end of a noose. No, Alexander, there are other ways of dealing with this.''

"Such as?"

Amelia took a deep breath, then said, "Society must deal with the symptoms first. What you need to do, Alexander, is reach the influential people of the government and try to sway them to your own beliefs.''

"Good Lord, Amelia," Alexander huffed, "do you realize the amount of time such a path would take? I could woo Parliament until I turn blue, and naught would come of it. No. A revolution is the only course to take—and I'll take arms in my own hand if it will end the suffering of the poor.''

"And if it doesn't?" Amelia pressed.

"Then God help me."

"My dear boy, God will be the only power to help you then."

Amelia had then left the study, not noticing Jocelyn, who quickly dodged out of sight, and Alexander had penned the note. Of course, the missive was to have been delivered not by Jocelyn, but by Randolph, the Grevilles' only household servant. But when Alexander had been called away to help oversee a difficult delivery at a nearby village, needing Randolph to manage the reins of his dilapidated coach, Jocelyn slipped inside the study and picked up the letter. She'd hesitated at first, for she knew next to nothing about what her father was involved in. Lately, Alexander had been spending an inordinate amount of time away from the house—and he hadn't been spending this time with his many patients. Jocelyn could only surmise that her father was truly devoted to this secret society. The fact that Amelia found this involvement disturbing caused Jocelyn a moment of indecision. Should she deliver the letter or not?

But even though Jocelyn had thought about the dangers of such an outing, she also thought of the excitement. Jocelyn had been bored for too long. The past summer had crept by with barely a party for her to enjoy. And now, with winter approaching, Jocelyn thought of all the dull evenings she would be forced to endure while the Cotswolds were blanketed with snow, and travel would be out of the question. What she needed was an adventure of her own—if only for one night. What fun it would be to travel the dark roads, carrying her father's secret note with her!

The very idea sent a shiver of excitement coursing through her. Jocelyn had always yearned for some grand escapade, some great quest that would lift her out of the mundane march of life she knew.

Her decision made, Jocelyn had tucked Alexander's note into the pocket of her skirt and hurried for the door. Calling on Charles to accompany her, the two of them had struck out in Amelia's ornate carriage—without Amelia's consent.

"Well," Charles demanded, cutting into Jocelyn's thoughts. "Are you going to fess up or not? You know these roads are not safe at night, what with the Midnight Raider terrorizing anyone with money to burn! Heavens, cousin, but you're much too independent for your own good! I know you've been restless of late, and yearning for some excitement . . . but this is ludicrous! We could be killed or—"

"Calm yourself, Charles," Jocelyn cut in, half wishing she'd had the forethought to go the journey alone. She'd brought Charles along because the two had had great fun in the past. But lately Charles had become stuffy, preferring to spend his time preening in front of his looking glass.

"*Calm myself?* How can I? We're perfect prey for any thief! I demand that you tell me why we are racing with the wind and heading directly into the eye of the storm!"

Jocelyn winced, for they very well might be heading into the eye of a storm, but not the storm to which Charles referred.

Suddenly the coach lurched to a breathless halt. The abrupt motion forced Charles to topple forward against Jocelyn, who was thrown back into the velvet-covered cushions.

"What the devil—" Charles began, but his words were cut off as the angry shouts of the coachman filled the air. A scuffle atop the box outside the coach ensued. Jocelyn distinctly heard the ominous rasp of a flintlock being pulled from its position near the driver.

"*Stand and deliver!*"

The authoritative, masculine shout cut above rumbling thunder and the frightened whinnies of the horses.

"Good heavens!" Charles expounded. " 'Tis that notorious highwayman out there!"

Jocelyn's breath left her in a rush. Too frightened to speak, she stared wide-eyed at her cousin.

"No, no," Charles began, righting himself immediately. "Don't go swooning on me, cousin. I'll take care of things, not to worry. Can't say as I didn't expect something like this to happen—damned foolish of us to be out on the road at this time of night. But it's happened and I'll just take care of the matter. Here now, that necklace you're wearing, take it off and put it in your slipper! And your ring, dear girl, off with it as well!"

Jocelyn instinctively put her hands to her neck, digging out the long heart-shaped pendant that had once belonged to her grandmother. She fumbled with the clasp, her hands trembling. She watched as Charles swiped five of his most treasured rings from his own bony fingers and unceremoniously tucked them under his bottom, hiding them securely from sight beneath the tail of his coat.

But just as Jocelyn had the clasp of her treasured necklace undone, the carriage door was boldly thrust open. The fine gold links of Jocelyn's necklace spilled, unnoticed, down into the palm of her right hand.

"Greetings," a tall man said. Although refined, the tone of his voice held an undeniable warning. His face was hidden from full view by an incongruous mask. Cold gray eyes peered at Jocelyn through the demonic covering. "If you would be so kind as to hand over your jewels and any other valuables you carry, I'll leave you to your business." The bandit's gaze slipped from Jocelyn's frightened face to her trembling hands.

She blinked in astonishment. "I—I have naught but this necklace . . . and my grandmother's ring," she whispered, struck by the man's stormy gaze.

Across from her, Charles hissed, "Hush, Jocelyn. I'll speak with this—this bit of a beggar." Sitting ramrod straight on the velvet cushion, Charles turned his attention to the bandit. "We've nothing of value, sir. Be gone with you before you feel the brunt of my outrage. How dare you accost a helpless young woman and her escort!"

Charles's valor surprised Jocelyn, but what startled her more was the low laughter of reply from the bandit.

Reaching inside the door with one long hand, the masked man relieved Jocelyn of her jewelry, then grasped

Charles by the coat sleeve, pulling him through the opening. "Out with you," he said to Charles. "I will be the judge of whether or not you've anything of value."

Jocelyn's fears of being robbed—or worse—were immediately overridden by concern for her cousin's welfare. Poor Charles had not even the stomach to ride with the hounds on a hunt, and yet he was gentleman enough to speak on Jocelyn's behalf. Without considering the consequences, Jocelyn grabbed hold of Charles's other arm and pulled his scrawny body toward her. "No!" she cried to the highwayman. "Don't harm him! He is in this coach only at my insistence!"

The masked man halted his movements, releasing Charles, who'd gone into a paroxysm of coughing. Charles, an asthmatic from his day of birth, gasped for air. His pinched features turned a ghastly shade of white, further alarming Jocelyn.

"Charles!" Jocelyn said, easing her cousin back against the cushions. But he merely brushed her hands away, for when she'd pulled him inward, she'd yanked too hard. Charles's hidden booty of rings was revealed.

The highwayman instantly spied the glitter of gold. "Nothing of value, hmmm?" He swiped the rings off the cushion with swift precision, then handed the treasures to a person Jocelyn could not view. The masked man then returned his attention to Jocelyn. "If you would be so kind as to step outside?"

Jocelyn hesitated. Charles continued his pathetic wheezing. But his color returned to normal after he'd managed, with quivering hands, to loosen the tight cravat at the neck of his shirt.

Jocelyn looked directly at the masked man. "We've nothing more of value, truly."

He was very tall, and the black coat he wore did little to conceal the powerful breadth of his shoulders. "Come forth, and we shall see."

Jocelyn did as the man commanded, deciding it best to get this horrid experience behind them. Perhaps if she faced this band of cutthroats, then poor Charles would have a moment in which he could catch his breath. Cursing herself for involving her delicate cousin in such a dangerous mission, Jocelyn stepped out of the coach.

The highwayman's warm, gloved hand closed about her elbow as he helped her to the ground.

Once there, Jocelyn stared about her. Two other thieves rode astride long-legged chestnuts. The men's clothes, though not so perfectly tailored as their leader's, were as nondescript as the man who stood so near to her. They, too, wore black masks about their faces. They said nothing, though one held a small pistol aimed at the coachman, who still sat atop his box.

"Forgive me, Miss Greville," the coachman, Jives, said. "I did not mean for this to happen."

Jocelyn nodded. "Of course not, Jives. How could you know?"

As Jocelyn and the coachman exchanged their brief words, the masked bandit had climbed into the coach to search for hidden treasure. He found none, of course. When he came back to stand at Jocelyn's side, he held the sealed envelope Jocelyn had forgotten in the chaos.

Jocelyn drew in a sharp breath at sight of it. "That belongs to my father," she said quickly. "Please, give it to me at once."

As the masked man stared down at the seal of wax, Jocelyn detected an immediate change in him. His body stiffened. An odd light came and went in those unfathomable gray eyes.

"Please," she said again, fearing the man might take the message with him. "The envelope contains no money, only a letter."

The man glanced up at her. Beneath his mask his eyes narrowed. An odd hush fell over the group. Thunder rumbled, the sound drawing ever closer as it swept over them. Charles's wheezing could no longer be heard.

Just as she lifted her hand to reach for the letter, Charles leaned out of the opening. He held tightly to the side of the door with one bony hand as with the other he waved a small pistol he usually kept hidden in his coat.

"Be gone with you!" Charles shrieked. His brown eyes were wild, filled with a recklessness Jocelyn had never known her cousin to display. "Be gone or I'll blast those masks from your faces!" As though to prove his point, Charles aimed into the air above the tall highwayman's head and fired.

The small pistol spewed forth a cloud of blue and yellow flame. A loud *crack* filled the air, frightening the right coach horse, who crowhopped to the side, fighting against his bit. The left horse bolted forward at the abrupt movement of his companion. Jives, having laid his own gun across his legs at the insistence of the robbers, had let his reins fall slack in his hands. With no guiding reins to stop their flight, the two horses shot forward, throwing Jives off balance. The old coach driver yelped in dismay as he was caught off guard. His gun clattered to the ground, firing on impact. The second blast sent the horses into an even wilder frenzy. With a burst of fear-induced speed, the twin horses charged ahead and took off into the night.

Charles gasped as he was thrown backward into the coach, the door slamming shut behind him.

As the coach whizzed past, Jocelyn found herself being pulled to safety by the solid grip of the tall highwayman. Not wasting a moment, the man grabbed Jocelyn by the waist and swung her up and away from the huge carriage wheels. Her breath was forced from her lungs as the man, lunging away from the moving conveyance, fell to the ground, cushioning Jocelyn from the hard impact.

Immediately Jocelyn tried to scramble to her feet, but her confining skirts were twisted about her legs. Her face burned with embarrassment as she felt the lean length of the man's body beneath her. Acutely aware of every inch of him, Jocelyn stayed where she was. The warmth of his breath brushed the small wisps of hair dangling near her neck, throwing her scattered thoughts into further chaos.

The man inched his way from beneath her, maneuvering her carefully to the ground.

Restricted by the tight cut of her sleeves, Jocelyn could do no more than wait for the bandit to disengage himself.

He righted himself, and then quickly stood up before her, offering his hand.

Had Jocelyn been able to stand up without any assistance, she would have done so. But that feat was impossible. She lifted her hand to his, felt their palms touch as his fingers curled about her hand, and allowed the renegade to help her to her feet.

As she stood before him, a wintry fear gripped her. She was alone now. Totally alone in the midst of these midnight raiders. The clattering sounds of the runaway coach grew dim, as did Jives's loud shouts to his frenzied beasts.

"We'll catch them," the masked stranger said, reading the stricken look on her face. To one of his men he commanded sharply, "Go after them!"

"Aye," the smallest of the two answered. "That I'll do, but—" and here he paused, cocking his head slightly. " 'Tis the midnight coach, I think. Nearly fifty-five minutes late, at that."

The tall highwayman turned toward the rumbling sounds of an approaching coach. "Of all the inopportune moments," he muttered. He glanced once at Jocelyn, studying her closely. He reached for her with his free hand, still holding the letter in one tight fist. To his men he said, "You know what to do. I'll be in the glade, with the lady. Should you have need of me, just give signal and I'll be at your side."

Jocelyn stepped away from his touch. "Wh-what do you intend?" she demanded, fearing now for her virtue.

His lips curled into a grim smile. "For the moment only to whisk you from harm's way. But of course, if you would prefer to be witness to a robbery, we can ride with the others."

Aghast, Jocelyn shook her head.

"Very well then." He took hold of Jocelyn and, before she had a chance to deny him, whisked her astride his huge horse. Swinging his body up behind her, he gathered the reins and then slapped the beast into a gallop.

With the sudden forward motion of the horse, Jocelyn

was forced back against the highwayman. *Sweet Heaven!* she thought. *This can't be happening!*

To Jocelyn's horror the man veered abruptly off the roadway, urging his mount through a tangle of whipcord branches. The smell of wet earth and pungent horseflesh filled her senses.

The darkness of the night increased as a thicket sprang up on all sides. But the man did not slow his beast, and the horse seemed accustomed to such a hindered path. The wild growth was like an enveloping cloak, creating an intimacy that set Jocelyn's nerves on edge. Finally he brought the horse to an abrupt halt.

Not waiting to guess what the renegade's next move would be, Jocelyn fought to free herself. With a strength that surprised her, she shrugged out of the man's hold and jumped to the ground, intending to run back the way they'd come.

But she wasn't quick enough. As soon as her feet touched ground, Jocelyn felt the tight clamp of the man's hand on her left shoulder. He yanked her backward, swinging his lean body off the horse in the same motion.

Jocelyn screamed as she was whirled about. She lashed out at him, her fists flying.

"Unhand me!" she shrieked. "Unhand me now or—"

"Or what?" the stranger demanded, curling one arm about her waist and dragging her lithe body against his. With his other hand, he drew the pistol from his gun belt and pressed the barrel of it against Jocelyn's cheek. "Tell me," he whispered in a frightening voice. "What will you do?"

Jocelyn stiffened, closing her eyes as he dragged the cold metal of the gun across her cheek. She could smell the oily stench of the barrel, could feel the man's heartbeat against her breast, and she wondered what it would feel like to have a pound of shot burrow into her head. Jocelyn only hoped it would be clean and quick, and that she wouldn't be left to a slow death upon the wet earth of the thicket.

But something was wrong, she realized suddenly. It was taking too long for the man to pull back on the hammer.

Jocelyn snapped her eyes open. He wasn't going to kill her! He'd pulled his pistol only as a ploy to keep her quiet while his friends robbed the coach!

"You sneaking dog!" Jocelyn whispered, incensed that he should play such tricks. "You've no intentions of killing me."

The man let out a slow grunt of laughter. "No?" he asked. "And how can you be so certain?"

How indeed? Jocelyn wondered, but she immediately snuffed out her fears. Never in her life had Jocelyn backed down from anything. Both her father and Amelia had taught her to be bold. She'd never faced a gun-toting stranger, but then again, she'd never been afraid of any kind of challenge. She'd set out this night to deliver her father's note, and she would, come hell or high water. At the moment it appeared she was facing both.

Feeling more reckless than she had a right to be, Jocelyn said, "Were you bent on the notion of doing away with me, you'd have pulled the trigger by now."

"Are you challenging me?" the man asked, a note of amusement—or perhaps approval—in his voice.

"I'd be a fool to do such a thing. You appear to be a man who has a weakness for challenges."

He smiled at her reply, and for one frightful moment Jocelyn saw a handsomeness in his mask-covered eyes. Though a highwayman, the man's stormy eyes showed a spark of undeniable beauty. For a fanciful moment Jocelyn wondered what the man would look like without the mask.

From behind them came a flurry of commotion. A gunshot blasted into the air. Horses screeched in fright. Another shot was fired.

Jocelyn seized the moment to flee. As her captor stilled and listened to the wild sounds coming from the road, Jocelyn slammed one elbow into his stomach and then ran.

Brambles caught at her skirts and arms, tearing both fabric and skin. But Jocelyn paid no mind to the burning pain, instead plunging forward into the maze of vines and thorns. She very nearly made it to the road, but the highwayman caught her just before she broke free of the coppice.

Before Jocelyn knew what was happening, he had her in his clutches again, muttering a string of strong words that burned her ears. Not even Amelia could curse so profusely!

"Stay still!" the man demanded. "Unless, of course, you want to catch a stray pound of shot in your spine."

Jocelyn whipped a strand of copper hair from her face, her cheeks burning with rage and fear as she glared up at the stranger. "You filthy robber!" she cried, then lashed out at him. Though she'd intended only to shove away from him, her hand caught at the base of his mask and she ripped the covering from his face. That, Jocelyn knew, was her worst mistake.

The skittering clouds above parted for only a moment, revealing a swollen moon caught in the play of wind, and in that instant Jocelyn had a clear view of the man's face. His bold, aristocratic features looked stark in the telling light of moonbeams. Broad, flat cheekbones melded into a strong jawline. His lips appeared carved from Cotswold slate, so tight were they with rage, and his gray eyes were spiked with long, black lashes.

Jocelyn had never viewed a face more frightening and handsome in all her life. His eyes, so stormy, rivaled the elements, and she knew she was the cause of his ire. But she didn't care. She felt transfixed by the sight of him, caught in the sudden and fleeting light of the moon.

Immediately the man wrenched her wrist and forced her to turn about. "Damn you, you shouldn't have looked at me," he said lowly.

"Damn *you*!" Jocelyn shot back, wincing in pain as he dragged her arm up behind her back, just as she managed to bring the heel of her right slipper down on the man's toe. Of course, the leather of his riding boot was too thick for him to have felt the crunch, but she felt a small victory giving him as good as she got.

"Let go of me, you filthy, rotten son of—"

"Take care what you say about me, wench."

"You're nothing but a damned thief!"

Dash heard the young woman's curse and nearly choked in disbelief. The lady was a firebrand in spite of her pampered appearance and wide-eyed innocence. He felt like a beast for treating her so roughly, but if he hadn't grabbed hold of her she very well might have found a round of shot in her chest had she run out on the road. Highway robbery was a dangerous affair, after all.

"Be still, will you?" Dash demanded, wondering how in the devil he would deal with this very unwanted yet very desirable intrusion. He'd thought they'd stopped Robert Mowrey's coach, not one transporting a spirited woman and her escort!

"And quietly allow your cutthroats to rob the coach?" she demanded in that high-pitched voice of hers. "I will not!"

No, Dash thought, *you wouldn't.* He tightened his hold on the fiery young woman and soundly cursed the winds of Fate. A moment ago, when the she-devil had peered up into his unmasked face, Dash had been given full view of her charms. Swathed in a gown of crushed velvet, the cloud of her long, coppery hair falling free about her animated face, she had appeared to be an angered angel come to plague him. Her witching green eyes threw daggers at him from her lovely heart-shaped face. And the moonlight showed to great advantage the spattering of freckles across her nose and cheeks. The women in Dash's past would never have left their sitting rooms with their freckles showing. Hell, the women in his past would have *swooned* had he even so much as shown his pistol to them!

But not *this* woman. No. She'd gathered her courage and had spit it right back at him!

Dash smiled at the thought. Lord, but she was pretty. Too pretty. And she was young—probably no more than seventeen. Dash had no doubt that she came from a landed background, for the coach she'd been riding in had been adorned with ornate gilt appendages and pulled by prime horseflesh. It was Dash's sore luck to meet up with someone of this woman's ilk.

Well, Dash decided, holding the young lady tightly, fearing she would bolt into the line of fire should he let her go, he had no choice but to keep her with him. She'd seen his uncovered face, and he clapped a hand over her mouth to keep her from screaming.

Another shot rang in the air. Clearly, his comrades had met with a bit of trouble in robbing the midnight coach.

Dash swore again. Nothing was going his way this night! "Come," he said to the young woman who was wildly fighting his hold. "Let's get you away from the road." He dragged her back toward his horse—with quite a bit of effort. Certainly not one of the class of women Dash had been forced to spend time with, this young lady was not about to be taken where she didn't want to go. To his consternation, she got her mouth free.

"And what do you intend to do with me now?" she demanded.

Dash grunted in answer, breathless from their struggle.

"What did you say?" she demanded hotly. "Speak up, man! If you're going to rob me, rob me! If you're going to shoot me, shoot me!"

Dash couldn't believe what he was hearing. This little spitfire was actually demanding him to shoot her! Did she truly think he could do such a thing? As he stopped beside his horse and eased his hold on her, she spun around and glared up at him. Dash felt thunderstruck. She should be cringing, crying for mercy. But she wasn't.

"You thief! You filthy rot of baggage!" she shrieked at him. "Give me back my letter!"

Dash blinked in surprise. And then he did the only thing he could think of that would shut her up.

He kissed her.

Two

Stunned, Jocelyn felt the man's lips cover her own. There was no tenderness in the kiss. It was all power and fury. Jocelyn had never known the feel of a man's mouth on hers, let alone the leap of excitement such closeness between a man and a woman could breed. Confused, disoriented, and mad as a hornet, Jocelyn brought her left fist up against the man's chest. But he didn't pull back. Instead, he deepened the kiss, and Jocelyn's senses careened out of control. His lips slammed over hers, his tongue pushed through to collide with her own.

To Jocelyn's horror, she felt her knees buckle and her mind grow dizzy. He tasted of hops and his scent was as heady as the air filled with an impending rain. Fresh and wild, that was what he was, Jocelyn thought, drowning in the kiss.

Abruptly Jocelyn pulled herself up from the depths of his spell. He dragged his mouth from hers, then stared down at her with heavily-lidded eyes. Jocelyn felt lost in those slate-colored orbs. Suddenly the robbery didn't matter. Her cousin's whereabouts didn't matter. Not even her father's note was of consequence to her. She only knew of the aftermath of this stranger's kiss, could feel the sting of it on her lips and the effect of it on her heart.

"How dare you?" she whispered, when actually she wondered how dare *she*?!

"I dare to do anything. I'm bold and I'm desperate . . . and I'm taking you as my prisoner."

Jocelyn stiffened. "Don't be absurd! My cousin and footman will return soon. They're armed. You won't get far."

"So you say," Dash countered. "I've another view of the situation. If your footman were such a crack shot, he would have taken me down the minute I came upon your carriage."

"Jives is a decent man!"

"And I'm not?"

"No!" Jocelyn cried. "You're a vile dog who preys on others, and I loathe you—"

Just then the sounds of hoofbeats could be heard, charging through the thicket. Dash glanced in that direction, then scowled as his men came toward him.

"Disaster," the smallest of the two said. He was bent over at the waist, his right hand covering a blood-spattered portion of his coat and shirt. "I've been hit."

"And you?" Dash demanded, looking to the second rider.

"Unscathed. I've got the cache. But we must ride fast, Dash. The driver is reloading as we speak."

Dash grabbed hold of Jocelyn, directing her up onto the saddle of his horse.

Jocelyn held back. "No!" she said firmly. "I won't go."

Dash was in no mood for her show of bravery. If he wanted to get Caleb back to camp before the boy bled to death, then he had to hurry.

"Forgive me, but you haven't any choice," Dash said, and then, without ceremony, he hoisted her up to his saddle while she shrieked in protest. Quickly he pulled himself up behind her, then kicked his horse into motion.

Jocelyn fell back against him, but immediately righted herself. Terrified, she watched as the land sped by them, and though she wished otherwise, she was taken farther and farther from the road.

The highwayman led his cohorts through a maze of

twisting paths. The going was slow in some spots and too fast in others. Jocelyn felt her skirts being ripped, and her hands had myriad scratches upon them by the time the man brought his horse to a breathless halt.

The moon, totally obscured by thunderclouds, did not shine upon the robber's camp. The darkness was broken by only the light of a small campfire. Jocelyn was quiet as the man led his horse near the fire. He dismounted, then offered to help her to the ground. Jocelyn ignored his proffered hand, instead dropping to the ground on her own.

She looked about her. It was a crude camp, set in the midst of nowhere. An arch of barren trees created a sort of roof above while the perimeter of the area was a tangle of brambles. Jocelyn could hear the gurgle of a stream nearby, and could see a crude tent set up off to her right.

"Pretty Boy!" the leader yelled. "Caleb's been shot."

Jocelyn watched as several men stood up from their positions near the fire and went to help the young man named Caleb. They pulled him off his horse and then carried him toward the tent. Caleb was a young man, probably no more than fifteen, Jocelyn guessed. In fact, many of the men in the camp were young, which startled her.

"My God," she said, turning toward the man who'd abducted her. "Haven't you the power to hire men instead of boys? Must you take young lads and force them to do your dirty work?"

Dash heard the censure in her voice, and the sound of it cut deep. "Look here," he began, but didn't get a chance to finish his sentence, for she'd already started off for the tent. "What the devil?" he muttered, then trailed after her.

Jocelyn, knowing she could aid the injured lad, pushed her way into the makeshift tent. A stub of a candle offered meager light, but Jocelyn could see well enough the ugly show of blood on the boy's side. One man fumbled ineptly by the lad's pallet, mumbling apologies to him as he tried to staunch the flow of blood. Good heavens! Jocelyn thought, critically eyeing the scene before her. The lad will die if someone doesn't take charge. Jocelyn tightened her mouth as the lad screamed in pain, then she moved forward.

"I'll need a lantern," Jocelyn announced, startling the thieves. "And a basin of boiling water as well. And be quick about it," she added sharply, bending down beside Caleb.

Jocelyn saw the crude, growing splotch of blood on his coat. Gently she lifted the material. A gaping hole, circled by the fragments of his tattered shirt, was revealed. Jocelyn forced herself not to blanch. She'd gone with her father on many of his rounds and had seen far worse than this. But her father wasn't here to help the young man.

"Have you a surgeon among your ranks?" she asked.

One of the thieves laughed, a guttural sound, then spit onto the ground beneath them. "I've got whiskey in a jar. That's all," he said.

Jocelyn sucked in a quick breath of air. "Then it will have to do. Bring it to me." When the man didn't move, she added, "Now!"

The man quickly shuffled off to do her bidding as the others cleared the way for Jocelyn, surprise upon their dirty faces.

Dash entered the tent just as Jocelyn began pouring some of the whiskey down the boy's throat; the remainder she used on the wound. Caleb shuddered convulsively, grabbing tight to the filthy blanket beneath him.

"Easy there, Cal," Dash whispered, moving to hold the boy in place. To Jocelyn, he asked, "Do you know what you're doing?"

"My father, Alexander Greville, is a doctor. I've learned a great deal from him," she answered, quickly ripping a portion of her underskirt and then pressing the swatch of cloth to the wound. "The shot went clean through him," she continued. "But we'll have to close the wound. I'll need a needle and some—"

"Haven't got it," Dash cut in.

Jocelyn met his eyes. "What *do* you have?"

Dash said nothing for a moment as he gazed down at Caleb's ashen face, then slowly he reached into the top of his riding boot and withdrew his knife. "This," he said grimly.

The blade glittered briefly in the candlelight, and Jocelyn felt her stomach tighten. She'd seen Alexander close a wound with a blade that had been dipped in fire, but she wasn't certain she could do the deed herself. To sear the wound shut meant sending a scorching-hot blade into the hole.

"We haven't any choice, do we?" Jocelyn whispered, thinking of her father, who was more than an hour's distance away. Even if this renegade leader would allow her to ride out for Alexander, Jocelyn knew the lad would most likely bleed to death before help could arrive. "Very well then," Jocelyn continued, taking a deep breath and gathering her courage. "Ready your blade. I'll need help holding the boy still—and if you have more whiskey, he'll need that, too."

Dash rose to his feet, watching as the young woman bent over Caleb and whispered words of encouragement. Dash admired her strength of character. Though he'd brought her here against her will, she was now putting her own fears aside to help the boy. How many other women, in her position, would do such a thing? Dash wondered as he left the tent. Not many, he was certain.

After ordering one of his men to take more whiskey into the tent and to ready another blade, Dash knelt beside the fire and pressed the tip of his blade to the hot coals. As soon as the tip glowed a menacing red, Dash hurried back to Caleb's bedside.

"Pretty Boy, take hold of his legs. Granger, you hold his shoulders," Dash commanded as he moved beside the young woman. She'd already given Caleb a strip of cloth to bite down on, and the flask of whiskey that had been brought in lay opened near Cal's head. Dash quickly handed Jocelyn the knife.

"I'll help you," Dash whispered, seeing indecision clouding her eyes.

Jocelyn glanced up at him, surprised at the tenderness in his voice. This man had treated her roughly, had held a gun to her face—and yet now he seemed the polar opposite of the frightening figure he'd cut while robbing her coach.

"Are you ready?" the man pressed.

Jocelyn nodded, and then, before she could dwell on what she was about to do, she slipped the hot blade into Caleb's side. The boy convulsed, cried out against the cloth in his mouth, and struggled to be free of the intense pain. But Jocelyn held her hand steady, forcing herself not to pull it back. The stench of burning flesh curled upward, assaulting her senses. Jocelyn felt the tender skin give, then meld together. Just as she drew the blade out, Dash took it from her hands and pressed another fire-dipped knife into them.

Jocelyn quickly seared the wound closed as Dash pawed through a saddlebag near the pallet. He yanked out a clean shirt of expensive lawn, ripped it into strips, then passed them to Jocelyn. He watched as she carefully bound the boy's midsection, and listened to the words of comfort she quietly said to Caleb. For the moment Dash's mind swung back in time as he saw another of his friends lying injured and near death. In November of 1816 Dash's harsh words about the government and their disinterest in the plight of the poor had incited many people to participate in a meeting at Spa Fields. The meeting had soon become a riot, and soldiers had come tearing in on horseback, shooting people, even running them down with their horses.

Dash shook his head, trying to clear it of that awful day. He saw the death and destruction clearly, as though it were happening again. He felt responsible for the loss of life. If only he'd tried to aid the poor in another way. If only he'd kept his mouth shut . . .

Unable to stay in the confines of the tent a moment longer, Dash blundered outside just as the clouds opened up and let loose their store of rain.

Jocelyn glanced up at the two men who'd held Caleb, but neither offered any explanation for their leader's actions. Jocelyn didn't ask any questions. She might be told things she'd be better off not knowing.

Quietly Jocelyn said, "I'll need a warm blanket for the boy. And some cool water. He'll doubtless run a fever soon."

The man called Pretty Boy nodded, then moved to a corner of the tent, where he found a threadbare blanket.

"Thank you," Jocelyn said.

"He—he'll live, won't he?" Pretty Boy asked in a whisper as he glanced down at Cal's pinched face.

Jocelyn had learned from her father not to give false hopes. "I can't tell you that for certain," she replied. "But he's young, and if infection doesn't set in, then he has a chance."

Pretty Boy lifted his chin. He was indeed a handsome man, almost pretty, in fact. Eyes a deep brown flecked with gold, he had long lashes and a flawless complexion that was rare to behold. His wavy nut-brown hair hung past his shoulders and was tied like a pony's tail.

"I know my Caleb. He's strong, he'll make it through this."

"Is he family?" Jocelyn asked, curious about this group of renegades.

"We're all family," Pretty Boy answered. "All of us." And then, after another glance in Caleb's direction, he left the tent, his comrade silently following him.

Jocelyn spent the next few moments trying to make the lad more comfortable. Her thoughts skittered in all directions. Though she'd been terrified when she first entered the camp, that terror was now receding. She didn't truly believe these men would kill her, or even harm her. The fact that she'd helped Caleb was a bargaining tool for her, she knew, and she felt far from threatened by Pretty Boy's presence earlier.

As she kept a vigil over Caleb, Jocelyn thought again of her father's letter. The hour was late, and she knew whoever was to have met her this night was probably long gone. Her heart sank at the thought. She'd let her father down . . . and now she was in the middle of nowhere with a band of thieves. Her father would be out of his mind with worry once he learned of her abduction. Jocelyn

wasn't so much worried about herself as she was about
her family. She could take care of herself—or so she believed. She'd learned from her grandmother to be strong
and not panic in times of stress, and it was this inner
strength Jocelyn turned to now.

The wind had picked up, and the rain fell in heavy
sheets, battering the far side of the tent. Now and then
Caleb babbled incoherent words, and Jocelyn, sitting down
beside him, took his hand in hers.

"Hush," she soothed. "Just rest, Caleb."

"G-got to get the money. Need the . . . money."

"It's over," Jocelyn whispered. "Lie still." He was
possibly delirious, she knew, and he'd probably had too
much whiskey.

In the soft candlelight, Jocelyn studied the boy. He was
very young. Fair, curly hair framed his round face, and
streaks of dirt covered his buttonlike nose. He reminded
Jocelyn of the painted Cupids that hung in Amelia's sitting
room.

Just then the sound of riders breaking through the night
could be heard. Jocelyn jumped to her feet, thinking perhaps Charles and Jives had come for her. She hurried to
the opening of the tent and peered out into the rain-filled
darkness.

Three men on horseback galloped into the camp. Jocelyn could barely make out their faces, for the fire was
dying beneath the downpour. But she distinctly heard their
angered shouts. The man who'd abducted her—Dash,
they'd called him—walked out from under a shelter of trees
and met them.

Low words were exchanged, and even from Jocelyn's
vantage point she could see that Dash was upset with the
visitors. Finally he nodded his head, swung his arms wide,
as though inviting the men to stay, then headed in Jocelyn's direction.

Dash entered the tent, his face black with barely suppressed rage. "We've company," he announced to
Jocelyn.

Jocelyn backed away. He appeared to be filled with demons now.

"What do they want?" Jocelyn asked. "Are they friends of yours?"

"Hardly that," Dash shot back. He raked one hand through his sodden hair and Jocelyn could see that he was trying to keep his emotions in check. Suddenly he turned his attentions to her, saying gravely, "I'm afraid their arrival in camp puts you in a precarious position."

Jocelyn nearly laughed in irony. In her mind her position at this highwayman's hideout had never been anything but! "Oh?" she questioned. "And what do you mean by that?"

"Those men out there . . . they're a lawless lot. They'd sooner lop a man's ear off than listen to anything he had to say."

"And you wouldn't?" Jocelyn tossed back.

Dash's eyes narrowed. "I deserved that, I suppose. My apologies to you, Miss Greville." Dash noted her surprise. "Yes," he said. "I know your name. I hear everything and forget nothing. You would do well to remember that." He paused a moment, then added, "I had no intention of abducting you from your traveling companions, but—"

"But I've viewed your face, and now, because of your hasty decisions, I've seen your camp and your band of men as well. I guess one could say I've gone from the pan into the fire."

Dash watched her closely. "Your grace in the face of adversity is admirable."

"Admirable?" she said harshly. "No, I think not. To be frank with you, Mister . . . Dash, I'm very angry with you. In fact, should I live through this and find my way back home, I have every intention of seeing you pay dearly for your deeds."

"And if you don't find your way back home?"

Jocelyn stiffened, but lifted her chin, meeting the challenge. "Are you going to kill me?"

Her bluntness astounded him. "I'm not a murderer."

"And your men?"

"They follow my command . . . but our visitors—well, I cannot speak for them. I'm going to have to ask you to keep yourself confined to these quarters."

"I wasn't aware that I had other options," Jocelyn replied, meeting his gaze with an icy stare.

"Damn, you've a fiery nature, but let me make my point. Those men out there—and I shouldn't be telling you this, mistress, for you know too much already—they are none other than the Braden boys." At Jocelyn's surprised reaction, Dash added, "Ah, so you have heard of them. Good, then you'll know enough to keep your mouth closed."

"But they're thieves!" she said in a hurried whisper, then clamped her mouth shut tight, for Dash and his men were thieves as well.

"Well, they are that, and a good bit more. They've heard we were after the midnight coach. They're demanding part of the money."

"Will you give it to them?"

"No."

The sound of his voice indicated he was a man of steely determination, and Jocelyn had no doubt but there would be trouble ahead once the Braden men knew of his decision.

"Why did you invite them to stay?" she asked.

"I didn't. They insisted." Dash rubbed the back of his neck, then stared down at Caleb, who lay peaceably on the pallet. "How is he?"

Jocelyn moved to Caleb's side and brushed a cool hand across his brow. "He's warm," she answered. "A fever is setting in, I'm afraid."

Dash took in a deep breath of air, then blew it out. "*I* should have robbed the bloody coach!" he said, more to himself than to Jocelyn. "Dammit!" He slammed one balled fist against his thigh, then turned on his heel, pacing toward the far end of the tent.

Jocelyn watched him from beneath lowered lashes, a plan forming in her mind. Quietly she said, "My father practices medicine. If you release me, I'll tell my father what has happened. He'll be able to help. I could bring him here, but only if you promise to free us once he's had a look at Caleb.''

Slowly Dash turned to face her. "Let you go?" He shook his head. "I can't do that . . . not yet.''

Jocelyn refused to give up so easily. "Not even if releasing me will save Caleb's life?''

Clearly she'd hit the proper nerve with such a bargain, for Dash appeared to consider the idea.

Hoping to press her advantage, Jocelyn added, "If you return my letter to me, I—I won't go to the authorities with what I know. I can promise you that. And neither will Jives or Charles—they'll both do as I say.''

"And your father?" Dash asked.

"He'll just be glad I am safe.''

Dash eyed her critically. Lord, she was beautiful, all windblown and wild-looking in the candlelight. Her eyes were bright with hope, her breath coming in short gasps that caused the bodice of her gown to tighten across her breasts. Dash had to suck in a large gulp of air just to keep his mind on the matter at hand, and not on the sight of her. She was like no woman he'd ever known. But he couldn't release her—not until he'd made the rendezvous and delivered the booty from the coach. No, there was too much at stake.

Quietly he said, "You are quick to make promises you might not be able to keep.''

"But I *can* keep them!" Jocelyn said indignantly. "You don't understand—my father and I are very close. He'll do whatever I ask him. And my cousin Charles is like a brother to me! We've kept secrets before, believe me. I won't betray you. I'll forget what I've seen this night. If you just return my letter and release me, I'll forget you, your name, your face, everything!''

The words tumbled out of Jocelyn's mouth, but as she said them, she had to wonder if she would be able to forget this man. Certainly she could keep her promise not to go to the authorities, but would she ever forget the feel of the man's hands on her body, or the touch of his mouth over hers?

Dash weighed his choices. To set her free could mean imprisonment for himself as well as Caleb and Rourke, for the three of them had robbed two coaches this night. But to release her could also mean proper care for Caleb.

Dash glanced at the boy, who lay peacefully now, having drifted into a whiskey-fogged sleep. Fifteen he was, and the only man of his house. His father had been killed in the Spa Fields riots. The boy was needed at home to help his mother and his seven brothers and sisters. Dash hadn't wanted the lad to strike out on this dangerous quest, but Cal had been insistent and wouldn't take no for an answer. In fact, he had ridden hard to catch up with Dash and his men, and by the time Dash had known of Cal's presence, it had been too late to turn back, and too risky to allow the boy to travel home alone.

But though Dash wanted desperately to help Caleb, he couldn't allow this woman to go free. She'd seen too much, and until Dash had the booty on its way northward, and his men clearing the campsite, he had to keep Miss Greville with him.

Having made his decision, Dash said, "I admire your bravery, mistress." He saw she would argue with him, and raised one hand. "But, no, I cannot risk the lives of my men by letting you go too soon."

"But—"

"Listen, and listen well," Dash cut in, hearing footsteps outside the tent and knowing there might be trouble. "When Braden enters—and he will—you will act as though you're my mistress."

Her eyes widened in shock, then narrowed in disgust.

"You'll do it," Dash said with authority. *"Or you'll live only so long to wish that you had."*

Just then two men entered the tent. Encased in huge greatcoats streaming with water and weather-worn hats that hid their eyes from view, they appeared formidable.

"Greetings," the larger of the two said. He faced Jocelyn, sweeping the hat from his head and then giving her a deep bow.

Jocelyn wasn't fooled by his genteel gesture, though she nodded in acknowledgment.

"Had I known you were entertaining a lady, Dash, I would have come in here sooner instead of standing outside with your men." He smiled at Jocelyn, his thin lips curling up. Undoing the closures of his coat, he stepped toward her, then extended one hand. "The name's Lane Braden. And you are?"

Ignoring the proffered hand, she said, "Jocelyn Gr—"

Dash cut in, moving closer to her. "The lady's name is Jocelyn—*just* Jocelyn—and she's with me, Laney."

Jocelyn glared at Dash, then said, "I was just leaving."

Laney Braden laughed. "To go where?" he asked. " 'Tis a nasty night, not fit for man nor beast, and certainly not for such a genteel lady as yourself."

Before Jocelyn had a chance to reply, Dash stepped to her side and, surprising her, wrapped one arm possessively about her shoulders. "What do you want, Laney?" he demanded, his fingers cutting into the skin of Jocelyn's shoulder.

Clearly he was telling her, with his actions, to be quiet and to let him do the talking. Jocelyn had half a notion to shrug away from him, but she decided it best not to be too hasty.

Braden fixed Dash with a long stare. His feral eyes were the color of a mudhole, and his voice, when he spoke, set Jocelyn's nerves on edge. With little effort the man shed his outer coat, revealing an expensive yet sturdy coat beneath and trousers that were mud-splattered but equally rich.

Jocelyn had heard of the Braden gang. Rumors of their deeds were known throughout the Cotswolds. Lane Braden's reputation preceded him even in the countryside of England. He was known as the "gentleman robber," for he wooed the elite of London with one hand while stealing from them with the other. But not one person who'd been robbed by Braden and his men had seen their faces. As luck would have it, Jocelyn would now be able to boast having seen Braden in the flesh—but, of course, she first had to live to tell of the moment. . . .

To Dash, Braden replied, "I want only shelter from this wretched night, and perhaps a strong drink or two. Have you any brandy, my man? If not, I'll take some of that pathetic whiskey your boy Granger is so fond of."

Dash nodded toward the flask near Caleb's pallet.

"Good, good," Braden replied, motioning to his man to fetch the flask. When he had it in his hands, he took a long swallow, then wiped his chin with the back of one wrist. "I see you ran into a spot of trouble while taking the midnight coach. Tsk, tsk, Dash. You should know better than to send a lad to do a man's job. Thieving demands a certain skill—or the luck of the draw. How is the boy?" he asked, sending a perfunctory glance in Caleb's direction.

"He'll live," Dash assured Braden, though he wasn't so certain.

"I don't know why you waste your time with these people, Dash. You could ride with the Bradens and your backside would be safe."

Dash nodded. "So you've told me."

"The offer still stands."

"As does my answer."

Braden laughed again, then took another swig of the whiskey. Thunder rumbled, sounding as though it were cracking directly above the tent, and a sharp streak of lightning flared brightly.

Braden mimicked a shudder. "Frightful night. I detest storms. What do you say we pass the time with a bit of bone throwing, eh, Dash?"

Jocelyn was just about to announce that she had no intention of waiting around while Dash played a silly game of who knew what, but Dash tightened his hold on her shoulder, then nodded to Braden.

Before Jocelyn could object, Dash, Braden, and the third man settled down on the grass beneath the tent. Jocelyn would have moved away, but Dash reached up, took her hand in his, then, wordlessly, guided her down beside him.

Braden gave Jocelyn a private grin. "Your gentleman friend has found more than one victory at the London gaming tables, but he and I both know which of the two of us can best the other. I am forever telling him, 'Dash, you shouldn't be wasting your skills in the countryside. Come to London,' I tell him. 'And we'll dazzle the blue bloods with our combined prowess of both pistol and dice.' But Dash, he's a stubborn man. He would go hungry just to feed others, wouldn't you, man?" Braden asked.

Dash's lips curved in a small half-smile, and Jocelyn could discern that he was only indulging Braden for the sake of humoring him. "Get on with our game, Laney. It's been a long day for me."

"Ah," Braden breathed, a knowing look on his face. "So you've a yearning to bed down for the night. With such a comely wench at your side, I can't fault you."

"*Wench?*" Jocelyn exploded, her dander up.

But Dash smoothly intervened, running one hand atop Jocelyn's skirt-covered thigh. To Braden, he said, "She's in high spirits this night. Ignore her."

"But how can I?" Braden insisted, eyeing Jocelyn as though she were on display. "Disheveled though she may be, I've rarely seen a woman of such beauty."

"She's *my* woman, Laney," Dash drawled, his voice brooking no argument.

Jocelyn was close to spitting fire, so angry was she that the two of them could talk about her as though she were no more than some prime horseflesh being auctioned off! Not hiding her anger, she pushed Dash's hand from her thigh and glared at him.

Braden chuckled. "It appears as though your lady isn't as pleased by you as you'd like me to believe."

With a slow and easy smile on his lips, Dash slid his gaze to Jocelyn's. His eyes, however, bit into hers, and Jocelyn knew well enough the message in them. She'd gone too far, he told her with just a look.

But Jocelyn didn't care. She wanted to go home, *had,*

in fact, been told she could leave, and now this. Doubtless her father and grandmother would be worried sick once they learned of her abduction. And what of Charles and Jives? How did they fare?

"Oh, she's pleased well enough," Jocelyn heard Dash say, and then, before she could react, he pulled her hand to his mouth, pressing an intimate kiss on the inside of her wrist. "Aren't you, my dear?" he asked, staring deeply into her eyes, clearly demanding her agreement.

Jocelyn ground her teeth together, and then, knowing Lane Braden was waiting for her response, said, "Yes, I am."

Jocelyn could see the flash of relief in Dash's eyes as he released her hand and turned his attention to Braden. The touch of his lips still lingered on her wrist, making Jocelyn edgy, but she quelled the urge to wipe away the tingle.

Lane Braden still had his eyes on her as he withdrew from his coat pocket a pair of dice that appeared to be fashioned from human teeth. He smiled, noticing Jocelyn's discomfort.

"I carved them myself," he told her. "Pulled them from the mouth of a sailor who thought to rob me while I slept. Pity for him that I wasn't sleeping, but only resting my eyes."

Jocelyn shuddered visibly. Laney chuckled. His laughter set Jocelyn's nerves on end. She knew very well the man wished to unsettle her, which made Jocelyn that much more determined not to show her unease.

She watched as the men became engrossed in their game. Braden won the first two tosses, his companion winning the third. Dash took his defeat with grace, which made Jocelyn suspicious, for the stakes kept climbing.

For nearly an hour the men continued the game of chance and their drinking. As Jocelyn watched, she began wondering at Braden's good fortune. He won every toss. Jocelyn began to keep a tally of the combinations of numbers that ensured Braden the winning roll. Just as Jocelyn suspected, the combinations began to repeat themselves.

Before long Dash had depleted his own source of money,

and to Jocelyn's dismay, he used two of her cousin's rings as his next wager. With a warning squeeze to her knee, he stopped Jocelyn from making a protest.

Jocelyn kept quiet only because she could see for herself that Lane Braden was fast becoming drunk. In truth, the renegade across from her frightened her more than Dash ever had. But Dash lost the next toss as well, and Jocelyn watched as Braden pulled in his winnings, which included two of Charles's most treasured rings.

From his coat front Lane Braden produced a small pouch of coins, tossing it to the dirt. "I'll wager all of it," he announced, taking a long swig from the flask. "What have you to wager, Dash?"

Dash shook his head slowly. "Nothing to compare."

Jocelyn glanced at him in surprise, for she knew very well that he still held three more of her cousins rings as well as her gold locket and a very valuable ring her grandmother had bestowed upon her at her last birthday celebration. Both the necklace and the ring were worth more money than all of Charles's rings. Surely Dash must know this, Jocelyn thought. Thief that he was, he could probably price any piece of jewelry laid before him.

"I don't believe you, old friend. What about the cache from the coach?" Braden said.

Dash didn't blink an eye, but Jocelyn could see the jump of muscle along his jawline.

"The cache isn't mine to wager, and well you know it, Laney."

Lane Braden gave a harsh grunt of laughter. "You're too bloody noble, Dash. That's always been your trouble. Now, you know I'm not going to leave until you meet my wager." He nodded toward Jocelyn. "What about your pretty little piece here? You could wager her charms for a night."

Jocelyn itched to slap the man, but Dash closed one hand over hers before she could do so. He eyed her closely for a moment, warning her to keep still.

In an even voice Dash said to Laney, "If you're in a gaming mood, then I'll meet your wager . . . with this."

Slowly he released his hold on Jocelyn, then drew the signet ring from his left ring finger.

Braden's eyes rounded with interest. "The family crest? Ho now, Dash, do the cache from the coach and this wench here mean so much to you that you would rather wager such a treasure?"

Dash said nothing, only tossing the thing down to the dirt.

Jocelyn saw the flash of a cherry-red ruby as the ring rolled to a halt alongside Braden's pouch. It was a huge ruby, perfectly cut, and flanked by two shields which had elaborate markings upon them. Jocelyn tried to make out those markings, but couldn't. Clearly, though, the man who'd abducted her hailed from a titled background. She glanced up at Dash, wondering what had brought him to a life of thieving—and also wondering why he'd chosen to part with something of his own rather than toss down her jewelry.

Dash felt Jocelyn's gaze on him and cursed himself for bringing her attention to his signet ring. If it hadn't been the only thing of value on him, he wouldn't have wagered it. But he'd lost his own money during the first few rolls of the dice, and if he wished to keep Laney's mind off the cache taken from the coach—and off Jocelyn—then he knew he had no choice but to remove his ring. As for gaming with Jocelyn's locket and ring, he couldn't bring himself to do it. He'd seen the look of pain on her face when he'd first taken them from her, and had decided then that someday he would return them to her.

"Your roll, Laney," Dash said.

Braden clacked the dice together in the palm of his hand. Smiling slyly, he sent them spinning to the ground.

With a wary eye, Jocelyn watched as the pair tripped across the grass.

When she'd been barely thirteen, she had joined Charles and his friends in their weekly games of chance. Though the games had been harmless, with such things as worthless cufflinks with no match and odd buttons being wagered, Jocelyn had learned the subtleties of the game.

She'd even cheated once or twice herself, for to get away with cheating had been a mark of superiority. Her past experiences enabled Jocelyn to observe this particular game with a skilled eye. She watched closely.

Yes, there! Like a quick flash of lightning, Jocelyn saw an odd roll in the dice. It was as though . . . as though they weren't shaved properly on one side! Why, Laney Braden was a cheat!

Braden quickly swiped up his pouch along with Dash's ring as well as his companion's wager. "Luck is a fickle partner, eh, Dash?" he asked, chuckling.

Dash made no reply.

But Jocelyn, without thinking, cried, "Unfair! Those dice have been tampered with. You, Laney Braden, are a cheat!"

Three

A horrid silence descended as Lane Braden eyed Jocelyn with a mixture of contempt and intrigue.

"Do you realize the weight of such an accusation?" he asked. Jocelyn felt a stab of fear in her breast, but forced herself not to back down. Her only weapon was her courage. "I do," she challenged, not flinching beneath the man's heated stare.

Slowly Braden rose to his feet. "Then you would do well to apologize, lest I be forced to defend my honor."

"*Honor?*" she spat. "You probably haven't a smidgen of honor in your black heart!"

Braden's face contorted with rage, then he lunged drunkenly in Jocelyn's direction.

Instantly Dash uncoiled from the ground. With his head bent he crashed into Braden's body and sent him sprawling to the grass. But Braden rolled to his back and with a strength that took Dash off guard hooked his hands to Dash's neck and squeezed.

"You stupid ass," Dash muttered. Eyes blazing, he pried Lane's hands from his neck, then drove his right fist against Braden's jaw. Lane's head hit the hard earth with a thud, but before Dash could punch him again, Lane brought his left knee up and slammed it between Dash's legs.

Needles of pain flared up into Dash's brain. His stomach tightened and convulsed. Gasping for breath, he doubled over and waited for the pain to subside.

"Just like old times, eh, Dash?" Braden asked, getting slowly to his feet and rubbing his jaw.

Dash lifted his head. "You never could give a fair fight, Laney." He maneuvered himself into a crouching position. "Then again, neither could I." With that he hurled himself into Lane's midsection. The two men toppled to the ground, rolling once, fists flying.

Jocelyn stepped out of harm's way, backing up until she met with the side of the tent. "Enough!" she cried. The men didn't listen. They were too absorbed in their fistfight, which, to Jocelyn's surprise, soon evolved into friendly roughhousing.

After several more minutes of punching each other and rolling about, the men separated and sat a few feet apart. They grinned at each other.

"You're a damned sight, Laney," Dash said, nursing a swollen left eye. "Even your own mother would disown you if she saw you now."

Lane swiped away the blood trickling from the broken skin at the corner of his mouth. "Haven't you heard, Dash? My mother disowned me long ago. Said I wasn't fit to polish the family silver."

Dash grinned. "Your family has no silver and well you know it."

"Ah, that was before I took to the highways and byways, my friend. Damn, but it *has* been too long since I've talked with you." Lane staggered to his feet, reaching out to help Dash up. "Come, let us finish that rotgut brew you and your boys call whiskey, and I'll fill you in on my latest adventures. And," he added, glancing in Jocelyn's direction, "you can tell me where you found such a gorgeous woman."

"She's *my* woman, Laney. Remember that."

Jocelyn straightened, thoroughly intent on informing both men that she belonged to no one. But Dash broke free of Lane's hold and walked uneasily to where she stood.

"I demand you take me home!" she hissed at him.

Dash glowered at her. "We'll discuss this later," he said in a low voice meant only for her ears.

Jocelyn lifted her chin. "There isn't going to be a 'later,' " she replied. "I'm leaving. Or have you forgotten your promise to me?"

"I didn't make any promises."

He swayed on his feet, and it was then that Jocelyn noticed the pupils of his eyes were as tiny as pinpoints.

"You're hurt," she said.

"I'm fine."

"No, you're not. By morning your eye will be swollen shut." Jocelyn reached up and gingerly touched the tips of her fingers to the corner of his left eye.

Dash pulled back from her touch. Jocelyn knew well enough that he didn't want her fussing over him in front of Laney Braden.

"Fine," she said heatedly. "If you're foolish enough to engage in such child's play, then you deserve to be in pain."

To her dismay, Dash's lips tilted up in a crooked grin. "Concerned about me, are you?"

Jocelyn dropped her hand to her side. "The only thing I'm concerned about is returning home alive. If something should happen to you, I might not return home at all."

"True," Dash said thoughtfully. "But don't be misled by Laney's outburst. Actually, he can be a gentleman when he wishes. I'm certain that should something unforeseen happen to me, Laney would escort you to your father's door. But," he added with a grim smile, "I'm not saying your virtue would not be threatened."

Jocelyn peered past Dash's shoulder at Laney Braden. With a clean handkerchief pressed to his bleeding lip, he appeared not so formidable as he had a moment ago. In fact, Braden looked, surprisingly, out of place in the makeshift tent. The fine cut of his clothes, the sapphire flashing on his pinky ring, even the diamond stickpin jabbed into his shirtfront gave him an air of aristocracy. But looks could well be deceiving, Jocelyn knew.

She returned her attention to Dash. "The man cheated you, yet you heap him with praise."

"Praise? Hardly that. I said he'd return you to your home, I didn't say he'd leave you alone there. Doubtless, he'd dog your every step until you reciprocated his attentions. He's an intense fellow."

"Ho, Dash!" Lane called out. "Enough chattering! Where's that jar of whiskey? I'm thirsty, friend, and the night remains a virgin. Bring your lady out in the rain with us. We'll show her I'm not such a scoundrel after all."

"Impatient as always, aren't you, Laney?" Dash said, then, looking deeply into Jocelyn's eyes, asked, "Well?"

"Well what?" Jocelyn replied, wary of this change of pace in the two men.

"Will you join us outside? The storm is nearly spent. Or do you prefer to say warm and dry?"

"Prefer it to what?" she asked warily.

Dash's eyes slipped down her svelte figure, vividly reminding Jocelyn that she was his prisoner and that he could do what he would. His voice husky, he said, "You'll see for yourself . . . that is, if you join us."

Jocelyn half feared the man would decide to stay in the tent with her. Not wanting to be alone with the renegade leader, she said, "Very well. I'll come. But you should send someone in to sit with Caleb."

Dash's eyes warmed on her. "As you wish."

Jocelyn stepped away from Dash. She checked on Caleb, who stirred only once when she touched his heated brow. After cooling him with the wet cloth from the basin, Jocelyn joined Dash and Braden outside. A few of Dash's men had gone to stand watch in the woods, while the rest converged about the dying fire.

The rain had indeed lessened, coming down now in a fine mist that splashed the leaves of the trees. Pretty Boy tossed some twigs into the fire. The man named Granger produced several more jars of whiskey, while another man took a battered fiddle from its case and began to play a sprightly tune. A few men began to dance, stomping their booted feet atop the wet grass and turning in ungainly circles as they clapped their hands and hooted. Jocelyn was amazed that these men could be so lax at having her in their midst. What she knew about them, if she told the right people, could very well land them with their necks in nooses!

As Jocelyn watched the highwaymen dance, Pretty Boy approached.

"Are you hungry?" he asked, offering Jocelyn a square of starched linen filled with an array of meats. "From the kitchen of the Fox's Lair—the best meats in the Cotswolds."

Surprised by his generosity, Jocelyn smiled, then took the fare. "How did you come by them?" she asked, then immediately wished she could snatch the words back.

Pretty Boy shook his head. "They're not stolen, if that's what you're thinking. I've a younger sister who's a maid there," he explained. "She makes these herself, along with confections that melt on your tongue. My family's proud of Meggie. She fled from the factories when she was but thirteen and made a life of her own. . . . I should have been so wise."

"What do you mean?"

Pretty Boy stared into the shadows of the night. "I thought I could make a change if I followed my father into the factory. I thought, if I worked hard enough, long enough, I could be something more."

"And now?" Jocelyn asked, thinking of all her father had told her about life in the factories. Young, homeless children were rumored to be picked off the streets of London and pressed into service in the northern factories. They were forced to work long hours, given small rations of food and little comfort. It was a horrible life for young and old alike.

The young man blinked, as if pulling himself out of the tight hold of a past that had taken too much of him. "Now I ride with Dash," he answered with pride, then walked away from her.

Jocelyn watched his retreat, wondering at this band of thieves she'd fallen in with. Highwaymen they were. Men who could be hanged if caught by the authorities. And yet, as Jocelyn stood there in the misty rain with her hair clinging to her shoulders and her nostrils filled with the heady scent of earth and foliage, she was suddenly hard-pressed to view them in an unfavorable light. Certainly these men had robbed the midnight coach, had even robbed her own coach and scared poor Charles and Jives into a harried flight, but Jocelyn found that she was almost forgiving them their nefarious deeds.

How absurd, she thought, watching as some of the men danced a silly jig while others shared jars of whiskey. She should be damning the whole lot of them. But she wasn't.

Lane Braden interrupted her reverie. "May I be so bold as to ask you to dance?" he inquired, bowing. As he righted himself, he added teasingly, "Or are you more of a mind to whack me alongside the head?"

"The latter, of course," Jocelyn answered, narrowing her eyes. "You toss shaved dice and scrape into your hands ill-gained winnings. And if not for Dash's intervention, you most assuredly would have thrown me to the ground for calling you the cheat that you are. What have you to say for yourself?"

Lane frowned. "Only that I am deeply sorry that I upset you. I hope to start anew with you, mistress. The name's Lane Braden. My friends address me as Laney . . . as I pray you shall do."

Jocelyn fought to control the smile that played about the corners of her mouth. She'd known men like Lane Braden; poised and polite on the outside, hard as granite on the inside. She could see him for what he was, an opportunist who could charm a fox from its home and then snare the beast in an instant.

"You're a devil in a sheep's mantle," Jocelyn told him.

"I am," Lane admitted easily. "But we've a common bond, I think."

"Oh? And whatever could that be?"

"Dash."

"I don't know what you're talking about."

Lane laughed. "Of course you do. He claims you as his own—and I must confess that I'm jealous."

"Really, Mr. Braden—"

"Laney, please."

Jocelyn nodded. "Laney. There's nothing to be jealous about. Dash and I are . . . we've a tenuous bond. In fact, on the morrow I intend to be gone from this camp."

Lane Braden digested this information, and it was quite clear to Jocelyn that the man was extremely interested in whatever she might have to say about Dash.

"Well, then, if that's the case," he said, "we shouldn't tarry a moment longer. Will you dance with me or not?"

Despite her previous conclusions about Braden's character—of lack of it—Jocelyn found herself warming to the man and his ways.

"I couldn't dance with a cheating man," she replied.

"Even if this man returned his winnings of the night?"

"You'd do that? *All* of them?"

"If that is what you wish."

"It is."

"Then it's done," Braden replied, snapping his fingers. "Now come, dance with me before the fiddler looses his tune."

Before Jocelyn could reply, Lane Braden took the linen from her hands and swept her out into the circle of men. More than a little besotted with whiskey, Lane missed a step or two, but he managed to stay upright long enough to take her through several intricate steps of a ballroom dance that neither followed the fiddler's tune nor matched the ambience of the rainy night.

Jocelyn could hardly believe the ridiculous situation she found herself in. She'd been robbed, held at gunpoint, and had been whisked away from her cousin and footman only to find herself ensconced in a den of thieves.

From the corner of her eye Jocelyn caught sight of Dash. He stood apart from the others, his bruised face appearing mean in the glare from the campfire. He held a flask of drink in his right fist, the knuckles of which were caked with blood. Even from her vantage point, Jocelyn could see that he was angry.

Dash tossed back another swallow of potent whiskey, wincing as it burned a path into his belly. Damn, but he was suddenly in a foul mood. He had enough to worry about, what with getting the cache of gold on its way north, and now he had added abduction to his list of rotten deeds. If he'd known it wasn't Robert Mowrey traveling in the coach, he would not have stopped it. And then Jocelyn had gone and ripped off his mask!

Dash's mood darkened. He didn't like what Jocelyn's nearness did to him. Certainly she was a beautiful woman, but there was more to her charm. She was like a dancing candle in a dreary night—bright, lovely, spirited. She was compassionate as well, and far too brave for her own good. If Dash had met her under different circumstances, he'd be wooing her, he knew.

Not only had his night gone awry the minute he'd met up with *her*, but now his childhood friend had decided to reenter his life. Dash didn't trust Laney Braden. He liked the fellow, but he knew well enough not to entrust any confidences to the man.

Lane hadn't changed a bit, Dash thought, watching Jocelyn and Laney enthrall the others with their show of nimble feet. Hell, Dash thought miserably, *I* was the one to teach Laney how to dance with the ladies, how to flatter and please them! Dash thought back to the first time he'd met Lane Braden. They'd been mere lads then, both of them more interested in how to shoot a cap off a man's head than how to woo the gentler sex.

At thirteen Laney knew how to steal a watch fob from a gentleman's pocket. He could run faster than any of the other lads who roamed the streets of London, could snatch a valise out of a porter's hands, and could pilfer two quid from an aristocrat in a crowded street without ever being noticed. But what Laney lacked in deportment, Dash had had in overabundant supply.

The two boys had become fast friends the day Laney tried to pick the pocket of Lord Montague Warfield, the

very man who'd rescued Dash from a dreary life in the
streets of London. Like Laney, Dash had been a child of
the slums, stealing what meager allotments of food he
could get his hands on and going hungry when there was
nothing to take. At the age of seven, Dash had seen too
much pain and known more than his share of grief. His
mother, the only light of his life, had been murdered in
her sleep, her bottle of gin that she kept close at hand
stolen from her motionless fingers. Dash didn't—
couldn't—remember the details of that horrible night. He
only remembered being scared and cold, and wanting his
mum to wake up. But she never did open her eyes again.

The days following her death were a blur to Dash. A
man named Will fetched him from the dank coal cellar,
telling him someone would come and care for his mum.
Will had had to pry Dash's hands from his mother's stiff
form. "She's with God in 'eaven now," Will had whispered. Dash hadn't understood, nor could he understand
why his cat, Six Toes, couldn't come with him. "Ain't no
bloody cat here that I can see," Will had said, lifting Dash
into the air and carrying him out of the cellar.

And that was when Dash met the powerful Lord Montague Warfield. A bachelor by choice yet unhappy despite
his decision not to marry, Lord Monty desired an heir and
had chosen Dash to fill the void in his life. Wealthy, po-
litically active, and powerful, Lord Montague Warfield was
a man to be reckoned with among his peers. But Dash
learned patience from the man, a wealth of values, and a
sense of his own worth in the world.

Uncle Monty, as Lord Montague requested Dash call
him, had only kind words about Dash's mother. "I would
have married your mother," he told Dash on the day they
buried her. "Indeed I would have had she only given me
some sign that she would accept."

Dash had wiped the tears from his eyes and tried to be
brave as he threw the first clump of dirt atop his dear
mum's casket. "Why—why didn't she?" he asked, hic-
cuping in spite of his vow not to cry anymore.

Lord Monty had stared long and hard at the box of

wood and its highly polished brass hinges—no pauper's grave for Dash's mum, no siree. Uncle Monty had seen to a right and fitting burial, and Dash was eternally grateful.

"Because she loved another man," Uncle Monty finally said. "I think she believed that man would one day come back for her, but he never did. But your mother was a brave woman." He'd put his arm across Dash's bony shoulders, gazing down at him with pure love. "You are very much like your mother, boy. But hear me now, you'll never want for anything from this day forward. What is mine shall one day be yours. The Warfield name shall live on through you. I promised your mother that should anything happen to her I would take care of you."

And Uncle Monty *had* seen to Dash's every need. After the funeral service, Lord Monty had taken Dash to a tailor, where Dash was measured and fitted for a number of coats and trousers, shirts and underclothes. Dash had never seen such fine material in all his young life, and he'd been beside himself with glee to learn that he would now be outfitted like a son of royalty. That evening they'd dined on roast duckling, baby carrots, and a delightful array of fresh fruits, as well as sugary cakes for dessert. And they'd toasted his mum's memory with sweet wine. It hadn't been a day of mourning, but a day of remembering. Dash had fallen asleep, sending a prayer for God to take good care of his mum, and promising in return that he would become a man his mum would have been proud to call her own.

Out and about in Hyde Park on a rainy May morning six years later, Lord Warfield and Dash were tripping along in Lord Monty's spiffy carriage when they came upon a small boy lying prone in their pathway. At first Dash had thought the lad had been run over by a carriage, as did Lord Monty, but when Monty had gone to the lad's aid Dash had seen Laney pilfer not only Lord Monty's gold money clip, but his watch fob as well!

Dash hadn't blurted this out to Uncle Monty right away, but waited until Lord Monty had met up with several of his political friends for the proper moment to race after the ragamuffin who'd robbed his uncle.

With direct orders from Lord Monty to stay out of the dirt and out of trouble, and to return within the hour, Dash sprinted off into the park. After all, he'd reasoned, knowing he might have to leave the park grounds to find the little thief, his uncle no longer had his watch, so how was Lord Monty to know when an hour had passed?

Dash tackled Laney in a dead run. The two boys went headlong down a steep incline and landed squarely in a puddle of odorous mud. Dash came up sputtering; Laney with his fists flying.

"Och! You brat!" Laney had screeched in a high-pitched voice. "You've got me damned britches all wet!"

"You beggar!" Dash yelled back. "You stole my uncle's belongings!"

"You calling me a thief?" Laney cried. "Who the bloody 'ell do you think you are? I'm no thief! Why, I ought to blacken your eye for saying such a thing!"

"Try it and I'll see you rot in Newgate!" Dash yelled back.

And then the two boys had gone at each other with a vengeance. By the time their fight ended, Dash had indeed gotten a black eye—two, in fact—and Laney had the breath knocked out of him when Dash punched him in the stomach several times.

Lord Monty pulled the two apart, thoroughly aghast to find his proper, well-behaved Dash knee-deep in mud. Always one to defend the downtrodden, Lord Montague Warfield saw a crusade in reshaping the life of one Laney Braden. He took the urchin to the Warfield estate, fed and clothed him, and quite literally took Laney under his protective wing. Dash had been beside himself with joy, for he now had the sibling he'd wanted for so long.

For Dash there were no more dreary school lessons, with the pinch-faced and switch-wielding Mistress Welding, to be endured alone. Mealtimes became great fun as Dash and Laney sent Mistress Welding into a snit with their tossing of pudding and meats. And the outings in Hyde Park became adventurous explorations as the two boys spirited themselves off into the thick of the trees where they aimed their slingshots at hand-holding lovers along the pathways.

But those exciting, prank-filled days soon ended when Laney's mother showed up on Lord Monty's doorstep. In her wild cockney accent the woman had demanded the return of her child. Lord Monty had at first refused, charging the woman with abandonment of her son. But Laney had surprised them all by declaring that he wished to live with his mother, and so Lord Monty had no choice but to let the lad go.

Crushed at the loss of his playmate, Dash had been inconsolable for a fortnight, until his uncle announced that he intended to set up house for Laney and his wayward mother. Soon Laney and his mother moved into a London flat furnished and paid for by Lord Monty. But the relationship between the two boys changed. No longer did they share their meals or their schooling. While Dash was sent off to school in Cambridge, Laney stayed behind and soon fell back to his streetwise ways. When Dash returned from his many trips abroad and his final year of studies, he was far removed from the lad he'd been. Molded to take on the responsibilities of a government seat as well as the managing of Lord Monty's estates, Dash was now a man of the world. A sparkling and exciting life of politics and whirlwind aristocracy awaited Dash, while only poverty lay in Laney's future. Though Dash attempted to strengthen his bond with Laney, his friend turned a cold shoulder to him. While Dash entered the posh salons of London, Laney slunk through London's back alleys and reacquainted himself with the vagabonds of society.

Dash took another swallow of whiskey. Ten years. How had time managed to pass so swiftly? he wondered. The last time he'd seen Laney had been in a London gaming house. The two had wagered on the same toss of the die—and Dash had lost. They'd laughed about it then, but Dash had felt the distance between them. They were no longer the close blood-brothers they'd been. Laney's mother had died of consumption, and though Lord Monty had offered Laney employment within the offices of government, Laney had declined the offer, instead choosing a route of lawlessness.

Laney, the wild one, Laney, the boy without a home, had grown into an embittered man—and now he danced with a woman Dash held more than a passing interest in.

Tossing the flask to the ground, Dash muttered a curse beneath his breath, then stepped into the circle of men. He saw Jocelyn's eyes widen as he touched Laney on the shoulder.

"I'll dance with the lady," Dash said to Laney.

"That's not for me to decide," Lane replied.

Jocelyn saw the hidden demons in Dash's dark eyes. He was angry, that was clear. But why? She faced Dash with more bravado than she felt.

Dash didn't say a word. Instead, he took Jocelyn by the waist and led her away from Lane Braden. It was no ordinary dance he led her into, but rather one of his own making. He held her too close, the palm of his left hand fitting intimately to the small of her back while his right hand closed over hers in a sure grip. Jocelyn felt his warm breath cascade over her cheek, could feel her breasts touch his chest.

"Dash," she began.

"What?" he asked harshly, his stormy gaze peering down at her. "Would you rather dance with Braden? He's not to be trusted, you know."

"I'm well aware of that fact," Jocelyn returned, determined not to allow this man to unnerve her. "But I must admit I've never danced in this manner before."

"They dance like this in London."

"I've been to London," she replied. "I know how they move about the dance floor, and this is not the way—"

"I'm not referring to how the elite twirl about the dance floor. I'm talking about the seamier side of London . . . where a man and a woman can slide their bodies against each other in shadowy chambers." His left hand rotated in tiny circles at the small of her back as he drew her closer still.

Jocelyn closed her eyes, trying hard to will away the

odd comfort she found in Dash's embrace. He was a thief, nothing more, and she was a lady. So why, Jocelyn wondered, did she not push him away? Was it her wild thirst for adventure that made her curious about this man and his way of life? She'd always been reckless, true, but now her very life was hanging by a thread, and yet Jocelyn was intrigued. Perhaps Charles had been correct. Maybe she *was* too reckless for her own good.

Jocelyn opened her eyes, staring up into Dash's handsome face. She felt a queer squeeze of her heart as she looked into his eyes. The visible, naked pain there cut her to the quick.

"You're drunk," she whispered, wishing she'd had the nerve to ask him why he'd felt the need to immerse himself in drink.

"So I am." He moved her slowly across the damp grass, his hips brushing against hers now and then.

Jocelyn fought hard to keep her composure. She was more than just a little affected by his attentions. Though his touch was far too intimate, it was also gentle. For a flash of an instant Jocelyn wondered what kind of a lover the highwayman would be. It was a dangerous thought, but one that came into her head nevertheless. Would he be intense, as she'd seen him be during the raid? Or would his seduction be filled with a coaxing gentleness?

They danced passed Braden then, who watched them with hooded eyes, and Jocelyn felt Dash stiffen.

She asked, "Does Laney's presence bother you so much that you must drown your good sense in whiskey?"

"Laney, is it?" Dash replied, his voice harsh. "So he's charmed as well as intrigued you."

"I didn't say that."

"You didn't have to."

"I want to go home," she said.

Dash shook his head. "Not tonight—or rather, not until later this morning."

Immediately Jocelyn came to a halt. "But you promised me I could go home!"

Dash tightened his hold and forced her to continue his

odd and nearly indecent dance. "I told you I don't make promises."

He released his hold about her waist to touch his hand to her chin. He tipped Jocelyn's face up so that their eyes met. "There are things you don't know, Jocelyn."

"Such as?" she demanded, incensed that her blood began to tingle every time their bodies touched. Her breasts felt on fire, aching whenever her nipples brushed his chest. Even through layers of material, Jocelyn could discern the heat of him. He was like some burning flame that drew her ever closer.

"Such as why I cannot allow you to leave my camp for several more hours. I'm afraid you'll have to make do with my hospitality—at least until after the sun rises."

Jocelyn waited for some sort of explanation, but none was forthcoming. A part of her didn't really want to be privy to his reasons. The less she knew, the less danger she would be in. Or so she hoped.

"My father will be beside himself with worry," she replied, trying to maintain some semblance of composure. It wouldn't do to break down into tears in front of this man, she knew. Jocelyn had never been one for theatrics, but she was dreadfully tired and very close to crying. She was frustrated and much too affected by the man's closeness. He need only touch her, and Jocelyn felt like falling into his embrace!

"I am deeply sorry that I cannot spare your family the heartache of hearing of your abduction. But I've others to think about," Dash said.

"Who?" Jocelyn asked, then quickly added, "Never mind. I don't want to know why you've chosen a life of thieving. I don't want to know why you have a group of boys following your command or even why the infamous Lane Braden has graced your campfire. Tell me nothing and I'll be the wiser for it."

Dash's eyes lit with admiration, and somehow, though he said nothing, Jocelyn felt as though he applauded her reasoning.

Beneath a moon that peeked through fitful clouds, Dash

spun Jocelyn about on a dance floor of damp grass. They whirled by the fire, past the men who cheered and clapped in time with the fiddler, and by Laney Braden, who continued to watch. But their spectators became merely a blurred backdrop of unending color for Jocelyn. She had eyes only for Dash. And though she knew she was mad for allowing a thief to take her in his arms, Jocelyn admitted to herself that she'd never known such a thrilling dance partner in all her life.

Later, when the meats and whiskey were depleted, Dash left Jocelyn's side to have a meeting with a few of his men. Jocelyn wondered if the discussion had anything to do with her presence, for one of Dash's men gestured her way, scowling. Dash quieted the man with terse words, and then the meeting broke apart, with three of the thieves packing their saddlebags and then departing quickly. After that, the remaining men scattered to find some slumber. Laney walked toward Jocelyn.

"What is happening?" she asked.

"You don't know? Ah, and here I'd thought you and Dash were as thick as . . . well, thieves." He laughed at his own humor, then shrugged into his great overcoat. "I'm off to find some excitement while the night is still young. It was indeed a pleasure to meet you, mistress, but I suspect you'll be here when I return."

Jocelyn was about to inform him otherwise, but Dash approached them then. He gave Laney a hard stare.

"Take care what mischief you get into this night, Laney," he said, a warning note in his voice. "My boys have their orders, and they won't hesitate to pull their weapons."

"Ho, Dash," Laney said, sounding miffed. "Do you think I'd harass them?"

Dash didn't reply.

"Rest easy," Laney said, laughing and motioning to his two men. "I'm off in the opposite direction. I've a yearning for a warm inn and even warmer women." With that, he nodded to both Jocelyn and Dash, and then headed for his horse.

Jocelyn turned on Dash "Well?" she demanded. "Am I free to go now? Others are leaving, why not me?"

Dash looked at her as though he wished to turn her inside out. "No," he said flatly.

Jocelyn's temper flared. Thinking she might gain Laney's attention before he bolted off, Jocelyn headed his way. Perhaps she could entice Laney to return her home, for she knew her grandmother would have the money to pay the man's price. But Braden and his men were already astride and heading out of the clearing. Jocelyn intended to run after them. "Wait!" she nearly cried out, but Dash grabbed hold of her then and clamped a hand over her mouth.

Before Jocelyn knew what was happening, Dash slammed her body against his, one arm curled about her waist. "Don't get any ideas, Duchess," he warned quietly.

Jocelyn struggled to be free, listening as Laney and his men charged off into the night, and knowing she should have acted sooner. Damn! she thought hotly. What a fool she'd been. But Dash's hold on her had gentled in the span of only a few seconds, and suddenly Jocelyn wasn't thinking about her freedom or of Braden, but of the man who held her.

His body was firm and solid—muscled by the rigors of his lifestyle. She could feel the beat of his heart pounding with solid precision against her back. Slowly he eased his hand from her mouth, and Jocelyn felt his calloused fingers brush across her smooth skin. His thumb traced a line across her jawbone, then dipped lower to find her pulse along the column of her throat.

"You're brave, Duchess, I'll give you that. But you're also reckless," he whispered, taking his sweet time in letting her free from his hold. "Braden could eat you up and spit you out and not think twice about it."

Jocelyn sucked in a deep breath of air. "And what about you?" she managed, feeling his hand move lower still.

He didn't answer directly. The silence stretched on like a dream. Finally he whispered, "I could do the same. But you have to trust me—you have no other choice." He allowed his hand to skim the curve of her right breast before he released her.

Jocelyn took a step forward, trying hard to get hold of herself. Her breath came in fast gulps, and her heart felt as though it might fly out of her mouth. Caught between fury at his rudeness and a startling awareness of her own reactions to his touch, Jocelyn found she couldn't quite decide whether to rage at him or flee inside his tent before he had the chance to touch her again.

Dash made the decision for her. He stepped in front of her and with one finger lifted Jocelyn's chin so that she was forced to meet his heady gaze. "Don't challenge me again, Duchess."

Jocelyn pulled back. "And if I do?"

For a moment she feared he might throttle her. But just when she thought he would strike her, Dash cupped her face in his hands. Roughly he breathed, "Then I'd be forced to do this."

With that he drew her face to his and kissed her fully on the mouth. It was a volatile, intimate kiss, swift and furious. Though an innocent she was, Jocelyn's feminine instincts flared to life. His lust became hers, and Jocelyn felt her lips part as his tongue slipped inside of her mouth. Fire leapt through her veins. Her stomach tightened and her knees felt weak.

Dash pulled slowly away. "I could do anything I wanted to you," he whispered roughly, his eyes smoky with passion and danger. "Do not doubt that."

Jocelyn, for all her anger at his audacity, was stung even more by how easily the man could ignite her senses. Tears burned her eyes, but she was determined not to break down and cry in front of him. With more boldness than she felt, she lifted her chin and said, "I wish to God you'd never stopped my coach."

Dash's lips pressed tight together; a muscle twitched in his cheek. "Not nearly as much as I," he muttered, then motioned toward the fire. "Go on," he said. "You might as well make yourself comfortable. Nobody is going anywhere until my men return."

With as much dignity as she could muster, Jocelyn headed toward the dying fire.

An hour passed, time in which Jocelyn had a moment to calm her nerves. Dash jabbed a long stick into the glowing embers beneath the branches, stirring some life into the flames.

"You should rest," he told her.

Jocelyn shook her head. She was afraid to fall asleep, for fear of what might happen to her if she did.

"I'm not tired."

"You should be. It's been a long day."

"What about you?" she questioned. "Are you not tired?"

Dash tossed the stick into the fire, then settled back against a saddlebag beside Jocelyn. He, too, had had some time to deal with whatever demons were menacing him. "I'm accustomed to little sleep. When I was in school, I'd spend my nights reading, or causing trouble, depending on the time of year."

"I suppose you were a hellion in your youth."

"There are those who would claim I still am."

"Do you enjoy it? Robbing people, I mean?" When he didn't move or speak, Jocelyn chanced a glance at him. He stared into the fire with narrowed eyes, as though seeing other times, other places.

After another beat he said, "No. I don't enjoy it."

"Then why do you do it?"

"Must you ask?"

"Yes. You aren't penniless—I mean, you can't be. I saw what you lost to Laney tonight, and I also noticed the fine shirt you tore apart for Cal's wound. You're also educated. I doubt you've known much hardship in your life. Am I correct?"

"Partially."

"Which part?"

"You're damned curious, aren't you?"

"Yes. So why do you do it? For riches? Power? What?"

"None of those things." He shrugged, as if to ward off the weight of the world. "I don't steal," he replied. "I borrow from those who can afford to lend." He grinned sheepishly. "As I figure it, I'm deeply in debt."

"You make light of a serious situation."

"Do I?"

"You must if you view stealing as borrowing. Do you fancy yourself to be a Robin Hood of some sort?"

"Robin Hood was valiant."

"And what are you?"

He stared long and hard into the dying fire. "To some I am a ray of hope in a world void of light—to others, I am the devil in disguise." Finally he brought his gaze to hers. "The trouble is," he said softly, "even I don't know who is correct."

Four

Jocelyn shivered, though not from the chill in the air. She folded her legs at the knees and tucked her feet under her bottom. "You sound bitter," she said.

"Do I? Ah, well, maybe I am. I don't mind being painted in an unfavorable light."

"You are accustomed to it?"

"No—but I must endure the unpleasantries if I am to get what I want."

"And that is?"

Dash gave her a weary grin. "You don't give up, do you? You'll push a man until he gives the answer you seek."

"I think you *want* to talk about your life."

"No, I don't."

They were forceful-sounding words, but Jocelyn wasn't fooled. She settled back against a saddle and stared with Dash into the embers of the fire. She would press him no more, at least for now. Dash was clearly a man of mystery, and he appeared to enjoy the aura of intrigue with which he surrounded himself. But Jocelyn hadn't spent seventeen years under the watchful eyes of her grandmother and not learned something from the older woman. Any person with a secret was a person searching for a willing ear—or so Amelia had always told Jocelyn. Dash definitely harbored a secret or two. And Jocelyn being Jocelyn was determined to learn what they were.

But for the moment she was willing to let him be. The day had been eventful, to say the least, and she was just now feeling the effects of having sipped several mouthfuls from the many jars of whiskey that had been passed around from person to person. Jocelyn stifled a yawn, trying her best to focus on the light of the fire, but she was too exhausted to do more than just stare sightlessly at it. She shook her head once, trying hard to remain awake. She remembered only too well the feel of Dash's lips on hers, and it frightened her to think he might attempt something more should she fall asleep.

"I hated having to abduct you," Dash was saying as Jocelyn's head began to feel like a heavy slab of Cotswolds slate. "But I didn't have a choice, you know."

Jocelyn nodded groggily, then fell promptly asleep.

Dash didn't notice he was without an audience. "You shouldn't have torn my mask off. You should have been scared witless and then swooned like any woman would do who'd just been threatened by a heartless highwaymen. After all, I *did* have my pistol pressed to your—"

Dash's voice echoed around him. He turned to find Jocelyn sound asleep and snoring beside him. The little minx was *snoring*! Not loudly, but quietly. Dash stared at the sight of Jocelyn slumped against the saddle, her head lolling to one side. She was pretty even in repose, a portrait of sheer beauty. Her copper-colored hair had escaped its many pins and now framed her face in tiny ringlets. Her dark lashes were just a smudge above her high cheekbones, and her mouth was pouty and kissable as it opened to show a flash of even, white teeth.

Dash again felt his lust for her. Earlier, when he'd kissed her, he'd had to fight for control. He'd wanted nothing more than to take her then and there. Her lips had tasted sweet and felt too soft. Her body, so tiny, had felt just right in his arms. Dash could well imagine what a night with Jocelyn would be like—fiery and steamy, hot and exciting. He felt himself grow hard just thinking about it.

The freckles sprinkling the bridge of her nose were her greatest asset, Dash decided, watching her a moment.

Though, he admitted to himself, her witching green eyes
were a close second. Lord, but she was adorable, all soft
and tiny and able to spit fire as well as exude a plethora
of charm and innocence. Dash could well imagine her
family's grief and fear once they learned she'd been kidnapped.

He was nothing more than a snake in the grass, Dash
knew. How could he hold this woman-child against her
will? What had possessed him to treat her so roughly and
then bring her to this moldy campsite? She should be home
in her own bed, dreaming of parties and new dresses or
any of a dozen other things young women dreamed of.

But she wasn't. She was here, with him—and Dash felt
miserable.

"I hope," he said quietly, wondering if a part of Jocelyn's mind could hear him, "that one day you'll be able
to forgive me, Duchess."

Jocelyn reminded Dash of a determined flame that wa-
vered and danced but never lost its heat or its enchanting
incandescent light. Yes, she was a lady of fire, a woman
filled with a heat so searing she could be capable of sending a man over the brink of insanity. But she was also still
a child in many ways. And this was what bothered Dash
most. Would his abduction of her color her entire life?
Would he blacken her bright spirit by his touch alone?

Dash got to his knees, then lifted Jocelyn into his arms.
She shifted slightly, her dusky lashes fluttering as she fitted her body against his chest. Her light sigh of contentment—or perhaps it was of acquiescence?—filled his ears
and left him feeling distorted, torn in two opposite directions.

As he got to his feet Dash decided he would do well to
keep his distance from this tiny slip of a woman. Jocelyn
made him feel too much, made him want for things he
could never have. He carried her to the tent where Caleb
lay in sweating misery, then deposited her upon his own
pallet. Jocelyn curled up on her left side, folding her hands
beneath her chin, and continued to sleep deeply. Dash
hovered over her, fussing with a light blanket, taking care

to tuck it up and over her shoulder. Before he realized what he was doing, he kissed her temple and whispered a good-night to her sleeping form.

Only the truly innocent could sleep so soundly, he thought. Dash half wished he could be so pure of heart, but those days were long behind him now. He'd made his choices.

After checking on Caleb, he left the tent and stood near the fire for a long, long time. He found himself awake even when the sun rose.

Thieves, it seemed to him, could find no rest.

Jocelyn came awake with a start. At first she didn't know where she was. Her back felt stiff and sore. Every muscle in her body gave protest as she turned on the thin pallet and glanced about her. Suddenly she knew where she was: in Dash's tent, lying on his pallet.

She sat up and wiped the sleep from her eyes.

"Good morning," a male voice rasped.

Jocelyn looked at Caleb, who was looking at her. "And to you," she replied, memories of the hectic night roaring through her head. "How do you feel?" She didn't bother about her own disheveled state or the fact that her stomach revolted as she got to her feet. Her only thought was of Cal's state.

"It hurts," Caleb admitted as she came to his side. "But I'll make it through the day, I think."

Jocelyn smiled at the lad. "I know you will. Here, now, let me check that bandage."

Caleb cringed. "Do you have to?"

"I'll only look," Jocelyn promised. She lifted the blanket. There was only a small stain on the bandage. She touched Caleb's forehead and was relieved to find his fever had broken. "There," she said. "That wasn't so terrible, was it? You'll be right as rain in a few days."

Caleb gave her a hopeful grin. "You think so?"

"I do. Are you hungry?"

He shook his head, playing with the edge of his blanket with both hands. "No. Th-thank you. It was you who saved my life, wasn't it? I remember seeing your face just before I passed out from the pain."

"There's no need to thank me. You're a brave young man, Cal."

"My mother will want to thank you, too," Cal continued, not dismissing the aid she'd given last night. "She tells me I'm her favorite son—'course, I'm her only son, but that doesn't matter. I—I thought I was dying last night. You saved my life, yet I don't even know your name."

"Jocelyn."

Caleb gazed up at her as though she were some vision from heaven. "That's a pretty name. Just like you."

Jocelyn clicked her tongue and made a pretense of straightening his bedding. "My father calls me Joss. He tells me I'm his favorite daughter and his favorite son all rolled into one even though I'm his only child, so I know how you must feel when you hear similar words from your mother. I want you to rest today, Cal. Just lay there and dream about something pleasant, you hear? By noon you should be ready to force some broth down to your stomach."

"Will it hurt?"

"Hurt what?"

"My stomach . . . and my side."

"Yes," Jocelyn admitted. "But only when you swallow, or when you breathe." She smiled down at him, wishing she could take away some of his pain.

"You'll make me eat it anyway, won't you?"

"Every last bite."

Cal thought for a moment, then nodded. "I'll do it. For you."

"No, not for me, you won't," Jocelyn admonished. "You'll do it for yourself. Now, just lie still and I'll see if I can't find someone to get some clean water for your basin. You ran a high fever last night."

"Pretty Boy will get it for me, or perhaps Dash."

Jocelyn said nothing as she lifted the basin of dirty water. She was thinking of Dash and of the fact that he'd drawn a mere lad into his web of deceit. What kind of man would do such a thing? Caleb could have died. The boy was fortunate to be awake and talking!

"Just rest," Jocelyn finally replied, then pushed her way out of the tent.

She found Dash sitting beside the fire that had long ago gone out. He was gritty-eyed from lack of sleep. His long black hair hung above his shoulders in untidy disarray and there were mauve, telltale shadows beneath his gray eyes.

"Caleb needs fresh water," Jocelyn announced, tossing the basin down beside him. "And fresh bandages."

Dash glanced up at her, looking as though he'd had a few more drinks of whiskey after she'd fallen asleep last night.

"And he'll need someone to give him a bath as well." She purposefully wrinkled her nose. "As will others of this camp." She let the insult stand on its own.

But Dash didn't rise to the bait as Jocelyn expected. He merely nodded, then returned his bleary gaze to the spent fire. Jocelyn grew angrier by the moment. Her body ached like never before and she was hungry and impatient. She wanted to be home, having slept in her own comfortable bed, awaiting a hearty breakfast of fresh ham and eggs. She yearned for a hot cup of tea and a buttered slice of toast. She wanted to see her father and grandmother and Charles greeting her a good day. She wanted to don a fresh gown and then go out into her father's gardens for her morning's respite of reading and fresh air. She wanted, dammit, to be away from this horrid campsite and all it entailed!

"Well?" Jocelyn demanded, arms akimbo. "Will you get the water or shall I?"

She saw Dash wince as though her loudness had been too much for him so early in the morning, and she cursed him for perhaps the hundredth time since he'd taken her from her family's coach. Why couldn't he have let well enough alone? Why had he chosen her carriage? Why had he chosen *her*?

"Oh, very well," she spat. "I'll get it myself!" She was just about to spin away from him and tramp off into

the thick of the forest except for the fact that she didn't
know where she should head. Jocelyn had no idea where
they were, or in which direction lay north—or south, for
that matter. Was there even a stream nearby?

"Well?" she heard Dash mutter. "Why don't you get
going?"

Jocelyn simmered. "You think you're very smart, don't
you? You know very well I have no idea which way to
go!"

He motioned to his left.

Jocelyn glared at him. "*You* get the water," she exploded. "It's the least you can do."

Dash visibly stiffened, coming out of his stupor.
"Meaning?"

"Meaning it's your fault that boy is lying in there with
a hole in his side!"

Clearly, those were the wrong words to say. Dash came
off the ground like a shot fired from a gun and in less than
a second he stood before Jocelyn. He looked like the wrath
of God. It took all of Jocelyn's will not to tremble before
him. He was angry all right. Enraged.

"It—it's true," she managed to say, though barely.
"You should have been the one to rob the coach, not Cal!
He's too young to be a thief, too—"

"Pure?" Dash cut in.

"Yes!" Jocelyn said. "He is. You're a man, you know
full well what you're doing, but Cal is merely a boy. He
shouldn't be here. He should be home, with his family."

"Like you?"

Jocelyn whipped the hair from her face and stared at
him. "Yes, like me," she said, but wondered why her
heart tripped as she said the words. She was actually
thinking what it would be like to stay a few more days
with these highwaymen!

Jocelyn snuffed out that tiny voice of wildness that whispered now in her mind. She'd always been a creature of
feeling. She'd climbed trees, had raced her pony at the age
of seven, and all because she'd yearned for adventure.
She'd sneaked out of her bedroom at the stroke of mid-

night and had raced across the undulating fields of her father's home only because she wanted to do the forbidden. Just as her grandmother Amelia smoked a pipe and sometimes wore men's clothing to be different, Jocelyn had always felt some undeniable urge to go against the grain of what was expected of her.

And here she was, doing it again. A part of her was absolutely thrilled at being held captive in some thieves' den. And the robbing these men had done—gracious, but even that was appearing to be a lovely flower to be plucked from some forbidden garden!

To steal from another was a sin. To pull a gun on hapless victims could not be condoned . . . and yet Jocelyn still marveled at the thrill of it all.

She wondered if Dash could read the thoughts spinning through her mind. Could he perceive the wild streak that ran through her with such abandon? Could he feel the pulse of her reckless heart? Jocelyn tried her best to keep her face impassive, to remain cool beneath his scrutinizing gaze.

In a vain hope to turn the conversation away from her own wants and fears, Jocelyn said, "You should send Caleb home. He doesn't deserve this kind of life."

"Oh, and you think you know what's best for him? You think you know what it's like to walk in his shoes?"

"Better than you know!" she snapped.

Too late she realized those were the wrong words to say. Dash looked positively livid. Jocelyn half feared he would grab hold of her and shake her until her teeth rattled. She'd gone too far, that was apparent.

Jocelyn steeled herself, waiting for the inevitable storm. She knew not what she would do if he touched her. There lay cunning persuasiveness in Dash's capable hands. Jocelyn remembered only too well the feel of being in his arms, the burning heat of his mouth on hers.

"You expect me to strike you," Dash said quietly. It wasn't a question, but a statement, and the words held a note of astonishment.

"Of course I do," Jocelyn said. "I can expect no less.

You're a thief. You'll rob anyone unfortunate enough to pass you by!'' She didn't know where the words came from. They just spilled out of her and hung like a sharp knife blade in the air between them.

Dash leaned closer. "Hear me and hear me well, Duchess, when—and if—I decide to lay a hand to that pretty body of yours, you'll not be able to stop me." His gaze flicked down her lithe form, pausing overly long on the curve of her breasts. "I'll take you so quickly and so thoroughly that your head will spin and you'll be begging me for more." Slowly he brought his gaze back to her face. "As for Caleb—he's none of your affair."

Jocelyn knew the depth of his warning, and it chilled her to the bone. He *could* take her, she knew. And to her horror, she also knew that a part of her might succumb to his lust. She forced herself not to tremble, and not to think about what should become of her if Dash stole her virtue from her, and perhaps left her to bear an illegitimate child.

No, she couldn't think of such things. If she did, she might very well lose all of her nerve.

Not backing down she said, "Caleb is naught but a lad, I will concern myself with him if that is my wish."

"Then you will do so at risk of displeasing me."

"More threats?" she shot back, realizing that if she didn't stand up to him now, she never would. He'd taken her prisoner and had scared her poor cousin half to death. Jocelyn decided it was high time someone stood up to the man! "I grow weary of all these veiled innuendos. Now it's time you heard *me*! I will not be forced to play the trembling victim, nor will I leave a young lad prey to the likes of you! I am here because I haven't the strength to overpower a crazed leader and a half dozen of his men. But I won't grovel at your feet and beg for crumbs if that's what you're hoping! Nor will I," she added with fervor, "allow a young boy to be drawn deeper into this nest of thieves!"

Jocelyn was just about to turn away from him when Dash lashed out, catching hold of her wrist with one hand.

"Hold it right there, Duchess," he muttered. "Where the hell do you think you're going?"

Jocelyn tried to yank free, but couldn't. His grip was strong and unrelenting, just like the man. "Let go of me," she ground out.

"I asked you a question. I expect an answer."

"I'm going to London to view the prince regent, where do you *think* I'm going?" she shouted.

To her surprise she saw Dash's mouth tilt up into a small smile. He wasn't so angry that he couldn't realize the absurdity of his own question.

"Give him my regards, won't you? I'm certain the man would take a moment to listen to what words spilled from this pouty mouth of yours." He lifted one hand, running his fingers across her lips.

Jocelyn pressed her eyes shut tight, hating the desire that suddenly washed through her. All the man had to do was touch her and she responded! What was the matter with her? Was she a wanton? How could her senses take flight with just his nearness?

Finding composure amid her careening emotions, Jocelyn pulled free of Dash's grasp and started to walk toward his tent.

"Jocelyn," Dash called out to her.

She didn't pause, didn't even look back at him.

"Take care what words you whisper into Caleb's willing ears," Dash called after her. "He is, as you've so clearly pointed out to me, an impressionable lad. My guess is that a lady as intelligent as you could probably sway the boy in any direction she wanted."

Dash's point wasn't lost on Jocelyn. He knew, as well as she did, that once Caleb was on the mend, he would probably be convinced to help aid Jocelyn in an escape plan. And that, Jocelyn admitted to herself, was what she'd been hoping.

Feeling deceitful and miserable all at once, Jocelyn huffed into the tent and stood by the doorway for a full minute before she got control of her careening emotions.

Caleb came out of a light sleep, having heard her entrance. "Something wrong?" he asked quickly.

"Nothing," Jocelyn soothed, forcing the word out. "Nothing at all."

"You look angry."

Jocelyn shook her head, trying hard to regain her composure. "I'm fine," she assured the boy. "I, ah, I just had words with your leader."

Caleb lifted his brows in understanding. "Dash can be quarrelsome at times."

Quarrelsome? The man could be downright insufferable! But Jocelyn didn't say so. She wasn't about to pull the injured youth into her misery. "Yes," she agreed. "He can be that."

"And mean, too," Caleb said, adding, "but he has a good heart."

Jocelyn doubted that.

"Dash is like a brother to me . . . every man in this camp is. We're a family, Jocelyn. We take care of one another."

So why are you lying there with a hole in your side? she wanted to demand. But she didn't. Clearly Caleb looked to Dash as some sort of heroic figure, though why was not clear to her.

"You have to understand Dash," Caleb continued. "He wasn't always so . . . driven."

"What do you mean?" she asked, moving to Cal's side.

Caleb thought hard before answering, as though he wanted to get his words straight and was afraid of giving Jocelyn the wrong impression. "I mean," he said slowly, "though Dash claims to be nothing more than a thief, he is a great deal more. He doesn't steal to line his own pockets. He steals because—"

Dash strode into the tent then, breezing quickly inside like a bold wind that could not be stopped. In his hands he carried the basin which he'd filled with clean water.

Jocelyn cursed his timing, knowing very well that Dash wasn't about to leave her alone with Caleb for longer than was necessary.

Caleb ceased talking. Dash acted as though he made unannounced entrances all the time.

"Ready for a bath?" Dash asked the lad. Caleb nodded. To Jocelyn, Dash said, "Will you, or shall I?"

Jocelyn shot him a quelling look. "I believe he's in capable hands. If you'll excuse me?"

"By all means," Dash said with a satisfied smile. "Just don't wander away."

Jocelyn didn't give him another moment to gloat but hastened outside. *Don't wander away!* And where did his majesty think she might go? The borders of the camp were well guarded.

Jocelyn fumed for only a second before she decided to beat Dash at his own game. So he didn't want her wandering off, nor did he want her getting too close to Caleb. Well, then, she'd just do as he'd hoped and stay close to the tent—but she didn't have to like it.

Jocelyn's mood brightened once she'd made her decision. Several of the men were rising, Pretty Boy among them. Soon they had a battered pot of water on the now crackling fire to boil, and Jocelyn saw Pretty Boy extract several servings of tea from his saddle pack to brew. She marveled at the chain of command playing before her. One man saw to the horses, another to rolling up the pallets, and still another dug in the earth for fat worms that would soon be bait upon the line of a crude fishing pole.

Pretty Boy handed Jocelyn a tin cup of steaming tea. "There'll be fresh trout for breakfast," he told her. "At least, I hope there will."

"What can I do to help?" Jocelyn asked.

Pretty Boy seemed surprised by her offer. "N-nothing," he stammered. "I mean, it isn't your duty to help."

"Then what *is* my duty?"

He groped for an answer. "I—I don't know exactly. . . . I mean, we've never had a . . ." Again, he searched for the right words.

"A prisoner in your midst?" Jocelyn answered for him and was slightly relieved by the fact. She was glad Dash didn't make a practice of spiriting women away from their private coaches, but was just as vexed at learning she was the first. "Very well," she told him. "I'll find my own niche here."

With a determination that would have made even her grandmother proud, Jocelyn set to the task of making herself useful. Though she hadn't an inkling of how to hook a trout on the end of a horsehair line, she did know horses. She spent the next hour seeing to the beasts that were grouped a few feet from the center of the campsite. Jocelyn helped dole out oats to each horse and saw that they had enough water. In spite of her own dislike of Dash, she found herself lingering near his mount.

A mammoth horse it was, all black with only a diamond of white on his face. She sensed a certain restlessness in the beast, and that was why she favored him—or so she told herself. The horse ate his oats while peering at his surroundings with a watchful eye.

"Anxious, are you?" she crooned, rubbing a hand along the animal's smooth neck. She remembered how keen of sight and sound the animal had been in the depths of night. Some horses were bred for night, others for day, she knew. This beast, it seemed, had been tempered for both. He knew what shelter the night could bring, as well as danger. Daylight could be a hindrance, too. The horse sensed this. He acted as though expecting his owner to jump astride him and demand instant speed and agility.

Yes, Jocelyn thought, that would be Dash; expectant and demanding. And yet Jocelyn felt this animal had known a harbor of gentleness, had been reared with sweets and fresh apples and had known nothing but a gentle yet firm hand.

Jocelyn checked the animal's bit and found it was fashioned of the finest steel. The shoes of his hooves were solid and new. No doubt the animal had known a warm stall supplied with an abundant amount of hay and sparkling water.

Dash, shirtless and carrying a sliver of soap and a ragged bit of cloth, came upon Jocelyn as she inspected his horse.

"Does he meet with your high standards?" Dash asked.
Jocelyn immediately straightened, feeling her cheeks
turn pink. "Are you forever sneaking up on people?"

"And are you forever answering a question with a question?"

A fair enough response, but Jocelyn wasn't feeling very
agreeable. "He needs a good grazing pasture," she announced, nodding toward the horse. "And perhaps an un-
reined jaunt through an open field."

Dash frowned at her observation. "He had a good run
last night."

"Chased by the sounds of gunfire," she replied.

"A run all the same," Dash admitted, somewhat testily.

Jocelyn measured the man for a moment, then shook
her head in disagreement. "I'm not talking about a sprint
for his life, but rather leisurely laps about an unbroken
field. Anyone can see this animal is nervous. He's been
pushed to his limit on more than one occasion. He needs
to have a moment of freedom. A time when he can be
alone and wild."

Dash eyed Jocelyn closely, as though he was trying to
decipher if she, too, needed such an uninhibited block of
time.

"He needs to feel his own power in his own way,"
Jocelyn finished, wondering if perhaps the words she spoke
fell too close to the bone. "When was the last time you
let him go free?"

"Never," Dash answered.

That didn't surprise Jocelyn. "And you?" she asked
even before thinking, which was the usual way for her.
"When was the last time you walked this earth without
thought or plan?"

He appeared taken aback—though not for long. "I'm
not a person who gives in to flights of fancy. I haven't the
time."

Jocelyn thought otherwise, for she remembered well the
sight of him when he'd raided her coach and had pulled
his gun. He'd been wild then, giving a hint of what the

man might be like when partaking in something not quite so dangerous. Quicksilver, and bold, the man intrigued her. And his kisses—yes, they were reckless, too. Powerful and uninhibited, just like the man.

"What do you have the time for?" she asked.

"Mayhem," he answered simply. "I've time for that."

Jocelyn felt stung by the quick reply, though she guessed Dash wasn't being totally truthful. Could he actually enjoy robbing others? Or even abducting an innocent young woman like herself? If he did, then she wanted nothing to do with him. But if he didn't . . .

Jocelyn was loath to think beyond that point. She gave the horse one last stroke, then turned away from the beast. "I'm hungry," she announced. "And I feel gritty and dirty. I need a bath." Suddenly all the long hours she'd spent at the campsite came crowding in upon her. Jocelyn didn't like what Dash's nearness did to her nerves. She didn't like the thin line she walked while in his presence. And more important, she was uncomfortable with the push-pull attraction she felt for the man.

When Dash made no comment, she said again with more force, "I would like to get cleaned up. Would that be too much to request?"

After a beat Dash said laconically, "Not at all. But I'm afraid we haven't the accommodations. The men are used to taking a quick rinse in the stream."

Jocelyn hesitated. A sponge bath would have felt divine, but she knew there would be little privacy for her. "Never mind," she said. "I'll wait. After all, you did say I could go home soon."

Silence then.

"Well?" she demanded. "I _am_ going home today, aren't I?" When Dash didn't answer, she flew into a rage, "You sneaking little dog!" she yelled, incensed. "You have no thoughts of returning me to my home, do you? You think you can keep me for God knows why! What kind of a snake are you that you would keep me against your own word? I want a bath, I tell you! And I want it—"

Dash suddenly came alive. Without any warning to Jocelyn, he reached out and lifted her off the ground.

"What do you think you're doing?" she cried.

"I warned you not to push me too far," he answered, fitting her easily over one broad shoulder.

Jocelyn's hands slipped down over his bared back as she tried to get herself upright. But it was a useless gesture, for the man had made up his mind—though to do what, Jocelyn had no idea.

Five

Dash set his jaw as he swung Jocelyn's lithe body over one shoulder, then headed into the woods. Her screech of indignation nearly pierced his eardrums. Damn, but she was a vocal woman. He'd never met a woman who flapped her tongue as much as Jocelyn did. That high-pitched voice of hers was beginning to rub on his nerves like a sharp knife blade.

"Put me down!" Jocelyn yelled, pounding on his bare back with clenched fists. "Did you hear me? I said—"

"Hear you? Lady, I think everyone this side of London can hear you. God's teeth! How does your father endure you?"

She tried to wiggle free, but only managed to slip several inches down his back, nearly falling face first to the ground. Dash felt her hands grasp on to the top of his trousers as she fought to at least remain upright. Her long curls whipped against his bared shoulders as she swung her head about. There was little doubt in Dash's mind that she was glaring at him with the devil in her eyes, but he had enough to contend with at the moment. Just the feel of her in his arms sent his mind drifting to a dangerous course. Did she have any idea what the feel of her hands hitched to his trousers did to him? Or of what the scent of her luscious hair grazing his shoulders made him feel?

"My father is a decent, honorable man!" Jocelyn sputtered, pulling Dash's thoughts back to the moment. "He wouldn't dream of treating me so roughly!"

"Then he's been mighty lenient with you. I'd say you're long overdue for a good spanking."

Immediately Jocelyn quieted, which brought a smile to Dash's mouth.

After a full beat of silence she ground out, "You wouldn't."

"Wouldn't I? Don't tempt me, Duchess."

"Quit calling me that ridiculous name."

"It suits you."

"It doesn't!"

"There you go again, being quarrelsome."

"You're insufferable."

"So I've been told."

"And far too smug."

"I've heard that on numerous occasions as well. Believe me, Duchess, there are few insults you can heap on my character that I haven't heard before."

"And you're quite pleased with all of them, no doubt! Put me down! I've had enough of you and your arrogant ways. I've a mind to—"

Dash didn't hear her next words, for he'd reached the side of the deep, cold-water stream that cut through the floor of the forest in a zigzagging path. Without ceremony he tramped into the middle of the rushing water and deposited Jocelyn on her rear.

She went down with a plunk and a scream, water spraying up like a fountain on all sides of her. Livid, spluttering, she tried to stand up, but Dash wouldn't let her.

"The lady wants a bath, she'll have a bath," Dash said, pulling out a rag and harsh soap he'd brought with him from the campsite. Before Jocelyn could protest, Dash leaned over and pushed her back into the chilling waters. She went down with a howl of rage.

Dash suppressed a smile. He was almost enjoying this too much. Served her right, though, for she'd spent the entire morning complaining—and he knew why. Her ploy was to wear him down with her constant whining, to make him want her out of his life so badly that he'd pack her off to her father's home in no time. But of course, Dash couldn't do that, not until his men returned and he knew the cache of gold had gotten safely on its way north. Until then Jocelyn would just have to learn who was in command here.

Getting the rag good and soapy, Dash set to the task of washing her hands. Jocelyn batted him away.

"Take it easy," he said, clamping one hand to her wrist as he rubbed the grime from her hands. "I'm merely giving you what you asked for."

"I didn't ask for *this*!"

"No? That's not what I recall. You've been muttering about your plight since dawn."

"And with good reason!"

"Yeah, yeah." Dash took her other wrist and ran the washrag up and down it as though he were trying to wear through to the bone. He didn't trust himself to be more gentle. Her skin was soft and slick beneath his hands, and even though she'd ridden through the night at his side, she still smelled fresh and sweet. Too sweet.

"You're hurting me!" Jocelyn cried, trying once again to be free.

Dash frowned; hurting her was far from what his mind was telling him to do. "If you'd sit still, I'd be done by now," he replied moodily. "Now, be a good girl so I can wash your hair."

"I'm not a girl! And I'm fully capable of washing my own—"

Dash took Jocelyn firmly by the shoulders and dunked her head beneath the freezing water. He held her down just long enough to get that gorgeous mane of hair of hers wet. The coppery tresses floated on the busy water like streamers. Dash's fingers caught in the tangles, making him take care not to pull too roughly.

Droplets of water clung to Jocelyn's long lashes as she glared up at him with murder in her eyes. But she didn't fight him, which both pleased and puzzled Dash. She became still, her neck arched, her hair fanning out, her breasts rising and falling as she sucked in deep breaths of air.

Dash hovered above her, feeling the rocks of the creek bed cutting into his right knee, feeling the delicate weight of Jocelyn's body as he held her with one arm hooked beneath her shoulders. Such a feisty woman for one so tiny, he thought. He wondered where she'd learned to be such a firebrand.

"Is this the calm before the storm?" he asked, shoving one hand into the water to get the sliver of soap lathered.

A spark of mischief lit her green eyes as she thought for a moment. "Perhaps. Are you worried?"

"That depends. Should I be?"

Jocelyn lifted her winglike eyebrows in a coquettish gesture. "If you want to play my slave, I'll let you."

Dash gave a short grunt of laughter, which sounded pained even to his own ears. Her clothing had molded itself to her body, and Dash could discern every luscious curve of her. "I'm nobody's lackey."

Her pouty, kissable mouth formed an amused grin. "No? Then why have you taken it upon yourself to wash my hair?"

How Jocelyn had managed to turn the moment to her own advantage totally eluded Dash. He'd tossed her into the stream to show her who was boss, but quick as heat lightning she'd suddenly wrested the upper hand from him. Totally calm she was, even lounging back against his arm like a queen who expected this as her due.

Ignoring her question, Dash brought the soap out of the water and set to the task of lathering her hair, but again he'd underestimated the power of Jocelyn's aura. Just being near her was like breathing a heady elixir, but her essence was as elusive as that magical moment when night meets day. Dash didn't trust himself to speak. Jocelyn, he knew, was the kind of woman who could push him to do wild things. There was something about her, some uncapturable quality that could ensnare him forever if he should be so foolish as to let his guard down.

Her wavy hair was silky as a spider's web and the feel

of those tresses in his hands was almost more than Dash
could bear. He'd fantasized about running his fingers
through her hair last night—along with a few other secret
places of her body he'd like to touch and caress. But his
nighttime fantasies paled in comparison to the genuine
thing.

With unhurried strokes, he massaged the soap bubbles
into the copper-colored strands, working his fingers against
her scalp, then down through the long length of her hair.
Dash watched as Jocelyn closed her eyes, as though the
experience was not so unpleasurable for her. He felt his
loins tingle, grow hot. If he didn't stop soon, he might
find himself doing more than just giving her a bath in cold
water.

"Feel better?" he asked, his voice low.

Jocelyn said nothing, just nodded her head.

He wished she would open her eyes. But no, that was a
lie. If she opened her eyes he knew he would drown in
those delicious green pools. Lord, just gazing down at her
pearly skin, seeing the smattering of freckles across the
bridge of her prettily upturned nose, made him dizzy with
desire. Who would have thought that Dash Warfield, the
same man who'd held more than his share of women in
his arms, could be so enchanted by this slip of a woman?
Jocelyn was barely of marrying age, hadn't been much
farther than her father's lands, and was far from being
worldly. So why, Dash wondered, was he so taken by her?
Innocence had never been a character trait he'd sought in
his women. There was danger in innocence; Dash had
learned that long ago.

Carefully he lowered her upper body down into the cool
swirls of water. Her tresses caught in the whipping motion
of the stream and the soap bubbles drifted away. Jocelyn
dropped her head back a little more, allowing Dash a moment to rinse the soap from her. He took his time, unmindful of his own uncomfortable position. Over and over
he ran his fingers through the heavy strands until there
wasn't a bit of the harsh soap left, then he lifted her upright.

Finally Jocelyn opened her eyes and gazed up at him. Her eyes were a startling shade of green; guileless and fringed by dark lashes that held droplets of water sparkling like diamonds.

"Finished?" she asked in a throaty voice that nearly took Dash's breath from his lungs.

He nodded, mute, transfixed by the sight of her.

"Good," Jocelyn whispered, and then, before Dash realized her intent, she lifted her hands and pressed them hard against his chest. "Because now it's *your* turn."

With more strength than Dash thought she had in her, Jocelyn shoved him backward so that he fell on the seat of his pants in the middle of the stream.

"What the—" he started to yell in dismay, but Jocelyn didn't give him another moment to gather his bearings. She got up on her knees, then lunged at him like a wily cat, tackling him where he sat. Dash felt his bare back hit the water and then the hard creek bed of rocks below.

With her skirts hitched up to her knees, Jocelyn straddled his waist and finished the task, dunking *his* head beneath the water.

"How do you like it?" she demanded in between dunkings. "Is the water cold enough for you? And let's not forget the soap," she said in a voice that was filled with wicked glee as she groped for the sliver of soap that had wedged itself between two rocks when she'd tackled Dash. "We can't have you roaming the roads with a dirty head!"

Caught between rage and laughter, Dash felt his scalp scrubbed clean by a merciless, revenge-seeking woman.

"Whoa! Easy now," he muttered. "I wasn't so rough with you, was I?"

"I'm not one of your horses to be soothed with a 'whoa,'" she snapped. "And yes, you were rough." Barely giving him a moment to catch his breath, Jocelyn forced his head beneath the water and held him there.

One. Two. Three. Dash counted the seconds, half fearing she meant to drown him. He could, he knew, easily toss her off his body and do whatever he wished with her. But he wouldn't. Perhaps she knew he wouldn't, and that was why she was waiting to see just exactly what he would do should she choose to keep his head submersed. Six. Seven. Dash felt his lungs begin to burn. Was she that heartless? Ten. Eleven. His mind began to crowd with thoughts of what it would be like to find a grave in six inches of water. Fourteen. Fifteen. Aw, hell, he thought. He wasn't about to find out!

Dash grabbed tight to Jocelyn's wrists and came up out of the water like a bullet from a gun barrel.

"What the devil are you trying to do?" he shouted once he'd sucked in a breath of much-needed air. "Kill me?"

Jocelyn sat back, her sodden hair hanging in heavy ringlets about her face and her clothes plastered to her skin. "The thought had crossed my mind."

"Murder before breakfast? I didn't think you had the stomach for such nastiness."

Jocelyn whipped her hair back behind her shoulders, spraying him with water in the process. "Then you don't know me at all," she snapped, making a motion to get off of him.

But Dash wouldn't release her hands. The freezing water had blasted the desire from his fogged mind and now he was feeling frisky. "Not so fast, Duchess. I'm not done with you."

Her eyes narrowed suspiciously. "What do you mean?"

He tossed her a wide grin. "I haven't finished bathing you yet."

"You most certainly have! Let me go, Dash."

"Is that a warning I hear in your voice? Take heed, Duchess, I'm a man who rises to a challenge—especially one given by such a beautiful woman."

She paused a moment, as though his compliment had taken her by surprise. Showing a flash of uncharacteristic self-consciousness, Jocelyn glanced down at herself. "You can hardly think me beautiful, with my hair hanging down my back and my dress—look at my dress! You've ruined it."

"It was ruined long before this moment. Forget about it. I'll purchase a new one for you."

She snapped her head up, all thoughts of her disarray forgotten. "I don't want anything from you!" she replied hastily.

"Nothing?"

"Nothing but my freedom."

Dash wiped the wetness from his face. "Ah, the one shining gift I am, at present, unable to afford you."

Anger flared on her gorgeous face. "But I thought I could leave this morning! I thought—"

"I know what you thought, dammit. You needn't remind me," Dash shot back, suddenly impatient. He hated to have to hold her against her will, but he couldn't change the facts. He had to make another raid tonight—perhaps two, and then his men had to deliver the goods to Fritz, another of his allies, who lived in Manchester. All in all, Dash figured, he wouldn't be able to release Jocelyn for at least a day or two more—maybe longer. "You're stuck with me, Jocelyn."

"For how long?" she cried.

"I don't know."

"What do you mean, you don't know? How can you not know? Whatever can you gain by keeping me here? My father can't afford to pay ransom money! He isn't a wealthy man."

"I don't want your family's money," Dash said heatedly, bothered that she would even think such a thing. Did she truly believe he was such a beast of a man?

"Then what *do* you want?"

The question was a fair one, Dash knew. He also knew he couldn't give her a truthful answer. What he wanted was to make long, delicious love to her. What he wanted was to remove every stitch of her clothing and lay her down on a sweet-smelling bed of grass and make her cry out in pleasure. What he wanted . . .

"I want to bathe," he answered testily, before his wayward thoughts totally took control of him. "So you'd best hurry up with the soap before I strip down to nothing and embarrass you."

Jocelyn slapped the water, furious, her eyes spitting

daggers at him. "Here!" she yelled. "Have your bath. I'm finished!" She threw the soap in the general direction of his head, then got up out of the water with more force than was necessary.

Dash watched her go, his trousers getting decidedly tighter across his loins as Jocelyn stood up and unknowingly gave him a lovely view. Her drenched clothing hugged every curve of her body. Her breasts, pointed and high, were quite visible, as well as her nipples, which had tightened into tiny buds from the chill of the water.

With head held high, Jocelyn turned her back toward him and headed for the stream bank, her shoes sloshing water as she went.

Dash couldn't help needling her one last time. He called, "Are you certain you don't want me to scrub your back?"

"Go to hell."

Dash chuckled, stood up, then commenced to whistle as he lathered his chest with soapsuds.

Jocelyn stood rigidly on the bank of the stream, silently cursing Dash with every breath she took. She'd actually told the man to go to hell! Heavens, what kind of person was she becoming? Never in her life had she uttered such words, and yet they'd come so easily from her lips! She could barely believe she'd just pushed the man down in the stream. But while her father had done his best to see she was brought up to be a lady, Jocelyn had inherited her grandmother's colorful ways. Somehow, in the past hours, Jocelyn had shed her genteel outer layer. She was now reacting like the free spirit she'd always been but had not had the opportunity to demonstrate.

"I'm becoming just like him," she whispered to herself. The realization was not so terrible. . . .

"What was that?" Dash asked good-naturedly from the middle of the stream.

Jocelyn didn't turn to look his way—didn't care to, actually. She'd heard the splat of his trousers hitting the ground where he'd tossed them. He was nude, naked as the day he'd been born! She knew he'd undressed just to rile her. There was absolutely no way she would allow herself to fall prey to his antics. He wanted her to turn around and see him in all his glory, no doubt. Well, he'd have a long wait!

"Not a thing," she called out over one shoulder, then plunked herself down on a moss-covered rock and began to finger-comb her wet and tangled hair.

The nerve of the man! He was an ogre, a lout! Ooooh, how she wanted to bring him down a peg or two. Jocelyn shivered as the cool morning air brushed over her. She'd catch her death if she didn't get out of these sodden clothes. Of course, Dash was probably hoping she'd do exactly that. Did he actually think she'd shed her garments and skip into the stream alongside him for a shared bath? Of course he did!

She had a good mind to get up and start walking home. Just as the idea sprang up in her brain, Jocelyn got to her feet. Somewhere behind her, Dash was whistling a hearty tune. Jocelyn smiled to herself, inching her way toward Dash's trousers, which lay in a heap on the bank.

Dash stopped whistling, clearly seeing her intent. "Jocelyn? What—"

Jocelyn scooped up Dash's trousers. "Enjoy yourself," she said in a singsong voice. She headed in a dead run for the campsite, her laughter floating out behind her. Dash's howl of outrage only made her laugh that much harder.

By the time she reached camp, she was breathless and her sides hurt from laughter. Pretty Boy stood up from his task of frying several trout for the morning meal.

"I'm not even going to ask," he said, spying Dash's garment in her hands.

Jocelyn smiled. "Your leader merely got what he deserved."

Pretty Boy shook his head. "He's going to be mighty angry with you."

"Yes, I suppose he is." She met his gaze and the two of them giggled like conspiratorial children.

"May I?" Pretty Boy asked, nodding to Dash's trousers.

Jocelyn handed them over. "Of course."

Pretty Boy took the pants to the tree nearest him, which held a hooked length of rope hanging from one of its branches. At night he would tie the packs of food to the rope, then hoist the packs off the ground so that no night-time predators could get at the food. Now, though, he used the rope to tie Dash's trousers and then dangle them there, for all the camp to see.

That done, he returned to Jocelyn's side. "Hungry?" he inquired casually.

"Famished," she replied, knowing she'd found a true friend.

By the time Dash returned to camp, Jocelyn was dressed in a clean pair of Pretty Boy's pants, as well as one of his shirts, while her clothes hung out to dry. At first she'd been aghast at the idea of wearing a man's clothes, but she was too cold to argue. In truth, wearing pants felt absolutely wonderful—freeing, in fact. When she'd been younger, Jocelyn had sneaked a pair of Charles's breeches and had then climbed the trees after him with ease. But now she wore men's clothing in a renegade camp, and Jocelyn could feel the covert stares she received from Dash's men. But none of them made any untoward advances, nor any rude remarks, so Jocelyn soon calmed her fears. It was Dash she had to worry about, she knew. What would be *his* reaction when he found her dressed so scantily?

She was just finishing the last bite of a very tasty meal of fresh trout when both she and Pretty Boy heard a loud and persistent "Psssst!" from the woods.

"Ho, is that you Dash?" Pretty Boy called innocently.

"You know damn well who it is!" came a familiar male growl.

Jocelyn ducked her head, pretending to be busy with pulling a fish bone from the meat at the end of her knife.

"My clothes, man, and be quick about it!" Dash yelled.

Pretty Boy gave Jocelyn a wink but didn't move from his spot.

"Did you hear me?" Dash shouted, his ire unmistakable.

Pretty Boy looked at Jocelyn. "Should I?"

Jocelyn shrugged her shoulders, thinking of Dash standing naked behind the trees. It wasn't such a terrible thought. "Only if you wish," she replied.

"Maybe we should let him stew for a while."

"Maybe," she agreed.

But another roar from Dash set Pretty Boy into motion. "I'll have your hide for this!" Dash yelled. "If you want your pay, then you'll get me my clothes. *Dry* clothes, too, and not those trousers of mine you've got swinging in the tree!"

Jocelyn almost felt sorry for Pretty Boy as he fairly tripped over his own feet heading for Dash's tent to retrieve the clothes.

"Don't be angry with him," Jocelyn called out to Dash, whose head she could just barely see within the line of dense trees. "He was only doing as I asked him to do."

She heard Dash's low growl of disapproval and suddenly wondered if she shouldn't be a little more worried about her *own* hide. Trying to make a peace offering, she called, "I saved a trout for you. And there's tea here as well."

Nothing but silence now. Jocelyn began to get nervous. What *would* Dash do to her? Perhaps she'd gone too far. Pretty Boy raced by her then, a bundle of clothes beneath one arm.

Two minutes later Dash walked out from the shade of the trees wearing only a clean pair of trousers. He had his shirt in his hands and a frightening look on his face. He walked straight toward Jocelyn.

Pretty Boy conveniently excused himself, and the rest of Dash's men scurried off to do God knew what.

Jocelyn quickly got to her feet, thrusting a plate filled with trout to Dash. "Here," she said. "Hurry and get something in your stomach. Maybe you'll be in a better mood then."

For a moment she feared he'd bat the plate away and

just go directly for her neck. A feast of her blood, yes, that's what he wanted.

"What the devil is this?" he growled, his wintry eyes raking over her figure.

Jocelyn forced herself not to cringe. "It's fish," she said, not being able to help needling him a bit more.

"I'm not talking about the food, and you damn well know it!"

Indeed she did. Jocelyn felt her cheeks grow warm as Dash took in her indecent attire. She felt as though she were standing nude in front of him. The heat of his angry eyes seemed to sear through her garments and slice directly into her skin. She wore no underclothes, for hers were too wet and cold and were now drying with her dress. Jocelyn felt her breasts tighten, and her stomach tingle. Damn the man for looking at her so intently! What right did he have to sit in judgment of her?

His face tensed, Dash tossed his shirt to her. "Cover yourself, before you cause a mutiny among my men!"

Jocelyn purposely let his shirt fall to the ground. "Your men," she said crisply, "were gentlemen and didn't even bat an eye at me." She wasn't about to tell Dash their true reaction, for she feared he'd force her to wear his coat for the duration of her stay!

He looked as though he'd like to turn her inside out, and that telltale muscle jumped menacingly in his cheek. "Get dressed," he barked. "Now."

Jocelyn stiffened. "I *am* dressed! Need I remind you that you tossed me into the stream and drenched my gown? Unfortunately for me, I didn't have the foresight to pack a valise before you abducted me."

Her words hit their desired mark. Dash grunted something unintelligible and took the plate and sat down. He wolfed down the food, gulped the scalding tea, and said nothing.

Not liking the silence, Jocelyn sat down as well and fidgeted. "Careful," she said, watching Dash shovel in another mouthful of trout. "The bones—"

"Afraid I might choke?" he asked gruffly. "Back at the stream your only thought was of drowning me."

Rude of him to remind her. "That was hardly my intention," she replied coolly.

"Oh? You could have fooled me." He sucked down another tin cup filled with tea, tossed the cup to the ground, then glared long and hard at her. "Look, Duchess, there are a few things we need to set straight between us."

"My name is Jocelyn, or rather Miss Gre—"

"Number one," he began, not letting her finish. "No more pranks. This isn't a fair. My men look to me as their leader. I cannot afford to have them see me made the fool."

Jocelyn lowered her face—not in submission or even embarrassment, but because she didn't want Dash to see the smile that was creeping up on her.

"Number two," he went on in a stentorian voice. "Keep your distance from my men."

At this, Jocelyn snapped her head up, all smiles of conquest forgotten. "And why should I do that?"

"Because I said so," Dash replied. "That's reason enough."

"Need I remind you that I am *not* one of your men?" Dash purposely let his eyes flicker over her body, which was encased in Pretty Boy's clothing, but Jocelyn didn't falter. "Nor will I take orders from you."

"Is that so?" Dash drawled, clearly getting angrier by the moment but determined not to let it get the best of him. "And need I remind you you're my prisoner?"

Jocelyn gave a snort of impatience. "I'm not! I'm only here because . . . because you won't let me go. A prisoner wears shackles and sits in an airless cell."

"Part of which I can arrange—if you ever try another stunt like the one you just pulled."

Jocelyn clamped her mouth shut tight, thinking of the length of rope that hung from his saddle pack. He could tie her up, if that was his wish. He'd do it, too, she knew. The man was heartless.

Dash seemed pleased with her silence. "So do we understand each other?"

"Perfectly," she ground out. "It's all very simple. I do exactly as you say and speak to no one but you."

"Very good."

Jocelyn lifted her chin, wanting nothing more than to slap him hard across the face. Someday, she promised herself, she'd get the better of him. Until then, though, it was apparent that she'd have to keep her spirited side in check. No more stealing his clothes and leaving him nude in the stream. She felt another spasm of laughter coming on as she thought of him walking naked back to camp. She covered the laugh with a cough.

Dash wasn't fooled. "A bone catch in your throat?" He made a motion as if to whack her between the shoulder blades, but Jocelyn dodged out of his reach, shaking her head.

"No," she managed, nearly laughing aloud. "I think I've caught a chill is all."

"Hmmm," Dash muttered, clearly unconvinced. But he let her go.

Just as Jocelyn stepped inside of Dash's tent where Pretty Boy had gone, the laughter bubbled out of her. She and Pretty Boy stood there giggling until tears came. No doubt Dash heard.

Six

Dash found his sour mood increasing as the day wore on. It wasn't so much due to the fact Jocelyn had outwitted him, but more because the woman was constantly on his mind. He could not erase the sight of her—standing in midstream, her velvet dress molding itself to her luscious curves—from his mind. Nor could he forget the softness of her body as he'd carried her to bed the night before, nor the way she'd snuggled close to his chest and had sighed lightly. And of course, the sight of her in Pretty Boy's clothes had nearly sent his lust out of control. The outline of her breasts and hips had been clearly defined beneath that garb, and Dash felt his loins tighten again with just the thought.

Dash swore in exasperation. He was acting like a love-sick lad! His men, those who had left under the cover of darkness, returned then, riding quickly into the clearing. Dash met them.

"Well?" he asked the first. "Any trouble?"

The man shook his head. "We met with Fritz and his boys. They've got the booty and are heading for Manchester, but just as you said last night, Dash, the cache isn't going to be enough. We'll have to make another run tonight."

Dash nodded, for he'd thought as much. "Very well," he said, thinking that after tonight's raid he'd be able to deal with Jocelyn. He would have to frighten her, though, to make certain she kept her mouth shut about him and his group of men.

"What about the lady?" the man asked lowly.

"I'll take care of her," Dash said, his voice grave.

"What if she talks? What if—"

"She won't," Dash cut in. "And if you know what's good for you, you'll steer clear of her. Don't speak to her. Don't go near her. Is that understood?"

The men nodded.

"Good. Now, get some sleep. We've got a long night ahead of us." Dash turned away then, thinking about his promise to his men. He wasn't totally sure he *could* make certain Jocelyn wouldn't go to the authorities with what she knew.

So what the devil was he going to do with her? he wondered. He knew what he *wanted* to do to her, and it wasn't deliver her to her father's door.

Needing to clear his head, Dash sat down under a tree and began to clean his flintlock pistol. With a patch of dried moss, Dash wiped the black powder residue from the barrel of the gun, poking the ramrod into the cylinder and swirling the moss about, then pulling the rod and moss back out. It was a mindless task, but he forced himself to concentrate. After cleaning the inside of the barrel, he set to buffing the bluish, case-hardened steel until it shone dully in the early morning light.

Dash's pistol was like a third hand to him; he felt naked without it. He'd won the flintlock in a game of chess from a Dutch mynheer who'd purchased the weapon while on holiday in the Black Forest of Germany. Dash liked to know the history of any weapon he carried. There came a certain power from knowledge, and when it came to firearms Dash never accepted second best.

Finished with the cleaning, Dash lifted the pistol and sighted it on a distant line of trees. Closing one eye, he aimed for a knot in the wood of a healthy beech tree. Jocelyn stepped into his line of vision. For a moment Dash thought he was just imagining her. His mind was playing tricks on him again.

She stood there like a woodland nymph, her rich, coppery-red locks spilling down to her shoulders in tumbling disarray. Even wearing Pretty Boy's clothes, she looked stunning. The man's shirt bloused about her small waist. She'd rolled the sleeves up to her elbows, and Dash could see her pale skin that was sprinkled with tiny freckles. But it was her eyes, the color of beryl fire, which caught and tugged at Dash's heart. They were clear in her face, and sad.

It was then Dash realized this was no fantasy show his mind played for him, but reality, for if he'd been imagining Jocelyn, then her eyes would have been smoky with passion. He slowly lowered his pistol, watching her.

Jocelyn blinked once, shifting from one hand to the other a spray of wildflowers she'd picked, along with a square of folded linen.

"Searching for a target?" she asked, her voice sounding far too husky for Dash's comfort.

Dash shook his head, wondering why his mouth went dry every time he looked at her.

"Then you're planning another robbery, is that it?"

Dash stood up, tucked his pistol into the top of his trousers, then walked slowly toward her. "Does that surprise you? I'm a thief—that's what thieves do."

"Is it so exciting that you must do it every night?"

He halted just a breath away from her. She smelled as pure as the outdoors. Pity that he wasn't good enough for her, that the two of them hadn't met under different circumstances. Softly Dash said, "You're very curious this day."

Jocelyn lifted her chin, not wavering beneath his intense stare. "It was a fair question. Are you going to answer it or not?"

"No."

The corner of her pouty mouth twitched minutely, as though she'd gotten the answer she'd wanted anyway. "Then you don't enjoy it."

"I didn't say that."

"You didn't have to."

Dash gave a short grunt of laughter, then nodded toward
the spray of flowers and linen in her hand. "What are
these for?"

"Color," she answered, her eyes softening. "I thought
Caleb might enjoy looking at them. And in here," she
added, flipping open one end of the linen, "are roots and
spiderwebs. They should help dry any infection in Cal's
wound—"

"You were out walking in the woods alone?" Dash interrupted, suddenly feeling testy again. "I thought I told you
to stay near the campsite. These are dangerous times. A
woman isn't safe—" He stopped himself from saying more.
He'd kidnapped her. What the devil was he doing rattling on
about safety and such when Jocelyn clearly felt like a fish
who'd gone from the frying pan into the fire?

Dammit, Dash cursed himself, seeing the softness leave
her gaze and a certain hardness creep in to steal the glorious light he'd just viewed. He'd gone and offended her—
again.

"I wasn't unchaperoned, if that's what is bothering
you," Jocelyn snapped. "Pretty Boy was with me. In fact,
he should be coming along shortly, so you can hear from
his own mouth how he dogged my every step for fear I
might flee with my life."

Dash felt like a perfect heel, but he wasn't about to let
Jocelyn see that. In Joycelyn's eyes he was nothing more
than a lowly thief and a sneaking dog. In order to ensure
she didn't try to escape or get to the authorities, Dash had
to keep an upper hand. He had to convince Jocelyn that
he was truly merciless and would have no compunction
whatsoever in doling out any punishment he deemed necessary.

Knowing he had to be gruff with her—for to do anything
else would be to fall prey to her innocent charm—Dash
fixed his meanest scowl to his face. With a terseness that
was forced, he said, "From now on you go nowhere without me. Is that clear?"

Jocelyn's eyes widened in sheer anger. "Nowhere?"

"That's right," he growled. "You want to pick flowers,

you come to me. You want to bathe, you do the same. If you want—''

Her hand flashed up before him, as if she wanted to bar the sound of his voice from entering her ears. ''You need not elaborate,'' she ground out. ''I'm your prisoner and you're my keeper. Things couldn't be clearer.''

''Good. I'm glad we understand each other.''

''Understand? Hardly.'' With that, she turned on her heel and stalked back to the tent.

Dash stood staring after her, watching as her tiny bottom swayed beneath those ridiculous pants she wore and wishing he could stop fantasizing about what her bottom might look like *without* those trousers.

''She's a damn witch,'' he muttered to himself, realizing no woman had ever gotten under his skin as Jocelyn had done in a little less than twenty-four hours.

''What was that?''

Dash tore his gaze away from Jocelyn disappearing behind the flap of the tent. Pretty Boy stood beside him. He, too, had watched as Jocelyn entered the tent.

Pretty Boy grinned at Dash. ''A witch, you say?''

Dash's scowl deepened. ''What the hell are you doing sneaking up on me? You want that fancy face of yours shot full of lead?''

Pretty Boy laughed. ''No sneaking involved. You just weren't listening. What's the matter? Did the lady get the best of you again?''

Dash grunted in answer. ''I don't want her wandering off. We can't risk letting her escape, and well you know it.''

''She's not going to squeal on us,'' Pretty Boy said with supreme sureness.

''And how can you be so certain?'' Dash demanded.

''Well, I . . . I can't, I guess. It's just a feeling I have.''

A long moment passed before Dash said quietly, ''A feeling, huh? The last time you had a 'feeling,' I found you near to death in the middle of the Spa Fields riot.'' Dash's gut tightened at the memory, and he knew Pretty Boy felt the same.

That night had happened three years ago, but neither distance nor passage of time could erase the awful memory of finding his friends lying deathly still in a pool of blood.

Dash wished he could forget the horrid night. In fact, he would have sold his soul to the devil to forget. But remembering the riot of the Spa Fields would forever be Dash's hell. He'd been a part of the riot, even though he hadn't participated; he with his firebrand revolutionist talk and his burning desire to right the wrongs of the long oppressed.

Just like the factory workers of the northern countryside, Dash had once known a life of hardship and grief. He knew firsthand what it was to go to bed hungry night after night, to wake to a new day and know there wouldn't be any relief from his misery. He'd vowed then he wouldn't live like that forever. He'd also been determined not to let others endure such a hellish existence.

And then he'd met Lord Monty and his life had done a complete about-face. Like Uncle Monty, Dash had taken up the cry to aid the silent, suffering masses.

But while Lord Monty voiced his opinion in the spacious chambers where Parliament met, Dash had chosen to scour the lands of England and seek out his fellow man. And he'd found them in the shantytowns near the northern factories.

Dash winced at the memories crowding in upon him. Lord, what a fool he'd been! He'd gone north to help the less fortunate people of England, not incite them to riot. But riot they had! In droves they'd converged on the sprawling Spa Fields, shouting for reform, for justice . . . and King George III's loyal soldiers had cut them down. Many men and women had been trampled by horses, by humans, some driven through with blades, others shot in the back as they'd tried to run for cover. Death had taken its toll that night.

And Dash felt responsible. He should have kept quiet. He should not have gone to those small towns and talked of fairness and honor. He knew that now. The blood upon his hands had been a harsh and unforgettable lesson.

"Don't think about it," Pretty Boy said quietly, cutting into Dash's thoughts. "It's done with. Over. We cannot relive the past."

Dash glanced over at his friend. "But how can I forget? I was responsible."

Pretty Boy said nothing more, only walked away, his own memories binding him tightly to their ugly past.

Yes, Dash thought, he *was* partly responsible for all those people losing their lives. Even Pretty Boy knew it to be true. There would be no relief from the ghosts of his past, Dash knew. How could there be? He'd helped incite a riot—and he'd killed those people just as surely as if he'd trampled them with his own mount.

Feeling the need to be alone, Dash headed deep into the woods. He stopped when he came to a rotted log that lay atop the forest floor, half-mushrooms of fungus growing on its upper bark. Dash sat down and stared at nothing. A kingfisher tapped out a long and lonely rhythm on a distant tree, the sound echoing off into the distance. Horseflies buzzed about. A whippoorwill beat its wings and sang for a mate. Sunlight, filtered through the deciduous trees, painted a checkered path of light atop the lush ferns on the ground as well as the tiny saplings that struggled to survive in the dense woods.

The world was alive, its pulse beating all around, but Dash felt dead inside. A huge chunk of him had died that night, alongside the others on the Spa Fields.

From behind, Dash heard the sure footfalls of an intruder. Instinctively, and without thought, he reached for his flintlock pistol tucked into the waistband of his trousers. Crouching down behind the log, he quickly pulled the ramrod from beneath the barrel of the gun, then jammed a load of powder and shot he carried in a pouch strapped about his waist down into the barrel.

Eyes narrowed, his nerves taut, Dash watched, and waited. More footsteps, louder now. Whoever was approaching was coming closer, and at a fast pace. Dash drew back the hammer of the pistol. When he pulled the trigger, the hammer would snap against the flint and produce a spark, igniting the powder and spewing the ball of lead outward. And then a bluish smoke would follow, and if Dash had been on the mark, injury, or even death.

Death. Dash's stomach soured at the thought. He'd seen too much of it in his life, yet he seemed to chase that very thing. He'd lived by his wits—and the power of his gun. When would it end?

Dash felt his forehead bead with sweat. Not much longer now. Whoever was coming toward him was nearly in view. Dash squinted his left eye and got ready to aim.

Laney Braden came tramping into his line of vision. "Don't shoot," he called amiably. "I know damn well you've got your pistol sighted on me."

Dash blew out a sigh. "You stupid son of a bitch," Dash replied, lowering his gun and getting to his feet.

Laney batted a whipcord branch of thorns from his way. "Watch what you say about my mother. She's probably rolling in her grave about now." Laney picked a bramble off his immaculate coat. "The campsite too wild for you, eh? You think you have to find some peace and quiet?"

Dash laid his pistol down. "I needed some fresh air."

"So breathe," Laney said, clearly disgusted at having to tramp through the woods to find his friend. "Fresh air is all around you. Can't get much sweeter than this."

"When did you get back?"

"Just now, and I came looking for you."

"You've found me. Talk."

"Did I say I wanted to talk?"

"That's what you're best at, Laney."

"That's not what the ladies tell me," Braden shot back with a grin.

Dash didn't return the smile.

"You're in a rotten mood. What's troubling you? Did your sweet little wench toss you out of your tent?"

"She's a lady, Braden. You'd do well to remember that."

"So I've been warned." Laney sat down beside Dash, then plucked a long blade of wild grass and clamped down on it with his teeth. "I've got some news for you, Dash. I thought it best that you heard it from me first."

Dash said nothing, only waited.

Laney laughed. "You aren't going to beg for it, are you, old friend?"

"I'm not a man to beg."

"No, that you aren't. You haven't been for quite some time now. All right, so I'll tell you. There are rumors circulating about the Midnight Raider. Ugly ones. Some of the upper crust have a description of him, which could or could not point to you. They want the Raider's hide."

Dash went cold.

"That's right," Laney continued. "They think it was the Midnight Raider and his boys who robbed Frances Keats and shot his son between the eyes. They've good reason to think so, too. I mean, what highway robber has such good aim? You've heard of the robbery, I'm sure."

"I've heard," Dash said slowly.

"Took place not far from here. About four leagues, as a matter of fact. Keats and his boy were heading back to London from a hunting trip in the north. He loved that boy, Dash. James was his name and he would have been seventeen this Friday—about the same age as that pretty piece you've tucked away in your tent."

Dash closed his fingers about the rosewood grips of his flintlock. "Jocelyn is a lady—"

"Yeah, so you say. Anyway, old friend, the elite of London are filling a hat full of coin—they've promised to pay a comely sum to the man who brings the Midnight Raider in alive. They want blood, Dash. James Keats was a bonny lad in their eyes. Now I'm not saying I think you are the Raider, but you and I both know you haunt these roads and that you'd steal from your own mother if she were still alive."

At that, Dash felt his palm itch. Without blinking an eye, Dash brought his left hand up and slammed it into Laney's jaw. Laney toppled off the log and lay sprawled on the forest floor. Dash jumped to his feet and towered over him, pistol in hand.

"Take care what you say about my mother. You know as well as I that I was not the one to rob Frances Keats and murder his son!"

"Do I?" Laney barked, nursing a sore jaw. "What the devil do I know about you or your boys? You're a stranger to me! The last I saw of you you were dripping wealth and rolling unlucky dice. How the bloody hell do I know how you came by such wealth?"

Dash couldn't believe what he was hearing. "How?" he thundered. "How do you think? 'Twas Lord Monty's money I threw about that night at the gaming tables! When have I ever had a quid to call my own?"

"When you were stealing," Braden answered.

Dash dropped his hands to his sides. Laney was correct. Damn him, but he was right! "Get up," Dash muttered. "And tell me more of this plot to see the Midnight Raider hanged."

"Hanged is the least of it," Laney said, climbing to his feet and flexing his jaw twice. "They'll roast his innards first—while he's still alive."

"Where did you hear this?"

"Where *didn't* I hear it should be the question. The description of the Raider is too close to a description of you, Dash. Even Lord Monty is beginning to get worried."

Dash cursed himself silently, knowing he'd been too long on the road and should have returned to London by now.

"Last I heard Lord Monty was moving fast to keep up with the rumors. Now if you *are* the Midnight Raider, Dash, then Monty's position in Parliament could be put to question. You'd do well to seek him out and prove to him you're not the Raider."

Dash sat down, his body rigid.

"You're a thief," Laney said, sounding almost as though he enjoyed the fact. "You have no right to bear the Warfield name."

Such a remark cut deeply into Dash's soul. From the moment Uncle Monty had taken Dash under his protective wing, Dash had felt unworthy. He'd merely been the son of a street waif and some faceless man, after all. Not even Dash knew who'd fathered him. And Dash's mother? She'd been pretty in her youth, and sought after by men who liked whiskey too much and the feel of a woman's body . . . but Dash was realistic enough to realize he was the product of hard times. His mother had gotten herself with child and had then done the best she could. Coal cellars and pickpocketing had been Dash's life before Lord Monty had come along.

But the Warfield name *did* belong to Dash—Uncle Monty had seen to that. Lord Montague Warfield had taken Dash as his son, legal and binding. And Dash had tried his very best to live up to what was expected of him. But what had been ingrained in him as a child had not been easy to get beyond. To forget his roots, to just leave the streets of St. Giles and never look back, was something Dash had not been able to do. And when he'd learned of the plight of the northern factory workers, Dash had been hard pressed not to give them his attention.

And so he'd chosen to put aside his rights to a cushioned life of ease and had joined the ranks of the revolutionists. The country of England screamed for reform . . . and Dash had been only too eager to see her claim that change.

"I have every right to bear the Warfield name," Dash said roughly.

"Think what you like," Laney said. "But you should be worrying about this description of the Raider. It appears someone is out to see you hanged for the murder of James Keats, whether or not you did the deed. If I were you, Dash, I'd head for the shores of Dover. You can board a ship there and be well away from England in a week's time. If you'd like, I'll send word to Lord Monty. He won't fault you for fleeing. He loves you. He'd forgive you anything."

Dash heard the note of bitterness in Laney's voice and realized dully that nothing had changed . . . nothing but his own precarious lot in life. Laney still slighted him for the fact that Lord Monty had chosen Dash to be his heir.

Suddenly it was horribly clear where he stood with his childhood friend. Laney had long been jealous of the attention Uncle Monty had poured on Dash.

"Yes," Dash said, looking Braden in the eye. "Uncle Monty *would* forgive me. And he would do all in his power to protect me."

"Precisely!" Laney quickly agreed. "And that is why you should get yourself out of the Cotswolds and safely to Dover. If you don't, Lord Monty will be forced to choose between you and his seat in Parliament and all that post entails. Do you want that, Dash? Do you want to force the man to give up his dreams only to save your neck?"

Dash's head became muddled with all his choices. Why was Braden pushing him to leave the country? Did Laney really care about him, or was Braden perhaps thinking of the roads that would be opened to him if Dash were not around? It was no secret between the two men that if Dash were not the center of Lord Monty's thoughts, Laney would then take that coveted position. It had always been thus. Dash had been the one showered with gifts and opportunities long before Laney had come to live with them. But Laney had been the second to come live with Uncle Monty, and for Laney that had been a fate worse than death.

"I'm not going anywhere," Dash announced, rising to his feet. "I didn't kill anyone, and I won't be forced into hiding as though I had."

Braden stood up as well. "Then you're more of a fool than I thought."

"I don't care what you think."

"No," Laney said lowly. "You never have."

Dash eyed his childhood friend for a long moment. "That isn't true and you know it. I've loved you like a brother—you *are* my brother as far as I'm concerned."

Laney faltered a moment, as though the admission took him by surprise. But in the next instant he rallied back, causing Dash to think he'd imagined his friend's hesitation.

"Yes, brothers," Laney said. "Through good and ill."

He clapped one arm about Dash's shoulders. "You've a difficult road ahead of you, but know that I'll be beside you every step of the way . . . just like the old days."

Something in Laney's tone caused a warning bell to go off in Dash's head, but he ignored it. He would not sully this moment by doubting the person who'd grown up alongside him. He couldn't.

"Then you believe I did not kill James Keats?"

"If you say so, then yes, I believe you."

At that moment Laney Braden appeared the only solid anchor in Dash's life, and he held to it like a man in a storm-tossed sea. "Thank you," Dash said.

Laney smiled, tightened his grip on Dash's shoulders, then led him back toward the campsite.

Seven

Once back at camp the day didn't get any easier for Dash. Pretty Boy all but ignored him as he went about his duties. It was clear to Dash where Pretty Boy's loyalty now lay—certainly not with him. And the same appeared to be true with Caleb.

"Don't be too hard on Jocelyn," Caleb said quietly as Dash brought some lunch to the boy. "She's lonesome for home."

"And you're not?" Dash asked.

"It doesn't matter."

"Oh? And how do you figure that?" •

"Because," Caleb said guilelessly. "I'm here to help my family and to see that they have food to eat during the winter. Jocelyn isn't here by choice."

That fact didn't sit too well with Dash. He went through the remainder of the day with the boy's words echoing relentlessly in his head. By nightfall, when the peepers started their unending chorus and even the hoot owls were restless, Dash began to feel the strain of all his worries. He couldn't go home; he was wanted for murder. He couldn't release Jocelyn; she knew too much.

"Dammit," Dash muttered to himself, feeling trapped. What he needed, Dash decided, was to engulf himself in his quest to help the factory workers. He had a mission to see to completion, and that much he could do.

So thinking, he saddled his horse and gave terse orders

to his men to prepare for another ride. But just when he thought he might find a moment's peace on the quiet roads of the Cotswolds, Dash heard Jocelyn's indignant shout of protest.

"I won't do it!" Jocelyn yelled, garnering Dash's immediate attention. "I won't sit idly by and allow others to be robbed!"

Dash pulled tight to the cinch of his saddle. "What the devil is the matter now?" he growled. "Pretty Boy! Can't you keep her quiet for even a few minutes?"

Pretty Boy stepped out of the tent, looking defeated. He waved his arms in the air as though he wished to wash himself clean of this particular fight, then moved away.

Dash's anger increased. "Granger!" he yelled. "See to my horse!" With clipped steps Dash marched toward his tent and threw open the flap. "Is there a problem?" he demanded, trying hard to keep his voice even.

"You're damned right there is!" Jocelyn yelled at him.

She stood in the middle of the tent, the bright lantern light fully illuminating her flushed face, and Dash thought she'd never looked so gorgeous. Her coppery-colored hair hung about her shoulders, all loose and free, looking soft and touchable, and swinging with her every gesture. And gesture she did!

"I've had it up to here!" she cried, slicing one slim hand in front of her throat, "with you telling me what I can and cannot do! I will not stay in this tent knowing you're out and about threatening innocent people! So thieves steal, do they? Fine! Steal from each other!" She jabbed one finger beneath his face. "Just don't think I'll allow you to steal from honest folk! I haven't spent the whole of my life helping my father look after these people just to see you sweep up their life savings in one single night! You are the devil in disguise, Dash! You should swing from a noose for all your thieving!"

Dash had to take a deep breath, telling himself it wouldn't do any good to yell back at her. "And well I might, lady," he said lowly. "But until I do, I won't endure your temper tantrums."

"Temper tantrum?" she shrieked. "Is that what you think this is? A tantrum?"

"What else?" he drawled, forcing himself to remain in control of his emotions. If he didn't, he might find himself pulling the luscious spitfire into his arms. Lord, but she was pretty when she was angry, and exciting, and desirable even. Dash figured he must be going mad, or at least be well on his way to it if he could find excitement in Jocelyn's theatrics. Had it been any other woman to thwart him, he wouldn't have paid her a lick of attention.

But Jocelyn Greville wasn't just any woman.

She threw Cal's basin of water at him, followed by Cal's bowl of uneaten broth as well Dash's bedroll.

"You told me you'd take me home!" she cried. "You lied to me! And now you expect me to be subservient and play the good victim while you head out with a loaded pistol to find unsuspecting travelers! Well, I won't do it!"

Dash ducked in time to miss the basin, but not the bowl, nor the bedroll. Jocelyn had a good aim, he had to give her that. But at the moment Dash wasn't feeling so generous.

"Why, you little—" He lunged for her.

Jocelyn didn't move. It seemed she wanted to meet him head on—wanted it very badly in fact. Before Dash knew what he was doing, he had his hands locked to her shoulders and was shaking her.

Jocelyn glared up at him, all fire and righteous anger. But she didn't cry out. She didn't even flinch. She would take her punishment, and then, Dash knew, try to give as good as she got.

Suddenly Dash felt the fight leave him. He couldn't hurt her. He didn't want to.

Caleb cried out from his sick bed. "Don't hurt her!" the boy shouted. "She's just afraid!"

Jocelyn's lips thinned. "I'm not afraid," she said, not batting an eyelash beneath Dash's heated stare. "Do it," she goaded Dash. "Throttle me. Show me who has the upper hand here."

Caleb whimpered in fright.

Dash barely heard the boy; he had eyes only for Jocelyn. "I *could* throttle you," he whispered. "Indeed, I could give you exactly what you deserve."

"What are you waiting for?" Jocelyn demanded.

Dash tightened his grip and felt her soft skin give beneath his fingertips. The musky scent of her drifted up to him, nearly knocking Dash off his feet. Her eyes, flashing fire, were provocative. Her breasts, heaving beneath her blousy shirt, proved to be nearly his undoing.

Dash said, "I should tie you to a tree until I return."

"You probably should."

"I should stuff a rag into that flapping mouth of yours."

"No doubt."

Dash felt his skin grow warm and his loins tighten. "I should toss you over my horse and take you with me."

A flicker of triumph lit in her green eyes. "Yes," she said. "That would probably be best."

In the end Dash didn't toss her over his saddle, but rather dragged her to his horse, then forced her up before him. Mounting behind Jocelyn, he scooped up the reins, then called his men to order.

With Jocelyn riding in front of him, Dash led the way out of the campsite and onto the road. Somehow, he knew he'd made the wrong choice. Doubtless, Jocelyn knew it as well.

Jocelyn held tight to the horn of Dash's saddle as the wind sliced through her teeth and snatched at the hasty braid she'd pulled her hair into. She smiled to herself as Dash kicked his mount into a gallop and they sprinted onto the rutted roadway. Her plans had gone swimmingly. In fact, she couldn't have been more pleased with the turn of events—except, of course, if Dash had given her her own horse to ride. But Jocelyn knew beggars could not be choosy. She was determined to make her escape this night, whether or not she rode the same horse as her captor.

Wearing Pretty Boy's clothes gave Jocelyn an added advantage. She'd be able to sprint away without having to worry about hitching up her skirts or having them caught in brambles. Yes, she decided, loving the feel of the wind in her face and the cloak of darkness pulling in around her, the night promised to be eventful.

"Don't get any ideas, Duchess," Dash muttered into her ear, as though he'd read her thoughts clearly. "Though I've got my mind on other things, I won't be so preoccupied that I'll give you a change to slip free."

Jocelyn stiffened in the saddle. "So you think I might try to escape, do you?"

"I'd be a fool not to." He slipped one arm about her narrow waist and held tightly. "Be forewarned: you cannot outsmart me."

Jocelyn tried to ignore the warmth and scope of his hand resting just above her hip, but it was impossible to do so. Glancing at him from over one shoulder, she said, "Are you trying to convince me . . . or yourself?"

"You, of course."

"And if I do attempt an escape?"

"Don't."

"But if I do—"

Dash interrupted her words with a low chuckle. "Oh, no," he said. "You'll not be hearing any more threats from me, if that's what you're hoping. Just know that you've been given fair warning."

Jocelyn harrumphed noisily, then trained her gaze on the darkness ahead. "Fair? I doubt you even know the meaning of the word."

They both fell silent then as Dash's horse raced into the pitch wall of blackness before them. The animal seemed to move by instinct alone. Bred for speed and loyalty, the beast took with ease to the free rein Dash had given him. Granger and Pretty Boy followed behind, as well as Laney and one of his men. A party of thieves they were, moving swiftly through the night.

Jocelyn had never felt so alive, so charged with energy. She told herself the reason was because she planned to escape, and not because she rode with Dash. Certainly it wasn't the fact that he had his left arm hitched about her waist, or because Jocelyn's bottom was fitted perfectly in between his muscled thighs. Nor could it be the fact that every now and then Dash was forced to remove his hand from her waist and uncoil her long braid from flapping in his face. After doing the deed four times in succession, Dash finally tucked the braid down the back of her shirt.

Jocelyn nearly jumped off the saddle when his fingers grazed the skin at the base of her neck.

"Easy now," Dash crooned into her ear. "I just don't want to be blinded."

Jocelyn clamped her mouth shut tight. The man clearly knew how much he unnerved her, and doubtless he enjoyed it. Determined not to allow him to ruffle her further, Jocelyn tried to concentrate on staying astride and keeping alert.

Laney came up beside them. "We should veer off the road soon," he said, keeping his horse even with Dash's. "The coach is due by at twelve forty-five."

Dash said nothing for a full beat of hooves pounding atop the uneven roadway. "I've a bad feeling about this," he finally said. "How did you hear about this shipment of gold?"

Laney grinned, his teeth flashing white in the night. "Same way I hear about everything, old friend. I eavesdropped on a certain conversation at the Fox's Lair. Smugglers along the coast have had a rich trade of late—what with the Corn Law and all—and tonight they believe they will get their rewards . . . but unfortunately for them, we'll intercept the transaction. You can do what you want with your share. As for me, I'll be heading to London to spend mine."

"Smuggler's gold, is it?" Dash muttered. "You're sure of that?"

"Sure as I'm slavering for the fine brandy that will be in the coach as well. Relax, Dash. No need to go nervous on me now."

"I'm not nervous," Dash snapped. "Just cautious."

Laney gave Jocelyn a conspiratorial grin. "The boy is always nervous, lass, don't let him fool you." To Dash, Laney said, "This will be the cleanest robbery you've ever known. Smugglers know a brisk trade that will find no mention in ledgers. Who can they rage to once we've stolen their swag? No one, my friend, and that's the beauty of it! The authorities won't have their ears filled with this night's tale, that's for certain.''

''And what about the smugglers?'' Dash asked. ''Don't think they won't come after what is theirs.''

''Oh, they'll try, all right,'' Laney agreed with wicked glee. ''But we'll be long gone. This will be like taking a sugar tit from a baby.''

Jocelyn could sense Dash did not think so. And Jocelyn's reservations were beginning to mount as well. She'd thought Dash and his men had been planning to rob another coach from Chipping Campden, not a private coach transporting ill-gained fortune to a group of faceless smugglers! Heavens, robbing from a group of miscreants would present its own set of problems, she surmised.

So thinking, she said, ''Won't these men be fully armed? Won't they be expecting trouble? I—I mean, they're smugglers, after all. They are accustomed to hazard.''

''As am I!'' Laney shot back, his voice filled with laughter.

Jocelyn found the man's enthusiasm frightening. Clearly Lane Braden thirsted for trouble. When the man dropped behind to chat with the others, Jocelyn chanced a glance at Dash. She could barely make out his features, for the night was moonless and thick.

''You don't trust him, do you?'' she asked.

''I rarely have.''

''Then why are you riding with him this night? Why let him talk you into robbing from smugglers?''

''Who better to rob from?''

Who indeed? ''I don't understand why you are a thief at all,'' she whispered, half to herself. ''You could be killed—or worse.''

''Worried for my safety?''

''Yes!'' she said emphatically, then added quickly, ''But only because you've the reins in your hand. If you find a shot of lead between your eyes, then I'll be left to handle this beast on my own.''

Dash pressed his lips close to her ear. ''But then you could ride for your father's home. You'd have your freedom, *and* be done with me.''

He was taunting her again, Jocelyn knew. But didn't he realize that what he said could actually happen? Jocelyn felt a shiver of premonition course up her spine.

''Cold?'' Dash whispered.

Jocelyn went rigid. ''No. I'm wondering if I'll have my head attached to my shoulders once this night is through.''

''*You're* the one who made such a fuss tonight. If you had kept that pouty mouth of yours shut, then perhaps I would have let you be.''

''Oh, so now it's *my* fault that I'm riding with a band of thieves?''

''It is and well you know it.''

''I know no such thing! You nearly threw me over this saddle and then barked your usual orders to everyone within earshot! One would think you'd been born to rule. You go about growling at everyone, and heaven forbid if they don't jump fast enough—''

''Shut up,'' Dash interrupted rudely.

Stung, Jocelyn snapped, ''Just who—''

''I said be quiet!'' he rasped, yanking hard on the reins and then calling out for the others to halt.

From behind, Pretty Boy said, ''What's the matter?''

''Up there,'' Dash replied. ''There's light ahead.''

Jocelyn squinted her eyes, peering hard into the night. There was indeed a spiral of torchlight blazing in the near distance.

''What do you think it is?'' Pretty Boy asked.

Dash shook his head, jerking the reins to keep his horse at bay. ''Could be nothing . . . or it could be a problem. Laney!'' he called in a hoarse whisper.

Braden came up beside them again.

''What do you make of this?'' Dash demanded.

''I don't know. Maybe our victims-to-be are expecting

us or maybe they've just stopped to uncork some of that brandy they're carting with them."

Dash was silent for a moment. "All right," he said, having made his decision. "We break apart here. Granger. Pretty Boy. You two take the left. Braden and I will take the right. Stay well away from the road until you hear my call. If these smugglers are just enjoying the fruits of their labor, then we'll ambush them from both sides."

"And if it's not the smugglers, but another coach, what then?" Granger asked.

Dash said, "Then I'll decide whether or not we'll take them. If you don't hear my call within fifteen minutes, head back to this spot. I don't want to waste our time on petty trinkets, not if the coach we want will come up behind us."

With that, the party broke apart, and Jocelyn felt her insides heave. This was it. She was actually going to take part in highway robbery. It was glaringly apparent that Dash had no intention of depositing her in the forest to wait for him, and that, Jocelyn knew, was her own fault. If he hadn't known she fully intended to attempt an escape, he might have been swayed to leave her alone while he did his dirty business. But that avenue of opportunity was soundly closed to Jocelyn.

She felt sick and excited all at once. With steadied slowness and absolute silence, Dash led his horse into the thick line of trees that reared up along the roadside. Laney came behind them. As they moved perpendicular to the road, Jocelyn could begin to make out two and even three torches that had been lit, then stabbed into the soft mud of the road. The torches blazed brightly, hissing and sputtering.

"Would you look at that!" Laney breathed. "Just waiting for us, they are!"

In the middle of the lane lay an overturned coach. The horses had been cut free of the conveyance and grazed without hindrance upon the grasses that shot up from the side of the road. Three men, dressed in dull and wrinkled clothing, attempted to reaffix the wheel of the coach that had come free from its axle. Like one giant machination, they heaved the wheel off the ground and lugged it toward the battered coach.

Laney let a soft whistle through his teeth. "This will be far too easy," he whispered. "Look, they've even unloaded their store of brandy and gold! Our job is half finished. All we need do is race out there with our pistols showing."

Dash halted Laney's rush of words with just a wave of his hand. "Quiet, Braden. Don't be too sure of yourself."

"And why shouldn't I be? We've got luck and the advantage of surprise on our side. It doesn't get much easier than this, Dash."

Jocelyn wasn't so certain. She could clearly see several rifles balanced against a single trunk that no doubt held the coveted gold. And the men who lumbered with the heavy wheel appeared to be quite capable of brandishing those lethal weapons. Big men they were, huge in fact, with beefy arms and stomachs full and round, and tree stumps for legs. Jocelyn guessed these men had been chosen to see the coach to its destination by their sheer bulk alone.

"This is madness," she whispered, unable to keep her thoughts to herself. "Don't do it, Dash. Don't—"

But Laney chose the moment to cup his hands to his mouth and imitate a quick and shrill bird call; the very sign that would send Granger and Pretty Boy into action.

Dash cursed soundly, then reached to his waist for his weapon. "You stupid son of a bitch!"

Laney grinned. "Not me," he said, pulling his own pistol out. Then he kicked his horse into motion and with a wild war cry, charged into action.

Jocelyn didn't have a moment to think. Suddenly she felt Dash's horse fly into movement.

"Hold on," Dash said, then slammed his boots to his horse's sides and flew after Laney.

Jocelyn fell back against Dash's frame with jarring force. But she righted herself, her eyes squinting shut as they careened through a tangle of branches. Whipcord, green limbs slapped her face, tearing her skin. Jocelyn instinctively hunkered down over the horse's neck. Dash did the same, and together they came tearing out of the line of trees. Granger and Pretty Boy broke free of the woods at the same time.

Pure mayhem reigned. The smugglers dropped the huge wheel, cursing and yelling, running for their weapons. Laney screeched like a madman, heading directly for one of the smugglers. The man lunged to the left, but not before Laney's booted foot met with his skull. The smuggler fell to the earth with a thud. Gunshots flared into the night. Acrid blue smoke billowed about. Jocelyn didn't know who'd fired first, but she guessed it was Laney. The man was wild now, a force of pure greed gone totally mad. He swung his pistol above his head, then brought his arm down as he swung his horse about and charged at yet another man. With brutal strength, he smashed the barrel of his pistol against the man's temple. The smuggler staggered, but didn't go down.

Laney circled the wrecked coach, came around, and charged at the man again.

Jocelyn screamed, seeing that Braden meant to beat the man to a pulp.

Dash yanked hard on his own reins. "Christ!" he muttered. "What the hell have I gotten you into?"

"He's going to kill him!" Jocelyn cried.

Dash made no comment, but swerved away from the fight, deciding to leave his men and take Jocelyn to safety.

"Don't look," he commanded her.

"But I—"

"Don't look!"

Jocelyn didn't have any choice, for Dash had confused his mount, first charging, then drawing back, and now the horse seemed indecisive, fighting at its bit. Jocelyn was having a hard time staying upright in the saddle.

"He's confused," Jocelyn cried, wishing she held the reins and not Dash. "Give him some lead! Let him calm down."

"I know how to handle my own horse, dammit!"

But Jocelyn wasn't listening. She leaned forward, trying

to keep herself astride. Just as she did so, a round of shot whizzed behind her. At least one of the smugglers had made it to the rifles!

Suddenly Jocelyn felt the horrid absence of Dash's guidance, and his weight was leaning precariously to one side.

"Dash! Are you all right?"

No answer.

Jocelyn came upright, whipping her head around. She saw Dash's grimace of pain, saw that he'd doubled over slightly and was holding his right side.

"I—I've been shot," he muttered.

"Oh, God," she whispered, her mind winging in a dozen different directions. "Hang on to me!" she called. "Dash!"

But he was slipping off the saddle, and the horse was wild now with the scent of smoke and blood. Jocelyn tore the reins from Dash's hands. Not meaning to do so, she yanked back, fearing if the horse bolted she would lose Dash. Just then one of the smugglers jumped in front of her, a rifle leveled at her chest.

"Get yer bloody arse off!" he yelled.

Jocelyn didn't have time to think. If she hesitated, she would be killed. With more bravery than she felt, Jocelyn ignored the order, tightening her thighs to the horse and forcing him forward.

The smuggler's face showed outrage, then shock as he dived to the right, out of harm's way. Jocelyn pressed her legs tight to the horse's sides. The beast surged ahead like a shot from a gun.

But just as Jocelyn broke free of the melee, Dash toppled off. She felt him sliding away and was powerless to help him. The gigantic horse was totally out of control now, having been given his head, and he charged away from the gunshots as though he'd never heard them before.

"Whoa!" Jocelyn screamed, yanking back once again on the reins. Dash's mount fought her. He halted, reared up on his hindquarters, and clawed at the air. Jocelyn groped to remain in the saddle. She was totally on her own now, forced to take control of an animal that was larger and stronger than any she'd ever ridden. Knowing her life depended on keeping a straight head, Jocelyn ground her teeth together and waited for the beast to have his fit. The horse whinnied, fighting at the bit, unaccustomed to his new master.

"Easy now," Jocelyn soothed, once the horse had all fours planted on the ground. She patted its neck, eased up on the reins a bit. "Easy."

Jocelyn glanced back, seeing Dash sprawled on the road, his blood spilling from him. Sheer fear gripped her. *He can't be dead!* her mind screamed, but she felt the absence of him—felt it like a knife blade twisting deep in her stomach.

Braden and his man dodged the smugglers, spewing fire from their pistols. Pretty Boy had been forced off his horse and now fought hand-to-hand with one of the smugglers.

Jocelyn watched the scene unfolding before her. She could ride away from all of it, she knew. She could slap Dash's mount into a mad flight and be well on her way home before anyone was the wiser.

But the sight of Dash lying wounded on the ground—possibly dead—stilled her flight. Jocelyn couldn't leave him. Though he'd treated her harshly and had met her head-on at every turn, Jocelyn knew she couldn't just turn her back on the man. Thief though he was, Jocelyn would not leave him.

Pushing thoughts of sweet freedom from her mind, she turned the horse about and plunged back into the thick of the fight. She felt a queer surge of power as she gained control of Dash's horse. The animal had become accustomed to her command and weight, and suddenly gave way to her direction. All fight drained out of the beast. He was one with her now. He would do as she commanded.

A heady euphoria engulfed Jocelyn. No longer did the cracks of gunfire startle her. No more did she fear a pound of lead crashing into her body. She felt focused, knew only she had to get to Dash and give him aid.

In a clatter of hoofbeats Jocelyn drew up alongside

Dash's form. In one swift movement she bounded down to the ground, kneeled at Dash's side, and called his name.

"Can you hear me?" she demanded. "Can you move?"

Dash twitched, grunted in pain. He was alive! Jocelyn didn't think beyond that. Without realizing what she was doing, she took up his flintlock that lay beside him and pulled back on the hammer.

Leveling the pistol with both hands on the rosewood grips, she aimed directly for the heart of the burly man who was approaching with rapid speed.

"Halt," she said with frightening force. "Don't move another step or I'll shoot."

Jocelyn could barely believe the sound of her own voice. But she was fighting for her life now—and for Dash's.

"Drop your weapon," she commanded. "Drop it!"

The man stared at her as though he couldn't believe his eyes. "A woman?" he yelled. "A mere woman is telling me to drop me weapon?" He spat at the ground near her feet, then lifted his rifle.

Jocelyn didn't hesitate. She couldn't. Pressing her eyes shut, she pulled back on the trigger. The hammer struck the flint, igniting the powder. Jocelyn felt the lead ball leave the barrel, felt the kick all the way from her wrist to her shoulder and then to her hip. But she didn't buck from the force of the shot. She held steady. When she opened her eyes, Jocelyn saw the burly man stumble backward, his rifle falling to ground and exploding on impact, the shot whizzing past her.

Stunned, sickened at her own audacity, Jocelyn lowered the pistol. She'd *shot* a man. She'd been taught by her father to cherish life and help aid others, not harm them! She watched as the man writhed on the ground, clutching his blood-soaked arm.

"God help me," she whispered brokenly. But it was too late. The deed had been done and could not be erased. Arms limp at her sides, Jocelyn hung her head and felt her stomach revolt. Bile spilled up into her mouth, burning her tongue. She spit it out, nearly choking on the acrid stuff. But when she righted herself the horror was still there, surrounding her, engulfing her.

Braden and his man had subdued two of the men. Jocelyn had taken care of the third. Through a fog of disbelief, Jocelyn watched as Pretty Boy and Granger took charge of the cache of gold, and then, at Braden's insistence, the crate filled with brandy. Nothing seemed real as Dash's men tied the three smugglers to their disabled coach—not the blood streaming from the one man's wounds nor their ugly shouts of revenge.

What had she become? Jocelyn wondered as she knelt beside Dash. What had she done?

"Dash . . . are—are you all right?" she whispered, barely able to speak.

Dash stared up at her, as though he were seeing his day of reckoning with the Lord. "Jocelyn."

"Yes, I'm here," she said, tears coursing down her face.

"I—I shot him, Dash. I—I could have killed him." Jocelyn didn't know whether or not Dash understood her words, but she needed to confess her sins, to have the weight of them lifted from her soul. "I shot him" she muttered again.

"Jocelyn," was all he said, and then he fell silent, unconscious. Or dead. Jocelyn didn't know which.

Eight

Jocelyn gave herself a mental shake, trying to fight off the fear and horror that gripped her with frightening intensity. She couldn't give in to the terror—not here, not now. Recalling all she'd learned at her father's side, Jocelyn leaned low over Dash. She could feel his warm breath against her cheek and a pulsebeat beneath the fingertips she pressed to his neck.

"Thank God," she whispered, quickly ripping open Dash's shirt to inspect how seriously he was hurt.

"What the devil are you doing?"

Jocelyn didn't even glance up at Laney. "What do you think?" she said, her voice clipped. "The man's been shot—"

"Nursing him will have to wait," Braden cut in. "Granger! Lot! Get Dash on his horse, strap him to the saddle if you must. Move quick, men! There's no telling who may come along and find us here."

Lot, Braden's right-hand man, forced Jocelyn out of his way. "Step aside, missy. Worrying over him while he spills his blood on the roadway won't do Dash any good."

"I meant to help him!" Jocelyn cried. But Lot wasn't listening. Clearly unconcerned about how much he hurt Dash, the brawny man swung his rangy body over one shoulder, then carried his burden to Dash's horse. "Be careful!" Jocelyn yelled, trailing after him.

Together, Lot and Granger positioned Dash over the

saddle, leaving his arms and legs to dangle on either side, then they strapped his body down with a length of rope. Jocelyn fussed at them as they made quick work of the job. "Don't tie him so tightly," she snapped, moving to loosen the knot Lot had just secured. "You've no idea what injuries he's sustained."

Lot growled at her, pushing her hands away from the rope. "Lady, those smugglers over there have friends, if you get my meaning. We'll all lose our lives if we waste our time pampering Dash."

From the other side of the horse, Granger said, "Dash is strong. He'll make it through this."

Jocelyn wasn't so certain, but she could see she was fighting a losing battle with Lot. "I'll ride with him."

"There's no room on that saddle for the two of you, missy," Lot groused. "Now, step aside and make yourself useful."

Before Jocelyn could protest, Lot snatched up the reins and led Dash's horse away. He mounted his own animal, and then, bellowing out a quick order for Jocelyn to get moving, he sped away, leading Dash and his horse in a fast gallop back toward the campsite.

Jocelyn was appalled. "He'll kill him for sure!" she cried, wondering how she was to make it back to camp without a mount. She stood there in the middle of the road, watching the dust the horses had kicked up settle beneath the glare of the torchlights. Behind her, Pretty Boy was stuffing his saddlebags full of gold as well as several bottles of brandy. Braden and Granger were doing the same.

Braden noticed her indecision. "If you're riding with me," he yelled at her, "then you'll grab some of this swag and be quick about it!"

Jocelyn didn't move. She'd already shot a man, and doubtless she could be tried before a judge for doing so! Help these thieves fill their saddlebags with gold? She wouldn't do it.

It was then she spied the two coach horses straining at the lines that held them to a sturdy tree alongside the roadway. Thinking quickly, Jocelyn headed their way. They were still in harness, and she had to unbuckle the straps and pull one of the beasts from its traces. The rein was too long, but she had no knife to cut it short enough to use. Gathering the thing up, she jumped astride the horse before Laney saw what she was about to do. There was no saddle, but Jocelyn didn't pause to worry. She'd ridden bareback before.

Kicking the horse into motion, she grabbed tight to its mane and urged the beast into a fast gallop, away from the nightmare of the night.

"God's teeth!" she heard Laney yell. "Would you look at that?"

To Jocelyn's surprise there came no whizzing of a lead shot, nor even a command for her to stop. Instead, she heard Laney's laughter filling the air. He was laughing, howling, in fact! Jocelyn didn't dare take a moment to glance behind her. She only knew she had to get away.

Darkness swallowed her. The wind cut through her clothes and chafed her skin. The strange horse beneath her was fidgety at first, confused by her sudden weight and reckless flight. But Jocelyn held steady, pressing her legs close against the animal's sides and showing him she meant to stay astride and in command. The beast fell into an easy gallop then, perhaps even relaxed once he realized he wouldn't be pulling a heavy coach behind him.

Jocelyn tried to relax as well, but couldn't. She felt disoriented. The night was too black, the road unfamiliar. She imagined sounds pressing in on all sides. At any moment she expected one of the smugglers' allies to jump out from the line of trees. And Dash . . . was he even alive? How could she just leave him?

The hoofbeats of the horse echoed loudly; indeed, it seemed to Jocelyn that all the world must surely be able to hear them. Her heart hammered against her ribs. Her mouth grew dry, and her hands trembled as she grasped tight to the horse's mane.

"Get hold of yourself, Jocelyn," she said aloud, hoping

to calm her nerves some. "You wanted your freedom and now you've got it."

But she had no idea in which direction she should go. Doubtless this road would sooner or later give way to a small town, or even a small outpost where travelers could find shelter for a few hours. But then again, she thought with trepidation, she might very well run into Lot.

Half of Jocelyn wished she *would* come upon Lot, for then she could see for herself how Dash fared.

"No," Jocelyn said adamantly. "I don't wish that. I'm glad to be free of the man and his pack of thieves!"

And yet, even as she sped along the darkened roadway, Jocelyn couldn't help thinking of the man who'd held her and kissed her and ignited within her a firestorm of passion. . . .

Dash came to with a start. He saw nothing but the black forest floor spinning beneath him. He groaned once, feeling his body slap against his horse's sides. Christ, he was sore. His chest felt on fire, and it hurt like hell to breathe.

He moved his arms. No bones broken there. What had happened? he wondered, trying hard to remember. And then memory served him. He'd been shot—or rather grazed, by the feel of his ribs on the right side. Obviously one of his men had tied him to his horse and was now leading him back to camp.

"Whoa!" Dash yelled hoarsely. "Hold up, will you?" Even those few words cost him much. He'd definitely cracked a rib—or two. "Stop the damn horse and untie me!" he managed to shout just before he nearly blacked out from the pain.

Dash felt the horse come to a jarring halt. Dash's body was forced to one side and he swore as another spasm of pain whipped through him.

"Sorry, Dash," Lot said, quickly jumping to do Dash's bidding. "Glad I am to see you're awake and talking, though. Your little lady was beside herself with worry—"

"Jocelyn! Where is she?" Dash demanded as Lot made quick work of untying the rope.

"Left her behind with the others," Lot replied. "You need help getting down?"

Dash slid off the saddle even before Lot could get the rope untangled from him. "No, I don't need any help!" Dash muttered, yanking himself free of the blasted rope. "I need to know where Jocelyn is. She didn't run, did she?"

Lot shrugged, eyeing Dash closely, as though he thought the man was delirious.

"For the love of God, man, where *is* she?"

"I told you. I left her with—"

"With Braden . . . and Pretty Boy?" Dash was yelling now, in spite of the pain arrowing through his rib cage, and in spite of the fact that he was getting dizzier by the minute. "Of all the rotten luck," he muttered, pulling himself back onto his saddle. "Braden won't keep an eye on her, and Pretty Boy, hell, he'll point the way home for her. Dammit! Why did I have to pass out?"

Lot blinked in surprise. "You were shot—"

"I've had worse happen to me. Get back to the others and help them with the cache," he commanded, clutching his ribs to support his broken bones.

"Where are you going?" a stunned Lot asked.

"To find Jocelyn."

"But I just told you I left her with the others."

"I know what you told me," Dash ground out, favoring his right side as he gathered up the reins. "And if I know Jocelyn, she's probably flying with the wind as we speak."

With that, Dash turned his mount about and kicked the beast into a fast gallop. He felt close to fainting, but forced himself to keep going. A thousand scenarios played their way past his mind's eye as he backtracked to the roadway. He first imagined Jocelyn being sternly ordered by Laney to stay put. But that hope soon dimmed. Braden would be too intent on getting the gold—and the brandy—to worry himself with Jocelyn. And doubtless, too, Laney would

probably think it great sport to watch Jocelyn slipping away
into the woods. No, Braden would not have stopped her
flight. Nor would Pretty Boy, Dash knew. That left only
Granger, and Dash knew well enough that Granger would
follow Laney's lead.

"She's heading for home," Dash muttered. "I'm sure
of it."

He couldn't ride fast enough. Once he reached the main
road, though, he couldn't decide which way to go. There
was the chance that Jocelyn had already passed this spot.
Too, she could have charged off in the opposite direction
from the site of the robbery. Or, Dash thought miserably,
she could have gone on foot through the woods, which
meant he might never find her.

Determined not to waste a moment's time on riding in
the wrong direction, Dash pulled up on the reins, then
eased off his horse's back. Breathing through the pain, he
hunkered down and felt the surface of the road for any
signs of Jocelyn's passing. The dirt was rutted with hoofprints. Too many. No, she hadn't fled by on this side of
the road. Dash moved to his left, and kept skimming his
hands across the dirt. If not for last night's rain, he would
have had a difficult time in deciphering new prints from
old. But the ground was soft, and finally Dash felt the set
of hoofprints he sought. They headed south. So, Jocelyn
had gotten one of the horses and taken flight.

Dash retraced his footsteps, then pulled himself back
onto the saddle. He was sweating now, beads of perspiration breaking out on his forehead and above his mouth.
The pain was nearly unbearable. He felt his blood oozing
out of the wound, but he knew he didn't have the luxury
of time to stanch the flow. Instead, he pressed his left hand
to his burning side and headed his horse south. The small
wool town of Snow's Hill lay just beyond the next bend.
He had to catch Jocelyn before she reached it.

Jocelyn nearly cried tears of joy as she spied a bevy of
lights flickering brightly in the near distance. Civilization!
She'd never been so glad in her life to enter a village as

she was now. Slowing her horse to a canter, Jocelyn came to what appeared to be a small mill town. The Cotswolds was known for its production of wool. She passed a long field wall that looked black and eerie in the dark night, then passed a number of tiny cottages.

Hoping she would soon come upon an inn, she kept going, unwilling to awaken strangers and thus alarm them. If her guess was right, it was nearing two in the morning. Finally Jocelyn came upon a squat, stone building. Two gas lanterns burned brightly on opposite sides of the doorway, and rattling in the slight breeze on iron hinges was a wooden sign: THE FOX'S LAIR, it read.

Jocelyn got down off her horse, tied it to a fence post near the road, then headed inside the inn.

The door was not bolted, so Jocelyn pushed the thing open and stepped into a warm common room that was lit only by a low fire in the giant hearth across from her.

"Hello!" Jocelyn called.

Commotion then. Jocelyn heard a crash of plates, followed by a woman's harsh curse.

Hoping to account for herself, Jocelyn headed for the sounds coming from the opposite room. She swung the door wide and found a young woman scooping a mess of broken pottery onto a dustpan.

"What do you want?" the woman barked, not looking up.

"I need help," Jocelyn replied.

The woman turned about and eyed Jocelyn through curly brown strands of hair that had escaped her oversize dustcap. "Help?" the woman nearly screeched. "Don't we all, luv. Well, then, come on in here. Don't stand there staring at my backside. Startled me half to death, you did, with that scream of yours."

Jocelyn straightened. "I merely called a hello."

"Shouted it, you did, as though you were deaf and thought the world must be as well! Come in, I said. *Are* you deaf?" The woman was shouting now, her voice rich and full of life.

Jocelyn shook her head.

"Addled, then?"

"What?" Jocelyn asked, thinking she must have heard wrong.

"Addled!" the woman replied, none too patiently. She twirled her fingers alongside her head. "A little touched—oh, never mind. Give me a hand here, will you? Davy will have my hide if I don't clean this mess before I leave."

Jocelyn hurried to do the young woman's bidding, thinking that she'd been the cause of the catastrophe. "Who's Davy?" she asked, holding the dustpan as the woman used a worn broom to sweep up the broken bits of pottery.

"He's the owner of this inn, and a slave driver to boot. You should hear the man when he gets angry. He could shout the roof off, he could. But he's not so bad, I guess. I could have a worse lot in life." The young woman stopped short, obviously realizing she was chattering. "Who *are* you, luv?"

"My name's Jocelyn."

"And what are you doing out and about so late at night?"

Jocelyn was about to say she needed to get home post-haste, but she didn't dare spill her sordid tale. She'd shot a man this night and had stolen a horse as well. "I—I need to send word to my family. I've been traveling, you see, and—"

"You need a place to sleep? Well, you're in luck, we've a *ton* of rooms upstairs. Scrubbed and cleaned every one of them, I have. You can take your pick, luv. Business hasn't exactly been brisk these past few weeks. People are afraid to travel—they think the Midnight Raider will rob them."

Jocelyn swallowed hard. "Midnight Raider?"

"You've heard of *him*, haven't you, luv? Lord, if you haven't, then you're more of a bumpkin than you appear. Where did you *get* those clothes, anyway?"

"My brother," Jocelyn lied.

The woman laughed. "Honey, if those belong to your brother, then I'm the next Queen of England!"

Jocelyn was stunned. "You don't believe me?"

" 'Course not. Why should I? You come waltzing in here looking like the cat who got chased by a pack of wild dogs, telling me you need a place to sleep. My guess is you need a place to *hide*, luv. Why else would you be going door to door at this hour?"

The woman was bawdy, but bright, Jocelyn decided, and she liked her. "You're right," Jocelyn admitted. "I do need a place to hide. Can you help me?"

"Help you? Lord, I'd like to scratch your eyes out. Look at you, luv, you're pretty even dressed in a man's clothes, and your freckled face smudged with dirt and scratches is far too beautiful."

"Then you won't help me?"

She took the dustpan from Jocelyn and carried the broken bits of pottery to a nearby refuse barrel. "Now, don't go putting words in my mouth. I didn't say *that*, I just said you're too pretty. I have to watch my own backside, luv. With Davy around, I can't be too careful. He's a womanizer, he is. He'll take one look at you and declare himself celibate until you go to bed with him."

Jocelyn's mouth fell open in shock, but she closed it quickly when the young woman turned around to face her.

"You can stay here," she announced. "But stay out of Davy's way, you hear?"

"Y-yes, of course I will."

The woman clicked her tongue. "Lord, luv, you haven't even *seen* Davy, yet you're agreeing to my terms."

"I'm not looking for a husband," Jocelyn returned, somewhat hotly.

"Nor is Davy looking for a wife. He's too smart for that, but he does hanker for a fine woman now and then. You'll be that woman, I'm sure. You've got that high-class look about you. Clean the dirt from you, and I'm sure you'd be a sight for sore eyes."

Jocelyn didn't know whether to thank the girl or become indignant. She did neither, though, for just then a loud bellow came from the outer room. Before Jocelyn could ask who it was, a tall, rangy fellow strode into the kitchen, breathing fire.

"Meggie, you slut, why aren't you done with your chores yet?"

Jocelyn jumped at the sound of the man's voice, but she narrowed her eyes on him as he entered.

"Go play with yourself!" the woman named Meggie shouted back. "I've been heeling to your yells all the day long. Don't you ever take a *rest*, Davy?"

"You're too slow!" Davy yelled in reply.

Meggie didn't bat an eyelash. "I'm the best maid you've ever hired, and you know it. Now, shut that trap of yours and greet your latest guest. Jocelyn, meet Davy the Terrible."

Jocelyn gave the man a crisp nod.

"Well, well," Davy murmured, his tone softening. "Jocelyn, is it? Welcome to the Fox's Lair. You just let me know what you need, and I'll—"

"Watch yourself," Meggie warned the man. "Don't go all doe-eyed on her. She needs only a room and a meal in the morning. *I'll* see she gets both. Now, get your ass out of here so I can finish my chores and get to bed myself."

Davy ignored his maid's demand. He eyed Jocelyn with all the cunning of a hawk aiming for a rabbit's tail. Moving closer to her, he lifted Jocelyn's long braid of hair, saying, "So you need a bed, do you, lass?"

Feeling more brazen then she felt, Jocelyn said, "A bed, *not* a man."

Davy took the message. "Pity," he said, giving up his pursuit even before it had truly begun. "Ah, well, I'm too tired to woo you, anyway. Perhaps tomorrow night?"

Jocelyn gave him an icy stare, but said nothing.

Davy laughed, dropped her braid of hair, then turned to give Meggie's bottom a quick pinch. "Finish up, dear girl. I'll see you in the morning."

Meggie scowled at his retreating back. "Not because I want to," she muttered.

Both Jocelyn and Meggie watched as the door swung shut behind him.

"Never have trusted him as far as I can spit," Meggie declared. "But he's not so bad. I've known worse."

"Oh?" Jocelyn asked.

Meggie nodded. "A girl doesn't grow up in the shantytowns near the northern factories but she doesn't find trouble. I came to Snow's Hill because I wanted to get away from those hellholes. I don't have it bad here, either," she said emphatically. "I earn a decent wage for my troubles. Davy isn't so terrible. A girl just has to know how to *protect* herself."

Something clicked in Jocelyn's mind. Suddenly she remembered the conversation she'd had with Pretty Boy. "My God," she whispered. "You're *Meggie*!"

"That's right. I told you so—what's the matter with you?"

"Nothing! I—I mean, I've met your brother. Pretty Boy."

"Jonathan? That's his given name, but everyone has forever called him Pretty Boy. You've met him? I can't believe it. Where? How? I'd thought he was riding with—" Meggie stopped short, unwilling to say more.

"With Dash?" Jocelyn supplied.

"You *know* him?"

Jocelyn nodded.

"And what exactly do you know?" Meggie asked, her eyes narrowing.

"Enough," Jocelyn said. "Pretty Boy is a friend."

Meggie didn't appear convinced. She made herself busy with cleaning up the kitchen, not looking at Jocelyn.

"Pretty Boy told me about you," Jocelyn chanced, wondering if she could learn something more about Dash and his men from this woman. "He even shared some of the food you'd given him."

At that, Meggie gave Jocelyn her full attention. "You *are* a woman of contradictions. Here, sit down, and tell me what you know about that brother of mine. Is he well?"

"He's fine . . . I mean, the last time I saw him he was."

"When was that?" Meggie demanded.

Jocelyn hedged. "Well, uh—"

"When?"

"A few hours ago."

"You *saw* him, at this time of night?"

Jocelyn nodded. "I—I was riding with him, and his friends. I know what he does at night, Meggie."

Meggie stiffened. "And?"

"And what?"

"Dammit, girl, are you friend or foe? Tell me now, or I'll be asking you to leave. I won't have you dragging my brother's name through the dirt—"

"I told you," Jocelyn interrupted. "I'm Pretty Boy's friend. I won't be telling anyone what I know about him."

Meggie appeared visibly relieved, but it was clear that she wasn't about to flap her tongue about her brother's business.

"You can trust me," Jocelyn said. "I will swear myself to secrecy."

Meggie stared at her hard and long. Finally she said, "I believe you, luv. I haven't seen my brother in a fortnight. He comes and goes, leaving me a pouch of coins now and then. These are difficult times, Jocelyn. A man has to make choices. I told Pretty Boy he'd be hell and gone from all his troubles if only he hitched up with Dash and his men. They're the best at what they do."

"They're robbers," Jocelyn said flatly.

Meggie nodded. "But good at it."

"It's a crime, punishable by hanging."

"Don't think I'm not worried about them," Meggie said. "I just wish . . . well, it doesn't much matter what I wish. Dash, my brother, and the others are good men, though. At least they steal only from those who can afford to be robbed."

"So that makes it honorable?"

"I never said what they did merits honor. Hell, they'll probably swing from the gallows before they're through, but at least they'll have made a difference."

"How so?"

"It's simple, luv. The money Dash and his men steal goes to feed and clothe the poor folk of the northern countryside. Every quid,'' she added proudly. ''My brother takes only what he needs, nothing more. And Dash? He takes none of it. Doesn't need to.''

''Why not?'' Jocelyn asked, her curiosity about Dash getting the best of her.

''You don't know?'' Meggie replied. ''Then I can't be the one to tell you. Here I'd thought you knew all there was to know.''

''You mean you aren't going to tell me?''

''And have to explain to Dash? No way, luv, not *me*!''

''Now, wait just a minute,'' Jocelyn said, getting to her feet. She'd been so close!

But as she stood up, there came a banging on the back exit of the inn.

Meggie rolled her eyes, heaving a sigh. ''Who the bloody hell could that be?'' she muttered, crossing the kitchen to open the door. She popped the thing open.

Jocelyn gasped.

Dash stood leaning against the stone framework, his face pinched with pain, murder in his eyes. He held fast to his right side which was stained with blood. ''Thought you'd get away from me, did you?'' he muttered, staring directly at Jocelyn. ''I told you once I might be the devil in disguise. Now you know it's true.''

Jocelyn didn't pause to think. She turned and raced through the door to the common room, then headed for the front portal. But Meggie was hot on her heels, and Dash as well.

''Stop her!'' she heard Dash yell.

Jocelyn lunged for the latch of the front door just as Meggie grabbed her from behind. ''Sorry, luv,'' Meggie said. ''But I've got my loyalties.''

''You don't understand!'' Jocelyn cried. ''He means to kill me!''

''*Murder* you? I can't believe it.''

''You must! He—''

But Jocelyn didn't get the words out, for Meggie had her by the arm and was dragging her into the middle of the deserted common room.

"She's a feisty one," Meggie muttered, heaving and hauling. "Did you truly say you'd *kill* her?" She spun Jocelyn about, barring her flight.

Dash frowned. "Of course I didn't say I'd murder her."

Jocelyn whipped the hair from her eyes. "You did!" she spat. "Let go of me, Meggie! My father is well respected in this area. He'll have your hides for this, mark my words!"

Meggie hesitated. "Is that true, Dash?"

"Hell if I know."

"Well, speak up!" Meggie demanded. "I'll not be helping you if it means my own neck is at stake!"

To the surprise of both women Dash grinned. "Very well," he said lowly. "Let her go, Meggie. This is my score to settle—and settle it I will."

Meggie released Jocelyn. "She's all yours, Dash. But I'm warning you, should you try to accost her, you'll have me to deal with."

"Warning taken. Go on up to bed, Meggie. Jocelyn and I have old times to discuss."

Meggie hesitated briefly, clearly unwilling to leave Jocelyn alone with Dash. "Perhaps I'll just linger in the kitchen for a while."

"Don't bother," Jocelyn cut in, seeing the stain of blood on Dash's shirtfront and realizing the man was in no condition to chase her around the common room. Also, she was miffed to think she might need to call on Meggie for aid. "Dash is correct. We *do* have things to discuss."

Meggie shook her head, clearly thinking this to be a lover's spat. "Suit yourselves," she said, then headed for the staircase and her own bed above.

Jocelyn met Dash's gaze head-on. "I'm no longer within your campsite," she informed him. "Nor am I your prisoner."

"That's right," he muttered. "You're not."

"And you have no say over what I do."

"None at all," he agreed.

Jocelyn became suspicious. "So what are you doing here?"

"Maybe I just wanted a cozy bed to sleep upon."

"And maybe you're a damned liar."

Dash grinned at her choice of words. "You've the mouth of a sailor."

"Or a thief," she mocked. "God knows I've had the best tutor."

"And you'll be spending more time with me," he said, moving toward her slowly. "I can't risk you going to the authorities, Jocelyn. You know that. Now, why don't you make it easier on both of us and just come with me willingly."

Jocelyn took a wary step back. "Never," she ground out, feeling his nearness and wishing she couldn't. "Touch me and I'll scream."

"Only if I don't cover your mouth first."

"You'll have to catch me to do so."

"Indeed I shall . . . don't doubt me, Jocelyn."

"You've been shot. You're bleeding all over the place. I hardly think you could catch me."

"Is that a challenge?"

Jocelyn glared at him. "I know better than to issue you a challenge."

"But you're doing it," he said. "You did so the moment you tore away on that stolen horse. I saw it hitched to the post out front, you know. Not a wise decision, Jocelyn. You should have hidden the beast well away from the road."

Damn, why hadn't she thought of that? "I hate you," she said.

"Do you? Somehow I doubt that."

"Then you're a fool."

"Yes," he acknowledged, moving closer still. "I am that."

Jocelyn backed up until she ran into a table. The wooden legs of it scraped atop the floor as she crashed into it. "Don't come any closer."

"Why?" Dash whispered. "What will you do?"

Jocelyn stiffened, preparing herself for a fight. With her hands behind her, she groped for a weapon of some sort, and to her relief she grasped on to a table knife Meggie had overlooked.

With dead seriousness, Jocelyn said, ''I'll kill you, that's what.''

Nine

She'd kill him all right, Dash thought miserably, but not in the way she intended. He was bleeding like a stuck pig because he'd ridden so hard and fast to find her. He'd even jumped the stone wall at the outskirts of Snow's Hill, cutting through the fields and taking a chance that Jocelyn would go straight to an inn instead of knocking on the door of a private cottage. Since the Fox's Lair was the only inn in the small wool town, Dash didn't have to waste time with second guesses. He'd raced toward the Fox's Lair, had spied the lathered horse, sans a saddle, and had deduced he'd find Jocelyn inside.

"Don't be rash," Dash told Jocelyn, both cursing and applauding her valor. Damn, but she was a spitfire. Why couldn't she just faint now and again like any other woman would do when faced with an irate and bleeding highwayman?

"Rash?" she shrieked at him.

Dash groaned. Clearly Jocelyn had no intention of going anywhere with him. He wanted to be able to tell her he'd take her home, but he couldn't do that. Even now a few of his men should be riding out to meet Fritz and deliver the goods from the night. Dash had to make certain Fritz was well on his way north before Jocelyn could go home. And the fact remained that Dash might never want to release Jocelyn. She'd ensnared him with her bravery and her spunk, as well as her beauty.

"Very well," he muttered, getting testy and closing the distance between them. "You've given me no other choice."

Jocelyn flared into movement, taking Dash off guard. With surprising speed, she swung her right hand up and out, tearing his shirtsleeve with the tip of her carving knife.

Dash stared first at his torn shirtsleeve and then at Jocelyn. "For the love of God! What do you think you're doing?"

"I told you to stay back!" Jocelyn yelled, her green eyes wild.

To Dash, she looked divine—and dangerous. "So you've a mind to lop off my ear, do you?" he asked, trying to calm his emotions. It wouldn't do to bully her. Also, he didn't know if he *could* bully her. Jocelyn had a marksman's eye along with that temper of hers.

"I'll take your ear and a good bit more, thief!"

"A thief, am I? And what are you?" Dash demanded, not moving closer, but neither stepping back. "Have you a bill of sale for that horse hitched to the post outside this inn?"

Jocelyn's face went pale. "I *had* to steal that beast! I had to get away from you and your . . . your cutthroat friends!"

"So you say," Dash drawled. "The question is, who will believe you?"

"Everyone! Anyone!"

"And if they don't? What will become of you?" Dash moved in closer, ignoring both the burning pain in his lungs as well as the knife in Jocelyn's fist. "Tell me, Jocelyn, what will you do if your people brand you a thief—even though you did the only thing you could? Will you accept their judgment, or will you fight them?"

Her gorgeous eyes widened as he came to just a hair's breadth from her body. Jocelyn didn't flinch but held her ground with glorious indignation. "They won't judge me."

"But if they did," he insisted, "what recourse would you have if no one but you understood your motive? Would stealing become second nature?"

"You're playing word games with me now."

"But I'm correct, aren't I? If you ever found yourself in need of transportation and spied a horse, you'd take it. Admit it, Jocelyn, you *would* steal again if you needed to do so. And that," he said quietly, his eyes looking deeply into hers, "is what makes us two of a kind."

"You *are* addled if you believe us to be two of a kind! I am no thief. In fact, I intend to return the horse—"

"You'd be a fool to seek out those smugglers"

"No more of a fool than I am for standing here and listening to this rot! Now, get out of my way, Dash, and let me be."

"I can't do that."

"You mean you *won't*."

"That, too," he said, feeling his head beginning to spin again.

Dash had an inkling the damned dizziness had more to do with the lady standing so near than with the amount of blood he'd lost. But Jocelyn was more than just a beautiful woman; she was brave and exciting, and she touched a chord in Dash that had never been reached by another person. Earlier, when he'd thought she'd escaped, Dash had realized then just how much Jocelyn Greville intrigued him. His wanting her by his side suddenly had very little to do with the fact she could send him to prison for highway robbery—indeed, Dash had to admit he wanted her for totally different reasons.

In a low whisper he said, "Let's go upstairs, Jocelyn. Morning will be soon enough to bicker." Dash saw Jocelyn's mouth fall open and her eyes ignite with beryl fire. In another second she'd be screeching again, and maybe swinging the cursed carving knife as well. Seeing he had precious little time to make his move, Dash did what he should have done the minute he saw her in the kitchen. With little thought of his injury or of Jocelyn's fury, he threw caution to the wind and swiftly took hold of both her wrists. He yanked once, then smiled with grim satisfaction as the knife clattered to the floor.

"You'll forgive me for this, I hope," he muttered, forcing her wrists together, then taking hold of them with one hand as he hefted her up and off the floor with the other.

Jocelyn did screech—and very loudly at that—all the way to the top landing of the staircase. She even kicked several of the doors they passed. A gritty-eyed Davy swung one door open and demanded to know what was going on.

"Nothing that interests you," Dash grunted as he heaved a reluctant Jocelyn down the hall.

"Jesus! I must be dreaming!" Davy cried, suddenly losing some of his sleepy-eyed state. "Dashiell Warfield, what the bloody hell are you doing here? Damned if I didn't think I'd never see you again. Thought the constables might have dragged you to the roundhouse by now."

"Not me, Davy. I'm too quick for anyone who hankers to put a noose about my neck."

Davy, looking ridiculous in a nightshirt and cap, leaned against the doorjamb, totally enjoying the scene before him. "I'd watch my arse were I you, Dash. Folks are getting downright nervous around here with the Midnight Raider running loose. Who knows, in the dark, all highwaymen look alike. People might start saying *you* are the Raider!"

Dash glared at Davy. "You've got a loose tongue, and a vivid imagination, Davy. Keep it down, will you? I'd rather not be run out of town tonight."

Davy laughed. "Not to worry, Dash. The inn is empty. Only Meggie and me here . . . and you and your lady. She's a pretty one, isn't she?" he asked chattily.

Dash managed only a quick nod to his old friend before Jocelyn sank her teeth into his arm that was hitched about her waist. Dash cursed her soundly.

Davy chuckled, delighted. "Got your hands full tonight, eh?"

"So it appears," Dash muttered.

Davy straightened, yawned, then said, "Do call if you find you've gotten in over your head."

Dash said nothing, which was just as well, because Jocelyn's rage increased as Davy swung his door shut.

"Call him?" she yelled. "*Call him?* I'd like to cauterize him! Would serve him right, too. And you as well, Dashiell Warfield!''

Dash tightened his hold. "I'd take care as to how often and how freely you use my given name.''

"I'm sure you would!'' Jocelyn snapped. "But I'm through taking any advice from you!''

"I didn't know you'd ever started,'' he said dryly, then quickened his pace.

Now that Jocelyn knew his last name, Dash would have to take extra care that she didn't let spill tales of his nefarious deeds. Davy and Meggie had a stake in what he and his friends did with their loot, so he knew they would keep their mouths shut. But what Meggie and Davy didn't know was that Dash was indeed the Midnight Raider. Before Dash had hooked up with Pretty Boy and the others, and before they'd devised a system of delivery between this area and Manchester, Dash had ridden alone, robbing only those men he knew could afford to be robbed, and who, he knew, had done some illegal business as well. Dash had robbed these men only to help the poor. He didn't like what he'd done and he wasn't proud of it.

But something had gone wrong. Though he hadn't ridden alone in nearly a fortnight, someone was haunting these roads and stealing from anyone who passed, and leading the victims to believe he was the Midnight Raider. Dash was being framed. The question was, by whom? Whoever it was had killed James Keats and was working hard to place the blame on Dash.

As for Jocelyn, Dash now had to wonder how exactly he was going to make certain she kept her pretty little mouth shut about the Warfield name. If any of Lord Monty's friends were to learn of his deeds, then Monty would be the one to suffer the most.

Dash didn't have the answer to that. He wasn't thinking any further than the room at the end of the hall. He banged the door open with his shoulder and swept inside the small chamber.

Jocelyn fought him like a wildcat. "Put me down!'' she screamed. "You boorish—''

Dash didn't hear another word. He made a straight line for the bed, deposited Jocelyn in the middle of the feather mattress, then promptly blacked out on top of her.

Jocelyn felt Dash's hard weight hit her with unerring force. Her breath left her lungs in a whoosh, and she knew then that he'd fainted. At least, that's what she *hoped* he'd done.

"Dash?" she chanced. Not receiving an answer, Jocelyn yanked her hands free from beneath him, then gently shoved his body to one side. He'd fainted all right. He was breathing—and bleeding.

Not taking time to think about her actions, Jocelyn quickly got to her feet and ripped his shirt the rest of the way open. "Good Lord," she breathed. "You've got more scars than an alley cat. You're nothing but a no-good renegade. And I'm nothing but a soft-hearted Nellie for aiding you!"

But aid him she did. She hastily lit a lamp, then got to work. His shirt was nothing but a tattered mass by the time she finished pulling it off his muscled chest. Using the clean but rough sheet for a bandage, she wiped the blood from him and then wrapped his upper body tightly. She was huffing and puffing by the time she'd worked the makeshift bandage beneath his back.

"Look at you," she muttered, working diligently. "That shot of lead must have cracked one of your ribs."

"Or two," Dash said, finally opening his eyes.

Jocelyn pursed her lips. "How long have you been lucid?"

"Well, now, let me think . . . probably never," he answered a tad too jovially for Jocelyn's mind. He winced as Jocelyn pulled the bandage tight and tied it. "Ow! That hurts!"

"Good."

"My, my. You're quite the little general now that you've got me flat on my back."

"You deserve to be lying prone! What possessed you to tear after me like you did? And to carry me up a flight of stairs! You haven't a brain between those ears of yours! You'll be fortunate if you haven't punctured a lung.''

"I'm breathing, aren't I?''

"Barely. You need a doctor.''

Dash glanced down at his chest. "It appears as though you've doctored me well enough.''

"I merely gave some support to your ribs. In a few hours you'll be wishing I'd done a great deal more.''

"I'll be fine,'' he rasped, trying to sit upright.

Jocelyn pressed him back down with one hand. "Oh, you'll be fine all right, until the constables catch up with you, then cart you off to a pillory. Do you know what they do with thieves? They carve their hands off, that's what! Unless, of course, they decide to hang you.'' Jocelyn shivered, visualizing the gruesome image. She wrapped her arms about her waist, fearful Dash might notice and thus deduce she had more than just a passing interest in his welfare.

"Take care, Jocelyn. If you continue to fuss over me, I might begin to think you actually care about me.''

Jocelyn dropped her hands to her sides and balled them into fists. "You enjoy playing the nasty highwayman, but I know better! What would happen to that tarnished reputation of yours if people knew you gave your stolen gold to the less fortunate?''

"Ah, so Meggie told you about that, did she?'' His eyes became hooded. "What other secrets of mine did she spill?''

Jocelyn shrugged her shoulders, deciding it would serve him right to stew for a while. "Worried?''

"I'm always worried about something. Highwaymen can't be too careful. What did Meggie tell you?''

Jocelyn toyed with the idea of pretending that Meggie had told her a great deal more than she had. But she was too tired for any more games. And the fact remained that Jocelyn was already far too involved with Dash and his wayward friends. Pretending to be knowledgeable about Dash's past and present could undoubtedly present more trouble than Jocelyn needed—or wanted.

Sighing, Jocelyn admitted, "Nothing other than the gold you steal is sent north to the factory workers." She looked him directly in the eye and asked, "Why didn't you tell me, Dash?"

"Would it have made any difference? As you've pointed out so many times, I am a thief, plain and simple. I doubt the authorities would show me mercy no matter what they thought I did with my part of the gold."

"But all this time I'd thought—"

"What?" he pressed, sounding distracted. "That I robbed solely for my own gain? Well, maybe I do. Perhaps I find a certain thrill in wagging a pistol beneath an aristocrat's nose."

"Don't talk like that," Jocelyn whispered.

"I think I should, lest I find you heaping laurels upon me for giving aid to the poor of England."

"I don't condone your actions."

"Then why bother to ask me my reasons for stealing?"

Jocelyn wanted to say *because I want to know the true man behind the facade*, but she didn't. She said nothing.

Quietly Dash asked, "Why *did* you stay? Why didn't you just flee when you had the chance?"

Jocelyn averted her gaze, wishing herself far, far away. But no, that wasn't quite true. If she'd wanted to go, she could have run out of the inn while Dash was unconscious. *Why had she stayed?* Because Dash had needed assistance? Or because she'd needed to remain near him, because she couldn't fathom being apart from him?

Angered by her own rioting emotions, she said quickly, "I could hardly leave you to bleed to death! I'm not that callous."

"No," Dash said. "You aren't." After a moment he added, "Thank you."

Jocelyn finally chanced a peek at him. He was sitting up on his elbows, a wave of hair falling down his forehead. He eyes were a deep gray in the soft light of the lantern. His skin was pale, his features tight, but despite all of that he was still stunningly handsome. A fine sheen of perspiration coated his upper lip, and Jocelyn could detect a shadow of a beard sprouting on his smooth skin. He looked haggard and worn, and damnably intriguing. It was his eyes, she decided, that made him appear so devilish. They harbored a spark of recklessness. He was that, yes, and wild. And yet those eyes also held a note of softness in them. It was as though she *knew* the man could be an attentive friend—and lover.

Lover? Where had *that* thought come from? But come it had, and Jocelyn could no sooner shake it than she could walk away from Dash and leave him for good.

"You need to rest," she told him.

"I can't. If I close my eyes, you'll leave."

Jocelyn shrugged her shoulders, trying very hard to remain nonchalant. "Then I'll wait," she announced. "You'll either faint again, or you'll fall asleep."

Dash gave her a lopsided grin. "Is that the doctor in you speaking?"

"I'm hardly a physician."

"But I'll wager you've worked at your father's side enough to know what kind of night I'll endure."

"You, Dashiell Warfield, are too quick to wager."

He grimaced at the sound of his name coming from her lips. "I wish Davy had kept his mouth shut."

"Is the Warfield name so well known that you need to keep it a secret?"

"Take heed, Jocelyn, the more you know about me, the deeper you become enmeshed in my troubles."

"As I see it, I'm up to my neck in your troubles. I did, after all, steal a horse to get away from you. Do you think the constables will give us nooses that match? Perhaps we'll swing alongside each other, and I'll be able to call a final farewell to you."

Jocelyn hadn't meant to sound so nasty, but she couldn't help herself. She was tired and cold, and she was worried about Dash. If he had punctured a lung, then he would need far more care than she knew how to give.

Dash frowned at her words. "Don't say such things."

"Why not?" she shot back. "I'm a thief, remember?"

Dash pushed himself upright, grimacing as he did so.

"Dammit, Jocelyn, you heard me. I'd meet my own death before I'd let anyone harm you."

The room became deathly still then. Dash's words echoed in Jocelyn's head, thrilling and frightening her all at once. Had there been a fire beneath her feet, Jocelyn would not have been able to move. Had she imagined it, or had there actually been a whispering of warmth in his admission?

"I don't want you to go, Jocelyn," Dash added.

Thunderstruck, Jocelyn could only stare at him. Was this another of his ploys to keep her in his company, to assure himself that she wouldn't run to the authorities with all she knew? Or did he truly mean what he'd said?

Trembling inside, Jocelyn whispered, "I can't stay. I won't be your prisoner, Dash."

"Were you ever? There were times when I thought I was *your* prisoner—like now." Without assistance, he pushed himself to his feet, swayed slightly, then found equilibrium. "I've only known you a few days, but I feel like you're some angel come to plague me. And tonight, when I was out there on the road, I couldn't think straight. I was supposed to lead my men, but I could think of nothing save you, and the feel of your body on the saddle in front of me." He lifted one hand, caressed her cheek, and said, "I can't let you go, Jocelyn. Not now."

Jocelyn's head swam. The touch of his warm fingers was all she felt. Suddenly her own weariness, the indignities she'd endured over the past forty-eight hours, fell away. She became a mindless being. His touch was soft and shimmered with promise.

Jocelyn pressed her eyes shut tight. "Don't do this," she said.

"Do what? Tell you how I feel? Or beg you not to leave?"

"I—I'm nothing more to you than a threat. You abducted me because of what I'd seen, and now you're keeping me because of what I know."

"True," he said softly, his hand dropping to her jawline

and then whispering atop the skin there. "But there are other reasons as well."

Jocelyn forced her eyes open. "Such as?"

"This," he said simply, then kissed her.

It wasn't a simple kiss, but one full of savagery and force, the total sum of all Dash was capable of and more. His tongue ravaged her mouth, arousing all the confusing and dizzying sensations Jocelyn had felt since first meeting him. A languid weakness stole through her limbs, sucking Jocelyn deeper into emotional turmoil. She'd never known a man like Dashiell Warfield. He thumbed his nose at propriety, yet he could be a supreme gentleman when least expected. He remained an enigma to Jocelyn. But his touch fired her in a sensual way.

Unmindful of the future, Jocelyn opened her mouth and met Dash's passionate kiss with one of her own. It was as though they were both starving for some unattainable goal, and Jocelyn felt that if she didn't make contact with him now, he would be forever lost to her.

Jocelyn's world exploded in a fiery conflagration as Dash's tongue met hers. She felt his warm breath on her cheek, could feel his body moving in against her own. She didn't think of tomorrow or even of what they might say to each other when the kiss ended.

Nothing mattered, nothing but the feel of his mouth on hers and the touch of his hands caressing her skin. It was as though everything she'd experienced in her life had led to this single moment. Wondrous, it was, an eternal second that had no end nor beginning.

Jocelyn wound her arms about Dash's neck, and she heard him sigh, or, at least, she thought she heard him sigh. Maybe it was her own sigh of contentment. It didn't matter. Jocelyn clung to him, arching her neck and allowing Dash to explore her fully. There was an intensity to the melding of their mouths, as though both of them knew this moment might never repeat itself. And so Jocelyn allowed herself the joy of it all. Total abandonment consumed her.

Dash lifted his lips to whisper, "I can't let you leave. Tell me you'll stay. Say you won't go."

Jocelyn met his gaze and saw the hunger there. She wanted to say she'd not be leaving. The words didn't come, though, for his mouth touched hers once again.

Dimly Jocelyn thought she should put a stop to such intimacy. But though she'd been terrified of Dash when he'd first abducted her, she had somehow come to trust him in some primeval way. He wouldn't hurt her—she knew that he wouldn't, for he'd had far too many opportunities to cause her physical harm. So thinking, Jocelyn allowed her muscles to go slack and melted against his lean frame.

Dash drew in a sharp breath at her acquiescence. He whispered her name against her mouth, then gently pushed Jocelyn away from him.

"What's the matter?" Jocelyn asked, wondering if she'd done something wrong. Had she displeased him in some way? Was her inexperience in such matters so glaringly apparent? Feeling unsure of herself and sickeningly naive, she said, "It's me, isn't it? I—I don't please you as your other women do."

"Lord, no!" Dash said, his voice quietly tense. Pressing one hand to his bandaged side, he eased himself back down onto the bed and sat there looking up at her.

She *didn't* please him, she decided, cursing her own virginity. She was seventeen years old and Dash had been the first man to kiss her, let alone caress her body. He must think her a fool, surely he must!

Cheeks burning, Jocelyn forced herself to say, "I know I—I'm . . . inexperienced, but if you'd just show me—"

"No," he cut in tersely.

"What? *Why?*"

Dash let out a sigh mingled with a laugh. "Indignant now, are you? Don't be. Believe me, Jocelyn, I would like nothing more than to continue kissing you, but"—and here he swung his legs up onto the bed, making a point to grimace as he did so, and inched himself back against the headrail—"I am a mass of aches and pains."

Jocelyn's face grew warmer still, but at least her pride remained intact. "Of course. Forgive me. Does your wound pain you too much?"

"I think I'll live."

"That's not what I asked," she said, regaining some of her earlier spunk. "I'll seek out Meggie, if you wish, and ask her if she has something to help you sleep."

"Don't bother. Meggie knows cooking and cleaning and little else. Knowing her, she'd hand you a broom and tell you to give me a knock alongside the head."

"I've had enough of unconscious highwaymen," Jocelyn said dryly, moving to the side of the bed to touch his forehead. "You're shivering," she noted.

Dash drew back from her touch. "It's this damned Cotswold air," he answered, his voice remaining tense. "It's good for sheep and grass, but not my bones."

Jocelyn wasn't fooled. Dash didn't want her to touch him, but not because he thought her too inexperienced for his tastes, she realized. Why, he was actually nervous! What was he afraid of? That *she* might seduce *him*?

Clearly that was what the matter was. Suddenly realizing her own feminine power, Jocelyn pressed her palm to his cheek and held it there, feeling the roughness of his shadowy growth of beard as well as the heated warmth of him.

"I'll build a fire," she announced, seeing the way his eyes turned smoky at the sound of her voice. "That should help you feel better." Turning away from him, Jocelyn moved to the hearth situated at the opposite end of the bed and made quick work of lighting the sticks heaped upon the grate. Soon there shimmered a hazy light in the small chamber. Shadows danced on the walls. The sounds of the crackling fire filled the silence that lay between them.

"I should have cleaned the skin near where the bullet grazed you," Jocelyn mused, watching Dash as he stared at the fire.

"I'm feeling better now."

"Still," Jocelyn insisted, "you'd probably rest better if you were cleaned up a bit."

Dash did look sleepy, Jocelyn decided, but she was nagged by the thought of his wound festering. She wished she'd paid more attention to her father's teachings, wished, in fact, that she, though a female, could have followed in her father's footsteps and learned to practice medicine. But Alexander Greville had been adamant about his daughter leading a genteel life. He'd wanted to dress her in satins and lace, had wanted her not to worry about anything but herself.

Jocelyn had never understood her father's intense desire for her to do no more than get up in the morning and go to bed at night. Alexander had been involved with the plight of the poor all of his adult life. He spent hours each day traveling in his carriage to the small wool towns of the Cotswolds to minister to the sick there. And he never took more than a family could give him in payment. But where Alexander had immersed himself in aiding the less fortunate, he had been bound and determined that Jocelyn should not do the same.

Feeling the need to do more to ensure Dash's comfort, Jocelyn said, "I'll go downstairs and see what I can find." Before Dash could stop her, she stepped out of the room and scurried down the stairs.

Actually, Jocelyn needed a moment to herself. She'd been much too close to allowing Dash to make love to her—not that he would have, she reminded herself. But all the same, she'd *wanted* him to—desperately, in fact. And that was what bothered her.

Rummaging about in the cavernous kitchen of the Fox's Lair, Jocelyn thought about her father and Dash, wondering why she would think of the two men as being somehow closely related. They both went out on a limb to help the less fortunate people of northern England, that much she knew. But where her father aided the simpler folk in a legal way, Dash did not.

Would the two men like each other were they ever to have a chance to meet? Jocelyn decided they might. Alexander Greville had blasted the English government on more than one occasion, charging the leaders of the land with disinterest in the welfare of their people. And Dash? He didn't waste time with words, Jocelyn knew. Dash was a man of action. There was little doubt in her mind that her father would silently applaud Dash for stealing from the rich to give to the poor. But then again, Dash had stolen *her*.

That particular thought brought Jocelyn up short. Her father would have his hide—if he could catch Dash. And, of course, Jocelyn had to return home first.

Trying not to think of such a volatile scene, Jocelyn swiped a large basin and pitcher from the stack of rickety shelves near the trestle table and then went outside in search of the water well. She stumbled once in the dark, tripping over a lopsided stair which gave way to a well-worn cobbled walk. The cool, early-morning air was rich with the scent of rose. Clinging to a tiny well was a rambling vine of wild roses, just beginning to bloom. Jocelyn cranked the handle of the winch, listening for any movement in the thick darkness beyond. But queerly enough, she wasn't afraid to be out in the dark alone. As Dash had said earlier, she'd ridden with thieves, and now, it seemed, the world should be listening for *her* approach and not the other way around. Odd, how experience had the power to tame fears.

The oaken bucket splashed into water below, and Jocelyn heaved it back up, pushing such thoughts out of her mind. She poured some of the water into the pitcher, then carried both it and the basin back into the inn.

When she returned to the room, she found Dash asleep.

"So much for all of my trouble," she muttered, but didn't actually mind.

She watched him for a moment, enjoying the way the firelight softened his handsome features. He appeared to be a painting, all beauty and life—like some powerful mythical god in repose. Jocelyn set the pitcher and basin down on the small stand near the bed, then checked his forehead again for signs of a fever. He was warm to the touch, though not too warm.

Thinking he would sleep until well into the morning,

Jocelyn stoked the fire, then moved the basin, which she filled with water from the pitcher, nearer to the fire. Taking her time, she washed her hands, face, and neck with the cool liquid. Its touch revived her, causing goose bumps to flare on her skin.

Chancing a peek at Dash and seeing he was still asleep, Jocelyn undid the buttons of her shirt and shed the garment. It felt divine to splash her bare breasts and arms. And, she had to admit, it felt deliciously sinful to bathe herself knowing Dash was so near but unaware of her actions.

Smiling to herself, Jocelyn shed the remainder of her garments and cleaned the stains of harried flight from her body. As she stroked her own limbs, she imagined what it might have been like to have Dash do the deed. His hands had felt so good. Jocelyn did not doubt Dash would be a consummate lover. Pity that they hadn't gone further in their explorations of each other. What would it have been like to have him touch her *here*, she wondered. Or here? She smoothed her palms over her body, slowly, closing her eyes as she imagined the touch of Dash's capable hands.

Excitement bubbled up inside of her. Jocelyn's breath quickened. Her skin grew heated. What *would* it have been like had Dash not thwarted her advances? Damn him for playing the gentleman—for that's what he'd done, she knew. He'd pushed her away because she was a virgin. But was that *her* fault? Jocelyn wondered wildly. She'd been torn in two different directions all of her life. Her father had yearned to raise a well-mannered lady, yet her grandmother had shown Jocelyn that a woman could make her own choices in life. Grandmother Amelia had never been one to walk the smooth roads. She'd instilled in Jocelyn a deep thirst for adventure and reckless acts. And though Alexander had thought he'd done the exact opposite, he hadn't. Not always. Her father allowed her to climb trees while her girlfriends were learning to stitch a straight line on handkerchiefs. He'd bought her a pony for her fifth birthday and seven days later had challenged her to jump the hedge in the west gardens—which Jocelyn had done with swift ease.

No, Jocelyn decided, turning about and facing the bed in all her nude splendor. She wasn't a prim and proper lady, nor had she ever been one. She was a woman, she thought vehemently, who had urges and—

"Lord, I hope I'm not dreaming," Dash whispered, his eyes fully opened and staring somewhere far below Jocelyn's neckline. "You look like a Grecian goddess in need of an attentive lover."

Ten

Aroused and startled all at once, Jocelyn could only stare at Dash. He had that smoky look in his eyes—the one that made her limbs feel weak and her head giddy. She wondered if perhaps he was delirious, but quickly decided that he wasn't. He was definitely lucid—and as physically aroused as she, Jocelyn could see.

Slowly she reached down and lifted the shirt she'd tossed to the floor. She pushed her arms into the sleeves and shifted the material over her shoulders.

"How do you feel?" she asked Dash in a whisper.

"Like something the cat dragged in . . . but I suspect an improvement coming."

Jocelyn smiled, noting the way Dash's jaw flexed slightly as she left the buttons of the shirt undone. He was actually nervous!

Enjoying the newfound power she had over him, Jocelyn nodded toward the basin. "I brought some water in. Would you like a bath?"

Dash's brows lifted, then he drew them low over his eyes. "I know firsthand what a terror you can be with a washrag."

"Is that a no?"

"Lord knows it should be."

Jocelyn laughed—a husky, yet nervous sound that lingered in the toasty room. Boldly forgoing the rest of her attire, she picked up the basin and walked to the side of the bed. As she placed the bowl onto the nightstand, the openings of Pretty Boy's shirt fluttered, allowing Dash full view of her breasts.

Jocelyn heard Dash's sharp intake of breath and could detect the stiffening of his body as she carefully sat down beside him.

"Relax," she told him. "I haven't any washrag. Only my hands."

"Jocelyn." There was a thread of warning in his voice, but Jocelyn knew the warning was more for his own peace of mind than for hers. "Don't," he added.

She shook a wave of coppery hair from her face. "But I want to," she said simply, then dipped her right hand into the cool water. With deliberate slowness, she swished her fingers through the water, then flicked a few droplets from them before reaching out to touch his face. With a gentleness that was borne deep inside of her, Jocelyn caressed his cheek, his jaw. The shadowy growth of his beard tickled. Dash tensed. Jocelyn smiled.

"Is this really so terrible?" she whispered.

His nostrils flared as he tried to remain in control. "Torturous is more the word. You're courting disgrace and dishonor. You know that."

"Whose dishonor? Whose disgrace?" she asked guilelessly.

"You know of what I speak, dammit. You're a lady! If your father knew—"

"But he doesn't know, nor does he need to know." She trailed a path down the corded length of his throat. He was as tense as a bow string about to be plucked. She wished he would relax. "Are you afraid of me, Dash?"

He nearly choked on a strangled laugh. "Hardly. I just don't make a policy of debauching innocent virgins."

"I'd thought thieves had no code of honor."

Dash glowered at her. "You make light of a serious situation. Do you realize what you're doing, Jocelyn?"

"Yes."

The single word hung between them like a knife blade. Dash grit his teeth, then snatched her wrist in his hand.

"That's enough," he said tersely. "Get up and get dressed, else you'll rue this night for the rest of your life."

"Perhaps I won't," she whispered, pulling her hand free and letting it slip down across the bandage on his chest, then to the flat expanse of his warm stomach. "Perhaps I'll cherish the memory." She ran her fingers through the arrow of coarse hair there, moving lower as she did so.

But Dash would have none of it. He swiped her hand in his, this time holding it with a death grip. "Think what you're saying," he ground out. "And doing. I'm not a man to be toyed with, Jocelyn. If I make love to you, it will be fierce and intense, and afterward, I'll want you again and again. But hear me, and hear me well—I will not marry you. Is that what you want? To be a thief's whore?"

Jocelyn felt as though the air had been knocked out of her lungs. His grip was strong and hurting and gave no indication that the man had just been grazed by a bullet. Despite her boldness of the moment before, Jocelyn was suddenly chastised. *What had she been thinking? That he would propose marriage?* The idea was clearly ludicrous.

A thief's whore. The words were dirty, disgusting. But still, Jocelyn could not deny her desire for the man. Her body burned in places she'd never acknowledged before meeting Dash. She wanted desperately to cuddle against him, to feel his hands caress her most secret spots. Was she then a whore for wanting such things?

Jocelyn stared down at Dash, at his lean, whipcord body emblazoned with scars from various skirmishes—and she knew keen desire. She looked at his calloused, sun-darkened hands and knew a deep longing. At the last she lifted her eyes to his and gazed deeply into the stormy orbs that were fringed in black lashes.

Quietly she said, "I never expected a proposal from you. I—I only wish to find pleasure with you. When you kiss me, Dash, I—I feel something wonderful and new inside of me. If that makes me a whore . . . then so be it."

Dash said nothing for several beats of her heart. At first, she thought he might push her from the bed, so wild was the look in his eyes. But he didn't.

"Christ," he said. "You make it difficult for a man to turn you away."

Jocelyn shook her head, the cloud of hair fanning her shoulders. "Not any man, Dash. You." And those words, Jocelyn knew, were what pushed him over the edge.

With a gruffness that was both sweet and frightening, he reached up and pulled her lithe body down beside him. He brushed the curls from her face, smoothed his hands down atop her shoulders, then forced her shirt all the way open. "So beautiful," he murmured. "I don't deserve this." But he kissed her all the same.

A wondrous kiss it was, charged with potent energy and filled with all of his pent-up emotions. His tongue flicked over her lips, pressed between them, and smoothed its way into the moist recesses of her mouth, all the while his hands explored her uncovered breasts. He teased her nipples into tight buds, sending delicious spasms down deep into her belly.

Jocelyn pressed back against the mattress, overcome by the riot of his assault. But she was an attentive learner, and she felt her body relax beside him as she soon became enmeshed in the wordless rhythm of his touch. His opened mouth consumed her, it seemed, pulling her deep into some hot void of pure ecstacy. Over and over he kissed her, finding new and delightful ways to entice her with just his mouth on hers.

Jocelyn murmured her contentment against his lips, her tongue meeting his own. Breathless, Jocelyn arched her back, rubbing her breasts against his chest.

Dash pulled back. "Wait," he gasped.

Instantly Jocelyn stiffened. "What?" she whispered, concerned. "Have I hurt you? Oh, God, I'm sorry. I'm being selfish. I—"

"Hush," he murmured, smiling at her. "You haven't hurt me. I just—I can't reach you in this position. Here, get on the other side of me. That's it, love," he whispered, helping her to move over him and get settled on his left side. "Much better," he said, touching her intimately once again. "You're so tiny and soft. I'm afraid I'll hurt *you*."

Jocelyn shook her head, cuddling against him. "No. Don't stop, Dash. I couldn't bear it if you did."

"I can't stop. Not now." He buried his face in her swath of hair, breathing deeply, then letting his tongue dart inside the shell of her ear. "I want you, Jocelyn. I want to take you here and now."

"Then do it," she nearly begged.

A small, tortured laugh escaped him. "So eager, yet so young."

"I'm not young. I'm seventeen . . . soon to be eighteen. Nearly all of my friends are married and rearing children."

"That's just it. I don't want to leave you to grow heavy with child. You deserve better."

Jocelyn didn't want to think about him leaving, or of having to return home to her father and grandmother and her cousin, Charles. She wanted this night to go on forever.

"But I'll take care," Dash was saying, his voice whispering into her mind. "I won't spoil your chances for a proper marriage."

Jocelyn was barely listening. She knew only the feel of his hands and the warmth of his breath on her skin. With practiced skill, Dash stroked her, fed her passions, and carried her senses higher and higher. He kissed her temple, her cheek, her lips, as he murmured husky, sensual words of love. Jocelyn opened to him like a petal to the morning sun, and her soul blossomed. Though he was nothing more than a highway robber and could give her nothing on the morrow, Jocelyn knew she'd rather be no place but in his embrace.

Her world became hazy and fuzzed as Dash worked his hands across her breasts, then down to her stomach and beyond. "Relax," he whispered, his mouth taking up where his hands left off. "I'll please you, love. Trust me."

Jocelyn did trust him. With her very life.

He drew one nipple into his mouth, sucking gently. Jocelyn's tormented pleasure increased. Her breathing grew raspy, her heart strumming wildly. Her entire body cried for release.

And then he touched her *there*—her most intimate spot. Jocelyn gasped at the contact, but Dash did not pull away. He stroked her, gently at first, drawing out of her every level of excitement. Gradually the motion of his fingers increased. She grew warm and ready for him.

Moaning, Jocelyn struggled against him.

Dash lifted his head, smiling down at her, his stormy, passion-filled eyes hooded.

"Dash," she gasped, gazing up at him. "I can't take much more."

"You don't have to," he whispered, then kissed her on the mouth, slowly, surely. "Just let go, Jocelyn . . . relax and let go."

Jocelyn pressed her eyes shut tight. Dash's fingers strummed against her, slipping deep inside of her, and Jocelyn felt as though she were being led through some sensual maze that was deliciously confusing. But she *did* relax, for the feel of Dash's mouth brushing across hers made her giddy with wanting and aching for surcease. Dash held the secrets for which she longed. He would bring to her the delights she sought—he, with his skillful hands and burning kisses . . .

Jocelyn's hips moved of their own accord against Dash's hand. Her breathing became just a pant. She grew moist and slick. God, the wanting! Jocelyn felt herself being borne higher and higher until suddenly she was balancing upon some pinpoint of volatile feeling. She was frightened by the fierceness of it, and in her mind she remembered Dash's warning, that his lovemaking would be intense . . . and that he would come for her again and again.

"No," she gasped, afraid of what would happen should she let go. But it was too late. With just another caress of his fingers Jocelyn felt herself being hurtled over a high summit of pleasure. Explosions of ecstasy ripped through her, shredding all poise, all thought. Her body convulsed, racked with heady shudders of pure delight.

"Dash!" she gasped, pulling his head down to hers and kissing him deeply. "What you do to me is so . . . so wonderful! I want you to touch me like that again and again and—"

Dash laughed against her mouth, playing a sensual game with his tongue. "You little vixen," he whispered.

"It was beautiful," she said. "It was everything I expected and more . . . but what about you? I thought the man derived more pleasure than the woman . . . I thought—"

"Hush, will you?" Dash said, seemingly overcome by her ardent hold. "You'll have me bleeding again."

Jocelyn released the pressure her arms had on his neck. "I'm sorry. I just thought . . . I mean, did *you* enjoy it, too?"

Dash grinned, though his mouth seemed to be a little too tight. "Believe me, Jocelyn," he said, "were I to enjoy myself more, I would ruin you for marriage."

"To hell with marriage," Jocelyn blurted out. "I told you once I'm not worried about that."

Dash winced at her choice of words. "You *have* been too long in a renegade camp," he said. "You should be worried, love. The men in your circles want a virgin in their marriage bed, not a woman who has known such pleasures."

Jocelyn frowned. "Why is it a man's privilege to sow his oats—but not a woman's right as well?"

"It's always been that way."

"Well, it isn't fair," Jocelyn announced, collecting herself, then sitting up on her elbows. "If this is what men have been enjoying while we 'decent' women twiddle our thumbs, then I want nothing to do with being decent! I want to please you, Dash. I want—"

"No," Dash said forcefully, touching his fingers to her lips. "And I won't be swayed in my decision. Now, lie down and try to get some sleep. We have a long ride in the morning, I'm afraid."

Jocelyn knew better than to argue the point with him. Besides, she decided, seeing the shadows of fatigue beneath his eyes, Dash needed to rest. She shouldn't have forced herself on him, even though she was glad she had.

"All right," she conceded. "I'll rest. But from now on, Dash, I won't play your prisoner. You needn't fear that I'll go to the authorities with what I know about you and your friends. I wouldn't do that."

"Not even if the authorities came to you?"

Jocelyn shook her head. "Not even," she declared. She reached for his right hand and clasped her fingers with his. "I don't condone what you do, Dash, but neither will I be the one to betray you. I wasn't raised to be a traitor."

Dash pressed a kiss to the tip of her nose, his eyes not giving away her feelings. "Good night, Jocelyn," he whispered. And then he settled back against the pillow, fitting his left arm beneath her neck and stroking her shoulder as he fell asleep.

But Jocelyn did not find slumber so easily. She lay awake thinking about all that had transpired between her and the mysterious highwayman. Dash was the notorious Midnight Raider. He stole from the unsuspecting elite, then carted off his ill-gained wealth to the north. He could be hanged for his deeds. Or rot in a prison. Either way, Jocelyn might never see him again.

She swallowed heavily at such thoughts. How could she leave him now that she'd known such splendor in his arms? She'd left her father's house because she'd wanted to deliver a message for Alexander. But she'd not seen the all-important note since Dash had abducted her. Had he burned it? Thrown it away?

Odd that she hadn't thought much about the note until now—until she realized that soon she'd be saying goodbye to Dash.

Jocelyn snuggled closer to him, listening to the even beat of his heart and feeling his bandage scrape against her cheek. He was an outlaw, yes, but he was something more than that. He was a man with a past, and one who was striving toward some secret goal.

Jocelyn wanted desperately to know what that goal was. She wanted to share in his secrets, and his pain. Dash had brought to her a wealth of knowledge about herself. During the short time she'd been with him, she'd come to realize that she *could* take care of herself and that she held the power to ensnare a man's attention. But she wanted more. She wanted to know that she could hold a man's interest. Jocelyn wanted the confirmation that she could be more than just a love interest for one night.

She wanted to be Dash's friend.

Jocelyn fell into a fitful sleep, dreaming of all the tomorrows that would come. Frighteningly enough, those days did not include the dashing Dashiell Warfield.

Dash awoke with a pounding headache. It wasn't just a normal headache. This one split his head in two and made his stomach sour and queasy. He glanced down at Jocelyn, who lay snuggled beside him, her gorgeous hair flowing about her shoulders and shielding a portion of her face. He had to quell the urge to take her in his arms again and finish what they'd started last night. Lust pounded through him, making his head ache even more.

Lord, he thought miserably. He'd nearly taken her virginity last night! It had taken an inordinate amount of willpower not to roll on top of her and enter her sweet, hot body with one single thrust. If he hadn't been nursing a gunshot wound, Dash knew Jocelyn would not have known another day of being a virgin. Fortunate for her— or him, he didn't know which—that he'd been in far too much pain to take her.

Trying not to awaken Jocelyn, Dash eased his sore body out of the lumpy bed.

"Christ," he muttered, standing up on shaky legs. "I'm getting too old for this line of work." He hobbled around for a moment, trying vainly to get the kinks out of his body. Using a bit of the water Jocelyn had brought in earlier, he splashed his face and neck and made a valiant attempt to face the world.

Looking out of the small window of the chamber, Dash

saw only a dreary, overcast day. There was no sun to be seen, only miles of heavy, mammoth gray clouds hugging the rolling lands of Snow's Hill. After stoking the fire, Dash went downstairs in search of a warm meal.

Meggie, in her silly, oversize mopcap and too-tight bodice and skirt, was hefting a bowl of duck eggs onto the trestle table. She jumped when Dash entered the kitchen.

"Och! You filthy robber, you scared me half to death!"

Dash managed a grin. "You're too tight for your corsets, Meggie dear."

"I don't wear such a thing, Dash, but little would *you* know. That travelin' eye of yours has never bothered to look up *my* skirts!"

"You're Pretty Boy's sister. I could hardly seduce you."

"No? Try me, Dash." She clicked her tongue when he made no answer. "Let me guess. You got yourself all wrapped up in that pretty, freckle-faced Jocelyn. She's a dangerous one, Dash," Meggie warned, cracking several of the eggs into another bowl. "She might as well be the wife of an earl or a baron. Either way she's too good for the likes of you."

"Spare me the lecture," Dash said dryly. "I came in here for a bite to eat, not a bite of that tongue of yours."

"Men!" Meggie breathed. "What good are you? No good, *I* say."

"You just haven't met your match, Meggie."

"And I won't either, if I have any say in the matter. What'll it be, Dash? Scrambled?"

"Just cooked is all I ask."

"Ah, you always were easy to please."

Meggie whipped the broken egg yolks, then poured them into a heavy skillet and set it on the cookstove.

"I take it you've heard about the Keats murder," she said suddenly, her voice hushed. "I'm telling you, Dash, the Midnight Raider bodes ill for you and your men. People are calling for justice. They want *all* highwayman hanged."

Dash felt his head throb anew.

"What are you going to *do*, Dash?" Meggie continued.

"Any highwayman who is caught will be charged with that murder. And what about your boys? Are all of you to hang for that crime?"

Dash eased his body down onto a low stool. "I don't know, Meggie. I haven't thought that far in advance."

"Well, you should! There's a great many people counting on you. If you find yourself dangling on a noose, what will become of us all?"

"Do you think I haven't thought about that?"

"Sure I think you have, so why haven't you got an answer? Thievin' is one thing, but murder is—" Meggie stopped short, staring at the door to the common room.

Dash looked up and saw Jocelyn standing there, looking dreamy and sleepy and too beautiful for words.

"Murder?" Jocelyn whispered. "Whose murder?"

"Dammit," Dash muttered.

But Meggie, with her usual gusto, waved Jocelyn into the kitchen. "Murder?" she nearly screeched. "Who said anyone was murdered? I was just telling Dash here that he'd best take care who he robs or there might be a murder—his! Now, girl, you just sit down and make yourself at home. I'm making Dash some eggs."

Dash watched as Jocelyn carefully entered the room, looking like she expected a lightning bolt to strike her down at any minute.

"Sleep well?" Dash asked.

Jocelyn smiled at him, a private, small tilt of her pouty mouth. "Yes," she said. "And you?"

Dash felt as though the sun had just exploded in the room. "Yes," he said. "You'll love Meggie's cooking. She's the best at what she does."

Meggie harrumphed noisily, but fluttered about the kitchen as though she were expecting a carriage load of guests. She served them their breakfast, with a pitcher of fresh milk to drink. "I've tea, too," she said proudly. "Just enough for the two of you." Dash held up his cup and Meggie obligingly filled it. "You?" Meggie asked Jocelyn.

Jocelyn nodded, watching as Meggie poured her a

steaming cupful of the brew. Jocelyn drank a sip and relished the taste. After a moment she said, "Must we return to camp today?"

Dash frowned, but nodded. "I've got to see that our shipment got on its way."

"And then?" Jocelyn asked.

Meggie conveniently slipped out of the room.

Dash took another drink of the tea. "And then I'll see you safely home."

Silence then. Dash could see Jocelyn was summoning her courage. Damn, but she was a brave young woman. She could go anywhere, he knew, do anything, and yet he feared his touch would blacken her world.

"What if I don't want to go home?" Jocelyn chanced.

Dash made a pretense of stuffing his mouth with scrambled eggs.

"Well?" she demanded.

No skirting the subject for Jocelyn! "You have to go home," Dash announced. "You belong there."

"But I want to stay with you."

Dash nearly choked on the eggs. He wiped his mouth with the back of one hand, hoping, with that small gesture, to impress upon her what a miscreant he was. "You can't stay, Jocelyn. You know that."

"But last night—" she began.

"Last night was a mistake," he cut in, hating that he had to be so cruel. "I shouldn't have touched you, let alone seduce you."

"You didn't seduce me, as I recall."

Pity, that she had to remind him of that fact. "It doesn't matter. You are still free to marry whomever you wish, Jocelyn. If I return you home now, then you'll be able to forget this mess and get on with your life."

Dash thought she might cry—she looked as though she would, anyway. Her eyes gathered with tears and her mouth quivered. Even her precious, tiny freckles seemed to quiver with her emotions.

"Don't fight me on this," he said tersely. "You're going home and that is that."

To Dash's relief—and also to his disappointment—
Jocelyn didn't argue. She merely sat there, her arms at her
sides, as she stared at the food on her plate.

When it was finally time to leave, Jocelyn still hadn't
eaten a thing. She said a quick good-bye to Meggie, then
followed Dash out to their horses.

"It's for the best, you know," Dash said, leading them
away from Snow's Hill and onto the country road that
would lead to the campsite.

Woodenly Jocelyn said, "Of course."

"There's no future for us, Jocelyn."

"I know that."

"Good," Dash said, aching inside. "I'm glad you understand."

But Jocelyn didn't understand, he knew, and Dash
cursed himself for ever having touched her so intimately
in the dark of the night. He should have had more control.
He should have bullied her and made her back away!
Damn! He was a fool for ever touching his lips to hers! It
would be his fortune to finally meet a woman who not
only aroused him, but dazzled him as well. Jocelyn was
unlike anyone he'd ever met. She was gutsy and daring,
but she had a vulnerability about her that could make his
heart ache. She was filled with sweetness and light, and
she made Dash experience emotions he'd buried long ago.
With Jocelyn, Dash knew, he could be compelled to let
go of his wayward life and set his sights to bettering himself.

But it could never be. They had no future together. He
was a thief, and she . . . she was a lady. Dash knew only
too well that he had to let go of her—he had to, before it
was too late.

They made the campsite shortly after noon. Dash was
sweating by the time they got there. His side hurt horribly
and his headache had increased to sickening proportions.
Jocelyn, on the other hand, appeared stiff and distant on
her horse.

"There's Pretty Boy," Dash announced, seeing the

young man posted on the outskirts of the camp. "Ho! Pretty Boy! What news have you?"

The young man came rushing toward them, his face etched with worry. "We've got trouble," he said, then smiled wanly at Jocelyn. "I found the lady's cousin tramping near our camp. He was in such a state . . . well, I felt sorry for the man, so I brought him back to the campsite."

"Charles?" Jocelyn cried, looking past Pretty Boy's shoulders.

"Yes," the man said. "He's here, and he's calling for blood. He's very worried about your safety."

Dash didn't have a chance to comment, for Jocelyn kicked her mount into motion and careened off through the trees.

"Charles is calling for your head on a platter, Dash," Pretty Boy said.

"I don't give a damn if he's calling for his pipe," Dash muttered, tearing off after Jocelyn.

"Well, you should!" Pretty Boy yelled. "The man has threatened to drag you in front of Lord Monty!"

Dash swore in exasperation. Charles knew his uncle? That would mean only trouble for him!

When Dash made the camp, he found Jocelyn dropping to the ground and rushing to her cousin. But to Dash's dismay, she wasn't crying and yelling that Dash had raped her. Instead she was laughing!

"I feared I might not see you again!" Dash heard Jocelyn exclaim. "I've missed you, Charles."

The man called Charles held his cousin apart from him. He stared, aghast, at the clothing she wore. "I'm hardly fit to find you in such a place, and dressed as you are, Jocelyn!" He quickly removed his coat and put it about Jocelyn's shoulders. "Are you well? Have these . . . these beasts harmed you in any way?"

"I'm fine," Jocelyn replied, squeezing his hand, then turning to face Dash. "Tell him, Dash," she demanded. "Tell my cousin you have shielded me from harm."

Dash bit down hard on his own guilt. Was this a game

she was playing? Or did Jocelyn mean to leave him without charging him with a heinous crime?

When Dash didn't answer, Jocelyn turned to Charles and said, "I'm perfectly all right. In fact, these kind men saved me from a fate worse than death. They—they intervened and saved me from the clutches of those horrible highwaymen . . . isn't that right?"

Jocelyn stared hard at Dash, forcing him to agree.

"That's right," he ground out, though the lie left a bad taste in his mouth.

But Jocelyn's smile was bright as she turned on her cousin. "These men came to my rescue, Charles. We should be thanking them, not questioning them."

Charles appeared to be at a loss for words, but he rallied back. He sketched a quick bow to Dash, saying, "You, sir, have my eternal gratitude—if, in fact, you did save my cousin from certain danger. I would like to repay you."

Dash pulled himself off the saddle, favoring his injured side. "That won't be necessary," he said. "But I would warn you not to travel these roads at night again. These are dangerous times."

"Indeed they are," Charles expounded. "Well, then, if you'll not be taking any monetary gain for your troubles, Miss Greville and I will be leaving. Thank you, sir. I am in your debt."

Dash felt his stomach churn. Jocelyn would be going home. He might never see her again. His bones ached, his blood tingled. God, how could he let her go? But he must. He had no other choice.

"Certainly," Dash ground out. "Good day to you."

And then he watched as Charles led away the only woman who had ever captured his heart. He saw the sunlight catch in her coppery hair, could remember vividly the fresh scent of those long tresses, and his chest tightened. He wished he could have touched her one last time. He wanted to hold her in his arms and know again the feel of her. He wanted to share a kiss with her that would last him the rest of his life.

As though Jocelyn could hear his thoughts, she turned

her head and glanced at him from over one shoulder. Their eyes met and held. She looked a vision—a face for a locket. She hesitated a moment, as though she had something she wanted to say before leaving. But Charles gave her arm a tug, and Jocelyn turned away.

As he watched her leave, Dash felt as though he were being sucked into a deep, dark hole and might never find his way out of it.

"Good-bye, Duchess," he whispered, knowing that she took a piece of his heart with her.

Eleven

"Are you certain those ruffians didn't harm you?" Charles demanded for the fifth time since he and Jocelyn had climbed into Amelia's gilt carriage. "I say, dear cousin, you look absolutely wretched! By God, if they touched so much as a hair on your head, I'll see them all thrown into prison! I have *connections*, cousin. I can have them all tried before a judge within a few days!"

Jocelyn arrowed Charles with a hard stare. "Will you cease your prattle? No, they didn't harm me, I told you that. A dozen times, at least. And the reason I look so 'wretched' is because *you* are giving me a horrid headache!"

"Tsk, tsk, Jocelyn, you needn't snap at me," Charles muttered, looking like a spaniel who'd been kicked. "I've been sick with worry about you! For heaven's sake, cousin, the last I saw you, you were being held by that horrid Midnight Raider! I feared I'd find you dead in some ditch with the crows picking at your eyes."

Jocelyn clicked her tongue. "You're far too theatrical, Charles. Those men back there . . . they came to my rescue and saved me from the Raider. They were preparing to take me home when you came. As you can see, I'm right as rain."

"I daresay you're not! Look at you, sitting there clenching and unclenching your fists and staring out the window like a forlorn Hero."

"How is my father?" Jocelyn asked, deciding she was getting nowhere with her assurances to Charles. "Is he well?"

"I only wish. He's not fared well in your absence. He had half the county searching for you. Didn't sleep a wink and hasn't taken a bite to eat since that frightful night. And Amelia! She paces about the house with that hideous pipe of hers clamped tight between her teeth while she awaits news from London. She has been furiously pulling strings, hoping to gain insight into your disappearance. Alas, no one sent her any news, which was when I decided to take matters into my *own* hands. Jives and I have been scouring these bleak roads since yesterday morning. I finally came upon some young man named Petty—or some such nonsense—and asked if he'd seen you."

"Pretty Boy," Jocelyn supplied, feeling extremely guilty that her family had been so overwrought with worry.

"Whatever," Charles said, waving one bony hand in the air. "The youth looked absolutely terrified when I told him our grandmother could be in contact with Lord Montague Warfield."

Jocelyn was startled to hear the Warfield name, but she kept her face well schooled. "So what did Pretty Boy tell you?"

"Nothing, and that's what has me so puzzled. He was stammering and stuttering about you when you and that man came riding into the camp. Really, Jocelyn, where had you *been*?"

Jocelyn kept her gaze fastened to the moving scenery outside the carriage window. "Riding," she said lamely. "We went after one of the horses that bolted away."

"Riding?! Had you no thought to ride toward *home*, cousin? Really!"

"That's enough, Charles," Jocelyn snapped. "I'll not have you berating me for the choices I've made. I'm on my way home now, doesn't that account for something?"

"Only because I came to fetch you."

"I'd have made it there sooner or later."

"It's the 'later' that worries me."

Jocelyn fell silent then, not wanting to discuss her abduction, or Dash. She knew she should be glad to be heading home, but she wasn't. She'd wanted to stay with Dash, if for only a day or two longer. Dash, on the other hand, clearly wanted nothing more to do with her.

The bitter reality cut deep into Jocelyn's soul. Last night had been beautiful, and yet Dash had turned her away, telling her their lovemaking had been a mistake. A *mistake*! How could he be so cruel? And how could she be such a fool for still wanting him? she wondered miserably.

By the time they reached her father's lands, Jocelyn was in a state of depression. Not even the sight of the sprawling honey-colored country house, with its crooked stone fence cutting through the rolling lands like a gray braid, could make Jocelyn feel any better.

Jives brought the horses to a grinding halt in front of the front steps, jumped down from his perch, then popped open the carriage door. "Welcome home, missy!" he said emotionally, looking as though he hadn't slept much himself. "Your father and grandmother will be mighty pleased to see you. And glad I am to be able to bring you to them."

Jocelyn forced a smile as she allowed Jives to help her to the ground. "Thank you," she said, feeling keen nostalgia and guilt overcome her. She kissed Jives's weathered cheek and gave him an affectionate hug. "I appreciate the trouble you've gone through to help find me."

"No trouble at all, missy. I was happy to help. I—I just wish I could have saved you from all of this the other night."

Jocelyn shook her head, feeling terrible that her loved ones had had to suffer so. "Please," she said. "It's over. Let's try and put it out of our minds."

Charles stepped down beside her. "So Jives gets a kiss while I get berated for *my* troubles."

"Don't pout," Jocelyn said to her cousin, threading her arm through his. "You know I'm grateful to you."

"About as grateful as a hound being bitten by a flea."

"Now look who's being testy."

"Of course I am, cousin. I canceled all social activities just to search for you."

"Then I'll just have to make it up to you, won't I?" she said, walking beside him up the smooth steps to the front door. "I'll make a fuss to all about how you came to my rescue, all right?"

"Even to Sally Warburton?" Charles asked quickly.

"Especially to Sally."

Charles appeared extremely pleased with that, and quickly stepped ahead of Jocelyn to reach for the door handle.

But the door was pulled open from the inside and Alexander Greville, looking disheveled and panic-stricken, cried openly at the sight of his daughter.

"Jocelyn . . . Thank God!" he exclaimed, then gathered her up in a tight hug. "I feared I might never see you again. I thought you'd been murdered or—"

"I'm fine, Daddy," Jocelyn whispered, her throat constricting with emotion. "Truly, I am."

Her father hugged her as though he couldn't believe she was actually in his arms. Jocelyn felt both guilt and happiness to be home. If Dash hadn't turned her away, she wouldn't be here, she thought. She felt cruel and heartless when she backed out of her father's embrace and saw how ragged and drawn his features appeared. She even thought he'd gotten a few more gray hairs at his temples since she'd seen him last. But how could that be? She'd only been gone a few days. Suddenly Jocelyn couldn't recall exactly how long she'd been gone. It seemed a lifetime, for she'd changed since being with Dash. She'd become a woman.

Could her father notice?

"Daddy?" she chanced. "Why don't you say something?"

Alexander Greville dug a handkerchief out of his wrinkled coat front and dabbed at his bloodshot eyes. "I—I'm overcome with joy and relief," he said hoarsely. He mopped at the beads of perspiration on his high forehead, then shook his head. "I can't believe you're here."

"I am. I'm sorry you've had to go through this."

"But what have you had to endure? My God, you're not hurt, are you? They didn't—" He faltered over his own words and began to cry again.

Jocelyn reached for her father's hands. They were cool to the touch and very smooth. But they seemed frail, which jolted Jocelyn. Her father had never appeared a frail man to her before. Jocelyn felt as though she were seeing her father clearly for the first time. His brown eyes, usually so warm and merry, were now filled with fear and deep concern. And his brown hair, lightly gray at the temples, did not have the healthy sheen she remembered. His clothes were damp and unpressed, and Jocelyn abruptly recognized them as being the same he'd worn that long-ago night she'd seen him pen the note in the study.

"Charles tells me you haven't been eating or sleeping," she said softly.

"Don't you worry yourself over me, dear. Now that you're home, I'll be fine. Now, come inside, out of the cool air. Your grandmother will want to see you. She's taken her mount out and is even now leading a search party."

Jocelyn was appalled. "Grandmother is *riding*? Oh, Daddy, she shouldn't be. The last time she rode Rosie, she fell and broke her toe!"

"Well, you don't think she'd sit idly by while the rest of us came and went, do you? She's been in and out these past few days and has every one of our neighbors called to arms."

Jocelyn digested the news and felt her guilt increase. She could well imagine her grandmother charging through the Cotswolds, sending sharp commands and forming her own posse of gentlefolk.

"Come, Daddy," she said. "You look as if you could use a warm meal and a hot bath."

Alexander Greville eyed his only child closely. "Nonsense. What I need is to know you are in good health. Randolph!" he bellowed, calling for the manservant. "My bag, and be quick about it. My daughter is home, man!"

No sooner had the portly Randolph come waddling into

the front room with Alexander's black bag than he dropped the thing and tripped over his own feet to greet Jocelyn.

"Ah, missy!" he said, tears misting his eyes. "Welcome home!"

Alexander snorted noisily as he retrieved the bag, then sent Randolph to the kitchen with an order to prepare a light broth for Jocelyn. "And some strong tea," he called after the man. "Jocelyn has been through an ordeal."

Jocelyn felt overcome to be the center of such great attention. "I'm all right, Daddy."

"I'll be the judge of that. Now, upstairs with you."

Up in her room Jocelyn allowed herself to be fussed over by her father. Listening to her heart, he demanded her to breathe deep, again and again.

"If I breathe any harder, I'll pass out!" Jocelyn said.

"Why? Do you feel dizzy? Look at me, Jocelyn." He waved one hand in front of her face. "Tell me how many fingers you see."

Jocelyn sighed deeply. "Seven," she said, trying for humor. But her father wasn't in a joking mood. He was trembling like a leaf in a stiff breeze. "Daddy, I'm fine."

"How can you be? Abducted by a highwayman and taken God knows where! Charles," he said to her cousin, who stood discreetly beside her bedroom door. "I want you to get the constable here, posthaste! He should hear what Jocelyn has to say. Don't you worry, sweetheart," he said to Jocelyn. "I'll make certain those robbers pay for what they've put you through."

Jocelyn didn't give protest. She would have to have time to think about what she would tell the authorities—if anything.

"I'm a little tired," she finally said when her father had assured himself that she wouldn't faint in a dead swoon. "Could I just eat in my room? I think I'd like to rest for a while."

"Of course," Alexander said, quieting somewhat. "What else would you like? A sleeping draught?"

Jocelyn shook her head. "Nothing. I—I just want to be alone."

Alexander fussed over her a moment longer and then finally left her to herself.

Jocelyn stared at her bedchamber. The room felt foreign to her. The snowy, frilly curtains hanging on the southern windows that looked out on the intricate gardens her grandmother had planned now seemed silly and girlish to Jocelyn. Even her huge four-poster bed, with its pink satin spread and pillow shams, looked as though a child of ten should sleep on it, and not a woman of seventeen. In the far corner was a cedar wardrobe, the doors thrown open and exposing Jocelyn's abundant supply of gowns, chemises, skirts, petticoats, and shoes, riding boots, and slippers. In the opposite corner, beneath the southern windows, was a rosewood desk, covered only with an inkwell, pen, and blotter. An embroidered chair was situated near it. A much-loved doll, with one eye missing, was propped against the cushion.

Jocelyn picked up the doll, staring down at it. Her father had bought it for her at one of the fairs, and Jocelyn had carried it everywhere from the time she was five until she was eleven. Only when Charles had teased her about it did Jocelyn delegate the doll to her chair.

Yes, it was a child's room she'd lived in all these years. But Jocelyn was no longer a child. She'd aged since she'd met the rash and rugged highwayman Dash. How could she continue living as she'd always lived now that she'd known the freedom of sleeping under the stars, and the heated touch of a man who wanted nothing more to do with her?

Oh, Dash, she thought . . . and buried her face into the soft dress of the doll, crying quietly.

Two hours later, after eating all of the broth Randolph brought up and having had a short nap, Jocelyn awoke to find her grandmother sitting on the desk chair she'd pulled nearer to Jocelyn's bed.

At first Jocelyn didn't remember where she was. She had to blink the fog from her mind, had, in fact, to stop herself from whispering Dash's name.

"Hello, Jocelyn," Amelia Greville said, smiling down

at her granddaughter. Dressed in a smart riding habit of crushed blue velvet complete with a small, stylish hat that sported a dyed plume, she appeared worldly and not a bit of her sixty years of age. Her watery blue eyes were sharp and clear as she looked over at Jocelyn. Her slim hands, encased in creamy-smooth leather gloves, were folded primly on her lap.

Jocelyn returned the smile, then sat up and rubbed the sleep from her eyes.

"I trust you had a good nap?" Amelia asked affectionately.

Jocelyn nodded. There was something different about her grandmother this day, but Jocelyn couldn't quite put her finger on what that something might be.

"And I see you've had a bite to eat," Amelia continued, nodding toward the tray on the stand near the bed.

Again Jocelyn nodded. Something was certainly amiss— she could see it in the shrewd eyes of her grandmother.

"Well, then," Amelia said, settling back into the chair and taking a small, hand-carved pipe from the drawstring purse that hung from a belt about her waist. "Since your father has doubtless poked and prodded you and seen to your welfare, I needn't pry about that. And by the looks of you, I can see you've been in good hands since I last saw you."

Jocelyn swallowed hard. Something was *definitely* amiss. Her grandmother, Jocelyn had learned long ago, was a woman who got to the heart of a matter without beating about the bush.

Amelia Greville packed the pipe—which was a decadent sculpture of a man and a woman involved in a very intimate act—and then touched a lit match to the weed. A fragrant puff of smoke curled about her striking features.

Without further ado, Amelia said, "You've been talking in your sleep again, dear girl."

Jocelyn inwardly groaned.

"Quite a bit, in fact."

"How long have you been sitting here?" Jocelyn asked, feeling her heart bury itself in the pit of her stomach.

"Long enough," Amelia said without censure, "to deduce that my granddaughter hasn't been an unwilling captive these past few days. Do you want to tell me about this fellow named Dash? Or shall I embarrass us both and pry?"

Jocelyn sank back against her pillow. "What did I say in my sleep?"

"Something about not wanting to leave him."

"Oh."

"Are you in love with the man?"

Jocelyn didn't answer.

"Ah, you are. Did you sleep with him?"

Jocelyn bolted upright, her face growing crimson.

"I can see that you did. Well, good for you, dear. Nothing wrong with a woman enjoying herself—you did enjoy yourself, didn't you? He didn't force you?"

Jocelyn was thunderstruck. She and her grandmother had never before discussed what went on between a man and a woman! But then again, Jocelyn had not asked, and she realized suddenly that she should have! No doubt Amelia would have answered all of her questions, and probably a good bit more!

"Jocelyn, did he force you?" Amelia pressed, pausing from taking another long puff of her pipe.

Jocelyn shook her head. "No," she whispered, and then she felt her reserve crumble and added, "I—I don't know if I can say I slept with him or not. I—I mean we did fall *asleep*, but I . . . I am still a virgin."

Amelia's thin brows lifted slightly. "I see," she said thoughtfully. "He was a gentleman, then?"

Jocelyn blushed. "Partly. I'm afraid I wasn't very much of a lady, though."

"Poppycock," Amelia admonished. "Don't berate yourself, Jocelyn. Ladies can enjoy themselves. Men don't always have to have their total fulfillment."

Jocelyn couldn't believe they were having such a conversation! But it became suddenly clear to her that her grandmother realized Jocelyn was no longer a little girl, and Amelia was making an attempt to treat her as an equal woman.

Feeling a tug in her heart, Jocelyn looked up and whispered, "I'm glad you're here, Gran."

Amelia blew out a tiny ring of smoke, then gave Jocelyn a wink. "Me, too. Now, tell me about this lover of yours. Is he the same man who robbed your poor cousin of his rings? And the same who leveled a gun at Jives? Heavens, Jocelyn, you should have seen the two of them that night! They were trembling in their boots and calling for justice. I assure you, it wasn't amusing at the time, but now that I know you're well and unharmed . . . well, I just have to say that this Dash must be quite a terror."

"He can be," Jocelyn agreed, then added softly, "But he can also be very sweet."

"Does he know that you're in love with him?"

"No! I—I mean, even I don't know if I *love* him. But it doesn't matter," Jocelyn said, taking a deep breath and gathering her courage to face life without Dash. "He told me our coming together was a—a mistake. He said he wouldn't marry me—not even if we'd . . ." Jocelyn couldn't finish the sentence. She started to cry. "Dammit!" she sobbed, angry at herself. "I don't want to cry over him, Gran. I don't want to miss him so much."

Amelia didn't even bat an eye at Jocelyn's choice of words. She merely placed her pipe on the table, then reached over to take Jocelyn in a gentle hug. "Go ahead and cry, my dear. And believe me, one day you'll be able to put the memory of Dash aside for a while and get on with your life."

"I don't think I'll ever be able to forget him," Jocelyn whispered.

"*Forget* him? Dear, I didn't say you'd be able to forget him. Nor should you, not if you enjoyed his presence."

"I did! Oh, Gran, I did."

Amelia patted Jocelyn's back but said nothing more.

The evening went by in a haze for Jocelyn. She joined the family in the massive, oak-beamed dining room for a late supper, but found she could only pick at the fare Randolph had prepared especially for her. She drank a little too much wine and skirted the issue of her abduction.

"We shall press charges, Jocelyn," Alexander Greville was saying. "If it takes every penny I have, I'll see those men get what they deserve!"

Jocelyn stared into the fluted glass of wine in her hand. She was barely listening. It had taken all of her pleading for her father not to force her to speak with the constable. Alexander had been aghast, thinking perhaps she'd suffered indescribable cruelties at the hands of the "cutthroat thieves," as he called them, and that that was the reason she didn't want to talk about her ordeal. But Amelia had intervened and Alexander had sent the constable home.

"Can't we just forget about all of this?" Jocelyn asked quietly.

"Forget?" Alexander exploded. "Certainly not! Those men could have killed you!"

"Alexander," Amelia soothed. "If Jocelyn wishes to put this ugly incident behind her, then I think we should respect her wishes."

"But who's to say those men won't come after her again? How can I ever sleep at night, worrying about my daughter's safety while her kidnappers are slinking about?"

Amelia was not to be swayed. "I'd been planning to take Jocelyn and Charles back to London with me for the winter season. She should be perfectly safe in my townhouse there, and if it will put your mind at ease, I'll hire someone to watch the house."

Jocelyn looked over at her grandmother, but Amelia did not return her glance.

"London is not to be matched in the winter," Amelia continued, having made her decision. "And Jocelyn will be so busy with socials and outings, that she won't have a moment to think about the past."

Jocelyn felt her depression deepen. So, her grandmother meant to cart her off to London in hopes that she would forget about Dash—and no doubt meet another man to take his place.

But, Jocelyn wondered, could any man ever replace Dash? Did there even exist a man as compelling and intriguing? And if there did, would Jocelyn even be interested?

Charles was in a tither of excitement, with thoughts of London swirling in his head. He talked in a rush about all the packing he had to take care of, and of course, he would have to wish meek Sally Warburton farewell, and wouldn't she just be crushed at the thought of spending her winter without him?

"But, alas," Charles ended, not noticing that he'd lost his audience with his chatter, "she shall have to make do without me. She can be quite tiresome with those doe-eyed looks she sends my way."

"She's quite taken with you," Amelia observed. "Perhaps you should ask her to join us?"

Charles turned a perfect shade of pink. "*Join* us? In *London*?"

"Yes," Amelia said. "Where else, dear boy?"

"Well, I, uh, I . . . Ahem!" Charles sucked down the remainder of his wine. "Yes, maybe I shall!" he announced finally. "I just might do that. What a splendid idea, Gran. Very splendid indeed!" He got dreamy-eyed then, and Jocelyn decided she couldn't take any more of the family gathering.

"If you'll all excuse me," she said, dropping her linen napkin atop her plate. "I think I'll read for a while before I retire."

Alexander got to his feet and helped to pull Jocelyn's chair back from the table. He kissed the top of her head, but he didn't ask her to stay longer at the table, as the family usually did.

Jocelyn walked slowly to her father's study and took a random book from the shelf that ran the length of one wall. Randolph had laid a fire in the grate and now the room was toasty warm, reminding Jocelyn of the room at the Fox's Lair. Without wanting to, she thought back to the night before and of Dash's touch, and the smell and feel of him.

No, she said firmly to herself. I won't think of him. I won't. And so she opened the book and started to diligently read all about raising sturdy Costwold sheep.

Her father came in some time later, peered over her shoulder, and shook his head. "I didn't know you took an interest in such things," he commented.

Jocelyn shut the book, her eyes strained and her neck aching from reading. "I don't," she said. "I just needed something to put me to sleep. And no," she added, seeing the concern creep again into her father's eyes, "I don't want a sleeping draught."

Alexander sat down in an overstuffed chair opposite hers. "Think I'm being overly worried about you, hmm?"

"Yes, but I would expect no less."

Alexander nodded, then stared at the fire in the hearth.

"Something more is troubling you, isn't it?" Jocelyn asked, noting again the fatigue on his features. "Your hands haven't stopped trembling since I returned home. I've never known you to be so nervous. What is it? What's troubling you? And don't tell me nothing," she said even before he had a chance to reply. "The last night I was home, I overheard you and Gran talking—or rather arguing. I know that you have been in contact with members of the Spencean society."

At mention of the secret organization Alexander jumped to his feet and quickly closed the door. "Hush, Jocelyn! Take care where you repeat that name!"

"But you *are* in contact with them, aren't you?"

"Was," Alexander said, giving emphasis to the word. "Your grandmother was correct, they are a lawless lot, and I've cut my ties with them."

"Why?" Jocelyn asked. "What have they done?"

"Nothing, yet," he said darkly. He sat back down, but leaned forward in the chair. "I will tell you this only because I fear for your safety and because you'll soon be traveling to London. I don't want you ever to repeat that name again, do you hear? Arthur Thistlewood—the man who is at the forefront of the group—is a Radical. Though I agree with his opinion that something must be done to help the less fortunate people of England, I do not agree with his methods. He—he is causing quite a stir with his firebrand talk. He wishes for a revolution, for the government to be jolted and to quit squandering England's riches on unnecessaries. He wants for the wealth to be distributed evenly, and for unemployed soldiers and sailors to be put to work. But I don't know how it can be done, Jocelyn—not without brute force.''

Jocelyn listened intently, pleased that her father was sharing his innermost thoughts with her. "And the letter you penned that night?" she asked quietly. "What was in it?"

"The letter? You knew about that, too?"

Jocelyn nodded, then admitted, "I took it, Daddy. I—I meant to deliver it to George Edwards, but I—"

"Good Lord, Jocelyn! I'd thought Randolph had destroyed the note. I ordered him to do so, but he must have forgotten about it in all the commotion of the night. Where is it, girl? Where?"

Jocelyn stiffened. "I—I'm not certain," she whispered. "I—it must be with—with the highwayman who robbed me."

Alexander went white. "My God," he breathed, sitting back in the chair and staring at nothing. "If that note makes its way into the wrong hands . . . I could be tried for treason."

Jocelyn felt as though the floor had dropped out from beneath her. Treason! "What was in the note?" she demanded. "What?"

But Alexander was muttering to himself, shaking his head.

"Tell me, Daddy! What was in the note?"

"Names of the members of the society," he whispered hoarsely. "And dates and places of a few of our meetings." He gripped the arms of the chair, as though his own world were spinning. "I was to keep track of this information for George Edwards. But it's just as well that Edwards never received the note, because I've heard he and Thistlewood have had a disagreement. But do you realize, Jocelyn, that if that highwayman reads the note, he'll be able to bargain his way out of the hangman's noose?''

"How?" Jocelyn asked.

"It's simple. Why hang a highwayman when you could arrest a dozen or so men for plotting to assassinate the British cabinet?''

Jocelyn's stomach churned, and bile rose sickeningly in her throat. "Are—are you telling me that Arthur Thistlewood and his men are planning—''

"Yes. But I don't know when—or how. Dammit!'' he exploded, slamming one fist against the chair. "Maybe I'm wrong. Maybe Thistlewood has had a change of heart. Perhaps he and his men have come to their senses and have realized that such an attempt would be suicidal.''

"And if they haven't?''

"I'll just have to find out.''

"No!'' Jocelyn leaned forward and grasped her father's hand. "No, Daddy, I don't want you to have anything more to do with this group. Please, promise me!''

"Jocelyn—''

"I don't want you to go near them! If they have murder on their minds—''

"I can't say for certain that they do. It was just an idea— one of many they've been contemplating. No,'' Alexander said, looking directly into Jocelyn's widened eyes, "I can't believe that Thistlewood would attempt something so dangerous. He wouldn't. I cannot believe that he'd go through with it.''

"Then you'll stay away from them?'' Jocelyn asked. "Tell me you will.''

"I told you I've cut my ties with them.''

"Very well,'' Jocelyn said, calming only a little. "I believe you. And the note,'' she added, seeing she needed to reassure her father, "I—I don't think the man who robbed me had much interest in it. No doubt he's done away with it by now. I mean, it was just a sealed letter taken from a frightened woman. He probably burned it, so there wouldn't be proof of his nefarious deed.''

Alexander thought on that a moment, and, clearly wanting to hope for the best, he said, "Yes, you're probably right."

"Yes," she agreed. "I am."

But later, after she said good night to her father, Jocelyn knew what she had to do.

She waited until well after midnight, until the house was quiet and even the sound of her own breathing echoed in her ears, then she opened the window of her bedroom and climbed out. She hadn't climbed down the trellis in a number of years, but it seemed like only yesterday. She was on the ground in a matter of moments. And then, like the thief she'd so recently been, she stole through the darkness and headed for the stables.

Twelve

Wisps of fog traced the land, looking like bridal lace in the wash of pale moonlight streaming down from above. The air was cool, and Jocelyn found it invigorating. She needed to be kept awake and alert. Dressed in Pretty Boy's clothes—the same she'd returned home in and had to explain to everyone how she'd come by—she cut through the spreading lawns and fields of her father's house. She'd pulled her hair up on top of her head and had secured it in a knot, then had pulled one of Jives's caps she'd found in the stables down over her head. No sense in letting people know she was a woman out and about alone, Jocelyn decided.

She reached the North Road in a little under an hour.

"It shouldn't be long now," Jocelyn said to her horse. Daisy was frisky, seemingly enjoying their clandestine ride through the night. Jocelyn patted the beast's neck, then slowed her to a canter as Jocelyn peered about for some familiar landmark.

"There," Jocelyn announced, spying a huge fir tree that had been split apart long ago by a bolt of lightning. "I think this is it."

She guided Daisy off the road, urging the horse into the thickness of the trees. Sinister shadows swallowed them. Jocelyn wished she'd brought a lantern—and perhaps a weapon with which to defend herself—but she'd been in too much of a hurry. She'd thought only of finding Dash and getting her father's letter from him. Odd that she hadn't given any thought to her own safety. There were other ruffians about, and not just Dash and his men, but evil wanderers who would think nothing of accosting a lone woman.

"Easy, girl," Jocelyn soothed the horse as she forced her through a tangle of branches. She was actually trying to soothe herself, though. "I think we're on the right path now."

But there wasn't a path, not really. Just a narrow line threading through the woods. It was difficult to recognize anything in the darkness. Every tree looked the same. And though she came upon an occasional birch or fir tree, Jocelyn couldn't be certain they were the same trees she'd passed earlier with Dash.

Just when she thought she'd veered off the road too soon, Jocelyn came into a small clearing. She pulled Daisy to a halt.

She'd found the campsite, all right, but it was empty.

Nothing remained but the telltale signs of trodden grass and the pungent scent of horse droppings. The campfire had been covered over and hidden beneath a pile of mulch. The tents were gone. All the gear had been picked up and stowed away.

"Damn," Jocelyn whispered. "I'm too late." She dropped down off the saddle, letting Daisy's reins fall to the ground.

Feeling deserted and alone, Jocelyn walked about the campsite, half wishing she'd find the much-sought-after note lying forgotten in the grass. It was a false hope, for Jocelyn knew Dash would not be so careless as to leave one shred of evidence behind. No doubt he'd scoured the campsite before leaving.

There seemed to linger ghosts in the area. As the wind whispered through the trees and the fog closed about with its eerie grip, Jocelyn imagined she heard Pretty Boy's laughter. She spun about, peering into the shadows. No one. Nothing. Anxious suddenly to be away, Jocelyn headed back to where Daisy was chomping on a mouthful of grass.

"That's enough, girl," Jocelyn berated the horse. "If I allow you your head now, you won't want to leave." She yanked on the reins, pulling up on them as she swung back up on the saddle.

But Daisy chose to be stubborn, whipped her head, then set about eating again. Not in the mood to endure a test of wills with her mount, Jocelyn gave Daisy a gentle kick and pulled back on the reins. "We're leaving, Daisy. And that is that."

But just as she swung the horse about, Jocelyn saw a masked rider at the edge of the clearing. At first Jocelyn thought it was Dash. Her heart leaped, and her stomach filled with butterflies.

"Dash?" she whispered.

The figure said nothing.

No, it wasn't Dash. The horse wasn't huge enough, and the man sitting astride was not so tall. Fear engulfed Jocelyn. She was unarmed and alone. No one knew where she was. She could be shot to death—or worse—and none would be the wiser. Knowing she had to react, and fast, Jocelyn slammed her booted feet against Daisy's sides and turned the horse in the opposite direction.

There, skirting the other side of the campsite, was another rider. And another to her left. Somehow these masked riders had stealthily surrounded her! In an instant Jocelyn checked her only route of escape and spurred Daisy toward a wall of thick brambles. They might be caught in those treacherous prickers, Jocelyn knew, but anything would be better than finding her death at the hands of these men.

Daisy flew forward, all grazing forgotten, and Jocelyn silently applauded her faithful horse. Go, girl, go! Jocelyn thought, feeling the wind tearing at her hair. They reached the thicket with swift speed. Jocelyn drew low over Daisy's neck, kicking the beast to urge her on, knowing Daisy might falter once she felt the pricks of thorns. Jocelyn pressed her eyes shut tight as the first layer of prickers slapped her face and hands. She felt her skin being speared by tiny, needlelike thorns. Tiny beads of blood welled up on her hands and cheeks. But Jocelyn didn't slow their pace. She was fleeing with her life.

"Go after him!" she heard one man call. "Stop him!"

Jocelyn's heart lodged in her throat. If they caught her and saw she was a woman and not a man—Oh, God! she didn't want to think of what would happen to her.

Get your wits about you, girl! she chided herself, knowing she had to keep her head clear. Sweet freedom was just a breath away. If Jocelyn could make it to the open road, then she had a chance of outrunning her pursuers. Daisy came from a long line of prime horseflesh. She'd been bred for speed and beauty, and in her long, lovely limbs was a latent power Jocelyn had only called to use on a few occasions. This night, though, Jocelyn would put Daisy to the test.

They came out of the tearing branches in a dead run. Daisy was wild now, her breath coming in fast, heavy blows.

"We've got to ride fast, girl," Jocelyn said, chancing a glance behind her. One of the riders had charged through the thicket after her but was now caught in the twisting vines. But the other two, wiser, it seemed, had veered around the mass of branches. The sounds of hoofbeats rattled in Jocelyn's head.

She wasn't going to make it, she thought fearfully. The riders were gaining on her, and she guessed the men had ridden these woods before, and so their mounts knew the terrain. Daisy, unfortunately, had known only far-flung green pastures and hillsides to romp about on. Jocelyn cursed her own cushioned lifestyle. She'd taken so much for granted; her freedom to come and go, her choice of staying abed late, or just lounging about her room all day, if she so desired. She should have challenged Daisy long ago! She should have trained the horse for such a harried flight, Jocelyn knew.

And she thought of Dash then and his own powerful mount. Dash need only whistle for the beast, and it would come to him. He'd taught the horse well. Oh, Dash! So brave, yet cautious. *He* would not have traveled through the night unprepared.

Jocelyn thought of all these things as she raced through the woods, praying to come to the road. But just when she got a glimpse of the deserted roadway, one of the riders came up beside her.

"Off the horse!" he shouted in a guttural voice.

Jocelyn tried to veer away, but another rider came beside her then, his face hidden beneath an ugly mask. And then Jocelyn's world went black as she felt a hard hit to the base of her neck. Black wings fluttered before her eyes. Her hands went limp, the reins falling free. And then *she* was falling as well.

Jocelyn came to with a start. For a moment she didn't know where she was or what had happened. She stared up into a pair of mud-colored eyes and thought she was seeing a glimpse from the past.

"Laney?" she whispered.

"Aye, it's me, lass," he said, frowning. "What the devil are you doing here? I thought you were a spy, hoping to ferret out some information about my boys and me. You're fortunate we didn't pull our pistols on you."

Jocelyn tried to sit up, but her head spun and her stomach revolted. Fearing she might lose the contents of her stomach on Laney's lap, she whispered, "I—I think I'm going to be sick."

Quick as a flash Lane Braden eased her head off his lap, then jumped to his feet. "Dammit, Granger!" he exploded. "Did you have to lop her alongside the head?"

Jocelyn barely heard the other man's reply, and apology.

"I—I'm feeling better," she managed, though she wasn't. Forcing herself not to throw up and make more of a show, she covered her eyes and sucked in a few deep breaths. "I was looking for Dash," she explained. "He— he has something that belongs to me." She opened her eyes and saw that Laney had crouched down beside her again.

"Dash is gone, lass. He pulled out shortly after you left today."

"Where to?"

Laney grinned, but shook his head. "Can't say, exactly. With Dash, one can never be too sure. If he knows what's good for him, though, he'll be heading for Dover and then the high seas."

"Dover?" she exclaimed, and this time she did sit up. "He's leaving England? Why?"

"Ho, take it easy. If he hasn't told you, then I can't be the one to explain."

"Nonsense," Jocelyn snapped. "You're a man of few loyalties, Laney Braden, and well you know it. Now, are you going to tell me, or am I going to have to head for Dover and learn on my own?"

"You'd do that, wouldn't you?"

Jocelyn nodded, though it hurt to do so.

"Damn, but you're a gem of a woman. Why is it Dash always finds the sweetest maids to share his pallet, when I find only doxies?"

Jocelyn skewered him with a heated glare.

"Sorry," Laney added quickly. "I didn't mean for you to take offense."

Jocelyn was in no mood for his talk, especially from the man who'd so recently scared the wits out of her. "Why is Dash leaving England? Is he in trouble? Has—has he been found out?"

"In so many words, yes," Laney replied darkly, suddenly turning serious. "A description of the Midnight Raider is circulating through London. This description could or could not—depending on who is doing the looking—fit Dash's appearance. The Midnight Raider is wanted for the murder of James Keats. There's a price on his head."

Jocelyn's head swam.

"That's right, murder," Laney emphasized. "James Keats was shot through the eyes about a week ago. Along this very road. If the authorities catch Dash and decide he fits the description they've been given, then Dash will be shown no mercy.''

"So he's headed for Dover?''

"If he knows what's good for him. But you know Dash, he isn't one to tuck his tail and run.''

"But what about the gold he wanted to give to the northern workers?''

"Taken care of,'' Laney replied. "Pretty Boy and the others saw to that after you left.''

So it was true. Dash was out of her life—forever. Jocelyn couldn't bear the thought of it, and yet she had to. "When does his ship leave?'' she demanded. "On what vessel will he sail?''

"I can't say . . . whoa, you're not thinking of tearing after him, are you? I wouldn't do that, lass. If he's caught, and you're with him, you could be tried alongside him.''

"But I have to talk with him!'' Jocelyn cried. "He—he has something that belongs to me. I must get it back!''

"Are you talking about the jewels he stole from you?''

Jocelyn hesitated only a moment. "Y-yes,'' she whispered. "I want my cousin's rings and my pendant returned to me.''

Laney narrowed his eyes. "Or could it be the note you were carrying that night?''

Jocelyn stiffened. "Wh-what note?'' she asked innocently.

"Come now, don't play me for a fool. After you left, I saw Dash pull a letter from his saddlebag.''

"Did he open it?'' Jocelyn asked, far too quickly.

Laney's interest was piqued. "Not that I know of. He merely looked at the thing, then tucked it away. Should he have opened it?''

"No!'' she nearly screeched, but then forced herself to slow down. "What I—I mean to say is that the note was just a silly love letter I'd written. I would be most embarrassed should anyone read its contents.''

"A love letter, hmm? Well, I wouldn't worry that pretty head of yours. What you should be worried about is getting home in one piece. I take it no one in your family knows you are here?''

Jocelyn shook her head, feeling a trifle guilty.

Laney offered her his hand. ''If you're up to it, I'll escort you home.''

''No. You needn't do that. I'm quite capable of finding my own way home.''

''I don't doubt that,'' Laney said, taking her hand firmly in his anyway. ''But my boys and I are staking out these parts in hopes those smugglers might return looking for their gold. I'm in the mood for a fight, lass, if you understand.''

Jocelyn didn't understand, but it was none of her business all the same. ''My father's house is an hour away.''

''No bother. We'll join you for the ride. Can you stand up?''

Jocelyn got to her feet. ''Of course,'' she said, unwilling to let her dizziness get the best of her. ''I'm not a child, Laney.''

''Ho, I didn't say you were! I know better than that, lass.''

Jocelyn grinned at his show of humor, then moved toward Daisy, who had quieted from their mad dash and was now grazing happily again. As soon as she gathered up Daisy's reins and climbed onto the saddle, they headed for the road.

It was nearing four in the morning by the time they reached her father's land. The fog had thickened considerably, and Jocelyn's hair and clothes felt damp. She was shivering from the cold when she turned Daisy down the long drive to the country house. But Laney and his men didn't follow her.

''Aren't you coming?'' she asked. ''I can't very well leave you out here.''

''Certainly you can,'' Laney replied easily, trying to get a glimpse of the house. ''I'm a night owl, lass. I enjoy the cold and the dark. I was born to ride these roads and trouble innocent folk.''

His words set Jocelyn's nerves on edge and brought into

focus the fact that she was riding with thieves. But Laney's friendliness was infectious, and Jocelyn found she could not condemn him for his way of life, though neither could she condone it.

"You could rest your horses," Jocelyn offered, absently wondering how she would explain Laney and his friends to her father, let alone Charles!

"Not interested," Laney replied, then lifted one hand in a gesture of farewell. "Until we meet again—and I hope we do."

Jocelyn returned the wave. "Good-bye. And thank you."

But Laney and his men had already turned their mounts about and were charging down the bleak road.

Jocelyn watched until they were no longer visible, then she set Daisy to a walk and headed for home.

Once inside the stable, she made quick work of rubbing Daisy down and scooping out a generous ration of oats into her trough. She patted the horse's side, feeling weary to the bone. Daisy, on the other hand, was very alert and seemed to have enjoyed the madcap night of adventure.

Jocelyn grinned at the horse. "So you think you'd like riding the midnight roads, hmm? Sometimes I like it, too," she added in a whisper. "There's nothing to compare with the excitement. Maybe that's why Dash does it," she said. "Perhaps the pull of a thief's life is too much to turn away from."

Jocelyn fell silent, thinking about Dash. He was wanted for *murder*. Had he done the horrible deed? Or had one of his men? Was Dash the Midnight Raider? Jocelyn couldn't believe any of Dash's men could be so cruel as to murder someone. No, it had to be a mistake, she decided sternly. Dash was always so careful. And yet he hadn't been so careful as to stop a young woman from tearing off his mask. . . .

Jocelyn left the stables, closing the heavy door solidly behind her. But as she hurried toward the house, she felt as though she was being watched. Stopping in a shaft of telling moonlight, Jocelyn looked back. There, above the stables, was a light in the window. Jives, who lived in the rooms up above the animals, was standing in full view, staring down at her.

Knowing she couldn't very well act as though she hadn't seen him, Jocelyn gave a meek wave to Jives—which he didn't return—and then she headed for the main house. No sense in climbing the trellis now, she decided, and entered through the back door.

The house was hushed, a silent hulk of rooms. Jocelyn tiptoed up the back stairs and heaved a sigh of relief once she'd entered her own room.

But she didn't fool herself into thinking all would be right. Jives had seen her. And Dash still had her father's letter. Life, it seemed, could be damned difficult!

"Are you going to sleep all *day*, cousin? Get up, I say. We've a long day ahead of us!"

Jocelyn opened one bleary eye and saw Charles's tow-head peeking inside her bedroom. "Go away," she groaned.

"But it's half-past ten! You should have been up *hours* ago! Are you planning to lay abed till noon?"

"If it pleases me, yes!"

"Tsk, tsk, cousin, but you're a lazy bag of bones."

Jocelyn answered by throwing her pillow at him. The thing hit him squarely in the face, and Charles howled in outrage.

"Fine!" he huffed. "Stay in bed, but don't be thinking I'll bring your post to you!"

At that, Jocelyn bolted upright. "What did you say?"

"Nothing," Charles replied testily, ducking out of the room. "Go back to sleep."

"I got a letter?" Jocelyn asked, bounding out of bed. "Dammit, Charles, get back here and talk to me!" She groped for her robe, which she'd slung across the bottom of her bed, and hastily shoved her arms into the sleeves. The long robe billowed behind her as she hustled after her cousin.

Jocelyn found him lounging in the hall, waving a battered envelope beneath his nose. "Looking for this?" he asked, far too sweetly. "It came by special messenger early this morning. *Very* early, in fact. The man was *breathless*, cousin. Said he had to give this to you personally. I told him he was daft, that you didn't rise before eight o'clock. I had to actually *argue* with the man, not to mention give him a blasphemous sum, just to be on his not-so-merry way."

"Stop blathering and give me the letter, dammit."

Charles's mouth dropped open. "I say, Jocelyn, you're in a snit this morning. What's the matter? Didn't sleep well? Dream of riding with Petty and his friends, did you?"

Jocelyn grit her back teeth together. "His name is Pretty Boy, and no, I didn't dream about him! Now, quit acting like a bloody lord and give me my letter."

Charles nearly went into a wheezing attack. Jocelyn had to pat him on the back to get him into form again.

"You've become a little urchin since your abduction," Charles said, looking miffed as he handed her the envelope. "Don't let your father hear you talking like that."

"I'm sorry," Jocelyn said. "I—I have a headache, that's all." And she did. A horrid one, in fact. Granger certainly knew how to knock a person from a horse. "Thank you," she said when she finally had the envelope in her hands.

"Aren't you going to open it?" Charles asked.

Jocelyn stared down at the bold script on the envelope. *Miss Jocelyn Greville.* The words were clear and rich with detail. She knew it must be Dash's handwriting, for it had a certain flair about it—like the man. A part of her trembled, but she forced herself to open it. Inside was a smaller, more familiar envelope secured with her father's wax seal, which hadn't been broken. Jocelyn felt both relieved and disheartened. There was no note from Dash inside. No sweet good-byes. Nothing. Her chest tightened at the realization. Would she ever stop missing the man?

Jocelyn folded the envelopes and stuffed them into the pocket of her robe, intending to give the letter to her father as soon as he returned from tending to a patient. The other envelope she would keep to herself. She felt closer to Dash just knowing she could look at his handwriting now and then. "I'll look at this later," she said.

Charles eyed her closely. "You've become very secretive of late, cousin. What *did* happen to you while you were away? Do you want to talk about it?"

Jocelyn forced a small smile to her lips. "I'm fine, Charles. I just thought—I thought to hear from one of my friends, that's all. Come, now," she said, lacing her arm with his. "What is it you have planned for the day?"

Charles didn't appear to be fooled by her sudden good mood, but he was kind enough to let the subject drop anyway. "We've got only a few days before we must leave for London, you know. And I thought the two of us should decide on our wardrobe. It wouldn't do for us to be caught out of style."

"Certainly not," she agreed, pressing her head against Charles's shoulder. "We'll just have to rifle through our wardrobes and see what we find."

"Precisely," Charles said, already forgetting their spat. "We'll start with mine!"

"Where else?" Jocelyn caroled, and allowed herself to be led to Charles's room, where she spent the next two hours nodding or shaking her head as Charles pulled one suit after another from his cavernous closet.

By noon Jocelyn was feeling cross-eyed. She left Charles to begin packing and went in search of her own haven. After dressing in a gown of crushed velvet—for she was still chilled from her nighttime ride—and sweeping her hair into a loose chignon at the nape of her neck, she ventured downstairs.

She found her father in his study. "Good morning, Daddy."

Alexander rose to his feet, then came around his desk to give a chaste kiss to her cheek. "You mean good afternoon. You slept quite late, Joss."

Jocelyn only nodded, then handed him the crumpled envelope. "I believe this belongs to you." She'd kept the larger envelope—the one with Dash's handwriting—tucked deep in the back of her wardrobe. She would never part with that, she decided, for it was her last connection with Dash.

Alexander stared in disbelief at it. "What? How?"

"Charles tells me it was delivered this morning by special messenger. It would appear, Daddy, that the Midnight Raider is not totally without a conscience."

Alexander had to sit down to get his bearings. "I can't believe it," he muttered. "Thank God! Why, the seal hasn't even been broken!"

"That's right, Daddy," Jocelyn said, standing beside him and touching his shoulder. "So no one, save the two of us and grandmother, need know of your previous involvement with Thistlewood and his men. And as far as I'm concerned," she added with fervor, "you never were involved with that group. It's behind us now. You can destroy the letter, and we can get on with our lives. You said yourself that George Edwards, the man you wished to send this letter to, is no longer involved with Thistlewood, so I don't think he'll miss getting this note."

Alexander nodded, though he was still visibly shaken. "Yes, you're quite right. I should burn this foul letter and that will be that."

Jocelyn watched as her father rose, then walked to the hearth, where a small fire crackled. He tossed the letter into the licking flames, and the two of them were silent as the envelope—and its contents—became nothing but ashes.

After a moment Jocelyn said, "The Midnight Raider returned the letter, so I hope you'll reconsider your desire to press charges against him and his men."

"But—"

"No buts, please," Jocelyn whispered. "We both know what could have transpired had he opened that envelope."

Alexander bowed his head, clearly at war with his own emotions. "But he abducted you, Joss. He—he held you at gunpoint!"

"It's over with," Jocelyn said forcefully. "I'm alive and I'm home. Let's leave it at that."

Alexander appeared about to protest, but Jocelyn would have none of it. She couldn't bear the thought of Dash being chased for kidnapping—he had enough worries at the moment! "No, Daddy. I won't discuss this any further. Tell the constable that I've changed my mind. Tell him anything you want—just tell him to stay away."

"Are you certain this is what you want, Jocelyn?"

"I'm positive," she stated flatly.

"Very well. I'll do as you ask." Alexander put his arm about her shoulders and hugged her. "You're a brave young girl, Jocelyn. You're mother would be proud of you."

Jocelyn smiled shakily, thinking of her mother, Margaret Greville, who'd died of a broken neck from a fall from a horse seven years ago.

"You're a great deal like Maggie," Alexander was saying. "She, too, was fierce in her convictions. She knew what she wanted, your mother did. She wasn't afraid of life, or of loving."

Jocelyn pressed her eyes shut, afraid she might cry. She wanted so much to be like her mother, and yet she was terrified of tomorrow, of what she might learn of Dash's whereabouts. Would he be hanged for murder? Or would he make it safely to Dover and out of England? Either way, how could she go on without him?

"You're wrong, Daddy," Jocelyn whispered. "I could never be as brave as Mama was."

The two of them stared into the fire then, both silent, both thinking their own private thoughts. Jocelyn's mind was filled with memories of Dash, of his touch, of his scent. She longed for him still, and knew that would be her own silent hell to endure.

He'd tried to warn her, that night at the Fox's Lair. Somehow, Dash had known that if they'd made love, Jocelyn might never be able to forget him. Even though he'd left her a virgin, Dash had been right. Jocelyn couldn't forget him. She wouldn't. He'd brought her too much. She'd known both joy and sorrow in his arms. She'd had a taste of complete freedom and of the bonds of intense feeling.

Wherever Dash was now, he carried a portion of Jocelyn's heart with him.

Five days later, on a cool late-fall morning, Jocelyn bid her father good-bye and climbed into the carriage behind her grandmother. Charles was the last to alight, and his face was animated with excitement.

"To London!" he exclaimed, looking fresh and handsome in a suit of wool. He wore a group of new rings on his hands, and he'd speared his neckcloth with a diamond stickpin. He was clearly prepared to take the teeming city by storm.

Jocelyn, though, was sullen and quiet. She didn't like leaving her father alone with only Randolph for company. Alexander had become moody in the last days before their journey, and Jocelyn had to wonder if indeed he'd cut all ties with the Spencean society.

"He'll be fine, my dear," Amelia said, trying to reassure her granddaughter. "And so will you," she added. "Once we're in London, you'll be too busy to think about all that has happened."

But Jocelyn wasn't so certain. She waved to her father, who stood on the steps, and watched him until he became obscured from her view. "He shouldn't be alone," she murmured.

"And why not?" Amelia asked. "He has the house and the animals to keep him busy, not to mention all of his patients. He'll be fine, Jocelyn."

"Yes, but even so, I wish he could join us."

"Poppycock," Amelia replied, patting her granddaughter's knee. "Your father never could digest the city. He hates all the noise and dirt. He's far happier in the country, running here and there and seeing to his business. Now, turn around, dear girl, and enjoy the scenery. London awaits you!"

Jocelyn did as she was told. She watched as the rolling Cotswolds swept by, and she felt a tug on her heart. These lands had been her home for seventeen years, and yet she'd never felt truly alive until she'd met Dash and had ridden with him along a darkened roadway.

Well, he was out of her life now, and she had to accept the fact. What better place than London to help her forget?

Thirteen

Almost a week after he'd watched Jocelyn walk out of the campsite, Dash found himself on a high hill not far from the Greville house. He sat atop a slab of Cotswold slate and stared intently down at a ribbon of exposed roadway. He barely took notice of the receding hills dotting the distant land and looking like blue-gray humps in the cool light of dawn, nor did he pay much attention to the huddled homes fringing the Greville property. It was the moving carriage, familiar to Dash even from such a distance, that caught and held his attention. Jocelyn was in that coach, Dash knew. He'd made it his business to learn as much about her as he could since she'd left the hideaway camp—but unfortunately, that hadn't been very much.

"Why are you going, Jocelyn?" he whispered to himself. "Why are you going to London?"

"Eh? What's that you just said?"

Dash glanced up at the man who stood a few feet away. Suddenly tense, Dash demanded, "Why the devil is she going to London, Granger? I paid you in gold to bring back information about the girl!"

"That you did," Granger said quickly. "But I told you, Dash, folks around these parts wouldn't say much—especially not about Jocelyn Greville. You'd think the girl owned a duchy the way people clammed up when asked about her! Her friends know she was missing for several days, and now they are rallying around her, not willing to talk about her. You're fortunate I ferreted out the fact that she's headed for London with her grandmother.''

"But why London?" Dash said, getting slowly to his feet as he watched the carriage pull out of sight far below. "What could she possibly have to do in London?"

Granger shrugged his shoulders. "Same as any gentle lady would have to do—enjoy herself."

"I doubt that," Dash muttered.

"Say, you don't think she's going to London to rat on you, do you, Dash? I—I mean the lady wouldn't be so nasty as that, would she?"

Dash scowled. "Why not? I abducted her, didn't I? I robbed her of her jewels, and—" He almost added that he'd very nearly taken her virginity as well, but stopped himself just in time. "Jocelyn Greville has good reason to hate me. I wouldn't be the least bit surprised if she and her grandmother were heading to my uncle's house."

Granger gave a low whistle. "And to think you even did the honorable thing by returning the lady's property to her." Granger shook his head, adding, "It ain't fair, Dash. Not at all."

Dash said nothing. He was thinking about Jocelyn's pendant and her cousin's rings, which he was carrying in his saddle pack. He hadn't returned *those* to her. He knew he should have sent them with Granger along with the letter, but at the last minute Dash had decided against it. For a reason he hadn't yet admitted to himself, Dash wasn't ready to part with Jocelyn's property. Unfortunately, though, his omission of returning her jewels might very well have been the impetus that sent Jocelyn on her way to London. If so, Dash's future was bleak indeed. Not only was he being framed for a murder he didn't commit, but if Jocelyn had an audience with his uncle, then Dash might find himself disinherited.

"Let's go," Dash grumbled.

Granger popped to attention. "Where to?"

"To London, where else?"

"That's a risky thing to do, Dash, and you know it,"

Granger said. "Now, I'm not saying I think you're this Midnight Raider who killed James Keats but—"

"I'm going," Dash said tersely, heaving his still-sore body onto his horse. "You can stay or you can come. It makes no difference to me."

Granger hung his head and kicked at a bit of dust with the toe of his boot. "Well, uh, I, ah—you see, Dash, if you *are* caught, and I'm not saying you will be. But if you are, then I could be hauled to prison right along with you. I've got a family to think of, Dash. I—"

Dash lifted one hand. "Say no more," he said. "I understand. Well, then, I guess this is good-bye." Dash extended his right hand down to Granger. "I was proud to have you ride at my side, friend. Take care."

Granger hesitated. "Damn," he muttered. "I—I can't let you go to London alone."

Dash could see he was putting his old friend in a rotten situation. Knowing what he had to do, he said gruffly, "Then consider this an order; keep your ass in the Cotswolds, Granger, and stay out of trouble."

"But, Dash—!"

"An *order*, Granger. Now, get out of my way. I've a race to win with that coach." With that he nodded to Granger, then gathered up his reins. If he was lucky, he might reach London before Jocelyn did. But then again, with the way his side was hurting, he might not.

Always one to take on a challenge, Dash rose to the occasion and sped away from the slack-jawed Granger with a cloud of dust.

London. Jocelyn couldn't help the flutter of her heart as she peered out her window, gazing upward at the rows of terrace buildings that stretched like gay dollhouses along the street. Jives clicked the weary horses on past the modest "two-up, two-down" houses, which had only two small rooms on each level. Spiked, wrought-iron gates flanked the front doors of each dwelling, and indeed, to Jocelyn, each house looked much like the other. But she didn't care, it was the people who soon caught her interest. *Doz-*

ens of pedestrians swarmed through London Town, walking at a leisurely pace, or clipping along with the quick city strides Jocelyn would come to know. Dozens of colors swam in front of her eyes: deep crimson, the palest pinks, dazzling whites. It seemed fashion reigned on the streets of London. Fine ladies in striped taffeta and beribboned bonnets, others in wonderful satin creations and hats adorned with feathers, walked with an air of knowing their place in life. Even the men, with fancy top hats, appeared to have stepped from the plates of a fashion journal. There were flower girls hawking their wares, and ragamuffin children darting through the parade of pedestrians. And though the scent of the river wasn't far off—and not very pleasant—Jocelyn thought London to be a grand place.

"What do you think?" Amelia asked.

Jocelyn shook her head in wonder. "I'd quite forgotten how alive the city is."

"Then you are pleased you've come?"

Jocelyn nodded. "I think this is what I need, Gran. But then, you always did know what was best for me."

"Poppycock!" Amelia snorted. "I've fallen over my feet too many times to count when it came to raising you and Charles."

Charles, sitting opposite them, grinned. "We've turned out well enough, Gran. You should be proud. Ah, look!" he exclaimed, slightly lifting his walking stick to motion at a shop window they were passing. "Wellington's! Finest leather goods in all the city," he announced. "We'll have to pay the proprietor a visit, Gran. I'm dreadfully overdue for a fresh pair of riding gloves."

Jocelyn rolled her eyes. By her own count Charles had packed at least *five* pairs of riding gloves into his overflowing trunk. He'd even had her sit on the thing so he could latch it shut. Her weight hadn't been enough, and so the both of them had had to trounce atop the trunk while Charles bent forward to snap the latches into place.

"And there's Elsom's baked goods!" Charles crowed, his mouth watering at the sight. "Finest pastries around!" he added.

Jocelyn sat back on the cushions and listened to him point out every tiny shop they passed. Each place was, of course, the very best of its kind. Knowing her visit to London would be filled with her cousin's chatter, Jocelyn gave herself up to his talk and tried to be a good listener as he prattled on and on. Even Amelia appeared exhausted by the time they'd reached the townhouse.

The trio alighted from the carriage, and Amelia and Jocelyn went inside while Charles stayed on the street to inform Jives of the finest alehouses London had to offer.

"Finally!" Amelia declared, removing her gloves after being greeted by her London house staff. "I truly detest that long ride. Binnie will bring us some tea, then you and I can get started on penning notes to my dearest friends."

"Notes?" Jocelyn echoed.

"Of course, dear girl. How will anyone know to invite us to their gatherings if they haven't a clue we're in the city? And of course," Amelia went on, somehow regaining her energy between removing her gloves and opening her mouth, "we'll want to get busy planning Charles's birthday celebration. He'll be nineteen come next Thursday. And you know how miffed he'd be if we didn't *surprise* him."

Jocelyn pretended a tiny shudder. She well remembered the last time the family had overlooked Charles's birthday. That had been seven years ago, and Charles had thrown a fit worthy of a petulant crown prince.

"No, we wouldn't want to forget his birthday," Jocelyn agreed.

"Certainly not, my dear! Now, come along. We've *plans* to make!"

Jocelyn followed her grandmother through the front hall and into an adjacent sitting room. The small chamber, along with the hall and the dining room, took up the front of the ground floor, while the kitchen and Binnie's quarters took up the back.

The narrow sitting room, with its four richly embroidered chairs and two round side tables, was decorated in splendid style. Paneled in cedar and smelling lightly of that wood, the room was enhanced with exquisite gold leaf, which ran between all four corners. The two street-facing windows, which reached from floor to ceiling, were draped with curtains of fine white wool.

Amelia sat down and took a moment to catch her breath before Binnie, the waddling housekeeper, whose girth was wide and full, came in with a silver tray of tea, pastries, and a large stack of notepaper.

Binnie poured them each some tea, then added sugar to Jocelyn's cup.

"Binnie, you remembered," Jocelyn said, surprised.

Binnie beamed. " 'Course I did, Mistress Greville. You haven't been away too long that an old woman would forget."

Amelia reached over and patted her granddaughter's knee, seemingly pleased to know Jocelyn would be kept busy with old acquaintances and new while in London.

The next few hours went by swiftly for Jocelyn. She filled her stomach with Binnie's sugary pastries and delicate tea, and then wrote notes until her hand was cramped.

"That ought to do it," Amelia announced, flicking through the pile of letters they'd addressed. "Oh, dear, I almost forgot one person—or rather two." She clucked her tongue, admonishing herself. "Monty would be absolutely livid to think I'd not invited him to my first gathering of the season."

"Monty who?" Jocelyn asked, settling back in her chair and yearning to kick off her shoes and wiggle her toes. She was exhausted, but she knew better than to say so. Soon enough she'd be able to slip upstairs to the comfort of the guest room.

"Lord Montague Warfield," Amelia said.

Jocelyn nearly slid out of her chair at the name.

But Amelia didn't seem to notice. "Monty's a dear, dear friend of mine. A bachelor he is, after all these years. He never married, but he did claim an heir. What *is* that boy's name? Ah, yes, Dashiell. Haven't seen him in *years*, Jocelyn. He was, let's see. oh, about eighteen the last I saw him. And dashing! Pity that you were only a small child when I met Dashiell. But I daresay I wouldn't have done more than introduce the two of you, for Dashiell was a mischievous boy in his youth, and far too reckless to boot. Anyway, dear girl, I must send word to Monty that we're in the city.''

Jocelyn was barely listening. Lord Montague Warfield's heir was none other than Dash, Jocelyn was certain! My God, she thought, thinking of all the implications. Dash was haunting the byways of England, yet he was of the aristocracy! Her head spun at the realization.

''You intend to invite both men to Charles's surprise party?'' she asked.

''Indeed,'' Amelia murmured, already setting pen to paper.

Jocelyn's heart leapt at thoughts of seeing Dash again. She'd thought he was out of her life—but then again, Amelia had no idea what Dash was involved in. As far as Amelia knew, Dash was living with Lord Monty, when in reality he'd been camping under the stars and riding the midnight roads.

That night, as she snuggled down in the spacious bed on the second floor of the townhouse, Jocelyn fell asleep remembering the touch of Dash's hands and the fervor of his kisses. She nearly wept at the memory. He'd touched her as no one ever had. He'd shown her what a man and a woman could share, and Jocelyn's body burned to be with him once again. She'd desperately wanted to forget about Dash, but she couldn't. She'd come to London to get away from the memory of him, and yet she found he followed her still.

The next few days were filled with a whirlwind of excitement. In preparation for the celebration, Jocelyn and Amelia journeyed out into the streets of London Town in hopes of purchasing accessories for their yet-to-be-stitched party gowns. Since it was rather warm—at least for late fall—the two decided to walk instead of taking the carriage, and Jocelyn's eyes grew wide as she gazed into the shop windows.

''There's so much to choose from!'' she exclaimed,

thinking of the tailor whom her father employed, who would ride in from London and bring with him fashion dolls for Jocelyn to decide which dresses she would have him create for her. Though her father was only a country physician, Amelia had been born into the landed gentry, and so she more often than not paid the bills for the family.

"Take your time," Amelia said, caught up in the flurry of activity along the streets. "We needn't do all our shopping in one day." Amelia spied a flower girl at the end of the walk and her eyes lit up. "Ah, just what the front hall needs!" she said, and then, telling Jocelyn to browse, scurried down the street to purchase a bunch of wildflowers.

Jocelyn enjoyed her moment of unchaperoned freedom and moved closer to a millinery shop, peering in through the soot-covered window at the display of bonnets. As she was admiring a stylish riding hat festooned with a plume of dyed feathers, she was jostled by a fast-moving man.

"Forgive me," the gent said, nearly toppling Jocelyn to the ground. He was dressed in crumpled clothing and wearing a battered, tall crowned hat with a curled brim. "I'm so sorry! I—I am on an errand of great importance, and I—"

"No harm done. I'm fine," Jocelyn assured the stuttering man. "Truly, I am."

"You're certain?" he asked, not convinced.

"Quite." Jocelyn noticed the handbills in his left hand. "Are you advertising a play, perhaps?" she asked, thinking she and Charles might enjoy a night at the theater.

The man shook his head. "Not at all! This is a grave matter, mistress. Take one," he insisted, shoving a piece of paper in her hands. "And if you have any information about this man, please contact someone at the address below." He sprinted off before Jocelyn could say a word.

"Londoners," Jocelyn muttered, shaking her head. But her blood froze when she read the words on the paper. "Oh, dear God," she whispered, feeling nauseous. In bold script the bill called for the hanging of the Midnight Raider for the brutal murder of James Keats on the fifteenth day of October 1819. Jocelyn's eyes blurred as she read on. A handsome sum was being offered by Frances Keats and by the friends of James Keats. There was also a description of the Midnight Raider—a description that could certainly fit Dash if one had a mind to point an accusing finger at him.

"My dear girl, what's the matter?" Amelia cried, returning to Jocelyn's side and seeing her granddaughter's ashen face.

Jocelyn dropped her hand—and the note—to her side. "Nothing, Gran," she said quickly. "I—I'm feeling a bit under the weather is all. I think it's all the excitement."

Amelia eyed her granddaughter closely, but didn't press the matter. "Do you see anything that takes your fancy?"

"What?"

"The hats, my dear. If you like one, we'll go inside and purchase it."

Jocelyn thought of turning down the offer, but knew very well her grandmother would find it odd that she wished to go home and discontinue their shopping spree. And so, forcing a smile when her heart was tripping with madness, Jocelyn nodded and pointed to the riding hat she'd been admiring earlier.

"What a grand choice," Amelia crowed, and pulled Jocelyn inside the shop.

Three hours and several shops later, Jocelyn found herself back at the townhouse. Charles was teasing Binnie about her plum pudding, while Amelia wandered into the small but luxuriant garden behind the house to "feel a bit of the country," as she put it. So Jocelyn crept upstairs to find some solace. Once she was alone, Jocelyn set the piece of paper to flame and tossed it into the grate in the guest room.

But even though it soon became ashes, Jocelyn knew there were probably a hundred more of those bills circulating through the city. What would happen to Dash if he were caught? Would the authorities decide his description fit that of the Midnight Raider? *Was* Dash the Midnight Raider? And if so, had he truly killed James Keats? Oh, God, Jocelyn thought, Dash would certainly be hanged.

Jocelyn tried not to think about the horrid possibilities. Her head pounded and she felt sick with grief. Life could be cruel and unfair—she'd realized that long ago when her mother had been taken from her life so swiftly. Also, Jocelyn had to remind herself that Dash had taken up a life of thieving. It mattered not that he stole to help the poor. He was a highway robber, pure and simple, and as such was prey to the hard fist of justice.

But Jocelyn couldn't believe that Dash had actually murdered a man. No, the image was too gruesome to contemplate.

By dinnertime Jocelyn had come to no conclusions. She both damned Dash and worried over his safety. She forced herself to eat Binnie's rich stew and flaky biscuits, and then to eat a small portion of her luscious plum pudding. Binnie had gone to great lengths to make both Jocelyn's and Charles's favorite foods. Afterward, when Charles joined Jives for a night of fun, Amelia and Jocelyn retired to the sitting room.

Jocelyn halfheartedly read through the replies they'd received from Amelia's friends.

"We've heard from nearly everyone, my dear," Amelia preened. "I take it my good name has not been tarnished by my lengthy stay in the country."

"You know you're a divine hostess, Gran," Jocelyn said. "Why *wouldn't* your friends respond?"

"Who knows?" Amelia said absently, still thumbing through the notes she'd received. "People can be most mysterious—not to mention quarrelsome."

Jocelyn lifted the last note of the pile. It was sealed with a heavy, embellished crest of wax. Flicking it open with Amelia's silver letter knife, Jocelyn read the contents.

My dearest Amy, it said in flourishing script. *Welcome home. I will indeed join you on the tenth. How could I not? And yes, Dashiell shall be with me. My heir is a man*

*in his own right now, and I fear I shall be competing with
him for your attention. Forever and always yours, Monty.*

Jocelyn stared long and hard at the words. Monty . . .
Lord Montague Warfield. He was coming to the celebration—with Dash! Jocelyn's chest tightened. She'd seen the
guest list often enough to know that the elite of London
would soon be flowing in and out of the townhouse. But
surely none of those people would think Dash to be the
Midnight Raider, would they?

Still, Jocelyn felt the urgent need to warn Dash about
the handbills and the hazy description given on them. She
had to do something.

And then it hit her. Glancing up at Amelia, she said,
"Gran, what would you think of making Charles's birthday party a masquerade?"

Amelia blinked, clearly astonished. "Well, I—I hadn't
though of that, dear. Why, we've already made plans for
our gowns, and the decorations . . ." Her voice trailed
off, her watery blue eyes lighting with all sorts of possibilities. "Charles *would* like that, wouldn't he?" she said.

Jocelyn nodded eagerly. "We could stage a grand affair.
Binnie could serve the guests dressed like Nell Gwyn—
given her penchant for the theater—and you and I, we
could be anyone we wanted to be."

"You'd like that?" Amelia questioned, still debating the
idea.

"Oh, yes. And you know Charles! He'd be beside himself with glee thinking up a costume. We could tell him
we'd been invited to a masked ball, and while he was
dressing we could be down here greeting our guests!"

Amelia sat back in her chair. "I like the idea," she
finally said. "Yes, indeed!"

And so, even before they'd finalized plans for a secret
birthday celebration, Jocelyn and Amelia began to pen another batch of notes, informing all that it would be a costume party.

That night Jocelyn fell into bed exhausted, but feeling
hopeful. If Dash *did* come to the party, he would at least
be incognito—and then Jocelyn could warn him about the

description of the Midnight Raider that was circulating the streets of London.

On the sprawling lawns of the Warfield estate, nearly an hour out of London, Dash stood talking with his uncle.

"I'm not interested," Dash declared, balancing a huge falcon on his gloved hand and feeding the bird a snack of raw meat. "I know enough of those gatherings your friends call parties, Uncle Monty. I'd be bored to tears even before the punch bowl was set out."

"What's the matter, boy?" Lord Montague Warfield argued. "Have you so had your fill of frolic in the past six months that you can't at least do your uncle a favor and join me for a simple costume party?"

Dash laughed, rubbing his left forefinger along the beak of the falcon. "You mean cosset your cronies, don't you, Uncle? I'm getting too old for that."

"Pah! You're not too old until I say you're too old. Now, let the damned bird free and give me your answer. I haven't got all day, boy!"

Dash kept the falcon close to his hand. "Worried he might peck at you? He's tame enough, Uncle Monty. You should know, you trained him yourself."

"*I* didn't do the dirty deed, Prentiss did. Now, do as I say and set him free. He's glaring at me, I swear."

Dash chuckled, knowing his uncle's peevishness when it came to birds of prey. Lord Montague Warfield couldn't stand the sight of blood—let alone his own blood. "Have it your way," he said, forcing the bird from its perch. The falcon gave a thunderous pounding of its wings, then careened straight up into the air and out of sight. Dash watched it for a minute, coveting the bird's complete freedom, then pulled the heavy gauntlet from his hand.

"Now, what's this about some silly surprise party, Uncle? Give me details, else I'll be forced to decline."

"No, you won't" Montague expounded. "You're invited, you'll be there, and that's that. Had you any plans?"

Dash lifted his brows. "Would it have mattered had I said yes?"

"Not in the least," Montague shot back in his usual brusque manner. "There have been some foul rumors circulating about you, and I want them to end. If you hadn't gone tearing off to meet with those Radicals, none of this would have come about."

"I had to go, Uncle Monty," Dash said with force. "And you know why."

"Of course *I* know, but must the capitalists and the aristocracy know as well? Dammit, boy, you can't walk in our circles as well as brush elbows with the poor. You know that."

"Am I to turn a deaf ear to their pleas, Uncle?" Dash demanded. "It was barbaric for Parliament to enact the Corn Law. These people cannot afford such high rents, and now they can't even afford bread for their families!"

"I know the situation well, Dash," Montague said, his tone softening somewhat. "But you have to understand what a fine line we walk. I can speak for these people, but only if I keep my good name with my peers. You must be patient."

Dash's features turned hard. "Patience, as you know, has never been one of my virtues."

"I know that, boy, but if you are to become a champion for the people, then you must learn how to deal with the Tory Cabinet. It's as simple and as complicated as that. I want you to keep your opinions to yourself—at least until all this hullabaloo about the Midnight Raider has died down. Why, people are actually whispering that you might be the Midnight Raider! Tell me it's rubbish, boy!"

Dash said nothing. He couldn't lie to his uncle, and yet he very well couldn't tell him the truth. To do so would place Montague in a precarious situation.

Montague shook his head, muttering about Dash's reckless nature. But he didn't ask him again whether or not Dash was indeed the Midnight Raider. And that, Dash knew, said all there was to say.

Montague turned away from the sprawling southern lands of the Warfield estate and headed back for the main house. Dressed in light wool trousers and sporting a coat that billowed about his heavy thighs, a pristine shirt of lawn beneath, he appeared a country gentleman who'd run into a lofty lord. And indeed, that is what Montague Warfield was. He'd found his niche in the upper echelons of London and had found a place in Parliament for himself. He had money to burn, but rarely did so. He was a man of fierce beliefs. With little time to squander, Lord Monty went from pillar to post in a flurry of excitement. He was an exacting man who expected respect from both employees and peers. But he never judged a man prematurely, and Lord Monty always had room in his big heart for the less fortunate of the world.

Dash walked alongside his uncle. "So whose house shall we grace this week?" he asked, knowing he and Monty would not be discussing the Midnight Raider ever again. His gunshot wound had very nearly healed, though it still smarted. But he was careful not to let on to his uncle about his discomfort of tramping across the wet lands of the Warfield estate.

Montague was eager to give a detailed listing. "The Barringtons' on Monday, the Watleys' on Tuesday. Wednesday we've a card game in the west wing, and Thursday we shall appear at the townhouse of Amelia Greville. You remember her, don't you?"

Dash felt his stomach do a crazed flip-flop. "Greville? Can't say as I do."

"Of course you do, boy! You met Amelia before you went off on your grand tour!"

Dash didn't remember, which didn't surprise him. In those days he'd gone through life on the tailcoat of his uncle and hadn't given a whit about whom he was meeting. Wouldn't it be just his luck not to recall meeting a Greville, of all people!

"Amelia's in the city for the social season," Montague went on. "She's planning a surprise birthday party for her grandson, Charles, and I expect you to be there." As if to add bait, Montague added, "I hear she has a fetching granddaughter, quite unattached at the moment."

Dash's ear pricked. Ah, so Jocelyn had no beau—or

beaux, for that matter. This tidbit of information pleased
Dash no end. But, though he hated to admit it, Jocelyn
was one person he didn't trust himself to be near. He'd
charged his way back to London, half-crazed with the
worry that he'd find Jocelyn filling his uncle's ear all about
his nefarious deeds. Dash had been definitely surprised to
find that the house hadn't fallen down atop him when he'd
come tearing through the front door.

But was Jocelyn merely biding time until she could meet
with Lord Montague? Was she even now planning what
tales she would tell? He'd scorned her that morning at the
Fox's Lair. He'd hurt her, he knew. Would she retaliate by
telling Monty all she knew? Dash had no idea . . . and
yet he knew he could do no less than find out.

"Are you interested, boy?" Montague was demanding.

Dash pulled himself from his reverie. "I'm always interested when it comes to the fairer sex, Uncle Monty."

"I'm not talking about some quick roll in the hay with
a street-wisened doxy!" Montague huffed. "Curb that
roving appetite of yours and listen well. Amelia Greville
is a dear friend of mine. I'll not be enduring any of your
foolish pranks in her presence."

"Pranks?" Dash said. "I take offense."

"The hell you do. You enjoy courting trouble wherever
you go. You always have. I'll never forget the wild antics
you and Laney undertook. How is he doing, anyway? Has
he settled down yet? Found decent employment?"

"You know Laney," Dash said. "He's always been a
wanderer."

"Pity. He could have *been* somebody. But you, Dash,
you always were the brightest and the best. One day this
will all be yours." He spread his bulky arm wide to en-
compass all of the Warfield estate. "I'll go to my grave a
happy man knowing you will carry on the Warfield name."

Dash saw the pride in Lord Monty's eyes, and the shim-
mer of tears there as well—and somewhere, in Dash's soul,
there came a squeeze of deep grief. What would happen
should Uncle Monty know of Dash's sins? The damage,
Dash knew, might very well be irreparable.

Quietly Dash said, "You know that I only want to please you, don't you?"

Montague clapped one arm about Dash's shoulders. "I know that, boy. I always have." After a few steps he said, "Now, are you going to Amelia's party or not?"

"I thought I didn't have a choice." Dash said.

"You don't, but a true politician never lets on to that fact."

Dash laughed, feeling closer to Montague than he had in a very long time. "I'll come," he said lowly, "if it will make you happy." Dash couldn't refuse his uncle. He would just have to worry about Jocelyn when the time came.

"Good! Then the matter is settled."

As they reached the stable yard and Dash headed inside the stables to check on his mount, Monty said, "Oh, and one last thing, boy. I almost forgot to mention it. Amelia is planning a masked ball, so come in your finest costume. We won't be removing our masks until midnight."

Dash felt as though a weighted chain had been lifted from his shoulders. A costume ball! What could be better? He'd be able to move in and out of the crowd and none would be the wiser. And if he took care in choosing his garments, perhaps not even Jocelyn would know he was within her reach.

Suddenly Dash's day was looking up. He began to whistle as he stepped inside the cool, cavernous stable. He couldn't wait for the party—and for his chance to woo Jocelyn not as the Midnight Raider, nor even as Dashiell Warfield, but as another person entirely!

Fourteen

On the day of the party Jocelyn was up early—much to Binnie's distress—and sending the harried Jives off to fetch the gown she'd requested for that evening. The seamstress had fussed and mussed about not having enough time to create the exact costume Jocelyn had ordered, but after a large sum of money had been thrust her way, the woman was only too eager to clap her hands and whip her sewing girls into a frenzy.

"It just isn't proper!" Binnie was saying, watching as Jocelyn gulped down a large breakfast of mouth-watering ham and eggs. "Mornings are for sportsmen and servants, not a lady as fine as yourself."

"Hush, Binnie," Jocelyn said with a smile. "And pass me that jam of yours. I think I'll have another biscuit."

Binnie clicked her tongue and spread jam onto the still-warm biscuit before Jocelyn had a chance to do the deed. "I've never seen you eat so much, child."

"I have a great many things to get done this day, Binnie. I need my strength." She popped the biscuit into her mouth and washed it down with fresh buttermilk.

Actually, Jocelyn was anticipating the long night ahead. She would have to play hostess alongside her grandmother, and Jocelyn knew such niceties would take up much of the evening. But she planned to corner Dash before midnight, and then hoped to spirit him out of the townhouse and tell him about the handbills. Jocelyn was almost certain she'd be able to pick Dash out of the crowd. They'd been too intimate for her not to notice him.

Her bright mood started to darken, though, when she thought about *how* intimate. Dash had hurt her deeply with his abrupt dismissal of her. He'd said they had no future, and that he would not marry her. Cruel words, considering how easily Jocelyn had fallen into his arms. He might just as well have taken his knife and twisted it in her heart.

So why am I so eager to help him? she wondered. But she knew the reason.

Somehow, Jocelyn had allowed herself to fall in love with the rogue Dashiell Warfield.

Evening soon fell across the city. The constant clatter of horses' hooves clipped atop the pavements outside the townhouse as sedans, smart carriages, and huge gilded coaches drew past. The lamplighters were busy lighting the gaslights along the streets, and a warm yellow glow seeped in through the window of Jocelyn's bedchamber.

She lay on her bed and watched as shadows played upon the walls. She hadn't lit her own lights. She wasn't yet ready to do so. She'd spent the morning seeing to all the little details of the party and trying her best to keep the curious Charles busy with silly errands. The afternoon had been filled with a long and not-so-leisurely tea with both Amelia and Charles, and it hadn't been until after four that Jocelyn had found a moment to herself. Her costume had been delivered promptly at five-thirty, and Jocelyn had scurried to her room with the huge boxes, anxious not to let her grandmother see the creation for fear Amelia would send the outfit right back to the dressmaker. It had been almost impossible to keep the costume a secret.

"I *will* wear the costume," Jocelyn said aloud to herself, hoping to find courage now that the hour had drawn near. It was one thing to plan such an outrageous scheme, and quite another to carry it through.

A knock at the door startled her. "Time to get dressed, Missy!" came Binnie's voice. "Your grandmother wanted me to help you."

Jocelyn got up quickly and opened the door. "That won't be necessary, Binnie. I can manage on my own."

Binnie was dismayed. "But you can't be dressing yourself! It isn't proper! And who will help you with the hooks and chemise?"

Jocelyn knew better than to inform Binnie that her garment had only a few hooks—and certainly not in the expected places—or that she wouldn't be wearing a chemise. Instead, trying to remain polite, Jocelyn said, "I'll manage, Binnie. If I need your assistance, I'll call you. Now, why don't you go help Gran? She's been nervous all day about this gathering. Go on. Scoot."

Binnie pursed her lips, but did as she was told.

Jocelyn heaved a sigh of relief and closed the door. Lucky for Jocelyn that Binnie was first and foremost a loyal servant. The woman would never think to argue with her employer's granddaughter.

"Well, I guess it's time," Jocelyn whispered, and took a deep breath before heading toward her dressing table. Once there, she lit the lamp and began to brush out her long coppery waves. She'd washed her hair with lemons earlier, and now the fresh scent hung lightly in the air. The lemons had brought out the golden highlights of her hair, and the strands shimmered in the glow of the lamp. Needing to tame the wild curls, Jocelyn dipped her hand in a pomade jar and smoothed a light oil between her palms, then ran her fingers through her tresses. That done, she swept her hair back and slightly to the left side, then braided the strands into a thick plait. She opened a tiny box that had come with the costume and lifted out several tiny stickpins with jeweled tips. She pierced a few into the braid, then put the remainder in strategic places throughout her hair. The effect was like a sprinkle of shimmering diamond tears.

Next Jocelyn began to apply her makeup. At first her hand wasn't steady, but she forced herself to calm down, and soon she found she was caught up in creating the precise effect she wanted. With a tiny brush she applied a very delicate line of kohl at the base of her lashes—not much, but enough to bring out the emerald of her eyes. From the many jars and pots she applied a light brush of powder, and then a gentle smudge of rouge to her high cheekbones. A clear gloss on her lips, and she was done.

Jocelyn stared at her image in the looking glass. No longer did she appear a young miss from the country, but rather a striking woman of the world. Her eyes were bright with excitement, and the diamond tears winked as she turned her head to one side and then the other.

Pleased, Jocelyn got up and walked toward the gown she'd spread across two chairs at the far side of the bedchamber. Slipping her robe to the floor, she stood in only her flesh-colored stockings, which were affixed to garters about her thighs. She felt sinful even before putting the dress on. Again, Jocelyn took a deep breath for courage, then put the costume on.

A dazzling creation of white silk, the dress had been fashioned to resemble the classic statues of Greece and Rome. Sleeveless, and caught at each shoulder with a gilded leaf of purest gold, the white, sheathlike silk whispered down over the curves of her body, fitting Jocelyn like a second skin. If not for the extra material that flowed to the floor beneath the leafed clasps, the gown would have been scandalous. But the added material gave a look of layers. Jocelyn tied a gold-colored rope about her slim waist, the ends of which were tassled and hung down nearly to her knees. Satin slippers, with a slight heel, elbow-length gloves, and a white, diamond-studded half-mask completed the outfit. She would wear no jewelry.

Fully attired, Jocelyn stood nervously in the middle of the room and reminded herself that it was a costume party, after all. Guests would come as whoever they chose to be, and what would it matter if Jocelyn had chosen to portray a Grecian goddess?

Heads would certainly turn, no doubt about it, Jocelyn knew. But she wanted only one man's attention this night, and that was why she'd commissioned this particular costume. She remembered only too well Dash's hoarse whisper upon awakening and finding her standing naked at the foot of his bed. He'd called her a goddess—and Jocelyn was determined to remind him of that moment.

She would, in this outfit, call to his mind all they'd shared—and had *almost* shared—in that room at the Fox's Lair. Dashiell Warfield would soon learn she was not a woman to be toyed with and then set aside!

Her purpose renewed, Jocelyn headed downstairs.

Thirty minutes into the party Jocelyn had still not spotted Dash in the crowd of shepherdesses, cavalrymen, knights in full armor, and several men dressed even as sailors. She frowned, wondering if he'd decided not to come, or worse yet, had been waylaid by the authorities.

"What's the matter, dear?" Amelia asked, coming up beside Jocelyn. "Aren't you enjoying yourself?"

Jocelyn looked over at her grandmother. Dressed as a Spanish lady, complete with high ruff and full farthingale, she looked divine, but a bit stiff.

She shook her head at Jocelyn. "I don't know how those women endured such costumes!" she whispered. "But this was the best I could do what with all the other preparations to be taken care of. But you, Jocelyn, you look simply smashing!"

Jocelyn felt a tiny blush cover her cheeks. "You—you're not shocked?"

"Certainly not! I'm pleased, in fact. How like you to commission a costume that would not be repeated. And you've that mischievous spark in your eyes, dear girl. Have you perhaps spied a gentleman in the crowd who takes your fancy?"

"No, Gran, I haven't."

Amelia took her granddaughter's hand in hers. "Ah, well, the night is young yet. Come, I want you to meet someone. I know there's to be no exchanging of names until the unmasking, but I just can't wait."

Jocelyn followed Amelia to the sitting room, where she found herself face to face with none other than Lord Montague Warfield. Outfitted as the infamous Henry VIII, Montague Warfield looked kingly in knee-length trousers

and a rich vest with its line of fur and flashing jewels along
the sleeves. He wore a heavy crested chain about his neck
and a jewel-adorned hat that sat upon his round head.
Three rings flashed on his right hand—one looking very
familiar to Jocelyn. It was of course, upon closer inspec-
tion, the Warfield family crest.

"Ah, it is indeed a pleasure to meet you again," Lord
Monty said, placing a chaste kiss to Jocelyn's outstretched
hand. "I feel as if I know you, for in her letters Amy
writes frequently of you."

Jocelyn lifted one brow at Lord Monty's pet name for
her grandmother.

Amelia tapped her fan atop Monty's shirtsleeve. "Now,
where is that boy of yours, Monty? I thought he was to
accompany you."

"As did I!" Monty said. "Dashiell is a constant source
of pride and agitation for me, as well you know. He should
have arrived by now. Can't say as I know what the devil
he's up to."

"I'd hoped he would be here to help surprise the guest
of honor," Amelia replied. "Charles should be here any
minute. We sent him off with Jives, and he was all aflutter,
thinking he and Jives were to enjoy a quick drink at one
of the taverns before meeting us. Won't he be in a snit
when he sees Jives brings him back to his own doorstep?"
Amelia glowed with anticipation just as loud a clanging
arose on the pavement outside. "Ah, that must be Jives
now. I told him to ring his bell as he came near." Amelia
then clapped her hands and gained the attention of her
guests. "They're here!" she cried. "Everyone into place.
Binnie! Douse the lights in the hall!"

Jocelyn was propelled to a spot near the door of the
drawing room, Lord Monty at her heels. Silence fell
through the townhouse as the partygoers got into position
and waited patiently.

Beside her, Jocelyn could hear Lord Monty's heavy
breathing, and wondered if the man was going to swoon.

"Are you all right?" she whispered.

"Right as I'll ever be," he managed to say in between

deep breaths. "It's my heart, I'm afraid—not as strong as it used to be. But not to worry, Mistress Greville, I'll not be falling dead at your feet."

Jocelyn smiled at his show of humor, but her worry didn't dissolve. "Are you . . . are you concerned about Dash?" she chanced.

She felt the man stiffen. "I'm always concerned about him. He's a reckless sort, forever taking off on some wild scheme."

"So I've heard," Jocelyn replied.

"You've met him?" Lord Monty asked.

Jocelyn hesitated a moment before answering. "Yes," she said. "Briefly. I was intrigued by his . . . intensity."

Montague gave a short laugh which sounded pained. "Intense, eh? Yes, he's that, all right."

Jocelyn heard the clank of metal links as Montague clutched at his chest. He wheezed heavily.

"Sir," Jocelyn said quickly, "shall I fetch you a physician? You sound as if—"

"As if I'm expiring? No, no, I'll be right as rain in a moment or two. My chest feels tight, is all. Nothing out of the ordinary, though. I haven't many days left, but I'll not be dying until I've seen to a few last details. I'm fine, mistress."

Jocelyn didn't have a chance to reply, for the front door was swung open then and Charles came bounding inside, screeching at the top of his lungs about the scatterbrained Jives and how the man didn't know if he was coming or going.

"Surprise!" a chorus of voices yelled.

The lights were lit, and Charles, pink-faced and slack-jawed, stood amidst a crowd of costumed guests.

"Gran! What a supreme schemer you are!" Charles crowed, clapping his hands together. He beamed, loving the moment. "I hadn't guessed! And here I'd thought you'd forgotten my birthday!"

Amelia hugged her grandson, then drew him into the heat of the gathering. "Forget your birthday? Nonsense, my dear boy! Now, come into the dining room and have the first glass of punch. We've a thirsty group here.''

Charles laughed, delighted, as he offered his grandmother his arm, then led her into the dining room, where the table was laden with delicacies and drink.

Jocelyn watched them go, then turned her attention to Lord Monty. He appeared flushed in the glow of the lamps. ''Why don't you sit down?'' she offered. ''And I'll get you something cool to drink.''

''No need to fuss over me, mistress. I'm fine now. Too much excitement is all.''

But Jocelyn wouldn't take no for an answer. She helped Monty to a chair and then went for the promised glass of punch. Charles was sipping a glass of the stuff when Jocelyn entered the room.

''You little conspirator,'' he said to Jocelyn, winking in mischief. ''You certainly pulled the wool over my eyes. And Jives! I thought the man was losing his mind. He took me for a turn down the Mall, then back up it once again before I was forced to lean out the window and demand what he was up to.''

Jocelyn smiled at the thought of poor Jives getting an earful from Charles. ''We told him to keep you entertained for an hour or two.''

''That he did,'' Charles replied, shaking his blond-haired head. He leaned closer to her and whispered, ''You're putting the guests into apoplexy with that costume of yours. If Alexander could see you, he'd be in a rage!''

Jocelyn pulled back, saying, ''Gran says I look smashing.''

''Gran, as we both know, is a bit too free-spirited for her own good.''

''I *like* what I'm wearing.''

''Do you also like instigating a riot?''

''Tsk, tsk, Charles, this is your birthday celebration. Loosen that cravat of yours and enjoy yourself.''

He harrumphed noisily, but Jocelyn knew he was teasing her all the same. With two glasses of punch in hand, she moved back into the drawing room. Lord Monty appeared to have regained his composure, for he was deep in conversation with a man in a devil costume.

"Nasty rumors, they are!" Lord Monty was saying. "Not an ounce of truth to them!"

"So you say, but either way, Montague, we must take heed. It wouldn't do for the Tories to get wind of this. Dashiell hasn't shown his face for weeks. How is he to speak for himself when he's nowhere to be found? It bodes ill for him, I say."

Jocelyn stepped beside the men and handed Montague his punch, then offered the other man the second glass.

Montague thanked her, then nodded toward the horned man near him. "Lord Barrington, this is Mistress Greville, Amy's granddaughter."

Lord Barrington sketched a bow, taking the glass of punch. "A pleasure," he said, his tone softening as he gazed at Jocelyn.

"Is there trouble?" Jocelyn asked brazenly, knowing very well they'd been talking about Dash. Jocelyn was determined to learn as much as she could about Dash's problems.

The stately Lord Barrington cleared his throat, clearly caught off guard by Jocelyn's question. But Lord Monty didn't hesitate.

"Nothing that can't be dealt with," Montague said quickly. "There are a few people spreading vicious rumors about my heir. Indeed, your own ear might be bent with some outrageous untruths about Dashiell this night. I'll warn you now to turn a deaf ear to the stories, mistress."

Jocelyn, never one to hold her tongue, and also knowing Montague was on Dash's side, said, "I've already heard some of those rumors. But I'll never believe that Dash murdered anyone."

Lord Barrington nearly choked on his punch. "Good Lord, Monty!" Barrington exclaimed. "What does this young lady know of Dash?"

Monty stared intently at Jocelyn. "I'm not certain. Mistress?"

Jocelyn moved closer to the two men and lowered her voice. "I know there are handbills circulating the city—handbills that have a description of the Midnight Raider. The description could fit Dash, as well as dozens of other dark-haired men. I believe if someone wanted to do Dash harm with this description, they could."

"Say no more!" Lord Barrington said hastily. "To what channels are you connected?"

"I told you she's Amy's granddaughter," Monty interrupted.

"Ah, then that explains a great deal," Barrington replied. "Well, what else have you heard, mistress? Have you any idea where Dash is these days?"

Jocelyn felt as though she'd shoved her foot firmly into her mouth. But Monty again came to her rescue, saying, "Dash has returned home, and he's assured me that he had nothing to do with any murder."

Jocelyn could see clearly that Monty was not telling the truth, for his breathing quickened again and he passed one hand across his chest. Lord Barrington, on the other hand, seemed to take Monty's word at face value.

"Good for him—and for you," Barrington whispered, and then, forcing his mood to lighten, added, "Enough of this kind of talk. We wouldn't want to start people buzzing. We want the rumors to die down, not flare up again."

"Quite right," Monty added quickly. The men then talked of lesser issues, drawing Jocelyn into their conversation.

Jocelyn spent the next fifteen minutes chatting with the gentlemen, and though the topic of conversation shifted from her country life, and then to what Jocelyn and her grandmother had been doing since arriving in the city, Jocelyn could feel a camaraderie develop. She knew both Lord Barrington and Lord Monty were fiercely loyal to Dash, and she admired their devotion. She learned, by catching tiny details, that Lord Barrington, a member of the Tory Cabinet, was not a staunch conservative, but rather open to the views of the Whigs and the Radicals. But where Dash and his followers were bent on seeing quick reform in the government, both Lord Barrington and Lord Monty realized that steady, yet tiny victories would lead to social change.

Jocelyn genuinely liked both men. She was pleased to think Dash had grown up under their tutelage.

Later, as she threaded her way through the crowd and made polite conversation with her grandmother's friends, Jocelyn couldn't help but wonder about Dash and his past. He'd been raised amid wealth and title, but Jocelyn suspected that Dash had known hardship at some point in his life. And Laney Braden? How had he come into Dash's life? The two men had been close friends at one point, she knew. They'd fought like brothers that long-ago night at the campsite. But if Dash had lived at the Warfield estate and been schooled at the finest institutions, then how had he come to be so close to Laney?

The evening wore on. The stroke of midnight was but an hour away, and still Jocelyn had seen no sign of Dash. Jocelyn retrieved her scarlet cloak, then wandered out into the small garden at the back of the house, needing to get some fresh air. A few couples sat upon the benches there, bathed in the flickering lights of the lamps. It was a cool night, but not bitterly cold.

Inside the house the musicians, after a short respite, returned to play, and the few couples left the garden to enjoy the music. Jocelyn stood alone near the back wall, listening to the merriment flow outside. She could hear her cousin's loud voice as he began to tell one of his famous stories, and she smiled. Charles was indeed enjoying himself.

From behind her the garden door was forced open. Jocelyn was startled by the sound, for no one but family and staff used the exit. Thinking it to be Jives coming in for yet his fifth glass of punch before he headed to a chophouse for a late supper, Jocelyn didn't get alarmed.

"Greetings," a low raspy voice whispered.

Certainly not Jives!

Jocelyn turned about. Standing just inside the garden gate was a tall, striking gentleman. He wore a flowing black cloak that was tossed carelessly back atop his shoulders and showed to great advantage the leather military jerkin beneath, and the lethal-looking sword strapped about his waist. Atop his black-haired head sat a dashing plumed military hat. It was cocked at an angle that lended him a rakish air. His breeches were cut off at the knee, and his boots, extremely wide at the top and folded down, were spurred. He appeared to be a swashbuckler who'd stepped out of the pages of a history text.

Jocelyn stared at the man with interest. She wished he weren't wearing a full-face mask, wished it very much, in fact, for she would have liked to view him fully.

Finding her voice finally, she asked, "Are you perhaps searching for a castle to storm?"

The man laughed lowly. "A London townhouse will do nicely."

Jocelyn smiled. "Then I must warn you, sir, there are six cavalrymen and three sea captains, not to mention the four knights in full armor, inside this house. At least," she added, "by last count there were."

"Then the lady is well protected."

"If indeed I need protection."

The man nodded, as if to applaud her show of spunk. His eyes—of indiscernible hue beneath the mask—swept down her lithe form. "It appears I have intruded upon a goddess," he whispered. "But which one? Are you Greek or Roman?"

The night, filled with shadows and a whispering coolness, seemed made for mystery, and Jocelyn decided to play along. It was a masquerade, after all. "I am Aphrodite," she said.

"Greek, then. The goddess of love . . . and beauty."

"And you, are?" she asked, her heart thrilling at the sound of his raspy voice.

The man held lightly to the hilt of his sword. "I am a wanderer, a man with no country to call his own."

"And do you always enter a home by way of the back?"

He shrugged. "I detest crowds."

"Then you made the proper choice, for as you can see, we are the only ones in the garden." She motioned behind her, then turned a nervous smile to the man. Their banter intrigued her, and the fact that they both wore masks made the exchange that much more interesting. But Jocelyn knew better than to be alone with the stranger. He could indeed be exactly as he claimed—a wanderer who had perhaps heard about the informal gathering and decided to pick a few pockets while getting a free meal. Jocelyn had heard of such goings-on.

But even though she thought of all of this, Jocelyn was loath to turn the man away. There was something about him, some indescribable essence of the man, that drew her toward him as a moth to a flame.

So thinking, she asked, "Would you like some punch, or perhaps—"

"I'd like to dance," the man said, startling her with his intensity.

Her nervousness increasing, Jocelyn said, "Here?"

"Here."

Slowly the stranger reached up to undo the inner cords of his cloak, then slung the garment over his shoulders. That done he said, "May I?" He motioned to her own cloak. "I would hate for you to trip over it."

Jocelyn's breath caught in her throat as the man moved close enough to touch her. He stood there for a moment, just looking at her, and then, when she didn't deny him, he carefully drew the cloak from her shoulders. Clearly taking his time, the man brushed his gloved fingers atop Jocelyn's shoulders, then down the length of her arms before he tossed the cloak behind her. The garment landed with a whoosh atop a box hedge.

Cool air assaulted Jocelyn's bared arms, but she wasn't given a chance to get cold. Before she could think straight, the man took her right hand in his, then drew her to the middle of the stone walkway.

Jocelyn's heart slammed against her rib cage as the stranger placed his left hand lightly to her waist. Wordlessly, they slipped into the rhythm of the music, and soon Jocelyn felt as though she were floating atop the walkway. She stared up at him, trying to imagine what he looked like beneath the leather mask he wore. But the eyeholes were merely slits and gave her no inkling of the man beneath.

"You wonder who I am, don't you?" he whispered in that deep, raspy voice of his that wreaked havoc on her senses.

"Of course I do."

"Don't. This is a night for fantasy." He tipped his face closer to hers, saying, "I am whoever you wish me to be, mistress."

Jocelyn wasn't certain what possessed her, but with the stranger's words, she felt herself relax. Without pause they danced from the end of one song right into the next. And with each passing minute their bodies moved closer together until there was barely room for air to pass between them.

Jocelyn felt bewitched, as though the stranger had cast some spell upon her. But she didn't care. She reveled in the nearness of him, the very scent of him, even. She was drawn to him, certainly, but she knew her interest in him was sparked by more than just the aura of mystery that surrounded him.

There was something familiar in the feel of his lean body. And his eyes, though she couldn't quite see them, seemed filled with a familiar, rakish light. Yes, Jocelyn was intrigued all right. Throwing caution to the wind, she allowed herself to fall into the weblike magic of the night—and of the man.

They danced as though they'd danced together a thousand times before. And in her dreams Jocelyn *had* danced with him. Through a blaze of starlight and sunlight alike, Jocelyn had moved with this man. She'd known his touch and had hovered in the delicious rapture to which he'd taken her.

Oh, God! Jocelyn thought, as the man tightened his hold and drew her closer still, she was drowning in his near-

ness! She had feared she might never see Dash again, and
yet he was here, holding her, touching her . . . or *was* he?

Jocelyn's mind grew fuzzy. She couldn't think straight,
nor did she want to. Should reason crowd in upon her,
she might flee from this enigmatic stranger. But he wasn't
a stranger—at least, she prayed to God he wasn't.

Suddenly nothing was clear to Jocelyn, nothing but her
own tumultuous thoughts and heated desires. She wanted
this man to enfold her in a tight embrace and never let her
go. She wanted to find the pleasure and sheer ecstasy she'd
known so briefly with Dashiell Warfield!

From inside the house Amelia's great clock struck the
hour of twelve. The musicians ceased playing. The chimes
rang loud and long. A cacophony of voices floated out to
the garden as the partygoers removed their masks and
laughed and joked with one another.

The stranger danced Jocelyn into the thick shadows of
the garden. He came to a halt, then gently toyed with the
fringes of Jocelyn's mask. "The witching hour," he whispered. "Time to unmask you."

"And *you*," she replied, sounding breathless to her own
ears.

Carefully he drew the studded party mask from her face.
Jocelyn heard his sharp intake of breath—though she didn't
imagine it was from his surprise. He dropped the mask to
the ground, then began to pull off his gloves.

"So beautiful," he murmured just before touching
warm, calloused fingers to her skin. "So very beautiful."

The words flared a bright memory into her mind.
Jocelyn pressed her eyes shut. She knew the feel of those
hands—knew it intimately, in fact. Her heart did an odd
somersault. Her blood roared through her veins. Searching
her soul for courage, Jocelyn opened her eyes. While he
touched her face, Jocelyn reached up and began to draw
off *his* mask.

"You probably shouldn't do that," he murmured
huskily.

Jocelyn found she was trembling, but didn't care. "Why
not?" she whispered. "I did it once before."

The man stiffened, then cupped her face with his hands, clearly fearing she would slap him away once she'd unveiled his identity. "And lived to regret it, no doubt."

"Is that what you think?" Jocelyn asked.

"Yes," he whispered, his voice sounding tortured.

Jocelyn pulled the mask free, and marveled at the handsome sight. *Dash—the man of her dreams.*

"Then you don't know me at all," she whispered, and before Dash could pull back from her, Jocelyn took his hands in hers, saying, "I've been waiting a very long time for this."

Without further ado, she pulled his hands to the pulse point at the base of her throat, then stood up on tiptoe and kissed him fully on the mouth.

Fifteen

Jocelyn's lips were sweet as nectar, soft and full. Dash groaned low in his throat, wondering if he'd gone mad. He certainly hadn't expected this response from Jocelyn once she'd seen beneath his face mask.

But then again, this was no time for wondering. Before Jocelyn had a change of heart, Dash wound his arms about her and held her fast, returning the kiss. But Dash's kiss wasn't nearly as gentle nor as sweet as Jocelyn's.

He'd been dreaming about this woman for the past few days—had, in fact, wished he could forget about her. But he hadn't forgotten, and now that she was in his arms again, Dash wasn't about to let her slip free.

He opened his mouth and pressed it against Jocelyn's, wanting nothing more than to drink in her essence. His tongue collided with hers, and Dash felt himself being sucked deep into the spell that was totally Jocelyn. Her neck arched back as she opened to him, and Dash had to catch one hand in the tangle of her thick braid to steady himself. He was on fire with wanting. He'd been celibate since he'd lain with her at the Fox's Lair. But it might as well have been a lifetime, for it seemed to Dash that he'd never known true desire before Jocelyn. Nothing could compare with the taste of her, the feel of her.

He ran his fingers through the plait of her luxurious coppery hair, pulling out the bands that held the braid in place. As the locks fell free, Dash could detect the subtle scent of lemons. He remembered well how she'd smelled of such freshness on the first night he'd met her.

"Christ," he muttered, dragging his mouth across hers, "you've staged this whole affair just to plague me, haven't you?

Jocelyn trembled in his arms, which only ignited him further. "Wh—what do you mean?" she murmured.

"You know damn well what I'm talking about. Look at you, dressed in next to nothing and looking like some sleepy-eyed love goddess! I can almost see through this gown . . . your nipples are tight and—"

"Dash!" she said, sounding horrified.

"What?" he demanded. "You and I both know you're wearing nothing beneath this dress. Why, Jocelyn? Had you hoped to seduce someone this night? Tell me, dammit!"

"Y—yes," she managed.

"And?"

"And what?"

"Who, Jocelyn? Who had you hoped to ensnare with your charms?" He thrust his fingers through the long strands of her hair, forcing the studded pins to fall to the ground. "Tell me, Jocelyn. *Who?*"

She pulled her face away from his, but couldn't get free of his tight hold. Her eyes blazed with beryl fire, looking gloriously enraged. "Do I detect a note of jealousy in your voice?" she demanded.

Dash wanted to throttle her just as much as he wanted to toss her to the stone and make long, earth-shattering love to her. "Possibly," he whispered, winding a strand of her beautiful hair about his hand. He drew her face back to his, nearly touching her lips with his mouth. "But I would have you tell me if there is another man who has touched you as I've touched you."

"And what if there is?"

Dash stared at her long and hard. "Then I'll draw my sword from its scabbard and challenge the gent."

"Then you *are* jealous," she nearly cried in victory.

"Yes," he breathed. "I guess I am." And then he

kissed her, slamming his mouth against hers with a force borne of strong desire. She tasted like ambrosia. Dash felt his loins tighten and his head swim with lust. Pulling his hand from her hair, he dropped it to the middle of her back, massaging his way there. She was as tiny as he remembered, and he reminded himself sharply to take care. She wasn't some street-wisened doxy, but a gentle woman who'd known only his touch.

Such a thought only fueled his want for her, though. With haste, he backed her farther into the corner of the garden, both of his hands working up and down her back.

"You've bewitched me," he whispered hoarsely, guiding her down to the ground. "I've thought of nothing save you these past days. How did you manage it? *How?*"

"I—I've done nothing," she murmured, going easily down with him to the cold stones of the garden. "You were the one to turn me away, Dash. I would have gladly stayed with you! I would have—"

"Hush, Jocelyn. Don't say the words."

"And why not? You needn't have pushed me away from you! I would have gone anywhere with you, Dash, done anything!"

He closed his eyes, fitting her lithe body beneath his bulk. He couldn't bear to have her pouring her soul out to him. He'd known well enough that she would have followed him wherever he went. And that was the trouble. He'd been nothing but a thief when he'd met her, yet Jocelyn would have given him her virginity in spite of that ugly fact. And now he was being framed for murder. How could he keep her with him when his own future was fraught with uncertainty?

He couldn't.

"Don't talk," he murmured, cupping her gorgeous face in his hands. "I just want to look at you. I want to remember you just like this, Jocelyn. God help me, but you are the most sensual woman I've ever known. You're honest and sweet . . . and I don't deserve you."

Her eyes darkened with passion. "But you want me."

"Yes," he breathed. "More than anything."

She smiled, a quivering tilt of her pouty mouth. "Then take me," she challenged. "Here. Now." And she arched her back and rubbed her breasts against his chest.

Dash growled, his own desire rock-hard between them. "You *are* a witch," he muttered.

"No, Dash," she answered, and ran her hands down his sides, stopping at the top of his breeches. She slipped her fingers inside, sending him over the edge.

Suddenly Dash wouldn't have cared if they were lying naked in Hyde Park for all to see. He knew only that he couldn't turn her away again. He whispered, "A lady you may be, Jocelyn, but you certainly know how to enflame a man's passion."

She laughed then, a rich, husky sound of pure delight. Dash smiled at the sound, his hands trailing down to pull up the hem of her gown. The sight of her long, coltish, legs, encased in flesh-colored stockings, did little to stop his wayward thoughts, or his wandering hands. He smoothed his hands over her calves, her thighs, and higher still. He nearly swooned as he realized she wore nothing to cover her most intimate spot.

He growled into her ear, caressing her between her thighs. "What if you'd found a different face beneath that mask?" he demanded roughly, arousing her with his fingers. "Would you have allowed another man to touch you like this?"

"I knew it was you," she admitted, breathless.

"When?" he asked harshly. "From the moment I stepped into the garden and took you in my arms?"

Jocelyn didn't answer right away, which enraged Dash. *"When?"*

Jocelyn's breath caught as his fingers pressed inside of her and did unspeakable, wondrous things. "Not—not long after that."

"Liar," he rasped, but suddenly not caring. She was here with him, giving freely of herself, and Dash would have it no other way.

Anxious now to penetrate her softness with more than just his hand, Dash fumbled with the closure of his breeches. "Damn intricate garments those swashbucklers wore. I pity them," he murmured.

"And their ladies," Jocelyn agreed, giggling when she had to help him.

They were like two naughty young teenagers then as they strove to free themselves of their costumes. But Jocelyn's costume had been created for lovemaking, and Dash again both cursed and applauded her forethought.

"You're a vision this night," he whispered. "When I first stole into these gardens and found you, I thought I was dreaming. And when you so easily slipped into my arms and danced with me, I'd thought you'd forgotten about our night together."

"I didn't forget," she murmured. "Oh, hurry, Dash. I don't want this moment to be taken away from me, too!"

He couldn't deny her, he realized. He could deny Jocelyn Greville nothing. He pushed the skirt of her gown higher still and propped himself on his elbows to see her fully. Her garters were just a lacy band, studded with diamonds and holding up her stockings. And at the apex of her thighs was a thatch of red gold—as fiery as the hair on her head. Again, Dash touched her there and watched as Jocelyn's face registered the impact. Her kissable lips parted, showing a flash of pearly teeth as she sighed with desire. Dash lowered himself slowly, touching his mouth to hers and pushing her legs apart. He felt himself grow harder still as he positioned his body and prepared to enter her.

But just then, the doors to the garden burst open and Amelia Greville stepped beneath the far lamplights. "Jocelyn!" she cried. "Jocelyn? Are you out here?"

Jocelyn went rigid. "My grandmother!" she whispered quickly. "Quick, Dash! Let me up!"

Dash didn't have a choice, for Jocelyn fairly pushed him off her body, then shoved her gown down to its proper place. Jumping to her feet and motioning for Dash to stay hidden, Jocelyn called, "Yes, Gran, I'm here. What's the matter?"

"Everything!" Amelia Greville cried. "It's Monty! I—I think it's his heart! Someone just now left to fetch Monty's physician."

Jocelyn shot a worried look toward Dash, then hastened to her grandmother's side. "Where is he?" Jocelyn asked.

"It's such a mess, dear," Amelia replied, looking haggard and full of concern. "He wouldn't stay here, but insisted on being taken to his London house in Grosvenor Square. His carriage just left. Would you see to my guests, Jocelyn? I want to be with Monty. He—he needs me. Jives is pulling the carriage around front."

Dash's blood froze when he heard the news. He listened as Jocelyn assured her grandmother that she'd see to things, and then felt numb as the two women scurried inside the townhouse.

Dash felt as though his past was repeating itself. *Monty dying?* No, he couldn't believe it. This couldn't be happening! He remembered only too well his mother's swift death and knew he couldn't face Uncle Monty's death as well.

Dash straightened his clothes, then swept up his gauntlets and cloak, intending to exit the way he'd come. But Jocelyn came rushing back into the gardens then.

"Wait!" she cried. "Don't leave without me."

Dash turned to face her, demons in his eyes. "Your grandmother needs you here," he said flatly.

"Charles will see to things," Jocelyn said, then took Dash's hand in hers and headed for the back exit. "You needn't face this alone. I'll be with you."

Dash said nothing, only led the way through the door and onto his horse that he'd tied to a post along the street.

Jocelyn felt her insides revolt as Dash helped her atop his saddle. She didn't care that the hem of her gown was hitched up past her knees or that she must look a fright sprinting through the streets of London with Dash. She was thinking only of Monty, Amelia . . . and Dash. Poor Dash.

Jocelyn could see clearly that Lord Monty meant the

world to Dash. She remembered her own mother's death and prayed to God that Monty would live through this.

"He—he'll make it, Dash," she said turning to look at him over one shoulder.

Dash's face was a mask of misery. "I don't know. He's been warned to keep himself calm, but Uncle Monty never was a calm man."

From King Street they raced straight past Hanover Square then straight for Grosvenor Square, where Lord Monty's London house was situated.

The massive, gray-stoned structure was ablaze with lights by the time Dash heaved his horse to a halt and he and Jocelyn dropped to the ground. Dash fairly flew up the front steps, Jocelyn hot on his heels.

Jocelyn didn't even have a moment to take in the grandeur of the place, with its huge front hall and warren of rooms snaking off to the sides. Dash raced up the curving staircase, pulling Jocelyn alongside him.

They found Lord Monty, lying deathly still atop a huge four-poster bed. Amelia stood beside him, holding one hand. A manservant hovered about. Another came and went, bringing extra linen, another pillow—anything he could think of to keep his employer comfortable.

Amelia glanced up at Dash's wild entry, her eyes widening when she saw Jocelyn following.

"How is he?" Dash demanded, moving to the opposite side of the bed and checking Monty's pulse.

Amelia held her questions in check, saying, "He's holding his own."

Dash nodded grimly, wiping the back of one hand across his mouth in a nervous gesture.

"I take it you are Dashiell," Amelia said. At Dash's nod, she added, "Monty was asking about you. He thought you hadn't made it to the gathering."

"I made it," Dash said woodenly.

"Good," Amelia replied quietly. "Monty will be pleased by the news. Tell him you're here, boy. He's been fretting about you."

Dash looked over at Amelia, who gestured toward Monty's motionless form. "Go on," she said again. "He needs to know he has family about. Don't be shy. No good ever came of pulling away from a loved one in need."

Dash appeared flustered, but did as Amelia bade.

Relieved, Amelia turned to Jocelyn, saying, "Let's give them a moment alone, shall we?" With that, she led Jocelyn out of the room, down the hall, and then into a small sitting room that was furnished with a number of chairs and a small settee.

As though she knew her way about, Amelia ordered Jocelyn to sit down and then poured them both several stiff fingers of brandy.

"I think you'll need this," she said, handing a snifter to Jocelyn. "Lord knows I do."

Jocelyn took a long swallow of the fiery brew. "Is—is he going to live, Gran?" she asked quietly.

Amelia stared into her drink. "I don't know," she said frankly. "His heart has been troubling him for years. Indeed, Monty has surprised even himself by living this long."

"But will he live?" Jocelyn asked again, needing assurance from the one woman who had given her that very thing over the years.

Amelia Greville gathered her composure. "It's doubtful," she admitted finally, and there came a mist of tears in her eyes.

Jocelyn stared at the floor, feeling a wave of grief wash over her. "Oh, Gran," she whispered. "I don't know if Dash could handle losing his uncle. He—he's feeling guilty, I know. I believe he thinks it's his fault that Lord Monty has taken ill."

"But it isn't," Amelia soothed. "It's no one's fault. Monty . . . Monty has always been a fiery man." She swallowed the remaining brandy in her glass, then added, "Monty has lived a full and fiery life. He's championed numerous causes and has fought Parliament on many fronts. My dear, he poured his lifeblood into seeing Britain through the war with Napoléon. But like so many of us, he thought England would reap a time of peace and prosperity, when in fact she found herself thrust into a postwar depression. I'm not surprised Monty's heart has acted up now. He—he's been living on the edge for too long.''

Jocelyn felt as though Amelia were speaking of Dash. She wept then, unable to help herself. "I'm so sorry this has happened,'' she whispered. "I'm sorry for Lord Monty, and for Dash.''

"Hush,'' Amelia soothed, moving to comfort her granddaughter. "Monty would not want you to mourn for him, but rather to herald his triumphs! He's a wonderful man, Jocelyn, and I pray to God you have a chance to come to know him.''

"I feel I do know him, Gran. Dash is so like him!''

"Dash,'' Amelia said, recalling the name. "He was the one to abduct you, wasn't he?''

"He—he saved me from—''

"From himself!'' Amelia cut in, clearly not wanting to waste time with falsehoods. "Don't lie to me, Jocelyn. Dash is indeed the Midnight Raider. He stopped you and Charles and then carted you off to his hideaway. I know it's true, so don't give me that wide-eyed look of yours. Really, Jocelyn, I thought what we had between us went deeper than grandmother and granddaughter. I'm your friend, for pity's sake!''

Jocelyn felt like a fool, and a heartless being as well. "You're quite right,'' she whispered. "Dash did abduct me, but only because he had to.''

"Of course,'' Amelia said dryly. "Only because he had to cover his tracks.''

"No!'' Jocelyn cried, then quieted. "All right, so he *did* have to cover his tracks! But he isn't a murderer, Gran! And he only robs from the rich because he wishes to aid the oppressed! He a fine man, Gran. And I—I love him.''

"You what?'' Amelia demanded.

Jocelyn straightened in her chair and met her grand-mother's bold stare head-on. *"I love him,''* she said.

To Jocelyn's surprise, Amelia managed a small smile. "Now, there's the granddaughter I love and respect. Good for you, dear girl! If you love the man, be bold enough to shout it from the rooftops of London. Don't hide your feelings behind propriety and righteousness! Wear your heart on your sleeve and be proud of it! Don't do as I have done and bury it from all and sundry.''

Jocelyn was thunderstruck. ''What are you saying, Gran?''

Amelia's tear-filled eyes flashed. ''What do you think I'm saying?''

''Do you love Lord Monty? Is that what you're trying to tell me?''

Amelia reached for the decanter of brandy. ''Yes,'' she said, sounding angry. ''I do love him. I've loved him for more years than I can count.'' She looked up from pouring another snifter of the stuff. ''But I never told him that, Jocelyn,'' she said, her voice cracking. ''I never once told him, 'I love you Monty. I want to marry you.' And now he's dying, and it doesn't matter a whit.''

Jocelyn got to her feet, feeling closer to her grandmother than she'd ever thought possible. ''But it *does* matter, Gran. Tell him. Now. Tonight!''

Amelia shrugged away from Jocelyn's touch. ''He doesn't need to know of my feelings, Jocelyn. He needs to have Dashiell near him. He needs his family, not an old woman who has long since passed her days of youth.''

''Poppycock,'' Jocelyn whispered, using her grandmother's favorite word. ''You're a sensitive, desirable woman. I'm certain Lord Monty knows it, too. Go to him, Gran. It's not too late.''

For a moment Jocelyn thought Amelia might break down and weep openly. But the woman tossed back the brandy, gathered her composure, and said, ''You're quite right, my dear. I'm being foolish and stubborn and . . . I thank the good Lord that you're here with me to make me see the light.''

And with that, Amelia Greville straightened her farthingale and headed out of the room.

Jocelyn felt her heart swell with pride as she watched her grandmother.

* * *

It wasn't until near dawn that Lord Montague's physician declared Lord Monty would live to see another day. By eight A.M. several of Lord Monty's contemporaries had either sent a servant to inquire about his condition or had come by in person. By nine Dash was cloistered in the great library with several Tories, Lord Barrington among them.

"This is absurd!" Jocelyn said to Amelia, pacing about one of the small guest rooms they'd slept in, though only briefly, through the long night. "What could they possibly be questioning Dash about? They've seen for themselves that Lord Monty is resting peacefully. What more could they want?"

"Clearly a great deal," Amelia said softly. "Do sit down, dear, you're soon to wear a rut in the floor."

"This is serious, Gran! What if—what if those men *know* about Dash? What if they've come to cart him off to London Tower?"

Amelia said nothing.

"Well?" Jocelyn demanded.

"I haven't any answers, dear. If indeed the man is the Midnight Raider—which I gather that he is—then there isn't a great deal we can do for him. Jocelyn, highway robbery is a crime punishable by hanging. Surely Dash realized what he was getting himself into."

Jocelyn turned away, disgusted. She wasn't about to hear a lecture on good and evil. "Well, I for one cannot sit idly by while he's dragged before a hanging judge!" She headed for the door.

"Where are you going?" Amelia demanded.

"Downstairs to get some answers," Jocelyn replied, not looking back. To her relief, Amelia did not follow her. Jocelyn made her way to the huge doors of the library and stood there for a moment, trying to regain her composure.

The doors swung open then, and Lord Barrington stepped out into the hall.

Forgoing pleasantries, Jocelyn asked, "What is going on? Where is Dash?"

Lord Barrington looked weary, as though he'd not slept much throughout the long night. "Calm down, mistress. It will do you no good to worry yourself sick. And lower your voice as well. Dash's position, at the moment, is precarious at best. Come," he said, glancing down the long hall. "We'll find a place to talk privately."

Jocelyn gave in only so much as moving a few feet down the hall. "This is far enough," she said. "I'm not leaving Dash alone in that room a moment longer. His uncle nearly died last night, and he certainly doesn't need to be bombarded with questions at such an early hour."

"I quite agree with you, mistress, but, alas, I haven't much say in the matter." Lord Barrington speared her with a heated glare. "Dashiell is under suspicion for very serious crimes, among them highway robbery and murder."

Jocelyn didn't falter. "I can vouch for his character," she announced.

Lord Barrington was not impressed. "I'm sure you would, mistress. But take heed, it would be most unseemly for you to do so."

"Why?"

Frankly, Barrington said, "As I see it, you're in love with Dashiell, and I'm certain every other man in that room will see it as well. To come to Dash's aid would only sully your good name and perhaps ruin Dash's hopes of a fair trial."

"Trial?" she gasped. "Is he being charged then? I thought you just said he was under suspicion!"

"Calm down!" Barrington demanded once again. "No, he isn't being charged, not yet anyway. But you mustn't interfere. This is an extremely delicate matter. Dash is holding up well in there, but to have you bombard inside and shout about Dash's virtues would be obscene."

Jocelyn fell silent, feeling ridiculous and horribly naive. "I—I only wanted to help," she finally said.

"Then I suggest you return to your townhouse and stay out of Dash's life. If he deems it prudent to contact you, then he will, in his own good time."

''Prudent?'' she echoed. ''But I don't understand.''

''Come now, Mistress Greville,'' he said, straightening to his full height. ''Surely you must have some inkling about what I'm saying.'' When she shook her head, Barrington went on, ''I've had some distressing news through the night—not all of it concerning the Warfields. It appears, mistress, that one Alexander Greville has been consorting with a band of revolutionists.''

Jocelyn's blood went cold.

''That's right,'' Barrington said, his voice dangerously low. ''I've heard about your father and what he's been involved in of late. And that is the very reason why Dashiell should have nothing more to do with you. Whatever your own sympathies, mistress, your father is a Radical. To have you vouch for Dashiell's character would be, as I've stated, obscene. Now do you understand?''

Numbly Jocelyn nodded. ''Only too well,'' she whispered, thinking of her father and his involvement with the Spencean society. ''Thank you, Lord Barrington,'' she managed, then turned away and headed for the stairs.

It felt as though her entire world were crashing in atop her head. Alexander had promised her he'd have nothing more to do with Thistlewood and his group! Had he broken that promise? Or was Lord Barrington's newfound information outdated? Either way, Jocelyn knew she could have nothing more to do with Dash. She couldn't risk even talking with him again. She had to leave him, and quickly.

She found Amelia just coming out of Lord Monty's room.

''How is he?'' Jocelyn asked.

''Resting. How is Dash?''

''I don't know. We have to leave, Gran. Immediately.''

Amelia reached for Jocelyn's hand. ''What's happened, dear?''

Jocelyn pulled her hand away. ''Nothing . . . everything. Oh, Gran, those men downstairs, they're questioning Dash about his whereabouts of late. I fear they might know he's the Midnight Raider, but they don't understand why he's done what he's done. And I could never believe that he murdered a man!'' She took a deep breath, whispering, ''It's such a mess. L-Lord Barrington just told me that he knows Daddy has been involved with Thistlewood and the Spencean society. Don't you see, Gran?'' she nearly cried. ''That means you and I must be under suspicion as well! We can't stay here. To do so would be to put Dash and Lord Monty in a very difficult position.''

The undauntable Amelia did not bat an eyelash. She digested the information, then stood thinking for a moment. ''Dammit,'' she finally expounded. ''I told Alexander to wash his hands of the miscreant lot! Ah, well, the damage is done, and now it's up to the two of us to clear the air. Let me bid farewell to Monty. You go out and see if you can hire us a carriage.''

''Do you think Daddy is still involved with the society?'' Jocelyn asked, terrified suddenly.

''I don't know. For all of our sakes, I hope not. But— well, we can't stand here wringing our hands about it. Get going, girl. We've work to do!''

Jocelyn raced back down the stairs, not even pausing on the bottom landing. She wished with all of her heart that she could say good-bye to Dash. But that, she knew, was an impossibility.

Jocelyn and Amelia returned to the townhouse shortly after noon. Charles was beside himself with worry, fussing over the two of them and asking myriad questions about Lord Monty. Amelia, in her usual way, calmed him, then sent him to tell Binnie to prepare a light midday meal for the family.

Jocelyn wanted nothing more than to hurry home to the Cotswolds and see for herself that Alexander hadn't gone trotting off after Arthur Thistlewood and his firebrand group.

''Don't be ridiculous,'' Amelia said to Jocelyn. ''We can serve your father better if we're in London where we can keep an ear to the ground. We'll send Jives back to the country, with a letter telling your father what's transpired. Jives will know how to handle Alexander.''

Jocelyn, in the end, gave way to her grandmother's firm decision. "But what if Daddy doesn't listen to Jives? What if he goes tearing off—''

"He'll listen,'' Amelia cut in. "Your father will do nothing to put you in danger.''

It was true, Jocelyn knew. Alexander would lay down his life for her.

"Now I want you to go upstairs and rest, and then tonight, promptly at five-thirty, we'll head for the theater, after which we shall attend some social gathering where we can be seen.''

Jocelyn was horrified. "What are you saying?''

"I am saying, dear girl, that we shall continue on as if nothing out of the ordinary has happened. We do not want to hole ourselves up in this house as though we're guilty of something. We need to be seen, and to act normal.''

"Of—of course,'' Jocelyn whispered, feeling as though nothing would be normal ever again.

"Good. Now, off with you. I've some urgent letters to pen.'' Fishing her pipe and weed out of the pouch strapped about her waist, Amelia went into the sitting room and got down to work.

Jocelyn did as she was told. But no sooner had she changed into a day frock than there was a knock on her door.

"Pssst! Missy, are you awake?''

It was Binnie. Jocelyn popped the door open. "Yes, I'm awake. Does Gran want me?''

Binnie shook her head quickly. "No! There's a gentleman to see you. He's in the garden, missy, and he gave me direct orders to come straight to you.''

Jocelyn brushed the hair from her face, not needing any more of an explanation. "Thank you, Binnie.'' She darted out of her room and headed for the back stairs, which led to the kitchen. "You're not to repeat any of this, do you understand?''

"Oh, no, I'll not be repeating it, missy. You can count on me."

Jocelyn prayed the woman was telling the truth. Leaving Binnie in the kitchen—with a firm command to alert her should Charles or even Amelia come looking for her—Jocelyn stepped out into the cool garden.

Dash was waiting for her.

Sixteen

Jocelyn felt her heart leap at the sight of him. He stood near the back wall, his face tight with fatigue and worry. His eyes were stormy and filled with demons. He wore a shirt of lawn that was opened at the throat—his neck cloth forgotten—and a coat of black wool that looked as though it had been hastily thrown on. His trousers were creaseless, though, and his spurred black boots were shined to a high gloss. Hair windswept and looking tousled, he appeared a god gone wild.

"You shouldn't have come," Jocelyn whispered, moving slowly toward him.

He glanced up at her, smiling only a little as he shook his dark-haired head. "I couldn't stay away."

She reached his side and Dash took her hands in his even before Jocelyn had a chance to say another word. She nearly wept at the contact of their palms touching. His hands were warm, and rough—just as she'd remembered them. There was power in his grip. And pain as well. God help them, but she loved him!

"H—how did the meeting go?" she asked.

His eyes devoured the sight of her. "I didn't come here to talk about meetings, or of family illnesses, or anything at all. I just want to look at you, Duchess. No," he then murmured. "That's a lie. I need you, Jocelyn. I want to finish what we started last night. *I want to make love to you.*"

His words, spoken with such intensity, shook her to the very core. She wanted it, too, desperately, in fact. But Jocelyn now knew that she was a disability to Dash. To be near him could bring his death!

"I—I can't," she whispered, her voice breaking. "We can't."

"Says who?" he demanded roughly, pulling her body to his and wrapping his arms about her waist. He ran his hands up her back, then raked his fingers through her unbound hair. "My God," he breathed. "I've wanted you for so long, Jocelyn. Don't deny me now. I need you like I've never needed you. Last night, when I thought my uncle was dying, I realized then how precious little time all of us have in life. I am done playing games. I'm sick of pushing you away when what I really want to do is to drive myself into you so hard and so deep that I'll never forget the feel of you. I want to lose myself in you, Jocelyn."

He yanked her head back and slammed his hot mouth down on hers, burning her with a deep and heated kiss that was the sum and total of all he was. He drove his tongue between her lips and raked it across her own, filling her mouth, and telling her with the gesture that he was not about to be denied this day.

Jocelyn's head arched back. Her knees nearly gave way beneath her. She wanted to deny him—knew, in fact, that she must—but found that she could not. Trembling, nearly crying out, she wrapped her arms about his neck and kissed him back. Oh, God! the wanting, the scalding desire! Jocelyn wished she had a stronger will, but Dash was like a crazed man. He filled her and left her panting for more. How could she turn him away? How? This could be the last moment they might ever share!

So thinking, she pulled back and whispered, "I want you, too, Dash."

He didn't smile, nor did he say a word. He just gazed deeply into her eyes, so deeply that Jocelyn felt as though their souls were mingling and they were suddenly one being. Somehow she pulled herself out of the heady spell and motioned to a secluded corner of the garden.

But Dash shook his head. "Not here. I want to be alone with you. I want to strip every bit of clothing from your lovely body, and then I want to step back and gaze at you." He kissed her again, slowly this time, his mouth drinking in her essence. Not taking his lips from hers, he said huskily, "I want to kiss every part, every curve, every wondrous nuance of you. And then I want to watch your face as I enter you."

A heated shiver coursed up Jocelyn's spine. Was he mad? she wondered. Or was she? "I want that, too," she heard herself say. "But we can't be seen together, we can't—"

"Hush," he soothed, quieting her with two fingers pressed against her lips. "I've a carriage waiting for us beyond these garden walls. It will take us to a flat in the St. James area. We can stay there all day, just the two of us."

Jocelyn's heart fluttered. "All—all right. Let me tell Binnie I'm leaving."

"I told her," Dash said. "I'm to have you back here by five. That gives us four hours, Jocelyn."

Suddenly time was a thief. And she was thinking of Lord Barrington and all the others who would be watching Dash with a keen eye. "I—I don't know," she murmured. "What if we're caught. What if—"

But Dash wasn't listening, and it dawned on Jocelyn that she should have known better than to challenge him with *what ifs*. Dash was a man who lived on the edge of life. Without another word, Dash swept Jocelyn up into his arms, then headed for the back gate.

True to his word, a carriage was indeed waiting for them. A discreet driver, dressed entirely in black, and who kept his eyes averted as they came out to the small alleyway, sat atop the driver's seat. Enclosed on all sides, the curtains drawn, the two of them, once inside, were shielded from prying eyes. Jocelyn hadn't even a moment to catch her breath before the carriage jolted into motion and Dash had his arms around her once again. He thrust her back against the stiff leather seat, kissing her passionately.

"At last," he murmured, "I have you all to myself." He rolled to his back, fitting her body on top of his, and then he expertly undid the buttons of her dress.

"Dash!"

"I want to," he said huskily, pulling the garment open and then yanking the material down off her shoulders and arms. He undid her chemise, and worked that open as well, then ran his hands over her breasts. His palms whispered atop her nipples, toying with them at first, and then he squeezed them until they hardened.

Jocelyn closed her eyes, holding herself up with her hands planted on either side of Dash's head. "This is scandalous," she whispered.

"Do you mind?"

She shook her head, her hair falling down in a shimmering rain about their faces. Dash kissed the hollow between her breasts, his tongue darting out to trace a wet and delicious path to first one hard nipple and then the other. "I want to eat you alive," he muttered, taking one erect nipple into his mouth and sucking gently.

Jocelyn's head swam as she arched her back and offered herself to him. She felt wanton then, and the sensation was startling. She thought briefly of the crimes Dash had committed, and of the intense meeting that had taken place that morning. And, suddenly, she knew exactly what she wanted.

"Let's make love here," she rasped. "In the carriage. I want you, Dash. All of you." As she spoke, she moved one hand down to the closure of his trousers and worked the thing free. "Tell me you will," she said, slipping her hand inside the garment and finding him hard and erect. She nearly gasped at the feel of him.

Dash sucked in a breath of air. "Do you realize what you do to me, Jocelyn?"

She wrapped her hand around him. "I've a feeling I

do." Briefly she moved her hand away only to pull her skirts up and clear the way for their lovemaking.

If Jocelyn had any reservations about losing her virginity, they were soon swept away on a tide of heated lust. As the carriage bounded through the streets of London, heading for St. James's Place, Jocelyn and Dash came to know each other more intimately.

With just a caress of his hands, he soothed any fears she might have had. But Jocelyn was soon feeling her own careening desires. Gazing down into his smoky eyes, she impaled herself upon him, swiftly, cleanly. There was only a moment of pain. In truth she was ready for him, warm and moist. Dash buried his face in her cloud of hair.

"It's far better than I'd imagined," he said hoarsely, his hands moving down atop her smooth buttocks. He caressed her there, then pushed her down so that he was deep inside of her.

Jocelyn gasped, then quickened against him, her body swallowing the long length of him. "I've dreamt about this," she admitted, unashamed. "Time and again I thought about what this moment would be like. But never was it this wondrous. I—I can *feel* you, Dash. It's like . . . I can't explain it. It's wonderful."

He quieted her with a deep mind-numbing kiss that somehow caught the rhythm of their hips. Jocelyn molded herself to him, learning quickly what he liked and what made his breath grow ragged. "I want to please you," she whispered into his ear, tracing his lobe with her tongue.

"You are, love. You are." He tangled one hand in her hair, while he moved the other between their bodies and touched the sensitive folds of her flesh there.

Jocelyn nearly drowned in the ecstasy of it all. Her breathing became jagged, and her entire body seemed prepared for some wild, reckless flight. Higher and higher he drove her, until finally, just when she thought she could take no more, Dash forced himself deep within her. Jocelyn's world exploded. Showers of pure delight poured over her, through her. She felt his seed spill deep within as her soul spun and twirled in some distant, fantastic realm.

As they both quieted, Dash reached up and cupped Jocelyn's face in his hands, watching the play of pleasure across her features. His voice just a husky whisper, he said, "I believe I am falling in love with you, Duchess." He kissed her sweetly on the mouth, his lips soft and tender.

Jocelyn pressed her eyes shut tight, feeling tears gather. Some part of her, deep inside, trembled with a bittersweet mix of grief and joy. She returned his kiss, afraid to voice her own emotions, for to do so could mean Dash's death. A single tear slipped past her lashes.

"You're crying," Dash whispered, full of concern. "I've hurt you, haven't I?"

He tried to push her up so that he could view her face fully, but Jocelyn shook her head and sought his lips again. She kissed him hard and long, her salty tears mingling on their mouths.

But Dash wasn't to be fooled. Gently he pulled his mouth from hers, kissing a path to her ear. "Talk to me, Jocelyn. What is the matter?" He slid his hands to her back, caressing her with care. "Do you regret our love-making? Do you—"

The carriage ground to a screeching halt then and both Dash and Jocelyn were propelled off the seat and crashed to the hard floor beneath them.

Dash landed on his right side with a thud and a curse. "Blast that Henri! He never could drive this thing with any great amount of care!" He peered up at Jocelyn who was on top of him in a tangle of limbs and arms. "Are you hurt?"

"I'm fine," she said, caught between laughter and tears. "But what about you . . . your ribs?"

"They're still here, and in one piece I think," he muttered, then winced. "But your knee, Duchess, it's—"

Jocelyn's face turned pink. "I'm sorry," she said quickly, realizing just exactly where her knee was pressed. She shifted her position, then eased up onto the seat and began to straighten her clothing. She smiled as Dash tried to get his long limbs unkinked. "I suppose this is what we deserve for being so hasty," she murmured.

In spite of his discomfort Dash grinned. "Hasty, were we?"

"Very."

"But I've never enjoyed myself more." He fastened his breeches, then eased himself onto the seat beside her. "Here, let me do that," he said, brushing her hands away and taking over the task of doing her many closures.

His hands were warm against her skin, fueling yet again Jocelyn's desires. Would she ever have her fill of his attentions? she wondered distractedly. But she knew the answer. Dashiell Warfield had stolen more than her jewels on that long ago night—he'd taken her heart as well.

A loud banging came on the carriage door then. "Ahem!" Henri the driver cleared his throat loudly. "We are here, sir. Shall I help you out or—"

"No need, man!" Dash called out, looking as though he'd like nothing better than to throttle his driver. "Take that coin I gave you and find yourself a chophouse. Be back here at a quarter of five."

A moment of silence, then: "But the carriage, sir. Should I leave it here or—"

"Henri," Dash replied, a note of warning in his voice, "must I spell things out for you?"

"No, sir. Not at all, sir. I, uh, I'm on my way, sir."

Jocelyn heard Henri's quick footsteps as he moved on down the street. "He only wished to please you," Jocelyn said softly.

Dash nodded, reaching across her to open the door. "So he does, but sometimes I wonder if the man has a brain between those large ears of his."

"A hard taskmaster, are you?" Jocelyn teased, relieved Henri had inadvertently interrupted Dash's declaration of love for her. It would do no one any good for the two of them to speak of love—or even of tomorrow. They *had* no tomorrow. The thought made Jocelyn's heart contract.

"I'm the worst kind of master," Dash was saying as he popped the door open and slipped outside.

Jocelyn smiled as he offered her his hand. "Is that a promise or a threat?"

Dash stood on the walkway, looking far too virile with his hair ruffled and his shirt still opened at the neck. "Come inside and I'll show you."

Jocelyn found she could not deny him . . . and, in truth, she didn't want to.

Dash's flat, housed on the highest floor of a stately building, was smaller than what Jocelyn had expected for a man of Dash's station and wealth. There was no gentleman's gentleman to pamper him.

"Don't need one," Dash explained. "Nor do I want one. I come here to be alone. If I yearn for people, I go to Uncle Monty's home in Grosvenor Square, or to the Warfield estate outside of London. And if I want space, then I head for the northern countryside."

Jocelyn looked about her at the cluttered space. A mezzanine bedchamber could be viewed from the main room of the flat. Both rooms were filled with odds and ends that had probably been removed from Lord Monty's homes. There were several small bookshelves overflowing with books and papers. A dull brass clock sat on the mantel above the fireplace, stilled at the hour of twelve. The place was very chilly, and smelled musty, as though Dash hadn't taken up residence in quite awhile.

As Dash began to lay a fire in the ugly fireplace that was blackened with soot, Jocelyn took her time exploring, drinking in the feel of the flat. This was another of Dash's hideaways, a place where he found solace. Oddly enough, she felt at home.

"There's wine," he said, hunkering down and fiddling with bits of dried wood. "At least, I think there's some."

"Yes, here it is," she replied, spying a dusty bottle amid the papers on a small table. "You enjoy writing?" she asked, seeing the many quills and a large pot of ink on the scarred tabletop.

Dash glanced up. "Sometimes," he said. "Speeches,

that sort of thing. Someday I hope to follow in Uncle Monty's footsteps. Since I was a lad, Uncle Monty has been grooming me for a life in government.''

Jocelyn stared down at the many papers. In his bold script Dash crusaded for reform of the law. He blasted the capitalists, the landed aristocracy, and even the members and controllers of Parliament. Frightening words they were—not so much because of the justice they cried for, but because by writing them Dash was fighting against the very thing he'd been raised amid.

Again, Jocelyn felt a tight squeeze of her heart. "I—I had no idea," she whispered.

The fire started, Dash got up and brushed his hands off. He glanced at her and saw that she'd read some of what he'd written. "Does this change your view of me?" he asked.

"I'm sorry. I shouldn't have read your work. It's none of my business."

"The plight of the homeless and the hungry is everyone's business."

"That's not what I meant."

Dash moved toward the table, rifled through some of the pages, then handed her one. "I don't mind sharing my opinions with you. In fact, I *want* to share them with you."

Hesitantly Jocelyn took the page. "These are powerful words," she whispered, once she was done reading.

"They are. I wrote that speech only days before the Spa Fields riot."

"You were there?" Jocelyn asked, astonished.

His face grim, Dash nodded. "I fear I helped to incite the people to riot."

Jocelyn didn't answer directly, for her mind was spinning with the revelation. She'd heard about the Spa Fields riot. Rumors were that Arthur Thistlewood had arranged the mass meeting, and then spurred the people to rage against the English government. Many people had lost their lives, having been shot or trampled by the king's men. Her own father had been beside himself with rage and grief after learning of the riot. It had happened over three years ago, but suddenly Jocelyn realized that that mass gathering must have been the deciding factor to propel Alexander Greville to unite with Thistlewood and his band of revolutionists.

Fearing even more for Dash's safety—and for her father's—she asked, "How involved are you, Dash?"

Moody now, Dash reached for the wine. "Perhaps too involved, perhaps not enough. I don't know. What I do know, though, is that something has to change. England cannot remain the supreme power that she is if her people are divided."

"But you cannot continue to rob in order to aid the poor," she nearly cried. "It would never be enough!"

"You think I don't realize that?" he asked, his features tight. "I've dipped into my own purse and those of others, and yet the suffering of so many has no end. I wish I could do more. I wish, dammit, that I had the might and the power, and . . . I don't know. It's just a vicious circle of wanting yet never having enough to give." He uncorked the bottle with a savage twist.

Jocelyn stilled his hand. "I understand," she whispered. "You're a noble man, Dash, and I admire you for that."

He laughed—a harsh sound. "It isn't admiration that I seek."

"I know that now. You rob from those who can afford the loss in order to give to those who can afford nothing at all. But don't you see, Dash? You cannot continue to place your own life in jeopardy. What good will you be if you're hanged for your crimes?"

Jocelyn hadn't meant for her voice to rise, nor had she meant to sound so desperate. But she *was* desperate!

"My God, Dash," she continued, "Lord Monty's peers could have charged you with highway robbery this morning, and they would have been correct! You escaped the noose only because of quick thinking and because no one has any solid proof! But what about the next time? What if someone *does* recognize you?"

"Stop it," he muttered. "Don't torture yourself with worry over me."

"And why shouldn't I?" Jocelyn demanded. "I care about you, Dash! I—"

She almost said *I love you*, but stopped herself before she did so. She couldn't force the words from her mouth for fear of placing Dash in an even worse situation. If he knew that she loved him, what would he do? Would he give up his midnight raids? Would he turn his back on all of his friends? If he didn't, then Jocelyn would be crushed, for then she would know that his cause was dearer to him than she was.

But if he did give it up . . . then what? Would Jocelyn forever have to live with the knowledge that she'd pulled him away from everything he held close? Would she be able to live with herself knowing such a thing?

"You what?" Dash asked, reaching out to tip her face up to his. "Say it, Jocelyn."

His touch was like a hot firebrand. He could arouse her with just a look, a gesture. And his voice, so husky and low, nearly put Jocelyn over the edge.

"I care about you," Jocelyn whispered, looking into his heady gaze. "You must know that."

His eyes devoured her. "I do. And that is why I brought you here."

"But, Dash, you must be careful. Promise me you'll not be taking to the roads again. Promise me that you'll put away your pistol and your mask. . . ." She stopped her spate of words, for Dash was moving in closer now. He let his hand slip down to caress the long column of her throat, pausing for a moment atop the point where her pulse beat a quick rhythm.

He said, "You want promises from me that I cannot make."

"But why not?" she whispered, seeing that he was going to kiss her. She wanted him to do so. Oh, yes. But they had so much to talk about, so many things to get clear between them. "You said yourself that the money you steal isn't nearly enough to help those who need aid."

"That's true," he murmured, dropping his left hand, with the wine bottle, to his side. He slipped his right hand behind her neck, sliding his fingers through her thick hair. "But I have to do whatever I can, Jocelyn, and therein lies my problem. Do not ask of me what I cannot do."

Jocelyn's head spun. He was too close. The scent of him, so manly and earthy, filled her senses. She thought then of Lord Barrington's warning and knew that she played a dangerous game with Dash. She should tell him that they had no future together. She should push him away and then leave at once.

But Jocelyn knew she wouldn't be doing any of those things. She would stay in the flat with him and enjoy the few hours they had together. And then, after they'd made love and he'd taken her to that secret, wondrous place where only he could transport her, Jocelyn would say good-bye. Forever.

Jocelyn closed her eyes as Dash covered her mouth with his. She forced herself not to think of the lonely hours ahead, nor of the pain of having to walk away and never see Dash again. Tomorrow, she told herself. Tomorrow would be soon enough to grieve.

Soft and gentle, his lips covered hers, and Jocelyn felt herself being carried off on a swift tide of desire. His breath caressed her cheek. His arms slid around her, enfolding her in a tight embrace.

Jocelyn melted against him, opening to him. Her own kiss was hungry, selfish. She wanted to burn into her brain the memory of this day.

Dash must have felt her desperation. "Relax," he whispered. "We've a few hours yet."

And that is all, she thought. "Love me, Dash," she murmured.

She didn't have to ask twice. Dash lifted her into his arms and carried her up the few steps to the bedchamber, then laid her down onto the mattress. He joined her on the bed, leisurely stroking her body, knowing exactly how to please her.

But Jocelyn, feeling chased by time, yanked at his shirt,

not caring that she tore a few of the buttons free. Hands trembling, she pulled the thing away from his muscular chest, then planted heated kisses across the wide expanse.

With her fervor she seemed to ignite a spark in Dash's soul, for he, too, became impatient. "Here, let me," he said, yanking the shirt from his body, then making quick work of divesting himself of the rest of his garments.

Jocelyn fumbled with the closures of her dress and was relieved when Dash reached over to do the deed for her. His eyes burned into her very soul as he peeled her garments off of her body. Jocelyn, at last free of the constricting clothes, moved into Dash's embrace.

"Not so fast," he murmured, his breathing ragged. "I want to look at you."

Jocelyn tried to still her roiling emotions, taking Dash's hand in hers and kissing his knuckles as he stroked her body with his other hand.

"So gorgeous," he crooned, his eyes slowly raking over her body.

Jocelyn was thinking only how handsome he was, and how much she loved him. She ran her fingertips across the pinkish scar where he'd been grazed by a smuggler's bullet. There were other scars as well, older ones. She wondered about them and wished again that they had more time to get to know each other. There was so much she wanted to ask him, so much she wanted to know! His healed wounds served as a reminder of what kind of life he'd chosen. They presented a distance between them— one Jocelyn didn't want to acknowledge.

So thinking, she lowered her hands and touched him intimately.

Dash quickened at the contact. "You're eager. But so soon? We just—"

"Hush," she ordered quietly. "Binnie is expecting me. We haven't much time."

Dash growled low in his throat. "No, we don't at that," he replied, and then rolled her over onto her back and began a delicious assault.

Dash wasn't a man to be hurried. He took his own sweet

time, slowly bringing Jocelyn to great heights of pleasure. He kissed every inch of her body, concentrating on her most sensitive places. Jocelyn writhed beneath him, feeling like a wild and untamed being. Scandalous were the things he did to her, but so very enjoyable. And she returned every kiss, every touch.

"You *must* be a witch," he rasped as Jocelyn pushed him onto *his* back and moved on top of him. He caught his hands in her long hair and pulled her face to his. "Where did you learn such things?" he teased.

Jocelyn impaled herself on his manhood, taking him deep inside. "From you, of course," she whispered, feeling the force of him sheathed in her body.

Dash gave a low growl, smiling up at her with heavily-lidded eyes. "You are a quick learner, Duchess."

"With you I am."

"I don't want this to end."

She said nothing as she gripped his shoulders and held herself above him. She didn't want it to end, either, but there could be no other way. The pain of knowing they must soon part was a vital force inside of her, nearly destroying her from within. But she would give to Dash one final memory to carry with him.

With rhythmic motion, she moved her hips and drew him with her into the sticky web of desire. Their hot bodies slid against each other and Jocelyn could feel Dash pulsate within her. Her breath quickened as her own senses careened out of control. When she thought she could not take another stroke, or that she would explode with wanting, Jocelyn felt her body quiver.

Together, they were catapulted into a distant sphere of intense delight. Dash gathered her against him, held her there. Jocelyn let go of all reason. This, she knew, was the very thing men fought and died for. She experienced a small death of her own. It was as though her soul had mingled with Dash's soul, and a part of her would be forever gone. But she didn't care. She melted against him, giving totally of herself.

It was her final gift to the only man she would ever truly love.

Later they shared a glass of wine—the only clean glass Dash could find in the flat—and sat in the main room, staring into the fire in the grate. They had only a few minutes before Jocelyn had to return to her grandmother's townhouse.

"I want to see you again," Dash said. "As soon as possible."

Jocelyn's stomach tightened. The moment to say good-bye had come. "I don't know," she whispered. "I—I fear I'm going to be very busy for the next few weeks. And Lord Monty . . . he's going to need you to be near."

Dash stiffened, pulling his gaze from the dancing firelight. "What the devil are you saying? Surely we can find a few stolen hours to be together."

Her heart felt as though it were breaking in half. "No, Dash, we can't." She chanced a glance at him. He was angry—and hurt—his eyes dark, a line between them. "I—I've been thinking about us," she continued, knowing she must give him some sort of explanation that would sever their bond. "I can't go on living like this. I can't be involved with a . . ."

"A thief?" Dash supplied, his voice suddenly cold.

"Yes, that's right," she said in a hurried whisper, wishing the moment could be behind her. "Life with you would be too tumultuous. I know, Dash. I've had a taste of it—the exhilarating highs and shattering lows. I—I can't live like that."

He leaned forward in his chair, not liking what she had to say. Not at all. "Didn't this afternoon mean anything to you?" he demanded, grabbing hold of her hands with a tight grip. "I told you I loved you, Jocelyn!"

She hated the pain she saw in his face, the fear in his eyes. But she forced herself to go on. "No, you said you believed you were falling in love with me. You said—"

"So I lied!" Dash said harshly. "I *do* love you, Jocelyn. I won't let you go."

Jocelyn met his gaze. "Think what you're saying. You're a highwayman, Dash. You pull your pistol on people and threaten their lives. How can you expect me to—to love a man who would do such a thing?"

His mouth tensed. "You know why I do it."

"Yes . . . but I cannot condone such actions. And there are rumors, Dash. People are saying that you might possibly be the Midnight Raider. I—I wanted to warn you last night. There are handbills circulating, handbills with a description that fits you."

"I know about them," he said darkly. "Barrington and his fellows gave me one this morning."

Jocelyn's heart tripped. "Then you denied being the Raider?"

"Of course I denied it. I'd be a fool not to."

But Jocelyn could see clearly that Dash had lied to Barrington and the others. The answer was there—in the way his muscle twitched in his cheek, and in the wintry coolness that seeped into his eyes. "Oh, God, Dash," she whispered, feeling as though she were being swallowed into the earth. "Tell me you're not the Raider. Tell me you didn't murder James Keats."

But Dash said nothing. He didn't deny the idea, nor did he claim innocence.

"Dash—"

But he would have none of her questions, her pity or concern. "You're right," he said suddenly, getting to his feet. "You shouldn't waste your time on a lowly thief. You deserve better, Jocelyn. God knows I wish I could give it to you." With that, he walked toward the door, opened it, and said, "Come, Henri should be waiting downstairs."

Jocelyn didn't know whether to rage at him or cry in despair. He hadn't denied being the Raider, and that, she knew, could mean only one thing. But had he murdered James Keats? Had something gone awry in the robbery, thus forcing him to shoot? Jocelyn's stomach heaved. She'd wanted to end their relationship, and to warn him about the rumors, but she hadn't expected *this*!

"Dash, we need to talk," she began. "We need—"

"As I see it, there's nothing more to say," he replied, his voice wooden. "You've made your choice, and you are correct. I'm no good for you. I never was." He motioned for her to go before him out the door.

Jocelyn wanted to hold back. She wanted another hour with him, another lifetime. But she'd already asked him not to haunt the highways again, and he'd said he couldn't make such a promise. There was, then, nothing more to say. He'd made his decision, and nothing—not even his love for her—could stand in the way.

Jocelyn gathered her courage. Tucking her despair deep inside of herself, she began to walk past him. "I wish things could have worked out differently," she said, pausing beside him.

Dash said nothing. Before Jocelyn had a chance to think clearly, she found herself back in the enclosed carriage—this time alone.

She sat atop the stiff seat and listened as Dash gave strict orders to Henri.

"Take her directly home. Do not leave until you see that she is safely inside."

"Yes, sir," Henri replied. "That I'll do, sir."

Jocelyn wished the windows weren't covered, she wished she could see Dash's face for one last time. The carriage bolted into motion. She pressed one hand to her mouth, trying not to cry. But it was too late, for the tears were already coming.

Jocelyn hung her head and wept as she left behind the man who had stolen her heart, and her dreams.

Seventeen

For Jocelyn the next few weeks went by in a daze. Her grandmother saw to it that the two of them attended every social function they possibly could. Jocelyn pasted smiles on her face and tried to get through as best she could. The only bright spot was in knowing that Jives had found her father safely at home and practicing his medicine. There would be no more political meetings for Alexander Greville, Jives has assured Jocelyn. She'd received one letter from her father, and from the words he'd written Jocelyn decided that Jives was correct. But still, though her father had seemingly cut all ties with Arthur Thistlewood and his political activists, Jocelyn knew she could not seek out Dash. She still posed a threat to him. To be seen with him could place Dash in further jeopardy.

But every morning there arrived at the townhouse packages for Jocelyn—and every gift was from Dash. Sometimes he sent hothouse flowers. Other days Jocelyn would find a poem, unsigned. One day she'd awakened to find a packet of heavy writing paper had been delivered, and on the next day there came a beautiful quill, and the next an inkpot. Jocelyn had been very tempted to write to Dash, using the gifts he'd sent, but she wrote the letters only to safeguard them in a small drawer in her room. He'd also written to Jocelyn asking her to meet him. Jocelyn never did. As bitter as the realization was, Jocelyn knew the best thing for Dash would be to have her out of his life.

And so the weeks turned into a month, and then another, and another. Winter deepened, bitterly cold, and all of London was coated with heavy blankets of snow. The political climate of the land was just as bitter. King George III, an old man who was known to be insane and who, for years, had been ruled under the regency of his son, the Prince of Wales, died. His passing was mourned by only a few as his final years in power had been marked by unrest. But even with his death there appeared no end in sight for the suffering of the country's masses, and the Tory ministry did little to alleviate the distress.

Jocelyn kept herself abreast of all she could. Never in her life had she taken such an interest in all things political. But she did so now, for the changes in the government could very well bring the arrest of Dash, and even of her father, she knew.

It seemed she was balancing on a fine line. The days and nights were endless for her. How much socializing could be expected of her? she often wondered. But always Amelia would be there to gently encourage her to keep up the facade, and Jocelyn did so because she had no other choice. She did not want to return home to the Cotswolds. To dwell in the same city as Dash was a comfort to her, though only a small one.

One day, late in February, Charles sought out Jocelyn as she sat in the drawing room.

"I say, cousin," Charles began as he warmed his hands near the hearth, "why don't the two of us have some *fun* today? You look as pale as the winter sky. I've told Gran that she's running you ragged, but she turns a deaf ear to my opinions. You aren't *ill*, are you?"

Jocelyn glanced up from the small square of linen she was stitching. "Ill?"

"Yes, sick, touched . . . you know my meaning. Look at you, doing needlework, of all things! Heavens, cousin, the last time you picked up needle and thread was *ages* ago, and you grumbled while doing so."

Jocelyn dropped the linen to her lap. Charles was correct. What had come over her? She'd hated stitching when she was younger, and she didn't fancy it now, either, but she had to do something or else her worry over Dash and her father would consume her. "All right," she announced. "What had you in mind?"

Charles beamed at her reply. "What do you say we find a noisy chophouse and have a bite to eat? And then we could take a walk in the snow, just like old times. I daresay I'm near bored to tears. I'd thought Sally Warburton would come to London once I sent word that you and Gran would be more than delighted to have her stay here. But I fear she's taken a shining to one of the country lads. Of course, she didn't tell me *who*, but I can well guess. No doubt it's Tony Peacham who's caught her eye."

Jocelyn could see Charles was saddened by Sally's dismissal. "I'm sorry," she said softly. "I know how much Sally meant to you."

"Did I say that? No, no, I wasn't in *love* with the girl. I just . . . well, I enjoyed her company is all."

And now you need to do something to keep your mind off the subject, Jocelyn thought, knowing only too well what her cousin must be feeling. She placed her needlework on the small stool beside her chair, then stood up. "A walk in the snow sounds divine, Charles. I'll get my wrap."

Charles's jaw nearly dropped to the floor. "Well, that was easy enough to convince you. Why hadn't I asked you sooner?"

Jocelyn gave him a winning smile, feeling better already. "I haven't a clue, cousin. But don't stand there looking surprised. The last one out of the door will have to eat liver for dinner!"

"Liver!" Charles replied, and mocked a shudder. "You know we both detest liver."

Jocelyn was out the door in a flash. "I know," she called. "Don't fret, cousin, I'll make certain you've a large tankard of drink with which to wash it down!"

Charles didn't need another warning. He darted after Jocelyn and they both raced up the narrow stairs of the townhouse for their rooms.

Jocelyn took time enough only to grab her scarlet cloak and her glass-beaded reticule. She reached the door downstairs just as she heard Charles running down the stairs.

"Foiled again," Charles muttered as he came to stand outside with her. "But, ah! you didn't even bring your gloves, Jocelyn. Why don't you get them, and I'll wait," he added in a teasing tone.

"And have you laugh at me while I choke down a portion of liver?" she shot back, knowing full well that her cousin would turn the tables on her should she go back inside. "Come, I'm looking forward to seeing you sitting before a heaping plate of the stuff."

Charles sighed heavily, but offered her his arm, and the two of them headed down the street.

For all of their teasing of one another, there was no liver to be had at the chosen chophouse. They made do with bacon rolls, which were chunks of bacon with delicious mustard rolled up on a bun. They sipped mugs of hot buttered rum and picked at the chips that were served with the bacon rolls.

"Now, this is the London I love," Charles said, leaning back in his chair and enjoying the commotion around them.

Jocelyn found herself relaxing as well. How nice it was to be swallowed up in the noise of a chophouse and not have to deal with polite small talk. "You don't miss home?" she asked.

Charles shook his head. "Not at all, actually. I'm perfectly content to hang my hat in Gran's townhouse every night, for the time being anyway."

"Wouldn't you like to move back to the Cotswolds and raise sheep?" Jocelyn asked, joking with him a little. She was feeling the warming effect of the rum as it settled in her stomach.

"Perish the thought," Charles replied. "I like to rag about the city with my friends—and I've made quite a few. Good chaps, they are. One even told me he might find me employment within the Bank of England. Could you fancy that? Me? Working in a bank? Goodness knows I have to find *some* sort of gainful employment. I can't continue pulling Gran's purse strings. Not that she minds, you know. But I've had my eye on a flat in Leicester Square.''

"Why, Charles,'' Jocelyn said, humor in her eyes, "you're growing away from me.''

"Never that, cousin. But it is no secret to me that Gran has more than just a passing interest in Lord Warfield. Who knows? Since Lord Monty is on the mend, he might very well propose marriage. Gran has been too long on her own. And *you*—sometimes I even wonder if I've ever truly known you. You've changed, Jocelyn. I can't explain it, but since last fall you've become a different person. You're very intense these days.''

"I—I'm just worried about my father. . . . He's all alone in that big house.''

"He has Randolph,'' Charles said. "And his patients.''

"Yes, but still—''

"Then why don't you return home?''

Jocelyn glanced up, caught between fabricating some excuse and telling her cousin the truth. Charles was so sweet and sincere, and there had been a time when the cousins shared everything. But life had a way of changing people, and Jocelyn knew she could probably never recapture the carefree youth she'd once known.

"I promised Gran that I would stay in London for the winter season,'' she finally said, thinking of Dash and aching to be near him. "I want to keep my promise.''

"Yes, of course,'' Charles replied, completely satisfied with her answer. He drank the rest of his rum, then noticed a friend in the far corner of the room. "Ah, there is Dick Cheltenham. He's the one I told you about who is employed at the bank. I need to speak with him for a moment.'' He waved his hand wildly, but did not catch the man's attention.

"Go and speak with him,'' Jocelyn encouraged. "I can sit here alone for a moment. I needn't have a chaperon every minute I'm out of the townhouse.''

Charles was already getting to his feet. "You're a dear,

cousin," he said, then gave her a brotherly peck on the cheek and was gone.

Jocelyn smiled, pleased to see Charles was finding his own place in the city. She had only a moment to herself before a man approached her table.

"May I?"

Jocelyn looked up to see none other than Lane Braden standing near her. "Laney!" she nearly cried. "What a surprise!"

He touched one finger to his mouth. "Not so loud, lass. I'm here incognito." He gave her a quick wink, then settled into the seat opposite her. "The last person I would expect to see in such an establishment would be you."

"I'm in London for the winter months—perhaps longer."

He nodded knowingly. "As is Dash."

"You've seen him?" Jocelyn asked, a bit too eagerly.

Laney grinned, then motioned for a barmaid. "Yes, as a matter of fact, I have." A buxom woman sauntered over to their table and took Laney's order. When she left, Laney continued, "He wasn't in very high spirits, I'm afraid. I saw him while I visited Lord Monty. Pity about Lord Monty, but the old man has Dash to fret over him. Dash is very good at hand-wringing when he needs to be."

"Meaning?" Jocelyn asked, hearing an underlying bitterness in Laney's tone.

But Laney shrugged, and when he spoke again, his voice was even and smooth. "Only that Dash is extremely loyal to Lord Monty. He should be, of course. The man has given Dash everything he could ever want in life."

"So what brings *you* to London, Laney?"

Braden was quiet as the barmaid placed a tankard of ale before him, and then he tipped her a handsome sum and watched her walk away. "Adventure," he answered easily. "Besides, the open roads are too cold for my taste these days. Nasty winters you country folk endure."

"We manage," Jocelyn said, half appalled at herself to be sitting with a man whom she knew very well to be a thief with little conscience. But he'd seen Dash—and Jocelyn was anxious for news about him. "And Lord Monty?" she asked carefully.

Laney wasn't fooled. "Come now, lass. Ask me what you really want to know. Ask me where Dash is and how he fares and if he's been thinking of you."

Jocelyn didn't bat an eye. She met Laney's bold gaze head-on. "All right, so tell me."

Laney swigged his ale, his many rings flashing on his fingers. "He is near here," he said finally, and a twinkle could be seen in his eyes. "In a tavern down the street. He's drunk—or rather, well on his way to being drunk. Doubtless I'll have to show the sot his way home. He's been drinking a good bit lately. I believe he's been taking to the highways again, too. In fact, just last week a man was robbed, and the thief even told him he was the Midnight Raider. Left a bit of poetry for the victim. Now, anyone who knows Dash well knows he is a man who loves the written word." Laney shook his head sadly. "Dash just isn't being careful. Why, people will soon start claiming *he* is the Midnight Raider."

Jocelyn felt her insides churn. Could it be true? Was Dash back to his old ways and now leaving a litter of clues behind him? But why would he be so careless?

"Pity that," Laney continued, either not realizing Jocelyn's discomfort, or not caring. "Lord Monty doesn't need to have his head filled with more rumors about Dash . . . but we both know how stubborn Dash can be."

Jocelyn stiffened. She hadn't thought Dash would be so reckless, but he was under a great deal of strain, she knew. And his heart was with the less fortunate people of England.

"Are you certain about this?" she whispered.

Laney nodded as he finished his ale. "As certain as I can be. Perhaps you can talk some sense into Dash." Laney leaned across the table, adding, "Midnight Raider or not, Dash is going to find himself in terrible trouble if he doesn't watch his step. What will it be, lass? Will you try and help him, or are you going to wash your hands of the whole mess?"

Jocelyn didn't know what to say. Clearly Laney was offering to take her to Dash and would most likely keep a keen watch while Jocelyn had a moment alone with him. But even so, did she dare attempt such a meeting? And if she did, would Dash even listen to reason?

Jocelyn weighed her options. She could continue as she'd done for the past months and hope that the cloud hovering above Dash soon disappeared. But this did not seem to be the best decision, for obviously Dash was falling back into his old way of life and would doubtless find himself dangling from a noose. But if she did go to him, she might be seen and thus place Dash in immediate danger.

"I—I don't think Dash would listen to me," Jocelyn said.

"I do. He's been at odds for the past weeks. Perhaps yours is the advice he needs."

In the end Jocelyn found she could not deny Laney's request. She'd been aching to see Dash for so long, and suddenly there seemed a perfect opportunity to do so. And if it was true that Dash was haunting the roads again, then Jocelyn could do no less than to try and dissuade him from such a life.

Laney left the chophouse first, then Jocelyn followed after she gave a hasty excuse to her cousin. Charles was caught up in his own conversation and seemed satisfied enough when Jocelyn told him she'd hire a carriage home and that they could have their walk another time.

Jocelyn met Laney outside. Dusk claimed the streets and snow fell in heavy flakes.

"I must see him alone," Jocelyn told Laney as they headed toward the tavern. "No one must see us, do you understand?"

Laney hunched his shoulders against the chill air. "I am a master of deception, lass. You want privacy, you'll get it. Trust me."

Jocelyn felt a fear of premonition steal up her spine with Laney's words, but she pressed forward. At the moment all she could think of was seeing Dash again. . . .

* * *

Dash tipped back his fifth and final ale and ignored the comely red-haired wench who came to take away the tankard and scoop up the coin he'd tossed to the tabletop. She tossed her curly hair over one shoulder, hoping to gain Dash's undivided attention.

Tempting him with a smile, she said, "I'll be finished here by midnight. I've got a room upstairs."

Dash looked up at her, taking in her come-hither look and shapely body. Normally such a proposition would have interested Dash, but not tonight . . . and quite possibly never again. There was only one woman he wanted to woo, and she, unfortunately, was out of his reach. He returned the wench's smile, but shook his head.

The maid shrugged. "You don't know what you're missing," she said, then moved away.

"I'm afraid I do," Dash muttered, thinking of another woman with flaming hair and a spirit to match. He'd thought of little but Jocelyn these past months. She'd not returned his notes, nor had she met him at any of the dozen places he'd asked her to meet him. Clearly she'd meant what she'd said that long-ago night in his flat.

His mood darkening, Dash was half tempted to order another ale, but he decided against it. He needed his wits about him. The tangled mess of his life had progressively worsened over the past few weeks. Though Lord Monty appeared to be recovering, Dash wasn't so blind that he couldn't realize his own secret past was weighing heavily on Monty. Dash had given up his thieving and had instead been giving only his own coin to help his friends in the north. But even so, there still trickled into London news of the Midnight Raider and his nefarious deeds. Someone was haunting the very roads Dash had once ridden, and leaving clues that would ultimately point to Dash.

Dash had been working night and day to learn the identity of this rider. He'd gone from tavern to tavern, linking up with old acquaintances who were privy to the gossip of the roads. But no one could tell him anything he didn't already know about the bogus Raider. Dash had done everything but ride out on the roads and try to track the culprit down. He couldn't risk such a mad scheme, not now when the government was in a state of flux and he and even Lord Monty were being watched from afar. It had taken all of Dash's skill just to get away from the house this night and outwit the man he knew Lord Barrington had hired to watch his comings and goings.

Dash cursed his luck—or lack of it—just as the barmaid returned. In no mood to deal with her flirtations, he said, "Look here, I told you I'm not interested—"

The girl frowned. "Now, don't go jumping to conclusions about me. I've got my pride, you know. I just came to deliver a message to you."

"A message?" Dash asked, suddenly suspicious. Though he'd learned little about the bogus Midnight Raider, he'd certainly heard more than a few tidbits about Arthur Thistlewood and his band of revolutionists. Tonight, if Thistlewood's plans went unimpeded, there would be bloodshed. "From whom?"

"Don't know, and I don't care to know. I'm to tell you only that someone wants to meet with you. Upstairs, second room on the right." With that, she turned away, leaving Dash to gather his own conclusions.

It could be a trap, Dash knew. Or perhaps Lord Barrington's man had found him out and now wanted to demand what Dash was doing in the tavern exchanging low words with vagrants. Either way, Dash wasn't about to leave without finding out.

He got up from the table, checked to make certain he wasn't being watched, and then moved cautiously toward the staircase at the back of the smoke-filled room. He glanced up at the narrow, dimly lit stairwell. It turned sharply to the right, and so Dash couldn't be certain if someone might be waiting for him near the top landing. So thinking, he reached into the hidden pocket of his waistcoat for the small pistol he carried there. His hideout weapon, it was a small gun that could be concealed with ease and proved extremely handy in situations such as this. Dash loaded it with quick precision, and then, pressing his back against the wall, he moved slowly up the stairs.

The old thrill of knowing his life might be threatened at any moment and that his wits and quick movements would be his only safety took tight hold of Dash. His heartbeat quickened, his senses became alert. How easy it was, after all, to fall back into that lifestyle. Though he was trying his best to put his life of thieving behind him, Dash realized there would forever be a part of him that loved the chase and the hunt. On the edge, that was where he enjoyed being—in love, and in life.

He paused a step away from the sharp turn of the stairs, and then, quick as lightning, darted up onto the landing, his pistol ready in his fist.

Nothing. No one. Just the dull glare of an old lamp sitting on a battered table down the hallway. Dash crept up the last few stairs. There were four doors flanking the hall—two on each side. Dash headed for the second door on his right. He found it ajar, opened only a crack. No light spilled out from inside. He could be ambushed if he chanced pushing the door open another inch or two. No doubt whoever waited for him was just as prepared for a fight as he was. With that thought in mind Dash made his decision. He lifted one booted foot, slammed it against the door, and then, pistol still in his grip and ready, he braced himself against the wall near the now-opened door. He heard an audible gasp, and the sound of shattering glass.

"Show your face," Dash said. "Or I'll fill you full of lead."

Silence then. He could hear nothing but the commotion coming from downstairs. "Get out here, dammit," Dash growled. "I want to know your name and your purpose here."

Another long moment passed, time in which Dash's finger grew tense around the trigger of his pistol. And then:

"Dash, it's me . . . Jocelyn. D-don't shoot. I only came here because—"

Jocelyn? What the devil was she doing here? Dash dropped his hands to his side, feeling his stomach turn. Jocelyn! He could have shot her. . . .

"Well," he heard Jocelyn demand sharply, "are you going to stand out there and plan your attack, or will you come inside?"

Dash felt his heart give a queer squeeze at the sound of her words. Yes, it was Jocelyn. He'd know that husky voice anywhere. And she was spitting mad, just as he remembered her. Dash quickly tucked his pistol into the top of his trousers, then reached for the lamp in the hall. He stepped inside the room, closing the door behind him.

Jocelyn stood at the far side of the room with what looked to be a shattered hurricane lamp at her feet. "You frightened me," she said. "I bumped into the bedside table, and . . . God," she whispered, closing her eyes a moment and visibly gathering her composure. "I—I didn't think I'd be so affected by the sight of you." She opened her gorgeous eyes then, looking confused and beautiful all at once. "I'm babbling, aren't I? I just . . . I had to come here, to see you . . . to talk with you."

Dash was trying to catch his own breath. The sight of Jocelyn standing there in her scarlet cloak, with her shimmering cloud of hair covered with melting bits of snow, was more than he could handle.

Needing time to sort through his emotions, Dash set the lamp on the floor, then bolted the door behind him. But even those small tasks did little to alleviate his throbbing desire at finding Jocelyn waiting for him.

"I must be dreaming," he whispered, so very pleased that she'd finally sought him out. He didn't care that she'd chosen a seedy tavern in which to do so. He didn't even care that she'd not given him any warning that she'd be here, on this night of all nights. He was only thankful that she'd come.

"We need to talk," Jocelyn said quickly.

"As I recall, our last conversation did not agree with me."

"I'm worried about you, Dash. You—you look tired."

"And you look absolutely stunning." He moved closer to her, unable to keep his distance any longer. He stopped when he was close enough to touch her. But he didn't

touch her, couldn't, for then the magic of the moment
might be broken if she pulled away. "I've been haunted
by the memory of you these past months," he said, his
voice thick with emotion.

"I received your notes. You shouldn't have sent them.
What if they'd been discovered, what if—"

"Hush," he whispered, finally reaching out to touch
his forefinger to her lips. "I took great care in sending
them."

She stiffened then, and Dash wondered what thoughts
were speeding through that quick mind of hers.

"You're being careless of late," she said sharply. "And
I'm a fool for coming here. But I *had* to talk with you.
I—I couldn't just allow you to continue on the path you've
chosen."

Dash figured she was talking of all his clandestine meetings. Doubtless she'd gotten wind of them through Amelia,
who'd heard from Lord Monty.

"I don't want to talk about that," Dash said, his own
voice turning stern. He didn't want Jocelyn involved in his
mess any more than she already was. And as for what he'd
learned about Thistlewood's group, well, he would not be
filling her ears with such sordid details. He asked, "Where
is your grandmother? And your cousin?"

"Home," Jocelyn replied. "At least, Gran is at the
townhouse. Charles is with his friends."

"And they don't know you're here?"

Her green eyes flashed. "Do you think I'm that stupid?"

Dash grinned at her show of spunk. This was the Jocelyn
he remembered. Quick to anger—and to love. "Not at all,
Duchess."

And then, as though just saying the oft-used endearment
he'd once given her could magically wipe away their last
disagreement, Dash found himself taking Jocelyn into his
arms. He held her close, held her tight, and buried his
face in her cloud of rich hair. God help him, but she was
as soft and lithe as he remembered. She smelled of violets
and a musky scent that was hers alone. Dash's mind reeled

with the impact of the feel and smell of her. He pressed his eyes shut tight and kissed her temple.

"I've missed you, Duchess."

"Dash—"

"Tell me you've missed me."

"Dash, we can't—"

"Tell me."

She drew in a ragged breath, trembling. "I—I've missed you."

"And what else?" he demanded, suddenly overcome as he rained hot kisses down to her cheekbone and then near her mouth. "Have you missed what we do together, Jocelyn? Have you yearned for the wonder we once found in each other's arms?"

"Dash," she gasped, slowly giving into his assault. "Don't do this."

"I can't help myself," he murmured, toying with her pouty, lower lip with his mouth. "Have you missed our lovemaking, Jocelyn?"

"You—you know I have."

"Then why didn't you come to me sooner?"

"You know why."

"No, I only know what you told me. You say you want nothing to do with a thief like me . . . but I can feel your response, Jocelyn. You want me just as much as I want you. Don't deny it."

"This—this is madness."

"You must mean love, Duchess."

"Or lust," she said, trying half-heartedly to pull away from him.

"The two make fine companions, just as we do."

He covered her mouth with his. A deep kiss it was, filled with all the roiling emotions that ensnared his heart. Dash had never kissed a woman so thoroughly, nor had he ever spoken with his soul as he did now. He kissed Jocelyn as though he might never see her again, which, Dash knew, might very well be the case.

This night he had a mission to see to its end. Even as he wrapped his arms about Jocelyn and plundered her mouth with his tongue, Arthur Thistlewood and his men were meeting in a loft on Cato Street, just off Edgware Road. They secreted their arms in this loft, Dash had learned while trying to ferret out information about the bogus Raider. Tonight, while the British Cabinet dined at the Earl of Harrowby's house, Thistlewood planned to ambush them. A murder plot, plain and simple. A mad scheme to do away with the powerful men of the government. Dash had also gotten wind of Alexander Greville's association with the Radical group. Dash had slipped away from home tonight in order to try and stop the assassination attempt, and to do what he could to see that Jocelyn's father would not be caught up in the turmoil.

It was a rash plan, Dash knew. How could he, just one man, try and stop a murder planned by a bunch of fanatics? And how in the devil was he to see that Jocelyn's father came to no harm—all without finding his own neck in a noose? It was indeed a tricky situation . . . and now Jocelyn had popped up in the middle of it all.

But Dash wasn't about to let her go, not yet. He wanted to savor the moment. He wanted to feel her body next to his and to love her as he had on that long-ago day in his flat.

"Damn but you taste sweet," he rasped against her mouth. "Too sweet. I've become your slave, Duchess."

"Then why is it *I* am trembling like a leaf in the wind? I—I didn't come here for this, Dash. Truly I didn't."

"No?"

She shook her head.

"No matter," he murmured, kissing her again. "When did the two of us ever waste time with 'what should have been'?" And so saying, Dash made the most of his short time alone with the only woman who had captured his soul.

Eighteen

Jocelyn wasn't quite certain what came over her then, but before she knew what was happening, she found herself melting in Dash's hard embrace. His muscled arms held her up, and if not for the steadying of his arms, Jocelyn was certain she would have crumbled to the floor. Her knees were weak and her stomach was giddy from excitement. Dash had always had this effect on her. Always. From the moment he'd stopped her carriage last fall—and even now, when she knew they could have no future together—Dash had woven a spell about her. He was all she could ever want—he with his mercurial moods and tender, loving hands.

"Oh, Dash," she gasped.

But he smothered her words with his mouth, and Jocelyn admitted to herself that it was not conversation she sought this night. She wanted to be a part of Dash and he a part of her. She wanted to take that dazzling journey with him into a hot realm of love and surcease. She wanted to forget the past few months and all their loneliness.

Dash seemed to want the same. With a swiftness that thrilled her, Dash began to undo the cords of her cloak. The garment fell away from her shoulders, slithering to the floor, forgotten. He swept his large hands up into her hair, pulling at the many pins until they fell free and her lustrous curls spilled down about her shoulders.

"So beautiful," he murmured, losing himself in the feel of her silky tresses.

Jocelyn was just as eager. Her breath coming in ragged gasps, she quickly slid his heavy coat from him, then began to work at his waistcoat, and then the buttons of his shirt. The feel of his warm skin was nearly too much for her. She ran her fingers through the coarse hair of his chest, painting from memory every sloping muscle and smooth dip of his skin.

Her gown, with its fitted undersleeves, was much too tight a garment for Dash to take off. Impatient, Dash slid his hands down over her hips, and then lower still until he found the hem of her dress. He hiked the material up as he pressed Jocelyn back against the wall. She wore no drawers—which were rarely worn—just her warm stockings, and they posed no barrier. Wild now, Dash undid his breeches, and soon Jocelyn felt the heat of him pressing against her thighs. She sucked in a sharp breath at the contact.

Dash smiled into her eyes, nuzzling her face with his. "I've dreamt of this for too long," he muttered.

Jocelyn felt a heady tremor shudder through her as he entered her. It felt so good, so right. Damn the world with all its chaos. Jocelyn didn't care that she'd vowed to stay away from Dash. She suddenly didn't give a whit that the two of them should not be together. She'd been very cautious this night. No one had seen her come up the stairs—no one but Laney. Lord Barrington and his peers need never know of this clandestine meeting.

The thought sent her soaring. These few precious moments would be her secret, Jocelyn knew. If she could not have Dash for all time, then she would take what little she could get, and she would cherish the memory.

Dash reached down and grasped her thighs with both hands, lifting her slightly as he drove straight and true within her body. Jocelyn clung to him, opening her mouth to his as he took her weight. She was on fire now, her body one with his. He moved within her, shattering all thought, fueling her desires. Jocelyn closed her eyes, drinking in the taste and feel of him.

And then it came, a release so filled with savagery and mind-numbing power that Jocelyn thought she would go mad. She shuddered with the force of it, holding Dash tightly as he filled her with his seed. Her world expanded. She felt omnipotent, showered with love. She could, she knew in that instant, accomplish anything. Jocelyn tightened her hold on Dash's neck, pressing her face into the crook of his neck and breathing deeply of the scent of him. She would never forget him, she knew. She would love Dashiell Warfield until her dying day.

Indeed, such words were on the tip of her tongue, but Jocelyn kept them in check. She could not tell Dash that she loved him above all others. She'd come to him this night to warn him away from his thieving lifestyle. She'd come to try and talk sense into him.

And she would, Jocelyn vowed silently to herself as they both quieted and their breathing became normal. But for the moment she allowed herself the beauty of just being with Dash. No words were spoken between them. They kissed and touched, and Dash gently set her down on the floor. He lovingly smoothed her hair, her skirts, and then cupped her face in his hands as he kissed her deeply.

"I love you," he said sweetly.

Jocelyn closed her eyes, feeling the tears gather behind her lids. She kissed him back, trying to show him with that gesture that she loved him too. She couldn't say the words, though.

Later, as Dash began to straighten his own clothes, Jocelyn said, "I came here tonight because I've heard you've taken to the roads again, and that you've been drinking, and—"

"What?" he asked, glancing up at her, his gray eyes narrowed.

"I've heard you've been in low spirits."

"Not that," he said, suddenly angry. "Who told you I'd taken to the roads again?".

"It—it doesn't matter, not really. What matters is that

I know, Dash, and I've come to beg you to give it up. Please, Dash.''

"*Who?*" he nearly thundered.

Jocelyn blinked at his harsh tone. "Laney," she admitted. "I—I saw him tonight while I was dining with my cousin. In fact, he arranged our meeting. He's very worried about you, Dash."

"Laney? *He* told you this?"

Jocelyn, nervous now, nodded. "Yes. He said you'd taken to drinking as well. He also told me the Midnight Raider has been haunting the roads north of here and leaving clues in his wake. Laney said the Raider recently left a poem with one of his victims." Jocelyn took a deep breath, then continued. "*You* sent me a poem, Dash. What are you trying to do? Do you wish to be caught?"

Dash looked as though he'd been hit in the face with a bucket of cold water. "A *poem*? I didn't send you any poem. I sent you flowers and paper, and notes begging you to meet me. Never a poem."

"But if you didn't . . . oh, my God," she whispered, ugly realization dawning. She remembered Laney's bitter tone when he talked of Dash and his relationship with Lord Monty, and how Laney had deliberately allowed her to think that Dash had indeed been continuing his midnight raids. "You haven't been on the roads, have you?"

Dash shook his head, his eyes stormy. "For months someone has been attempting to frame me for robberies I haven't committed, and even for the murder of James Keats."

"But who? Laney?"

Dash grimaced. "I pray it isn't Laney."

"But why would he even do such a thing?"

His voice ragged, he said, "There are things you do not know about Laney and me."

"So tell me, dammit," she nearly shouted, angry now to think she'd doubted Dash. She'd believed Laney when he'd said Dash had been drinking himself into oblivion and thieving again.

Dash took hold of her shoulders, holding her tightly.

"Listen to me," he said, his voice low. "I can't believe Laney is behind this. He can't be! It *must* be someone else. Someone who knows about my past and Laney's. We—we were like brothers once, Jocelyn. Lord Monty took us both under his wing, only I was the one chosen to be his heir, and not Laney. But Braden made his own way in life. He walked away from everything Lord Monty offered him. He turned his back on us. It was his own choice."

"But then who?" she asked, horrid fear clutching at her. "Who would want to see you hanged for crimes you didn't commit?"

"I don't know, Jocelyn. But I mean to find out."

"How?" she demanded. "What can you do? You can hardly go to the authorities!"

"True. But then I never have relied on others to see to my problems." He gazed deeply into her eyes, as though there was something more he wanted to say, promises he wanted to keep, perhaps. But then the moment slipped away and he released her. "I want you to return to your townhouse. Stay there until I get word to you, do you understand?"

Jocelyn didn't move. "Why? What are you going to do?"

He was agitated, she could see, and haunted by inner demons, but he tossed an emotional wall up between them, unwilling to let her through. "Don't you worry about me," he said. "I've some business this night, and then tomorrow I intend to get to the bottom of all of this. Go home, Jocelyn. Wait for me."

Jocelyn backed away from Dash, hating the distance that had suddenly formed between them. He was contemplating some mad scheme, she could see. But what? Knowing he wouldn't leave her alone until she gave in to his demands, she said, "Very well. I'll go."

He gazed at her long and hard. "Just like that? You'll leave?"

"Yes, of course. What *had* you expected? For me to grovel at your feet and demand answers?"

"Not grovel, but demand, yes."

"Well, you were wrong. I'm leaving, Dash. Just as you requested." Jocelyn bent to retrieve her cloak. "You will send word to me?"

Dash nodded.

"And you'll be careful?"

"I always am."

Jocelyn nodded, though she didn't believe him. He appeared a demon unleashed. There was a coldness to his gray eyes that unsettled her, and the telltale muscle along his cheek twitched. But she knew well enough that she had a role to play. She took his warm hands in hers, kissed his cheek, and said good-bye.

"I'll hire you a carriage," he said.

"No need. There's one awaiting me," she lied. 'You'd best stay here. We cannot afford to be seen together." And then she walked out of the tiny room and hurried down the dark stairwell.

Jocelyn fairly flew out of the tavern, then positioned herself in a doorway of a distant building and waited for Dash to exit.

Dash stood in the room, watching Jocelyn's hasty retreat. His mind turned with all he'd learned this night. Laney. That sneaking dog! He'd filled Jocelyn's ears with a passel of lies! Drinking to excess . . . haunting the roads again, leaving a litter of poems in his wake. There was only one explanation for such lies, and that was: Laney was pretending to be the Midnight Raider.

Laney Braden, the man Dash had loved as a brother, was framing Dash for the murder of James Keats, and for a string of robberies Dash hadn't committed. And for what? Dash knew the answer. Laney wanted Dash's inheritance. With Dash out of the way, Laney would be free to return to Lord Monty, with his heart on his sleeve, and Lord Monty, feeling betrayed by Dash, would doubtless give Laney everything he wanted.

Dash felt bile rise in his throat at the realization. He

reached for his pistol that he'd set on the table before taking Jocelyn in his arms, then headed out of the room.

Though he wanted nothing more than to find Laney and have it out with the man, Dash knew he had even graver matters to attend to. The hour was growing late, and Thistlewood and his men were no doubt readying for their raid on the Earl of Harrowby's house in Grosvenor Square.

Dash stepped out of the tavern and made quick tracks to his horse tied nearby.

Jocelyn stepped out of the shadows of the doorway, watching as Dash sped away. She cursed her own lack of foresight, but soon hailed a carriage. The driver was a huge fellow, wearing a scarf tucked about his neck and a woolen cap and mittens against the cold. "Follow that rider!" Jocelyn commanded, handing the man several coins. "And hurry!"

The man grinned, pocketing the money. He slapped his reins as soon as Jocelyn sat down on her seat. She was jolted by the quick motion, but was pleased to see she'd found a driver willing to race with the wind. And race they did! Dash set a fast pace, since he rode astride and could fly through the slick streets. Jocelyn leaned against the window, urging the driver to go faster and promising he would be paid for his trouble.

"Don't worry about me, mistress," he called back. "Ain't nobody can handle the reins like me. I even outran the Bow Street Runners," he boasted. "Now, mind you, I didn't *know* they were runners at the time, but that's not the point of my tale. I just took to the alleys and side streets and I found myself clear and free of them. Don't you worry," he said again, keeping a discreet distance between the horse and rider far ahead. "I'll get you where you want to go."

Jocelyn prayed he would. She feared Dash would find Laney and do him harm. The last thing Dash needed was to be arrested for assaulting a man!

The driver brought the carriage to a sliding halt. "He's

in the next street,'' the man said, popping off his seat to
help Jocelyn to the ground.

Jocelyn needed no assistance. She gave the man every
coin she had, then scurried off into the chilling darkness.
She didn't even know where she was, she'd been so confused by their breakneck speed. But she pushed forward
anyway, remembering Dash's dark mood when he'd heard
of Laney's involvement in bringing them together. Jocelyn
sneaked past a row of buildings, and then another, until
she spied Dash's tall frame ahead. She flattened her back
to the gate of one home, training her ear for any sounds.

The night was crisp and quiet, and she was close enough
to hear voices.

''Ho, who goes there?'' an unfamiliar voice demanded.
''Dash! You'd best get away from here, if you know what's
good for you.''

''Calm down, man. I'm looking for someone. Alexander Greville. Is he here?''

Jocelyn went rigid when she heard her father's name.

''Alexander?'' the unknown man replied, astonished.
''Haven't seen him in months. He's not here, nor should
you be here.''

Jocelyn watched as Dash then leaned closer to the man
who was swallowed in shadows. They exchanged more
words—words Jocelyn couldn't hear. Then Dash straightened, stepped back. He looked up and down the street,
then headed in Jocelyn's direction, toward his mount.

Jocelyn sank back against the building, praying Dash
wouldn't see her.

Just as Dash reached his horse, a loud commotion broke
out. Riders came tearing down the street far ahead of where
Dash had just been. Dash jumped on his mount, hissing
for the other man to run clear. And then Dash turned his
horse about just as Jocelyn spied the king's men charging
toward them.

Fearing the men had come to arrest Dash, Jocelyn darted
out from under her cover. ''Dash!'' she cried, her voice
nearly drowned out by the sounds surrounding them.

Dash pulled up on his reins, his horse skittering on the

slick pavement. "Jocelyn! What the—get over here!" he yelled glancing behind him.

Jocelyn didn't need further persuasion. She ran toward him, hitching her skirts up as she went. Dash's hand closed over hers, pulling her up onto the saddle, and Jocelyn threw her weight up and over the horse. Even before she'd had a moment to get settled, Dash whipped his horse into motion and the beast careened down the street, charging into the dark night.

Jocelyn held fast to Dash, clutching him about the waist as they took a sharp turn and raced onto a wider street that was rutted and wet.

"What's happening!" she cried.

"What the bloody hell are you doing here?" he shot back.

"Following you, what else?" she yelled, her teeth snapping together as they raced through the wet streets. "And what do you know about my father that you're not telling me? Damn you, Dash, I want some answers!"

"Shut up, will you?" he snapped, directing his horse through a sharp turn that nearly sent Jocelyn flying off the saddle.

She did shut up then, but not because she wanted to. By the time they reached Lord Monty's house, Jocelyn was in a rage. Windblown, her face and hands chafed by the cold air, she jumped down off the horse and whirled on Dash with righteous anger.

"Tell me what you know about my father," she demanded again. "And why were the king's men breathing down your neck back there? You could have been arrested! You could have been—"

Dash yanked her by the wrist toward the door of Monty's house. "Quiet," he snapped, moving quickly inside. "Do you want all of London to know what we were about this night?"

"And what is that?" she demanded, allowing him to drag her alongside him.

Dash shut the doors soundly behind him. "Prentiss!"

he bellowed, ignoring Jocelyn's question. "Where the devil are you, man?"

A tall, stately-looking manservant hurried toward them from the hall to their right. "I'm here, sir," the man said quickly. If he was surprised to see a windblown and furious woman with his employer, he made no show of it. He kept his blue eyes fixed to Dash's face and awaited his orders.

"See to my horse, Prentiss. See that he's rubbed down. And if anyone asks, I've been at my uncle's bedside for the past hour, is that clear?"

"Yes, sir."

Without wasting another moment, Dash took Jocelyn's cold hand in his and led her out of the great front hall and into the library. A fire burned low in the grate. A decanter of brandy and several glasses sat on a small table.

"Sit," Dash ordered Jocelyn as he reached for the brandy.

"Excuse me?" she raged. "I'm not one of your servants, Dashiell Warfield, and I'll not be ordered about. I want some answers and I want them now."

"Of course you do," he said darkly. "And you'll get them, as soon as I have this." He tossed back a swallow of the brandy, wincing slightly as it burned a path to his stomach.

But Jocelyn was in no mood to wait. In an instant she moved in front of him and snatched the glass from his hands. "Tell me what you know about my father, dammit!"

"You've the mouth of a sailor, Jocelyn. I should get some soap and wash—"

"Try it and you'll find your head soaked with brandy," she threatened.

For a moment Jocelyn thought Dash might indeed head out of the room in search of the promised soap, but instead there came a change in his expression, and his eyes twinkled slightly. "You're at your most gorgeous when you're spitting fire," he said matter-of-factly.

"And you," Jocelyn shot back, "are as insufferable as

always! Why is it every time I follow you, I find you knee-deep in trouble?''

"*Me?*" he thundered. ''You were the one out and about unchaperoned and with no way of outrunning the king's men. If I hadn't been there to whisk you from harm's way, you would have been at the mercy of the authorities. How would you have explained yourself, Duchess? Would you have told those men you were out getting some fresh air?''

Rude of him to remind her that she'd taken a foolish course. ''I followed you because I thought you might need me.''

''Need you? For what? To hamper my flight?''

''Now, see here,'' she exploded, filled with fury. ''It was your choice to order me astride your horse!'' She clamped her mouth shut tight, unwilling to verbally spar with him. Finally she said, ''Enough of these games. Tell me why you were searching for my father in that—that place.''

''That *place*,'' he told her, ''was none other than the loft where a band of Radicals stores their arms. And you, Mistress Busybody, could have very well been charged with attempted murder this night had I not been there to take you away from the chaos.''

Jocelyn blanched. ''Murder?''

''Of the Cabinet, no less.'' Dash ran one hand through his hair in agitation. ''Look,'' he began. ''I might as well tell you this now, for tomorrow all of London will be privy to the news. There is a group known as the Spencean society. They are a body of revolutionists, and their leader is a man known as Arthur Thistlewood. He—''

''He's a Radical orator, I know,'' Jocelyn whispered, knowing only too well. ''My father told me about him.''

Dash gaped at her in surprise. ''So you've known all along that your father is involved with Thistlewood?''

''Was involved,'' Jocelyn corrected. ''He cut his ties with those men months ago.''

Dash let out a long-held breath of air. ''For the love of—I went to the loft on Cato Street to save your father from imprisonment! Only tonight I'd heard a rumor that

Thistlewood was planning an outrageous scheme. Once before he'd been betrayed by paid informers, and no doubt that's what happened. I'd thought if I got there in time, I might be able to talk your father out of joining that lawless group.''

Jocelyn felt thunderstruck. ''You don't even know my father, yet you were willing to place your own life in danger to save him?''

''Yes.''

Jocelyn felt tears gather in her eyes. Brave, sweet Dash. How like him to rally to her family's side! ''Thank you,'' she murmured. ''But I wish you would have told me about your plans. My father is home in the Cotswolds. Safe.''

''Now you tell me.''

''You're angry?'' she chanced.

''Me? Angry? Why should I be? I only missed the hangman's noose by a mere inch this night. Nothing out of the ordinary for me, now, is it?''

''You *are* angry.''

He shook his head, a sad smile on his lips. ''I'm only sorry that we barely know about each other's lives.'' He gently took the glass from her, set it on the table, then took her hands in his. ''Look at us, Duchess. We've been as close as a man and woman can be, and yet what do I know about you?'' He ran his lips across her knuckles. ''I've thought of nothing save you these past few months. Yours is the face I see in my dreams, the name I turn over and over in my mind . . . and yet you are still a mystery to me. I hated the way we said good-bye in my flat. I wish—''

Jocelyn stiffened, his words sharply reminding her of the vow she'd made. She was a threat to him, to his very life. She couldn't be found here, with him.

''Don't,'' she whispered. ''Don't say any more. I should go. I shouldn't be here.''

''Why?'' he pressed, gazing deeply into her eyes. ''Do you hate me that much, Jocelyn? Is my character so reprehensible to you that you must find excuses to be gone from my side?''

Hate him? Never. She loved him more than her own life, and that was why she must leave.

"Please, Dash. My grandmother must be worried about me."

"Then I'll send one of the servants to deliver word to her. I'll tell her you'll be staying here as our guest. She won't mind, not with Lord Monty in the house to oversee us."

Jocelyn shook her head, feeling the intense heat of Dash's lips on her hands. "No. I—I can't stay."

"But why?" he demanded, his voice sounding harsh.

And it was then the tears Jocelyn had fought so hard to keep at bay came. She wept, bowing her head. "Oh, Dash, I don't hate you," she whispered, feeling as though a dam of emotion had burst within her. "I am nothing but a disability to you. Don't you understand?" She lifted her face and stared up into his stormy eyes. My—my father's past involvement with Thistlewood places me under suspicion. Lord Barrington warned me that I must keep my distance from you. He—he said if I didn't, then you might be charged with treason."

"Treason?"

"Yes!" she cried. "Lord Monty's peers know of your sympathies, Dash. They know you will do all in your power to help the oppressed . . . and they lie in wait for you to trip over your own eager feet. And that is why I must stay away from you. To have me—the daughter of a supposed Radical—in your life would be to place you in further jeopardy. I can't do that to you, Dash. I can't. I . . . I love you too much."

Dash appeared stricken by her admission. For an instant he pressed his eyes shut. He drew in a sharp breath. "Say it again," he demanded quietly. "Tell me again, Jocelyn."

A shudder ripped through her. She hadn't meant to declare her love for him, for to do so only complicated things further.

"Dash—"

"*Say it.*"

Jocelyn felt his steely grip all the way to her soul, and the fervor in his eyes did little to calm her. "I—I love you."

"Again."

"I love you." The words came in a choked whisper, filled with ragged emotion. He'd never let her go now, she knew. He'd want her beside him, possibly forever. The thought sent her mind soaring, and a painful ache formed in her breast. How she wanted to stay with him, to touch him and comfort him. But she couldn't!

"Ah, Jocelyn," he murmured, lowering his mouth to hers. "How I've longed to hear those words from your lips." He kissed her, sweetly, tenderly, showing her with the gesture that she was the only woman who'd captured his heart.

And Jocelyn, despite her own misgivings, opened to the kiss. Her tears mingled on their lips, fusing them, binding them together for all time.

"Don't cry," he murmured, enfolding her in a strong embrace. "I'll take care of this mess, my sweet. I'll see to it that we need never part again."

Jocelyn melted against him, wishing with all her heart that he could indeed make everything right. But the feel of his mouth on hers soon washed away her grief and her fears. On a warm tide of love she was swept away. Her tears continued to flow, but they were tears of relief. Finally, after months of having to deal with the pain alone, she had Dash to share the burden. He took the weight from her soul.

"Come now," he coaxed, pulling away from her. "You've had an emotional night. You need to rest."

"But what are you going to do?" she asked, fearing he meant to leave her.

"I'm going to stay by your side while you fall asleep," he soothed. "I'll take you to a guest chamber upstairs."

"No," Jocelyn said, not wanting to leave the warmth of the library. Nor did she want to be sequestered alone in a room without Dash. "Let's stay here. Please."

Dash gave in, helping Jocelyn to remove her cloak, then

covering her with the garment once he'd coaxed her to lie down on a small settee. He sat down on the floor, his back against the side of the thing while he held Jocelyn's hand in his and stroked it gently.

"Sleep," he told her. "In the morning we'll figure out how to extricate ourselves from this sticky web."

Jocelyn curled up on her side, watching Dash's profile in the flickering light of the hearth. He was so handsome with his unruly black hair and aristocratic features. Jocelyn thought again of all the external forces threatening them, but was happy for the moment to be alone with him. *Yes,* she thought, feeling her lids grow heavy, *tomorrow will be time enough to make sense of all the chaos.* She fell asleep, still holding Dash's hand.

Dash heard Jocelyn's breathing deepen. He chanced a look at her. Her dark lashes fluttered, casting smudged shadows atop her high cheekbones. Hers was a face for a locket, filled with beauty and charm. Dash felt his heart squeeze as he took in the pouty bow of her lip, the smattering of freckles across her cheeks and nose, and the fan of her fiery hair spread about her face. How he loved her: her spirit, her brave, feisty nature, and yes, her beauty. Jocelyn was all he could ever want in a woman, and more.

As he thought of all this, Dash felt his pulse quicken and his mind begin to spin in many directions. Jocelyn had left him once because she thought herself to be a threat to his welfare. How so very like Jocelyn to put her own wants and desires aside in the name of good. He admired her character, but was angered all the same.

He should have known better than to think he could turn his back on the life he'd once led! Always, his sins would haunt him. He could accept that. But now those same sins haunted Jocelyn as well. She'd been manipulated like a puppet by Barrington and the others.

Damn! Dash should have realized what was happening! He should have put two and two together, but he hadn't. He'd believed Jocelyn when she claimed she could never love a thief. All Dash's life he'd felt he wasn't deserving of the riches he'd found nor of the love he'd received . . . and he'd very nearly lost Jocelyn because of such insecurities.

But no longer, Dash vowed, thinking of Laney Braden and Lord Barrington, and all the others who were keeping an eye on his every move. Now that he'd finally puzzled out who was framing him, Dash was determined to do something about it.

Carefully he disengaged his fingers from Jocelyn's, then laid her hand beneath her cloak and placed a light kiss to her brow.

"Sleep well," he whispered. "And when you awaken, all will be well."

With that, Dash stood up, then headed out of the library.

Nineteen

Jocelyn, drifting on the fringes of wakefulness, heard Dash's words. They struck terror in her breast. Just as Dash closed the doors of the library, Jocelyn opened her eyes and sat up with a start. The room was lit only by the dying fire in the hearth, and she felt chilled by Dash's absence. He was leaving her . . . but to go where?

Not wasting a moment to second-guess him, she got up and put on her cloak, then hurried out the door after him. She met Prentiss in the hall.

"Where has he gone?" she asked the startled servant.

Prentiss blinked in confusion, then gathered his wits. "Mistress Greville, I was just about to check in on you. I was told you were asleep and that you weren't to be disturbed."

"Well, I'm very much awake, as you can see. Now, please, tell me where Dash has gone."

"Forgive me, but—"

Impatient, and knowing she hadn't a moment to lose, Jocelyn pressed, "Are you going to tell me or not?"

"I—I don't know where he's gone, I'm afraid."

Jocelyn skewered the very proper man with a heated stare. "But you've an idea, I'm certain of it. Please, Prentiss, you can trust me. I love Dash. I only want to help him. He could be heading directly into danger!"

The man hedged, folding his gloved hands and wringing

them nervously. "He—he mentioned something about the northern road, and about meeting a man."

"Braden?" Jocelyn asked. "Lane Braden?"

Prentiss pursed his lips. "Yes . . . I believe that was the name he mentioned."

Jocelyn needed no more direction. "Thank you, Prentiss," she said, then hustled out of the house. She had a devil of a time finding a swift way out of London. The hour was late, and she hadn't the time to hire a carriage—even if she could find a driver willing to take her out of London. More important, she knew she must take great care. She didn't want anyone to know what she was up to. So thinking, she did find a seedy-looking driver to take her to the stables where Jives kept Amelia's carriage and horse while in the city. Much to her discomfort, she was forced to sneak past the very drunk and snoring man who watched the stables. She made quick work of rousing the horse from its stall and quieted the beast with just a touch. Fortunate for her that he knew her touch and smell. She found an old saddle, telling herself she meant only to "borrow" the thing until she could return it. And then, hitching up her skirts, she headed out of London, hoping she would find Dash on the very roads he'd haunted months ago.

The sky above Jocelyn was filled with stars and a generous moon that coated the land with iridescent beams. The snow was deeper here than in the city, and the whiteness reflected the wash of moonlight and offered Jocelyn the ability to see where she was headed. Giving the animal its head, Jocelyn kept the beast to the ruts in the snow. As they charged through the night, Jocelyn fought to keep her fears at bay. The roads at night were no place for an unarmed woman. She had no way of protecting herself—nothing but flight.

"I won't turn back," she said aloud, needing to hear her own voice.

Dash was somewhere ahead, searching for Laney. What would happen when he found him? She cringed at the thought, remembering the last time Dash and Laney had fought. But this would be different, for Laney had betrayed his friend. There would be no casual roughhousing between them. No, this time, Jocelyn knew, the men would meet in a fiery battle.

And what if Dash *didn't* find Laney? What if Laney were able to continue the robberies, leaving further clues that would ultimately lead to Dash? Would Dash go to prison because of Laney's betrayal? Would he be hanged?

Jocelyn's head swam with the possibilities, and she found her hands growing clammy about the reins despite the chill in the air. Her lungs burned now, and her face felt raw from the bite of the wind. But she kept up her mad pace, knowing she had to find Dash. Ahead, there could be seen a sharp bend in the road. A warning bell sounded in her mind, warning her to slow down and take care as to how fast she charged about the curve.

Too late, though, Jocelyn found she couldn't slow the horse in time. There, in the middle of the road, was a dark rider on horseback—and he held a pistol leveled at her chest.

"Halt!" came a masculine shout. "Who goes there?"

"Dash!" Jocelyn cried, recognizing him then. She fought to get control of her mount, but the horse skidded on a patch of concealed ice. Jocelyn nearly fell from the saddle as the beast crow-hopped to the side, stepping out of the wheel ruts and into the deep snow. "Whoa!" she called, yanking hard on the reins.

Dash rode to her aid. He reached out with his free hand and managed to take hold of the reins and bring her mount to a stop.

Jocelyn's heart thudded with relief. "I—I feared I might not catch up to you," she said, sending him a tentative smile as her horse snorted in impatience and pranced through the snow.

Dash appeared in no mood to return her smile. "I'm not even going to ask," he muttered. "I should have known better than to think *you* would ever stay put long enough to be safe! Dammit, Jocelyn, are you ever cautious?''

"No," she shot back, not liking his angry tone. "Never, not where you're concerned. I came to help you, Dash."

"Help me? I nearly put a bullet through you! I thought I was about to be ambushed, or perhaps even caught by the authorities. When I heard the pounding of hooves, I pulled off at this bend and waited."

"With your weapon drawn, no less," she said, still reeling with the memory of seeing him pointing his gun at her. "Really, Dash, you're far too quick to draw your pistol."

"At least I have the good sense not to come out on the roads unarmed!" he said. "You foolish, headstrong, reckless—"

"I'm glad to see you, too," Jocelyn snapped, sounding miffed. "Are you quite finished flinging names at me? If so, then let's get moving. I didn't come here to argue with you. I came to help you find Braden."

"No," Dash said, shaking his head. "You're not coming with me. In fact, I'm taking you back to London." He tightened his hold on her reins and was just about to turn her horse around.

But Jocelyn wouldn't let him. "I won't turn back," she announced, lifting her chin. "You can talk until you run out of breath, but I won't change my mind."

"Coaxing you," Dash warned, "is not how I intend to see you safely back to your grandmother's house."

"How, then? Do you think you're going to tie me up and throw me over your horse?"

"If that's what it takes," he muttered.

Jocelyn whipped the hair from her eyes, challenging him with a bold stare. "I doubt you even have a length of rope with you."

A shadow of a grin played at the corners of his mouth as he motioned to his saddle.

Jocelyn lowered her gaze and saw a circle of rope hanging from his saddle. "You wouldn't," she said.

"You think not?"

"Dashiell Warfield!" she exploded, angry at the two of them for bickering when they should be searching for Laney. "Why must you always give me threats? Don't you see that I only want to help you? I followed you because—because . . ." She took a deep breath, and then in a rush, said, "because I love you and do not want to live without you."

Dash's mouth pulled tight, his nostrils flared, but Jocelyn was too intent with looking into his eyes and seeing just how much her admission shook him.

"I need you, Dash" she said softly. "I want to share everything with you—your joys, and even your pain." She covered his gloved hand with hers. "I realized something tonight, Dash, and that is that I'm tired of running away from my feelings for you. I'm sick of keeping them locked deep inside of me for fear someone might learn the truth and thus pass further judgment on you. So please, don't even think of taking me back to London. I'll just follow you again and again."

For the flash of a second Jocelyn thought Dash might cry. Her brave and bold highwayman actually had tears in his eyes!

"Are you so surprised that I don't ever want to be without you?" she asked, almost in wonder. "Surely you must have known—"

"I believed you that day when you said you'd not give your heart to a thief like me," he said, his voice husky with emotion.

"I had to say those things," she whispered. "I—I had to find a way to pull back from you, from your love. I was a threat to you. I still am, but I'm determined to clear my father's name and yours. I want to help you, Dash."

Dash swallowed convulsively, and then he lifted his hand, drew it behind her neck, and pulled her face to his. He kissed her, deeply, thoroughly.

Jocelyn nearly drowned in the sweetness of his touch. His tongue collided with her own, and she felt their souls fuse. She could have stayed with him like this forever and forever . . .

A loud *crack* filled the air then. Gunfire! Jocelyn's horse panicked, trying to bolt away. Dash broke the kiss, instinctively reaching down to grab up her reins as well as his own.

"I've got him," she said, quickly taking hold of the situation. "What's happening?"

"I can't be certain," Dash said darkly, managing his own beast that was suddenly eager to be in motion. "I want you to stay here, do you hear me? No, don't argue with me. Get off the road and get yourself hidden."

Jocelyn snapped her gaze to Dash's. "You know better than to tell me to stay put. I'm going with you, Dash."

"For the love of—"

"I'm going!"

Dash glowered at her, and then, seeing she would not be stopped, he reached inside his coat and withdrew his hideout pistol. "Then take this," he said. "And be careful. I loaded it when I heard you charging up behind me. You've fired a weapon before, correct?"

Jocelyn nodded, closing her hand about the cool casehardened steel. She well recalled the night she'd shot a man. But could she force herself to do the deed again? Even before she'd had a chance to come to a conclusion, Dash turned his mount about and the two of them headed toward the sound of the gunfire.

They went slowly, cautiously. Every sound seemed to echo through the bluish night, bouncing off the trees and snow. Jocelyn could discern voices in the distance. They picked their way closer to the sounds, and then, at Dash's insistence, they dismounted and crept along the sides of the roadway.

Up ahead, in the middle of the road, was an ornate carriage. The driver had his hands held above his head and was shaking visibly as a masked man on horseback held a gun pointed at him.

"Get down," the masked man was saying. "Open the carriage door and then stand aside."

Jocelyn's blood froze in her veins. She would know that

voice anywhere. It was none other than Lane Braden robbing the coach!

"Stop," Dash whispered to Jocelyn, taking her hand in his and pulling her down to a crouching position.

"What are we going to do?" Jocelyn asked, talking into Dash's ear as she watched the scene unfold up ahead.

Dash was quiet for a moment, straining to hear the words exchanged. Then: "I'm going to stop Braden before he makes his escape."

"But how? He's already astride, and—" She stopped her spate of words as a man climbed out from inside the carriage. "It's Lord Barrington!" she gasped.

Just as Barrington stepped to the ground, Laney Braden spoke. "Greetings. I am the Midnight Raider, terror of these roads. Your money or your life, and be quick about it."

Lord Barrington, a man of substance and titled bearing, did not cower before the masked bandit. Instead, he bravely faced the man. "This is madness," he said, his voice filled with authority. "I know who you are. Enough of this foolishness."

Braden gave a harsh laugh. "Now who is being foolish? You dare stand there and tell an armed and desperate man you know his identity? I should think a man of your station in life would have better sense than that."

"Put down your weapon, Dashiell," Lord Barrington ordered. "Your thieving days are over . . . as well any hopes you might have had for a life in government."

Braden tossed back his head and laughed loudly. "Did you hear that?" he said to the driver. "He addresses the Midnight Raider as Dashiell! Remember that, man. You might be the only surviving witness to this night," Laney said, then leveled his gun at Barrington, taking aim. "Deliver to me any valuables you carry."

"And if I do not?" Lord Barrington challenged.

"Then you'll wish you had."

Dash didn't waste another moment. He jolted into motion, determined to put an end to Laney's terrorizing.

Braden looked up, saw the fire in Dash's eyes—and the pistol in his fist—and he muttered a curse.

Lord Barrington spun around, and his mouth dropped open at the sight of Dash. "Dashiell!" he sputtered. "But I—I thought—"

"We know what you thought, fool!" Laney snapped. To Dash, he said, "You've the scent of a bloodhound, *friend*. Did you not get my message, the one telling you to go upstairs for a meeting?"

Dash said nothing, only kept walking, his insides churning with anger and the knife-twisting reality of Laney's betrayal. Jocelyn, unwilling to stay hidden and prepared to help Dash in any way she could, followed in his wake.

Braden spied her. "Ah, so you did get my message. Pity for me the two of you couldn't have entertained each other for an hour longer. Go home, Dash," Laney said, his voice filled with malice. "You don't belong on these roads. You never did."

Dash kept walking, nearly upon them now.

"I said go!" Laney shouted. Seeing Dash's rage and knowing the man wasn't about to back down, Laney leaned over and swiftly caught at the neck of Lord Barrington's coat. He dragged the man back against his horse's side, curling one arm about his neck and squeezing tightly. "Take one more step and he's a dead man," Laney warned, pressing the barrel of his gun to Barrington's neck.

Dash froze, his arms—and the gun in his hand—held ready at his sides. "It's over, Laney," he said. "You've thrown the dice one last time, and you have lost."

"You pompous ass," Laney hissed. "You always did believe you were better than me. And here we are, at the end of it all, and still you're believing you can outwit me. Think again. The tide has turned, my friend. No longer will I be forced to walk in your shadow." He tightened his hold on Barrington, his lips curling as he did so. "For years I have had to watch you rise within Lord Monty's circles. Dash, the bright one. Dash, the man who would try and make a better England for the less fortunate. Ha! Such lofty dreams, but you believed them, and Monty

adored you because of them. You were his golden child,
the one who could do no wrong. And when you began
sending money north and rallying the people to unite,
Monty looked the other way. That's right,'' Laney continued, his voice growing frantic as he spoke about the past.
''Monty could forgive you *anything*, even highway robbery. But not me. No, I was the vagrant who had no place
in his heart once I left his home. Suddenly I wasn't good
enough anymore. No matter that both of us had come from
the alleys and had lived in coal cellars. You, Monty could
forgive. But never me.''

Dash couldn't believe what he was hearing. How could
he have been so blind? All these years Laney had been
eating himself up with jealousy, and yet Dash hadn't realized. ''You're wrong, Laney,'' Dash said, taking a step
closer, and then another. ''Lord Monty loves you like a
son. As far as he's concerned, you *are* his son.''

''Lies!'' Laney shouted, his eyes glazed and wild now.
''He had no love for me. He gave it all to you.''

''That isn't true. You were the one who chose to leave.
For years Monty has been asking you to return to the Warfield estates. He even offered you employment, yet you
turned him down.''

''Ah, yes. 'Come home to us, Laney, and I'll find a
place for you,' Monty would say. *Find* a place for me.
How so like Monty. For me he had to search for a niche,
but for you there was always a place in his life and in his
heart.''

''You're distorting the truth, and well you know it,''
Dash said, standing directly in front of Lord Barrington
now. ''It wasn't that way. Not at all.''

''And what do you truly know about it?'' Laney demanded harshly. ''You were too busy touring the Conti-
nent, finishing your precious schooling, while I stayed in
London and watched as Lord Monty threw me a meatless
bone now and then! But no more,'' he said, looking like
a madman. ''My luck is about to change.''

''What do you mean?''

Laney gave him a warped smile. ''After tonight you

won't be around to get in my way. On the morrow some
hapless traveler will find your bodies, lifeless and stiff. I,
of course, will be in London, and won't it be fitting that
I should be the one to comfort Lord Monty when he learns
of your murder.''

"You're mad," Dash whispered.

Laney laughed, a devilish sound. "Yes, I suppose I am.
Nasty business this highway robbery is. People will say
what a pity it was that Barrington chose this night to travel,
and that somehow you and your lady came to be with him.
There will be those who will mourn you, Dash. Lord
Monty one of them. But there will also be those who will
whisper about the fact that you might have indeed been
the notorious Midnight Raider. They'll say it was your
presence that caused Lord Barrington's death. Doubtless
every unsolved robbery ever committed on these roads will
be linked to you. You'll die a legend, though a sullied
one."

Jocelyn, standing a distance away, listened to Laney's
wild talk. He was insane, utterly out of his mind. Did he
truly think he could accomplish such a wicked scheme?
Dash was armed, and even she carried a small pistol. But
Jocelyn knew, even if she could get a good aim on Laney
and not chance harming Lord Barrington, that her weapon
might not shoot far enough.

Laney, though, gave none of them a moment to think
through their advantages, however slight. In a swift move
he thrust Lord Barrington away from him, slamming the
man's body directly into Dash. Dash stumbled backward,
gaining his balance as he helped keep Barrington upright.

"Take cover!" Dash yelled to the others as Laney began
to ride a huge circle about the carriage. Laney fired a shot
toward the driver, who was diving for his own rifle. A
bullet whizzed through the air, missing the driver by mere
inches.

But Jocelyn was prepared as Laney came charging by
her. In her hands she held a stout limb that had fallen to
the roadway and that she'd spied while listening to the
exchange. Mustering all of her strength, knowing she had

one chance to unsaddle Laney, she lifted the thing and bashed it against Braden's side as he passed.

Laney, unprepared for the hit, was knocked off his horse, his gun falling from his hands. Jocelyn, too, was stunned by the force of her blow. She'd hit him so hard that her hands felt on fire and her arms and back burned as well. The folds of her cloak hampered her way as she strove to pick up the small pistol she'd laid on the ground as she'd grabbed the limb.

"I wouldn't try it were I you," Braden said, his voice filled with deadly intent.

Jocelyn froze, seeing Braden lying flat on his belly, his own gun once again in his hands.

"Step away from it, lass. Nice and easy. That's better. I actually liked you, Jocelyn," he said, almost chattily. Clearly the man had lost all sense. "What a shame you had to fall in love with Dash. I'm not surprised, though. He always did have the knack of doing me one better." Braden pulled back on the hammer of his gun, clearly intent on murdering her where she stood.

Out of the corner of her eye Jocelyn could see Dash approaching.

"Say good-bye, lass," Braden demanded, his finger nestling beside the trigger.

Just then Dash sprang off the ground and threw himself on top of Laney. The gun fired. Jocelyn spun away, throwing herself to the ground as she saw an explosion of bluish powder. The bullet winged through the air, hitting nothing.

Jocelyn scrambled to her feet as she saw Dash slam a fist against Laney's jaw. She heard the hit, the crunch of bone. But Dash wasn't finished yet. He hit him again, harder still. Dash looked like a god gone wild, his hair loose and windblown about his face. His eyes were filled with fury . . . and pain. Again he hit him. Blood poured from Laney's cut mouth and his face appeared misshapen.

"Dash, no!" Jocelyn cried, fearing Dash would beat Laney to death. "Enough! He's unarmed now. Stop yourself before you kill him!"

Laney glared up into Dash's tortured gaze. "You'd be a fool to listen to her."

"Shut up!" Dash growled at him.

"And when have I ever listened to you? Prepare yourself for battle, *brother*. I won't rest until I have you out of my life." With that vow, Laney thrust his knee up, intending to disable him.

But Dash, having fought Laney too many times to count, was ready. He shifted away from the vicious hit, taking Laney by his coat front and slamming his head against the earth. Laney grabbed hold of Dash's neck with both hands. He squeezed tight, his glazed eyes filled with wicked light.

"Remember the last time I tried to choke the life out of you at your camp? You thought I was just enjoying some brotherly roughhousing, I know. But I wasn't. I wanted to kill you then, Dash. Wanted it so much in fact that I could taste it. I should have gotten rid of you then."

"Why didn't you?" Dash asked, his voice choked as he clamped his own hands on Laney's neck.

"Because first I wanted to watch you fall from Lord Monty's grace," he gasped, baring his teeth as he tried to strangle Dash. "I wanted to watch you squirm as you dug your own grave. Dressed as the Midnight Raider, I haunted the same roads you rode, but I was not so choosy about the people I robbed. And then I happened upon James Keats and his father. The boy reminded me of you, Dash. He was filled with his own importance, was the apple of his father's eye. Such a sickening sight he was."

"So you killed him, just like that?" Dash growled, feeling his hands tighten on Laney's neck.

"No, it was an accident, actually. But after I'd done the deed, I was glad. *Glad*, do you hear?"

Dash felt bile rise in his throat, and if not for Laney's tight hold, the stuff would have spilled into his mouth. "You make me ill, Braden. God help me for ever loving you as my brother."

"Love? Don't speak to me of such an emotion. It doesn't exist. Not in my life . . . it never has." Laney came to life then. Filled with the power of his own hatred, he pushed up with his arms and attempted to push Dash off of him.

Dash didn't slacken his hold. Together, with their hands still locked to each other's throats, they rolled on the snow-covered road. Over and over. Dash felt his windpipe being crushed. His mind grew hazy from lack of air, and his lungs burned. They rolled for one last time, Dash coming out on top, and this time he squeezed his hands with all his might.

Laney had betrayed him. Over and over that single thought swirled through his head. Laney, the man he'd loved as much as his own mother and Lord Monty, had turned his back on him and had tried to frame him for murder. Dash felt suddenly as though his hands were a separate living creature. He couldn't control them—and a part of him didn't want to. He felt his fingers dig into Laney's skin, felt the man's throat give. Another moment, he thought, queerly detached from the scene, and it will be over.

"You—you can't kill me," Braden said, his voice reedy. "You haven't . . . the stomach . . . to do so."

Dash heard the words and knew Laney spoke the truth. He couldn't commit murder. Not now, not ever. Abruptly he let go, then reached up to pry Laney's hands from his neck.

Braden sucked in a much-needed breath of air, and then, with a demonic gleam in his eyes, he brought his head up and slammed it into Dash's face.

Dash's head snapped back with the force of the hit. White pain flared in his mind as blood sprang from his nose. Laney didn't give him a chance to regroup. He sent a fist to the same place. Again. Again. Through a haze Dash saw his opponent's ugly face. Laney appeared some evil monster from a deathly realm, and Dash realized in that instant that he'd never truly known Braden at all.

Dash grabbed him by the coat front with one hand and drew back his other. "You deserve far worse than this," he muttered just as he sent the hardest punch of his life. It landed squarely on Braden's broken jaw. The impact of it stung even Dash's hand, rippling all the way to his shoulder.

Laney, knocked senseless from the pain, fell back against the snow. Dash slowly got to his feet, wiping the blood from his face. He looked down at the man he'd once called his brother, and his heart felt as though it had been cleaved in two. Swaying slightly, feeling sick to his stomach, he turned his back on Lane Braden.

Jocelyn moved to his side. "Are you all right?" she whispered, reaching out to gently touch his face.

Dash pulled back, wondering if anything would ever feel right again. "I . . . I cannot believed this has happened. I loved him," he said hoarsely. "I would have done anything for him."

"I know that," she said softly. "But he isn't well, Dash. His mind—it must have snapped."

Dash didn't want to talk anymore, for a part of him felt responsible for what had become of Laney. His soul heavy with grief, he gathered Jocelyn in his arms and held her tight. The world, with all its chaos and cruelty, suddenly seemed leagues away.

Much later, once Laney had been revived, and, much to Dash's dislike, had been tied at the hands and feet and put into Lord Barrington's carriage, Dash led the small group back to London. He rode beside the carriage, prepared to deal with Laney should he try to escape. Jocelyn rode beside him.

Lord Barrington, who'd chosen to ride on the seat with his driver, glanced over at Dash. "I'm deeply sorry it has come to this, Dashiell," he said, his voice grave. "I'm as stunned as you to learn of Braden's sins. Lord Monty will be beside himself with grief."

Dash nodded, but said nothing, only kept his eyes trained on the road ahead.

"But there is one more truth that has come from this," Barrington continued.

Dash finally glanced at the man. "Which is?"

"That Braden, and not you, rode as the Midnight Raider."

Dash stiffened. "There is something you must know, sir—"

But Barrington wasn't about to listen to Dash's confession. "Glad I am to be finally free of this web of intrigue concerning your good name. Braden will be charged with the murder of James Keats as well as highway robbery. He robbed many innocent folk of their hard-earned money."

"Lord Barrington," Dash began again. "I—"

"As for the other robberies along these roads, they're best forgotten," Barrington interrupted. "You know as well as I the men who claimed they were robbed by the Midnight Raider had gotten their money in illegal ways. I see no reason why they should be compensated, considering the fact that they barely miss what was stolen from them. The matter is settled, Dash," he added sternly. "Do you understand what I'm telling you?"

"Yes, sir, I do," Dash said, realizing Lord Barrington was offering him a second chance.

"Very good," Barrington replied, straightening in his seat and looking very much like the titled man he was. "I'll expect to see you in my offices the first of next week. I've some ideas concerning the plight of the poor that I'll soon be presenting to Parliament. You're a good man, Dashiell. Our government could do with a few more men such as yourself."

"Thank you, sir," Dash said, warmed to know he had a friend in Lord Barrington.

"Now, don't go thanking me yet," Barrington shot back. "We've a long and difficult road ahead of us. And I warn you, I'll be watching your every step."

Dash suppressed a smile. "I would expect no less from you, sir."

Lord Barrington sat back on the seat, a pleased expression settling over his features. "I'm pleased we understand each other." To his driver he said, "Pick up the pace, man. I've work to do in London."

And with that, the company hurried on through the moon-washed night. Jocelyn sent Dash a small smile, reaching out her hand to him.

Dash took hold of it, feeling the warmth of her. He knew then that, no matter how dark the past few months had been, his future was suddenly bright and filled with promise.

Twenty

On a glorious late-spring morning, in a quaint little church in the Cotswolds, Jocelyn became Dash's wife.

Alexander Greville, looking very regal in coattail and fashionable hat, gave his daughter's hand in marriage, as well his blessings to the union. A tearful Amelia, flanked on her right by Lord Monty and on her left by Charles, looked on as her granddaughter moved down the aisle on her father's arm. Lord Barrington was there as well, a silent figure who appeared as pleased as the bride's father.

A grand affair it was, with family and friends alike filling the small church and whispering about the comely bride and her handsome groom. Gay ribbons decorated each pew, and sprays of wildflowers released their heady scent into the air.

But it was Jocelyn, in her elegant white gown and veil as fine as a spider's web, who held the congregation enthralled as she glided down the aisle. And Dash, so handsome in his black coattail and pristine shirt beneath, his eyes smoky with desire and pleasure, watched as his bride-to-be came beside him and joined her hand with his.

The service was lengthy, but Dash didn't mind. He recited his vows, looking deeply into Jocelyn's eyes. There could be no doubt in her mind that what he said he meant. And Jocelyn, her heart filled to overflowing, promised to love and cherish him above all others, and to be with him in this life and the one beyond.

She left the church in a daze, buoyed by love and hope. There was a mad celebration at her father's home. Guests had traveled from London and the small wool towns scattered through the Cotswolds. Drink flowed freely. An array of delicacies covered four tables in all. Numerous toasts were made—many by a beaming Charles, who had come to enjoy Dash's company nearly as much as Jocelyn did. But it was Lord Monty's toast that brought a tear to Jocelyn's eyes.

"To my son," he said proudly. "And to my newly acquired daughter, who outshines even the sun. I wish for the two of you a lifetime filled with health, happiness, and prosperity. May God smile upon you, and may you always be as happy and in love as you are on this day."

Jocelyn thought she might be unable to swallow the wine past the lump in her throat. But she did, and many times after that, for other guests added their own toasts. She was dizzy with drink by the time everyone had finished.

"You might have to carry me to our marriage bed," Jocelyn teased Dash when they were at last alone. "I fear I won't be able to climb the stairs."

Dash grinned, looking virile and very much in love. "I'd planned to carry you all along," he whispered, taking the last glass of wine from her hands and setting it down. "I'm tired of this celebration, Duchess. What say you we finish it in our bedchamber?"

Jocelyn, feeling heady from the many toasts, and drunk on happiness, tossed him a coquettish smile. "Shouldn't we see to our guests?" she teased.

"I'm certain they don't expect us to do so."

"But even so . . ." she said, letting her voice trail off.

Dash gave a low growl in his throat, pulling her close and then lifting her into his arms. "Need I remind you that you're now my wife? You must obey my every wish, wench."

"A wench, hmmm?" she said, trying to sound stern but failing miserably. "I'm your wife, Dash. You'd do well to remember that."

Dash nuzzled his face against her neck. "Warning

taken.'' With that, he carried her away from the celebration and upstairs to her childhood room, which had been transformed since the last time she'd been inside it.

"What is this?" she asked as Dash shoved the door shut with his foot.

"Amelia's idea," Dash replied, carrying Jocelyn to the new oversized bed that now replaced her old one. "Part of her wedding gift to us."

"A part?"

Dash nodded, kissing her prettily upturned nose with its smattering of gorgeous freckles. "She mentioned something about a prize bit of horseflesh for each of us. Said we should keep the beasts to the open fields, though. She wouldn't want us taking to the open roads again."

A small laugh escaped Jocelyn. "Just like Gran," she said. "Do you think she and Lord Monty will be married soon?"

"I don't doubt it. Lately they're as thick as thieves."

Jocelyn shuddered at his choice of words.

"Forgive me," he whispered, realizing his error. "I did not mean to remind you of the past."

Jocelyn snuggled against him as he sat down on the bed. "Don't be sorry. I don't want to forget the past—not all of it, Dash. There are moments I never want to forget, such as the first time we kissed . . . and the night at the Fox's Lair when you touched me and taught me how to love." She gazed up into his eyes, stroking his cheek, then moving her fingers gently across his nose, which had been broken during his skirmish with Laney. "You miss him, don't you?" she asked, unashamed to speak of the man who'd brought them so much heartache.

Dash closed his eyes, opened them, then nodded. "Terribly," he admitted. "But I've done all I can for him. Both Lord Monty and I have paid the jailor and seen to it that Laney has one of the better apartments in London Tower. He'll be tried soon. It will be up to a higher power to decide whether or not Laney is executed for his crimes."

Dash, Jocelyn knew, had finally come to terms with Laney's betrayal. He now admitted to himself that it wasn't his fault Laney had taken the path he'd chosen. The past few months had been hard on Dash and Lord Monty, but the two men had become closer because of their shared pain. No longer was Dash under suspicion for treason, or highway robbery. Jocelyn guessed Lord Barrington had had a hand in that. And as for Alexander and his association with Thistlewood, all had been laid to rest as well.

Arthur Thistlewood, along with several of his cohorts, had been taken to the tower that chilly night in February. Thistlewood and four of his associates were taken to Tyburn on the first of May and hanged. Thistlewood, hanged and publicly decapitated—but not quartered—had met his death without regret.

Jocelyn trembled at the memory. They'd certainly not gone to witness the execution, as so many had, but they heard about the gruesome details. And Jocelyn knew Dash worried the same might happen to Laney.

"We'll do what we can for him," she promised. "At the least, we'll know that his stay in the tower will not be as horrid as it is for others."

"My beautiful Jocelyn," he whispered, cupping her face in one hand. "How is it I was so blessed as to have found you?"

"Flattering me, Dash?" she teased, hoping to recapture the lightness of the afternoon.

"Only speaking the truth, my love."

She pressed her face against his palm. "Who would have thought, on that long-ago night, that the two of us would ever fall in love?"

"Certainly not me. I thought you were the loudest, most headstrong woman I'd ever had the misfortune to meet!"

"And I thought *you* were an insufferable rascal."

"And now?" he asked.

Jocelyn made him wait for an answer. "Well," she began slowly. "You *are* insufferable at times."

"Oh?"

"Hmmm."

"And a rascal?"

"You have been known to be mischievous . . . but I'd have you no other way. I love you, Dashiell Warfield."

He kissed her on the mouth. "Glad I am you said that, wife, else I might not have given you this." He leaned back, pulling out a beribboned box from beneath the pillows.

Jocelyn, her face wreathed in smiles, eagerly took the box. "Another gift? You'll have me spoiled in no time!"

"It isn't truly a gift," he said quickly.

But Jocelyn was barely listening as she tore off the lid. On a bed of white satin lay the necklace and ring Dash had taken from her last fall.

"I'd meant to return these long ago," he said, scooping the pendant out of its satiny bed. "But other things kept getting in my way."

"Oh, Dash," she whispered, her voice thick with emotion. Of all the things he'd given her of late—and they were many—the return of her grandmother's jewelry meant the most.

He said, "I hated myself for stealing them from you."

Jocelyn allowed him to place the necklace about her neck. "The only thing you stole from me was my heart. But no," she added, once he'd managed the clasp. "That isn't true, for I'd already given my heart to you. I think I did so from the first moment you kissed me." She gazed up into his passion-filled eyes, her own filling with unshed tears. "You stole my dreams that day, Dash. I'd always thought I'd marry a man who raised sheep, and that we would settle near the lands where I was raised."

"Are you sorry," Dash asked, "that you didn't fall in love with a man more accustomed to herding sheep than mayhem?"

"Not at all," she said truthfully.

Then Jocelyn did what she'd been yearning to do all day: she pressed Dash down atop the bed and covered his body with hers. "Why would I desire a man who tends to sheep when I can have you?" She became the seductress then, teasing him with her mouth, her hands.

Dash's breath quickened, his heart beginning to hammer in his chest. "Jocelyn!" he nearly cried, his eyes igniting with passion.

"Yes?"

Dash became putty in her embrace then. "Nothing," he murmured, matching her unbridled lust. "Nothing at all."

"I thought as much," Jocelyn whispered against his mouth. "I want to love you, Dash . . . I want—"

"I know what you want," he said, his voice a husky growl as he moved his hands to accommodate her.

Jocelyn did not have to tell him twice.